FROM THE DEEP OF THE DARK

Stephen Hunt has worked as a writer, editor and publisher for
a number of magazines and national newspaper groups in the
UK. He is also the founder of www.SFcrowsnest.com, one of
the oldest and most popular fan-run science fiction and fantasy
websites. Born in Canada, the author divides his time between
the UK, North America and Spain. His interests include
computer programming, the graphic arts and collecting comics.
One day he hopes to have a library large enough to house all
of his books.

By Stephen Hunt

STEPHEN HUNT

FROM THE DEEP

OF THE DARK

HARPER
Voyager

HarperVoyager
An Imprint of HarperCollins*Publishers*
77–85 Fulham Palace Road,
Hammersmith, London W6 8JB

www.harpercollins.co.uk

This paperback edition 2012
1

Set in Sabon by Palimpsest Book Production Limited,
Falkirk, Stirlingshire

Printed and bound in Great Britain by
Clays Ltd, St Ives plc

Go tell the Spartans passerby,
that here obedient to their laws we lie.

Epitaph carved at Thermopylae.

Prologue

Some years ago.

Luck. Her survival was all to do with her *luck*. That much Gemma Dark knew, such a small hope to cling to, clutching the old lucky shark's tooth so tight between her fingers it left an impression on her thumb. Not as much of an impression as its original owner had bitten out of the wooden paddle she'd used to beat back the great white, and certainly not as much an impression as – *BANG* – the thump of the distant depth charge echoing off her U-boat's hull.

'Exploding high,' hissed Gemma's first mate, wiping an oil-streaked hand against his forehead. 'And wide.'

Not quite high enough for her tastes. Captain Dark hovered behind the pilot and navigator's chairs on the bridge; an angel of death for submariners that believed in such things.

'Take us down deeper,' Gemma ordered, ignoring the rebuke sounding back from the hull, the creaking of straining metal.

1

'When our friends up there don't spot any wreckage, they'll start setting their fuses longer.'

Gemma's voice, so deep and rich like honey, even with the march of years, sounded hollow and tinny at their current depth. The air recycling was struggling, just like the rest of her beautiful, ancient boat. A trusted sabre to slice into enemies of the cause. But not like this. Damn the aerial vessel, a long-range Royal Aerostatical Navy scout, hanging out of sight to catch any privateer rash enough to raid the Kingdom of Jackals' surface shipping – like the richly laden merchantman Gemma had targeted. From hunter to hunted in one ill-starred transition. Gemma's pursuer only had to be lucky once with the depth charges they were rolling out of their bomb-bay slides, while the deeper Gemma drove her boat to escape, the more dangerous the impact of any concussion wave that found its mark.

She was ancient, their u-boat, the *Princess Clara*, practically a family heirloom. Hundreds of years old like all of the royalist fleet. And Gemma could hear her pain, the groaning from the hull growing louder as they sank, the ratcheting of the gas-driven turbines deep beneath Gemma's calf-length leather boots increasingly strident with every extra fathom of depth their screws thrust against.

The boat demonstrated her petulance by blowing a valve on the pipes at the far end of the bridge, two of Gemma's crew leaping to close off the venting steam that began filling their compartment. The *Princess Clara* was in the ocean's grasp, and the ocean was slowly crushing the life out of the submersible.

'We could jettison cargo,' said the first mate. 'Flood the torpedo tubes and send more junk towards the surface. We might get lucky.'

Lucky. Yes. But the clever dog of a skipper standing on the bridge of the airship would know the difference between a real hit and the *Princess* expelling fake wreckage. He was an experienced submersible hunter; any fool could see that from the position of his ambush and the classic stovepipe hat-shaped spread of his depth charges. Shallow brim with a deep side-band . . . and deep shit for all of them. He was a professional, this one. A shark, as sharp as the tooth Gemma was rolling between her fingers. Of course, *he* might be a *she*. A female airfleet officer. Someone like Gemma, a face once considered beautiful, hardened by the privations of age and the cause and the fight – not ready to be pensioned off yet, for all of her silvery grey hair.

Those who never experienced the pleasure of serving under Gemma often mistook her vivaciousness for greed, her appetite for life for swinishness. Curse the lot of them. Lubbers and cowards and weaklings, afraid of a strong-willed captain. Pirates and rebels. The two terms had become interchangeable long before she'd been born. Gemma stole every cargo she came across, and if she had to hang a couple of captured officers to make the taking of the next cargo easier, that was only to build her reputation. A privateer could never have too much of a reputation. That wasn't vanity – hardly any compensation for her age-faded beauty at all. Just cold economic sense. Manacle a crew to their ship and send her to the bottom of the seabed with a torpedo, and the handful of survivors you let out in the lifeboat would soon spread word that resisting Captain Gemma Dark was not a safe or sensible option. Did that make her a bad person? Her crew took fewer losses that way. And when continuing an uneven conflict between the royal family and their disloyal parliament that had been lost centuries ago, well, all was fair in such a war. Sailors might call Gemma the *Black Shark* in harbour-side taverns, for the predatory silhouette she'd added to her house's personal coat of arms after surviving the sinking of her uncle's vessel as a girl, but what was in a name? Gemma had cargoes to plunder. She had a crew to feed. Did the Kingdom's Parliament of filthy common shop-keepers think of that when they dispatched their clever dogs to hunt her titled head? Not a bit of it. And their cargoes were so luxurious . . . and profitable. Precious metals. Rare jewels. Fine wines. Expensive silks and spices. The latest mechanical advances from the Royal Society. And the squawks of their owners so fine as she attached a noose to a sail and watched their boots kick and struggle.

The crewman on the pilot wheel gave a yelp of alarm as one of the gas lamps illuminating the deep of the dark outside the u-boat imploded. Little pieces of hot glass showered the armoured viewing glass at the fore of the bridge.

'We can't keep this up,' cried the pilot, his eyes focused on the needle of the altimeter, the little needle pushing so far into the red at the right-hand side of the brass dial, there was nowhere left for it to go.

Before the pilot could do anything about it except bitch, Gemma Dark had a pistol out and shoved into his temple. 'Follow my damn orders. Down bubble. Gentle declination, keep on pushing deeper.'

A crack sounded behind her. One of the pieces of oak panelling that lined the bridge splintering as the metal it was riveted to tightened. The wheel shook in the pilot's hands as he tried to fight back his fear.

'*There!*' called the first mate. The black lines of an under-water trench lay revealed by the light of their two intact exterior lamps. 'It's a damn big drop, not on the charts either.'

No. None of this was on the charts. The retreat of the magma of the Fire Sea to the north was leaving a whole new topography under the surface of the sea. Underwater volca-noes, mountains and valleys to be explored. Not on their charts, and certainly not on the charts of Parliament's deadly airship circling above them.

Gemma had chased her luck, just as she always had.

'Head into the trench,' ordered Gemma, counting the seconds from the last thump of a depth charge in her head.

The wheel trembled in the pilot's hands. 'We'll die down there!'

'The correct response is *aye-aye, captain*,' said Gemma, pushing the pistol in tight against his temple.

'They won't set their charges deeper than the seabed,' growled the first mate as he realized what his captain was looking to do.

'No,' Gemma agreed.

'If we last that long,' said the first mate, his eyes settling on the creaking armoured crystal canopy in front of them. A single piece of chemically reinforced glass. If the screen gave way . . .

'Yes,' said Gemma. *If we last that long.*

All around them, the *Princess Clara*'s complaints swelled louder and louder as the darkness of the underwater trench swallowed the vessel up. A last wave of depth charges tumbled towards where the u-boat had just been, drums buckling under extreme pressure even as the charges detonated.

Then, as the avalanche into the trench started to rain down onto her u-boat's hull, Gemma Dark's luck finally turned.

CHAPTER ONE

This wasn't the normal quality of residence Dick Tull got to stake out. When you worked for the State Protection Board, the preservation of the realm was more often made in the great slums of the capital, blighted tenements their lowlife inhabitants called the *rookeries*. Where narrow streets and broken gas lamps simmered with the smoke of manufactories, and alehouse talk ran to rebellion and plots.

In the slums, it was easy to surveil such souls as Dick Tull's masters suspected of treason. Anyone with a room would gratefully accept pennies from a stranger in exchange for an hour or two at a cracked window overlooking a similarly rundown tenement. Peeping Tom, arsonist, murderer, stalker, State Protection Board officer. Owners hardly cared, as long as the coin provided proved genuine. Parliament's enemies bred like rats inside the filth and the poverty of the slums. But *here*? Waiting on the pavement of a well-lit boulevard? A long line of almost identical five-storey townhouses behind Dick, the fine wrought iron gates and high walls of Lord Chant's residence in front of him on the opposite side of the street. Dick could smell their money; smell it as only someone who had never had any could. From the shining copper spears of the railings to the way manservants would imperiously emerge to greet calling guests.

Bugger the lot of them.

Dick Tull was dressed in the dark frock coat of a hansom cab driver, warming his freezing hands on the brazier at the street's cab halt opposite his cabbie apprentice. That much of his disguise was genuine. Dick Tull was the master, while young William Beresford was standing in the apprentice's shoes Dick had occupied some forty years before. Eager and stupid and patriotic. Too dull to realize there had never been any shine in the great game; that he and Dick were just the weight of the manacles needed to bind the common people from getting above their station. Glorified watchmen, protecting the shiny bright railings of these expensive whitewashed buildings from the forces of anarchy. And like all good watchmen, Billy-boy had been set to watch, watch with his keen young eyes.

But what about Dick? What good was it being the state's muscle, when the muscles were growing old, aged and weak? Dick's thin hands covered with grey fingerless wool gloves, the ageing skin on his hangdog face almost cracking in the late evening chill. Watching, always watching. Just like the State Protection Board's motto bid them to: *See all. Say nothing.*

For most of his life, Dick Tull had been seeing all and saying nothing. And now he could see that he wasn't just training another fledgling officer in the arcania and tricks of the spying trade. He was training his replacement. And where would that leave Dick? Shivering out in the cold, no doubt, like the old nag clicking its horseshoes at the front of their fake hansom cab. One step away from the knacker's yard, that's all Dick was.

While Dick Tull's cheeks were pale and drawn, frigid under the long side burns, young William Beresford's cheeks were flushed a rosy red by the cold, his eyes eager and bright. Tull could bring a flush to his cheeks too. He drew out the dented brass hip flask from under his coat and downed a burning slug of its bounty, ignoring the disapproving look from his partner.

'Just my cover,' said Dick.

'There's a lot of cover sloshing about in there, sarge.'

'It'll be a long night,' said Dick.

And he was relying on the boy's young eager eyes to memorize the faces of any royalist rebels that might come calling at Lord Chant's place tonight.

'Jigger this for a fool's errand, anyway,' Dick spat.

'What makes you say that, sarge?' William asked.

Dick nodded towards the mansion gates. 'Why would rebels want to infiltrate Lord Chant's household? If they wanted to assassinate him, they wouldn't need to go to all the trouble of getting one of their people into his household, would they? They could just stand out here shivering their nuts off alongside us, and the first time his Lordship came out, well—' Dick patted the side of his frock coat where his pistol was strapped, '—a bullet in the head is a lot less trouble than play-acting as a butler and slipping poison into his nib's brandy glass.'

'I hear an old man talking, sarge,' said William. 'Where's your sense of imagination? Lord Chant is a force in the House of Guardians, keeper of the privy something or other. He has the keys to the parliamentary chamber. What if that's what they're after? The board ain't going to want a gang of royalist scum slipping a dozen barrels of liquid explosives under Parliament's floorboards, are they? Or they could be trying to blackmail his lordship, leverage his connections in the house.'

Yes, the boy had a point. Clever. Ambitious. Well educated. All the things that Dick was not. Give it a couple of years, and if by some good chance Dick was still on the payroll of the board, then he would likely be working for Billy-boy here. If not him, someone just like him. They all got promoted over his head. And here he was, shivering on a rich man's street, all these years later. The quality giving Dick orders, giving him long, tiring night-time surveillances with added apprentice-minding duties.

At some point in this long dirty trade, Dick had turned around, and when he'd glanced back, his life had passed him by. The worst thing was, in retrospect Dick could gaze back and see all the decisions he'd made, settlements that he could have remade, to nudge his life towards the better. The things he should have said, the people he should have talked to, the paths he should have gone down. There was a trend now in the penny-dreadfuls – cheap fiction from the stationers' stalls – for what were called counterfactuals, invented histories that could have been, but hadn't. Dick could see the counterfactual for his own life – a career where he had ended up as a senior board officer, with a fat pension and a big house and a plump happy wife, smiling sunny children waiting for him when he got home. And in that counterfactual, perhaps the Dick Tull in that world was dreaming of a thin, hungry doppelganger of himself, his hair running grey beyond his years, and nothing to return to of an evening except cold rented lodgings in one of the least salubrious parts of town. A shrew of a landlady who spied on him just as he spied on the enemies of the Jackelian nation. *It's never made easy. Not for me.*

Dick glanced down the street. As late as it was, the street was still surprisingly empty – only a few street hawkers trying to entice householders' servants to the doorstep for a final purchase of the day. And it wasn't just because of the thin white layer of snow and frost painting the cobbles and trees along the road. There was something else stalking the streets of the capital, if the newssheets were to be believed. *Vampires*. Tales like that should have been confined to the pages of the penny-dreadfuls that were one of Dick's more faithful companions in bed, but now the Middlesteel press was running with headlines as sensational as their editors' imaginations. Bodies were being discovered in the capital of the Kingdom drained of every last vestige of blood. In the east of the city where Dick's humble lodgings could be found, the people were patrolling the narrow streets in gangs of vigilantes – although they preferred to call themselves the 'city militia'. The Circle help anyone that got in their way. For, like Dick, the Middlesteel mob had never seen a vampire. In fact, until now, nobody who wasn't a fan of inferior literature had ever encountered a vampire in the Kingdom of Jackals. This presented something of a problem for the rough militia rabble . . . but one that had not proved insurmountable. With the mob's usual ingenuity, they were now resorting to the simple expedient of hanging any strangers who had the misfortune to be travelling unrecognized through the streets.

Of course, in a rich area like this, no militia had been formed of middle-class clerks, bankers, merchants and their household staff. The rich didn't get their hand dirty, that's what they paid their taxes for. Quite literally. For to be made a Lord in the Kingdom was not a matter of birth now, but a matter of money. The industrial purchase system. The revenue service kept a record of how much tax was paid by each citizen. Passing set amounts over your lifetime would automatically trigger a title . . . a small amount of tax earning a knighthood, a filthily large amount guaranteeing a dukedom.

'Here we go, then,' said Dick, the noise of iron wheels rattling on cobblestones given amplification by the cold night air. Around the corner emerged one of the more recent varieties of horseless carriages. Steam-driven, the carriage was wider, taller and a great deal less elegant than the high-tension clockwork driven vehicles that until recently had been the mainstay of traffic running through the capital's streets. But that was progress for you. Legislation had been passed last year in Parliament allowing these ugly, cheap, steam-driven brutes to share the road, and now the capital's crowded passages were filled with the smoke and noise of such things. The press had nicknamed them *kettle-blacks* and already the omnibus companies had pressed them into service for the conveyance of paying passengers. If Dick had been a real hansom cab driver, he might have been retiring in the next few years, he suspected. *Always change. Never for the better.*

Pulling to a stop, the vehicle's stacks melted a few flurries of snow drifting in the air. Down below, a heavy iron door jolted open, spilling yellow gaslight from the passenger cabin out onto the pavement. A hunched figure emerged into the light, a dull brown workman's coat pulled tight over his frame against the cold, the man coughing in the chill air after exiting the heat circulating from the cabin's boiler.

Dick Tull peered from the cab halt. *Damn my tired old eyes. Is that the man we've been waiting for, is that Carl Redlin? Ask the boy. The boy will know.* 'Is that Carl Redlin?'

'I think so,' said Billy-boy. Surreptitiously, the young agent used the cover of their hansom cab to inspect the images they had been provided of likely callers at Lord Chant's house. He located the sheet with their mark's likeness, excitedly tapped it, and then slipped the sheets back under the flap cabmen used to store their street maps.

Well, then, perhaps there was some truth to this nonsense assignment their masters within the board had assigned them. Captain Twist was an old pseudonym used by royalists when

11

they returned to the Kingdom with mischief on their minds. And now Captain Twist was abroad in Middlesteel again, with his rascally minions scuttling about the city. Dick was surprised. After all, nobody knew better than he did how far the card of the royalist threat was overplayed by Parliament to bolster its popularity. Yet here was a known royalist, Carl Redlin, calling at the residence of Lord Chant.

I should be relieved. Now they'll pull me off this sodding cold surveillance and put someone on the job who counts. Who would've thought it, after all these centuries, Captain Twist and his merry men back in the Kingdom?

In the wall by the side of the gate there was a recess with a wooden handle to pull, and the visitor placed his hand into the niche, gave the handle a tug, then yanked his flatcap down tight as the gates moved back on a counterweight. Their mark didn't wait for the gates to fully open, he was in too much of a hurry. As soon as there was enough of a gap for him to wriggle through the space he did so, and then he was off, down the path that led up to the white marble-fronted mansion, his footsteps dragging against the gravel. The distant barking of a dog greeted the man as the main doors swung open. Too far away for Dick to see who'd allowed him inside Lord Chant's mansion.

'Come on, sarge,' urged William, 'we can follow Redlin in. We might be able to see who he's going to meet if we can get to a window.'

'Are you joking me, boy?' said Dick. 'We haven't been ordered to do that. Now we know that the rebels have business inside the house, there's plenty of time to get a man inside on the staff. You don't want to be spotted creeping around the grounds – someone's likely to take a blunderbuss to you.'

What was the boy like? Plenty of time for an agent with

suitable references – perfectly forged, of course – to be inserted as a member of the household. Eager little sod.

It was obvious that Billy-boy was bridling against the older officer's orders, but he was the junior man on this watch and while he might be giving orders to Dick next year, tonight he had to bite his tongue and keep his peace.

'So, what do you propose we do, sarge?'

'We wait. When he comes out, we'll follow Redlin, see where he goes. Is that enough action for you for tonight?'

William shook his head in disgust, but Dick was beyond caring what the boy thought of him.

You'll see, Billy-boy. Give it a few decades, and you'll be where I am. Making some new young fool bite on the bit while you urge caution and pull your tired bones up into the cab of the hansom, lift your boots up onto the seat opposite, and take a few more hits from the flask you're keeping warm in your coat pocket.

'Is that it then? You're just going to sit up there in the cab and watch?'

'No,' said Dick. '*You* are going to watch, I'm going to catch up on my shut-eye now that our mark is safely tucked up over there. Just wake me up when he comes out again.'

Dick reached for his copy of the *Middlesteel Illustrated Times*. The front cover carried a large political cartoon of the head of the government, the First Guardian, bending over at the beach of a seaside resort while one of the underwater races, a gill-neck, was creeping out from behind the shadow of a bathing machine with a trident-like weapon to poke him up the arse. The politician's buttocks were painted with the Jackelian flag, and he was reaching for a coin washed in by the tide, while the speech bubble rising from the gill-neck's mouth read, '*Now, there's a fine pair of plums for the picking*'.

There was still a furore being raised by the newssheets over the new taxes the great underwater empire of the Advocacy was attempting to levy on Jackelian shipping – innocently crossing international waters, or aggressively trespassing across sovereign territory, depending on whether you were human or gill-neck. But however expensive shipments of plums and other fruits from the orchards of the colonies became, this was one conflict the State Protection Board wasn't going to be called into to provide intelligence for. There were a lot of foreigners an officer like Dick Tull could mingle with undetected, but lacking scales and the ability to breathe underwater, gill-necks weren't one of them. Dick folded the pages over his face to mask the glare of the gas lamps. With his liquid winter-warmer circulating through his body, Dick let the tiredness slip over him, the wooden curve of the cab keeping out the worst chilly draughts as he drifted off to sleep.

It hardly seemed any time at all until a rough shaking jolted him back into the cab's still interior. William's face was flushed, but not this time, Dick suspected, from the scouring wind of a long wait and the rude health of the boy's callow constitution. *He's panicked.*

'Our mark out of the big house already, is he?'

'No, it's not that.' There was a look on Billy-boy's face that Dick had not seen before. It was alarm mixed with confusion.

'I went over the wall—'

'You fool! If you've been spotted, if you've blown this job for us . . .' Dick jumped out of the cab, nearly slipping on the pavement's ice. As he angrily steadied himself, Dick saw that his stumble had been noted by a bookseller a couple of houses down the street, the hawker's tray of cheap novels covered with a piece of cloth to protect it against falling snow. The bookseller hurriedly looked away, no doubt not wanting

14

to test the aggressive reputation a hansom cab driver carried. There was something familiar about that face, something—

'No, I've not been seen, it's *what* I've seen, sarge,' continued the young officer, speaking so fast he was almost choking on his words. 'I was hiding in the formal garden when Lady Florence came running out, our mark Carl Redlin and Lord Chant close on her heels. They grabbed her, pushed her down into the snow, and then stabbed her with some kind of blade. Both of them. It only took a minute for Lady Florence to die, then they dragged her body back into the mansion and locked the patio again.'

'That doesn't make sense!' coughed Dick, all vestiges of drowsiness vanishing as he realized what he'd slept through.

His mind reeled. Lady Florence Chant, if he remembered their briefing correctly, was a forgettable society beauty, a clothes-horse, well mannered, without a political bone in her body. She didn't have access to Parliament. Access to her husband's guest lists for the boring suppers she was expected to host, perhaps. Royalist rebels didn't risk capture in the capital to help errant husbands murder their spouses, and certainly not by such an obvious route as stabbing. A fall down the stairs, perhaps. A heart attack induced by a crafty poison, maybe. But cold-blooded murder in a garden, run down like a fox to hounds when any neighbour could be staring out from one of the houses opposite?

'Sense or not, I saw it. *We have to do something*!'

'Not us, lad,' said Dick. He felt the lines of his greying moustache, as he was wont to do when thinking or nervous. 'We report it back up through the board. They notify the police. Let the common crushers go in there and stir everything up. If we charge into the big house, we'll tip off any royalist inside that we're onto them.'

'I'll send for the police now,' said Billy-boy.

'What if they arrest our mark? We need to follow him back to his nest of troublemakers, not have him locked up in Bonegate jail waiting for the noose.'

'Didn't you hear me, sarge? Our mark's helped murder someone,' said William. 'Carl Redlin won't be hanging around the capital after this. He'll be gone anyway, whatever we do.'

You've got a point, damn your eyes. 'Put up the sign, then,' sighed Dick.

The sign that would indicate their horse was lame. The sign that would tell their runner on his next circuit past that they needed to send an urgent message to the board. Getting the police involved in their business, garden-variety crushers from Ham Yard, that wasn't going to be welcome back in the board, back in the civil service's draughty offices at the heart of the city. What was the nickname that the other civil servants called the State Protection Board? *The peculiar gentlemen.* And this business was getting more peculiar by the hour.

Dick Tull made William hang back as the constables summoned from Ham Yard hammered at the door of the mansion.

One of Lord Chant's butlers opened the door, a curious expression passing across the man's impeccably haughty face as he took in the ranks of police lined up outside. 'How can I help you gentlemen?'

'That would depend now, sir,' said the inspector standing at the head of the coppers. 'We have had an account from a neighbour who reported Lady Florence coming to something of an injury inside your garden.'

Indignation mixed with displeasure as the old butler arched an eyebrow. 'If there had been an accident involving Lady Florence, I can assure you I would have been informed, and shortly thereafter, it would be her ladyship's personal physician attending our doorstep, not the officers of the Middlesteel constabulary.'

'That it is as maybe,' said the inspector, 'but a report has been made, and our inquiries must follow. Now then, be so good as to fetch Lord Chant.'

'If it is her ladyship's health you wish to inquire after, I shall not be troubling his lordship. I shall summon her ladyship, to quicken the removal of your presence and the disturbance you're creating this evening.'

Her ladyship? He's in for a shock, then.

Dick Tull angled his neck for a better view of the richly appointed hallway beyond the constables' peaked pillbox-style caps. So much sodding money. How much wealth had been spent in furnishing the vast space? Alabaster-white figureheads on columns engraved with victory scenes, the ancestors of Lord Chant, their humble tradesmen's origins unsurprisingly not reflected in the statues' noble poise, patrician robes hardly suited to the tradesman stock of a factory owner. Dick could feel the warmth flooding out into the night, underfloor heating pipes kept warm by some great boiler in the basement of the mansion, tended by stokers and eating up an expensive supply of shire-mined coal. Such waste, such extravagance. The fuel they were using to heat that hall that would have kept Dick's lodgings warm for a month.

I should have a hallway like this. Well, let's see them produce her ladyship. That'll wipe the superior smile off their man's face, suck some of the warmth out of Lord Chant's comfortable life. Fat rich sod. Let's see how he copes in a prison cell. It won't be warm inside Bonegate Jail. Nobody waiting on him hand and foot, no summoning breakfast with a pull of a chord by his bedside.

There was one thing that Dick Tull had to say about Lady Florence. She looked good for a dead woman. She certainly looked better than the image of her that he'd seen in their briefing. The daguerreotype hardly did justice to her long curled blonde hair, as elaborate as the gown of pure velvet that curved seductively around her arms and neck, her face as perfect and flawless as the statues she was passing.

'An unexpected pleasure,' she smiled as warmly as the heat of the air gushing out into the night. 'Old Cutler tells me that our neighbours across the road have concerns about my welfare. They are dears, but it was quite a minor slip on the ice in my garden. Nothing apart from a slight mud stain on my dress and the loss of dignity secured from the fall.' She stopped to indicate a long thin hound with yellow fur lounging around the top of her wide, sweeping stairs. 'But Brutus does need his exercise, or he makes the most terrible mess in the parlour.'

'You know that it's my duty to take the dog outside, your ladyship,' said the butler, in a hurt tone of voice, as if his personal honour had been offended. 'Especially in this ugly weather.'

'Then when would I take my exercise?' said the woman. 'I step from door to carriage and from carriage to door. My little darling keeps me company, and we exercise each other. Peace now, gentlemen, since you have taken the trouble to visit, I quite insist that you come inside out of the cold while old Cutler goes down the stairs to cook and fetches up a tray of tea and biscuits. You must warm up before you venture out once more to mind our safety. I certainly wouldn't want to be bitten by any of those dreadful creatures with their monstrous appetite for blood.'

Dick Tull didn't need the heat of a mug to warm him, as he held onto the bubbling outrage he was feeling towards one William Beresford. The young officer had made a fool out of him with his tale of Lady Florence's murder. When the board's runner had stopped at their cab halt, Dick had needed to confirm Billy-boy's story, and present it as his own as the senior agent on duty. After all, he hardly could have admitted that he had been snoring off the contents of his hip flask inside the hansom cab when he should have been alert and watchful. *It's never made easy. Not for me.*

So, this was the way the ambitious young tyke had found to get back at him. Making him look a fool in front of the board. He glanced around. Billy-boy had vanished. No doubt sniggering all the ways back to the board's headquarters. What would Dick say to the two new extra State Protection Board intelligencers waiting outside, waiting to see if their mark made a bolt for it? *Just a mistake. Sorry about that. A murder? No, it was a fall while walking the dog. It all looks the same when you get to my age.* And with a royalist rebel somewhere inside the building, no doubt cultivating contacts on the staff under the guise of being a relative or peddler. If the rebel troublemaker spooked, if he scarpered now, it would be Dick Tull's head on the block, not the royalist's.

Old Cutler appeared leading a pair of footmen, two younger versions of himself in black livery, bearing trays jingling with delicate porcelain cups and raisin-encrusted biscuits. Well, there was no need for the night to be a complete waste of time, not now that Dick was freed from young Billy-boy's disapproving gaze.

With the police constables' attention focused on the bounty of the unexpected brew, and the serving staff distracted by the presence of the constables, Dick expertly removed a pair of silver candlesticks from the mantelpiece and slipped them inside his great coat. He could tell from the heft of the ornamental showpieces that they were solid silver, nothing cheap about them. They would be worth a pretty penny in the pawnshop off Ruffler Avenue where Dick kept his lodgings.

19

That was the good thing about working for the State Protection Board, he was protected from the sort of questions asked when producing such candlesticks for sale – or even worse, getting the kind of lowball price offered to a common criminal trying to fence his wares. Dick just had to open his leather wallet and flash his silver badge of state, and all questions would gag to a faltering halt in the pawnshop owner's mouth.

Lord Chant won't miss it, not with factories full of toilers like me stamping out wealth for him every day. Sweating his workers in this cold, day in, day out. A new pair of silver candlesticks falling into his pockets every hour. Well, these two are for poor old Dick, so thank you, my lord commercial, here's to you and your fat pockets, padded with more money than you can spend in a dozen lifetimes.

Dick slipped back outside, to the cab halt where the hansom cab should be, finding only a single board officer waiting – with no sign of that sly little chancer, Billy-boy. Their cab had vanished, along with the second agent watching the gates. With a terse exchange of words, Dick discovered that their mark had come out of the mansion gates while he and the constables had been inside the house. Only a couple of minutes ago, the second agent had let their mark reach the end of the street on foot, then the agent casually set off in the hansom cab, taking Billy-boy along in case he needed an extra pair of boots to drop off and follow the mark through the streets on foot. Had the rebel been spooked by the arrival of the police? Pray he wasn't lost in the narrow alleyways of the capital.

Billy-boy's done his work well this night. I've been royally rogered. He'll get the commendation for following our mark back to his nest. I'll be left looking like an idiot. Perhaps he'll be giving orders to me earlier than I expected, now. Ambitious little sod.

Dick Tull put off the remaining officer's questions about the constables' business inside the mansion. Their masters in the board would hear about this night's tomfoolery soon enough, when the inspector inside the house got back to his warm offices in Ham Yard and started complaining about his time being wasted by the civil service, by the peculiar gentlemen.

Dick stood there for a moment, angrily brooding, as the remaining agent left now that he'd been updated on the surveillance. Dick was about to head off in the opposite direction when he noticed it. Such a small matter, but an obvious thing when spied from afar. The hawker with the bookseller's tray was still at the far end of the street, and he crossed the street before the departing officer reached him. As casual as you like, crouching by a lamp-post in the shadow of Lord Chant's high wall and sorting his stock out. *In the falling snow.*

The hawker had been watching them, coming and going, Billy-boy and Dick, then the extra two bruisers from the board, just a single cab at the halt, with a supposedly lame horse that was suddenly able to follow their mark exiting the mansion. Dick's frock coat exchanged for a nondescript great coat to blend in as one of the plainclothes' inspector's men when the police had turned up. The hawker had been watching the agents, and he'd pegged the peculiar gentlemen for what they really were, and now he was pretending to do a stock-take on the other side of the road so the agent wouldn't see his face . . . his face. *His face that had been one of the mugs on the sheets of known royalist rebels!* Rufus Symons, that was the bogus hawker's name. A descendent of the old aristocracy, the kind that hadn't needed to pay an industrialist's share of taxes to purchase their baronial titles. The forty-second Baron of Henrickshire, in fact. The county didn't even

21

exist any more, while the fury at being disinherited of its wealth centuries ago still festered on.

But why would a royalist covertly watch his fellow rebels? Did the silly buggers suffer from the same factional infighting that the civil service saw? Only one way to find out the answer to that question, and in its answer, perhaps a chance for Dick to divert the board's wrath when they brought him in to answer why the capital's constables had been sent calling on Lord Chant for the sake of a slipped heel in the garden.

Dick headed off in the opposite direction from the hawker and then doubled back on his tracks using the street behind the townhouses, following the rear of the crescent around to where he could catch up with the honourable Rufus Symons. As Dick suspected, once he'd left the cab halt, the fake hawker had wasted no time leaving the scene of his own watch. Symons hadn't been brave enough to trail the exiting mark, not with his fellow rebel being followed by the secret police – or attempt to warn him, for that matter, that the authorities were following his tracks. But perhaps that merely showed a measure of sensible caution. They were rare creatures, now, royalists – supplanted by the lords' commercial for centuries, hunted down and vilified with all the sins of the Jackelian nation still lumped upon their heads. You couldn't blame Symons for wanting to preserve his own skin, whatever his motive for mounting a surveillance alongside the secret police.

Dick hung back from the rebel, not wanting to get too close, the weight of the stolen candlesticks still swinging heavy inside his coat. When he had a moment, Dick changed the coat's pattern by reversing the garment, warm brown fur on the outside – the kind of garment that might be worn by one of the repair crew of patchers that climbed the city's towers. He changed his gait, too, a confident strut to match the expandable low-crowned John Gloater top-hat that was now covering his silver hair. There was no longer much of the hansom cab driver about Dick.

It wasn't difficult to stay out of the rebel's sight, following behind him and masked by the falling snow at night, the gaps between each gas lamp filled with shifting mists and vapours. It got easier still, once the rich residential district fell behind, pressing towards the heart of the city, where Middlesteel's streets still had patrons falling out of drinking houses and Jackelians whistling down cabs and climbing into private coaches as they exited theatres and gambling dens. Symons was spry on his feet, doing everything correctly to check if he was being followed. All the little halts and checks, the sudden changes of direction; stopping by the harp maker's window to snatch a quick look behind him in the reflection of the glass panes. Ducking through the tavern crowd in the *Crooked Chimney* and out through the drinking house's back entrance, into the side street where Dick was already waiting. But this was bread and butter to Dick. If he had an art, this was it. Wherever Symons looked, Dick Tull wasn't, all the way underground to the atmospheric line at Guardian Lenthall station, and then they were both just part of the throng crowding its way onto the platform. When the next capsule shunted through the rubber airlock, Dick waited for the rebel to board, spotting the heap of the hawker's jacket shrugged off on the platform and being trampled underfoot. Then the capsule's brass doors swung shut, a slight hiss as its airtight integrity was proved to the instruments on board, before being shunted through the rubber curtain and into the pneumatic tubes, the pressure differential building up until they were hurtling through the airless tunnels like a bullet. There was Symons, now wearing the black jacket of the middling sort of clerk who inhabited the towers of the capital's counting houses, no sign of his hawker's tray, his narrow cheeks having acquired a thin pair of spectacles to perch on the end of his nose.

Rufus Symons must have been comfortable that he wasn't being followed – there were no false exits by the door of the atmospheric capsule as it pulled into the concourses of other stations, no sudden step backs into the carriage as if he had changed his mind about his destination at the last minute. When the rebel did exit, there were enough people moving on and off the concourse that Dick's own exit didn't appear contrived.

Just a tired patcher returning home, but where was home? The answer to that appeared to be at the foot of one of the tall hills that surrounded the capital, the city thinning out into a cluster of village-like lanes at its outskirts, a couple of cobbled streets surrounded by shops and homes climbing upwards on a steep incline.

I've been here before. On the business of the board, too. When was it?

The feeling of recollection grew stronger as Dick followed Symons up the hill. There were large houses at the top of the hill, he recalled, with their own grounds. Not as expensive as Lord Chant's, but then this district was too near the outskirts of the city to begin to be considered fashionable. A place for independent thinkers, the kind of person who didn't care what others thought of them, who valued the view over the pneumatic towers at the capital's heart, haze rising into the sky from the heated water flowing through their rubberized skins. The sort of soul who had no use for society invites and could see poetry in the venting steam from the mills below curling into the darkening sky, obscuring the collision lamps of airships passing through heaven's command.

This is where I'd end up if I only had the money for it. If only I could go back in time and take my chances again. A nice clean ward. No thieves rattling my skylight, waking me up in the small hours, sending me reaching for the pistol under my pillow. No drunken singing in the middle of the night from gangs of full-up-to-the-knocker louts falling out of alehouses.

There was a village green at the top of the hill, a duck pond frozen enough that a couple of birds were skating over its surface, using the light spilling out from the crescent of houses and cottages on the other side to try to find a break and a drink of water. Dick's quarry was heading towards an arched opening in a brick wall on the other side of pond, the wall's shadow just taller than a man's height, foliage from an orchard rising up beyond the bricks, and behind that, a single large tower crowned with an illuminated clock face.

Dick didn't need to see the residence's name engraved in the brass plate by the entrance, just the sight of the folly rising like a landlocked lighthouse enough to shake the memory of his single visit here years before. Tock House. The State Protection Board knew well the true identity of the man who lived behind these comfortable walls; after all, they had been using it to blackmail him into working for the secret police for long enough. Commodore Jared Black. A royalist who had changed his identity so many times in his life on the run, it was a wonder he still knew who he was. And when he'd finally stopped running, the board had eventually caught up with him and sunk its claws in his tired old flesh. They had turned him and used him to their own ends.

You're meant to be our asset, Blacky, you old rascal. You had better not be playing both sides of the field. Backsliding with your old rebel friends.

Here was information worth having. But he'd have to tread softly. The commodore was as sly as a fox, and there were always wheels within wheels where he was involved. He might act like a blustering old sea dog, but the man was deadly with a sabre and cunning enough to have survived everything fate and the dangerous, unasked for duties of the board had thrown at him. There were those who played in the great game as masters, and old Blacky was one of them. Double agent, triple? Or more likely only ever on his own side? Dick'd have to play this one right carefully with the brass-buttoned officers back in the board – there were those who wouldn't take kindly to having one of their prize chickens plucked bare by a lowly officer of Dick Tull's standing.

Dick patted the side-pocket of his coat where the comforting weight of the two stolen silver candles lay, and then he smiled. *I'll be back for you, Blacky. See if I can't wipe that smug smile off of your wine-stained lips. Back to squeeze you for the truth of what you, Symons, and all your royalist friends scampering about the capital are up to. You've just become my ace card, you sod, and I'm keeping you tucked up my sleeve.*

CHAPTER TWO

'As you can see,' said Charlotte, her husky voice cutting across the assemblage, 'there is nothing tucked up my sleeves.'

Not that the mostly male audience was interested in looking up her decorated sleeves when she had left so much else on show, her powder-blue dress shockingly low cut for high society's current standards; fanning delicately over the sides of the purple crinoline skirt riding her willowy hips.

Distraction, it was all about distraction. Especially for the sponsors of this coming-out ball, who would hopefully never piece together Charlotte Shades' true involvement with what would really be coming out this night – and not just the dull debutante daughters of a mob of fat mill owners and merchant lords.

'But—' she continued, gesturing theatrically towards the member of the audience plucked up to the stage, '—while there is nothing up my sleeve, might there not be something in your pocket?'

There was a collective gasp of astonishment from the

audience as the man on stage tugged his gold pocket watch out of his pocket.

'It still works,' Charlotte reassured him. After having seen it wrapped in her handkerchief and smashed to pieces he looked at it doubtfully dangling from its expensive chain. 'But, alas, I couldn't fix it from being a minute slow. My skills in the sorcerer's arts do not extend to matters horological.'

'Upon my life,' huffed the man. 'It still works!'

Charlotte bowed as she took the round of applause, trying to ignore the shouts for extra acts of hypnotism. That was the trouble with owning a flashy stage name such as *Charlotte Shades, Mistress of Mesmerism*. It was catchy enough to act as a lure for invites into the grand mansions of the nobility (which proved lucrative in so many ways). But her clients always wanted to see tricks of hypnotism, and she was loath to reveal just how well she could perform her artifice. *Nothing to make you think too hard about me. Distraction, it's all about distraction. Just a performing curiosity, capering about the stage for your entertainment, my lords.*

She addressed the audience. 'I have found it advantageous to always leave gentlemen requesting an extra encore. Besides, I fear my account at Lords Bank may be cancelled if its chief cashier is once more made to believe he is a humble lamp lighter, and the notes in his wallet the wicks he must ignite.'

Hoots of good-natured laughter echoed around the chamber.

'Away. Away, I have detained you from your daughters and your better halves for long enough. And even the Mistress of Mesmerism does not possess the magic to transform a wife's ire into happiness if you miss the start of the debutantes' procession tonight.'

And I need to away too, before tonight's patron, his Excellency the Duke Commercial Edwin, discovers some disreputable rogue has transformed his prized private gallery into an empty strong room with a blank wall.

It was as the crowd broke up and began to disperse back to the mansion's ballroom that she caught sight of the man. It wasn't just that he was out of place here, runaday cloth on a bland suit without the assured stance of the wealthy and powerful – but his face was a policeman's face. They all had that stare, unflinching and jaded – a stare that had seen it all and kept on watching until it finally got tired of judging. A little island of self-awareness fixed in this aristocratic surf of egos and vanities, lonely among the preening popinjays floating around him.

Haven't I been careful enough tonight? What's he doing here, in the audience? Not a coincidence, not the way he's watching me. Someone hired by one of the many patrons who'd woken up in the morning to find their jewel boxes broken open and their safes emptied? Ham Yard, or a consulting detective specialising in private resolutions? She didn't need to discover what he was. Like all good conjurers, Charlotte knew when it was time to disappear.

Jumping down from the stage, Charlotte allowed herself to believe she had lost him, filtering through the flow of departing guests, but someone came up behind her and shoved her arm behind her back so roughly it made the jab of the pistol in her ribs redundant. She tried to protest, and in doing so caught a glimpse of her captor. Not the policeman after all, someone else . . . a short broken-nosed bruiser with the kind of face only a mother could love. Charlotte was frog-marched out of the chamber she'd been performing in, through a small wooden door and into a large private library with a hillside view down to a river running through a valley. Shutting the library door behind him came the simply dressed gentleman with a police-man's gaze, a velvet cape lined spilled blood-red flashing behind him as he locked the door with a clack.

Charlotte smiled her best innocent smile. If she could just get the two of them standing together . . . but broken nose was a shadow behind her, the pistol in his hand. 'I didn't know his Excellency the duke commercial operated a reading group, or that you were so desperate for new blood that you have to abduct his guests.'

'I prefer the newssheets to novels,' smiled the gentleman, very little warmth on his thin lips. He perched himself comfortably on the edge of a large mahogany reading table, both hands clutching a wooden cane. 'Fact is so much more informing than fiction. How do you think the headlines will read tomorrow, Damson Shades? Does the Mistress of Mesmerism also dabble in the art of precognition – is there, perhaps, a crystal ball among the possessions of your conjurer's chest?'

'Why sir, if I had the gift of future sight, I'd be following the racing season with wager slips in my pocket, not performing for the debutante season.'

'Oh, I don't know, Damson Shades. I think there is profit enough in performing under the duke's roof. Did you know he has a painting in his private collection, *Turn Back to Yesterday*, worth its weight in gold? I find Walter Snagsby's works a little chocolate-box for my tastes. All those bucolic scenes of village fields and cows and milkmaids.'

'An art critic as well,' said Charlotte. 'Who are you, honey?'

The gentleman lifted a newspaper out of a reading rack and laid it down on the table. 'My companion is Mister Cloake. You may call me Mister Twist. So, you have no magic incantations to allow you to see the future?'

Charlotte slowly shook her head.

Twist laid aside his cane and moved the palms of his hand over the open pages of the newspaper, as if he was divining for water, humming theatrically as he did so. 'Ah, the clouds are parting. I see . . . a robbery. The thief the papers call the Sable Caracal has struck again, leaving her mocking calling card tucked into an empty picture frame.' He patted his pockets, and with a false look of surprise pulled out an oblong of cardboard with two feline eyes embossed on it. 'And as if by magic . . .'

'Seeing as it's you that's carrying one of those, perhaps it's *his* mocking calling card?'

Twist spun the card between his long fingers. 'Well, most people think these cards are just a piece of theatre to taunt the police. But anyone with a deeper understanding knows that it's actually to announce which criminal lord's protection the thief is operating under – and which flash mob an interested buyer should contact to obtain a stolen piece. In this case, the Cat-gibbon and her gang of cut throats.'

Charlotte's heart sank. And only the Cat-gibbon had known she was here tonight for the painting.

I've been sold out. But who has the balls to lean on the Cat-gibbon? She'd dump the body of any police inspector who came calling in the river just for the cheek of asking her to give up one of her prize thieves.

Charlotte considered using the jewel nestled on a chain around her neck, the Eye of Fate, but it had been acting oddly ever since these two devils had appeared, throbbing like a piece of cold ice huddled against her skin. It had never done that before.

Scaring my jewel, scaring the Cat-gibbon – okay, consider me appropriately terrified Mister Twist.

'You're not with the police.'

'Certainly not the dull plodding kind that feels the collars of pickpockets for transportation to the colonies,' said Twist.

'So what do you want?'

'You've left your calling card,' said Twist, pushing the

oblong of card down onto the reading table. 'And we've come calling.'

His companion was still behind Charlotte, and she didn't need the cold burning weight on her chest to know that he had his pistol pointed at her spine.

'An engagement at your gentlemen's club, perhaps?'

'A more exclusive venue,' said Twist. 'The House of Guardians.'

Parliament! In terms of my usual venues, that's certainly a move up in the world.

'Do you think there's a ward where I could get elected?'

Twist shrugged. 'The bastard issue of Lady Mary's affair with the scandalous lord commercial, Abraham Quest. I suspect not, if that fact became known.'

They knew all about her. The Cat-gibbon really had given her up.

Charlotte felt a familiar twinge of old wounds being rubbed raw. 'I prefer illegitimate and reserve the term bastard for scoundrels like you.'

'Perhaps I am. Yet, it was your mother who stopped paying your foster parents shortly before she got remarried. Worried about the duke tracing the payments, finding out about you and calling the wedding off, I daresay.'

And hadn't they been quick to throw me out onto the streets when the baby farming payments stopped.

'The term for that, Mister Twist, is bitch, not bastard. At least it is, if it's my mother you're referring to'

'Oh, but it must rankle,' said Twist. 'You should have been the heir to one of the greatest fortunes in the Kingdom, blood as refined as any inside this house – well, at least on your mother's side, your father was quite the chancer. And here you are, flashing your legs and bosom on stage among bursts of conjurer's powder, your hand dipping into the cutlery tray for silver when nobody's watching.'

'I get by.'

'I would imagine that getting by is the thing that weighs most on your soul. Ever a guest, on sufferance at the feast. Have you been inside Parliament, the visitors' gallery perhaps?'

Charlotte shook her head.

'You would like it. Its chamber is packed to the gunnels with all the richest and most powerful people in the land. The ones who should have been your peers at some expensive finishing school. Instead, there you were as a child, scraping around for bones with meat left on in the dustbins outside the capital's hotels.'

I did a little better than that. Eventually. 'What's this about, honey? Nobody keeps their valuables in the House of Guardians.'

'Not quite true,' said Twist. He pulled a small wooden box out of his jacket, placed it on the table next to her calling card, and clicking open a pair of clasps on its side he opened it, an interior lined with cloth as crimson as the lining of his cape. On top of the cloth lay three or four punch cards, the heavy card edged with gold.

'To open locks?'

'Perfectly correct – locks in Parliament.' Twist lovingly brushed the tattoo of information that would slot into a transaction-engine's punch card injector, calculation drums turning to the beat of the cipher contained on the cards until heavy bolts withdrew from an armoured door. 'Enough open doors to create an opportunity for, what is it the *Illustrated* calls the Sable Caracal, the nation's most extraordinary and audacious thief?'

'One of their politer headlines. What's inside Parliament you want?'

'A little thing,' said Twist. 'A box under the speaker's chair containing three things. The two amputated arms of the present puppet monarch, stuffed of course—'

'Of course.' *He'd said 'puppet', were these two jokers royalists, then?*

'You can leave those behind. It's not Parliament's stooge raising arms against the people that the guardians need to worry about. The other item under the speaker's chair is far more valuable – the sceptre, the only one of the crown jewels to have survived being melted down and sold off during the innumerable economic crises of the last few centuries.'

'King Jude's sceptre!' Charlotte was incredulous. 'You think I can steal King Jude's sceptre? It must be priceless!'

'Purely sentimental value to me, I can assure you,' said Twist.

'So you two *are* rebels. You must be insane. There won't be a constable or soldier in the land that Parliament won't set on the trail of it if it goes missing.'

'I would be disappointed by anything less. It's a symbol,' said Twist. 'Of Parliament's hegemony over the royal family. Value far beyond the gold and jewels that the sceptre is composed of, and that value is substantial. Think of it, every First Guardian since Isambard Kirkhill overthrew the rightful king has appointed a speaker to sit above that sceptre, their fat arses sweating and wiggling on top of its jewels and crystals. By such acts are history made.'

'I thought the crown jewels were kept in a safe room below Parliament?'

'So they are. When the house is not in session, the box is lowered into a vault, very well protected by guards and traps and doors and thick walls of concrete and metal. We hold the punch cards here to many – but not all – of those doors.'

'Unfortunately, I don't work for sentimental or symbolic value.'

'Nor would I expect you to. You are an artist Damson Shades, and we are asking you to produce your masterwork for us.' Picking up a pen from an inkwell in the table he scrawled a figure on the calling card's blank slide, and pushed it across to her.

Charlotte's eyes widened when she saw the amount, and she worked hard to halt her face from expressing any flicker of interest. *The money helped, it always helped.* 'And the painting from tonight?'

'Already removed from the false bottom of the cabinet you used to saw the duke in half, and returned upstairs. We require the sceptre's delivery with the minimum of fuss; and the postponement of police interest until later.'

'The Cat-gibbon will not be pleased.'

'She is a pragmatist, like all the rulers of the flash mob. We have made, let us say, an accommodation with her.'

That would have been an interesting conversation. Wish I could've been there.

'May I say that one exists between us also?'

Charlotte slipped her calling card back into his lapel pocket. 'For art, Mister Twist. For my masterwork.'

Charlotte made to leave the room, but the man casually raised his cane blocking her exit.

'You appear to be practised in the arts of mesmerism, for—'

'For . . .?'

'For one so young, Damson Shades. Where did you learn such an art?'

'An old gypsy woman taught me.'

He shrugged and lowered his cane, disappointed. 'Well, hold to your craft's secrets then. We will be in touch through the contact woman you use to intermediate with the Cat-gibbon.'

No, really. A gypsy woman.

Twist's broken-nosed companion lowered his pistol as the door closed. 'Do think she believed you, sir?'

35

'Not everything, Mister Cloake. I sense there is a little more to her than that which she professes to be. But she will do the job for us. That is all that matters.'

'We could get the sceptre ourselves, given time. Steal more pass cards; threaten the guards and the people protecting the vaults.'

'Time,' sighed Twist. 'I think we have waited long enough, don't you? Better it looks like a robbery. No questions asked about how the thief got so close to the sceptre. Nothing to implicate us and our friends until it is too late for events to be stopped.'

'And if she is successful?'

'Charlotte Shades trade is a high-risk occupation. It wouldn't do for her to be captured and coerced into telling others who she sold the sceptre to. If she succeeds, it will be time for her to retire, Mister Cloake.'

The bruiser licked his lips as he pocketed his pistol. Retiring people like her always provided such good amusement.

CHAPTER THREE

In Greenhall, the heart of the Jackelian civil-service, you could always hear the beat of government – even here on the top floor of the jumble of buildings that sprawled for miles, the throb of the transaction-engines housed in the underground chambers could be felt underfoot. Unlike the great towers of the capital's business district, the natural order of the placement of offices was inverted here. Those government departments with the most pull and political capital got the rooms closest to the eternally warm underground chambers housing the house-sized thinking machines. Those with the least got the unheated rooms near the top of the civil service's spread out complex. It was not by accident that the State Protection Board occupied the unheated rooms under the great glass palace that formed the roof.

Dick Tull looked out of the crystal panels as he waited for his meeting with the head of the service, playing with the edges of his greying moustache. If he looked carefully through the forest of chimneys venting steam, he could just make out the network of canals running between the Greenhall buildings, navvies with axes chipping away at the ice. Even now,

in the depths of winter, the great engines of government needed
to be cooled with water.

*Miserable, cheapskate jiggers, those engine men are.
Sweating in comfort down in their echoing caverns, shovelling coal into their furnaces while they let me freeze up here.
They get paid more than me too, closed shop with guild
exams to get in. Sods. That's why they give out regimental
ranks in the board, so they don't have to pay me civilian
civil service rates.*

And here, walking down the corridor, was a prime example
of the board's officer class. Another one of the chinless wonders
who had joined after him, then unfairly risen so far above
Dick's position in life: Walsingham. He stopped before Dick,
scratching his dark sideburns, his neat moustache twitching
as if it had a life of its own. Walsingham's face was so vague
and nondescript that in his absence you could usually only
recall him by his fussy manners and over-neat clothes, every
fold tucked, every crease ironed to tight angles. Never what
he looked like. A little walking blank passing through life
unremembered.

'Sergeant.'

'Major.'

'Last night,' said Walsingham. 'The surveillance at Lord
Chant's residence. It was badly done.'

'Sorry, sir.'

'Were you drinking?'

Had that young sod Billy-boy ratted Dick out about his
hip flask too?

'Of course not, sir. Is Beresford not coming in with me to
see the head?'

'He's been reassigned, Tull. To someone who can tutor to
him in more than the art of skiving.'

Of course he has, conniving young sod. Already William

Beresford was being pushed onto a trajectory that would carry him far beyond Dick.

'I'll try to manage without him, major.'

'Better you had. Watch what you say in front of the head, he's feeling a little . . . withdrawn, today.'

Circle's teeth, not another one of the old steamer's funny turns?

Dick tapped the side of his nose. 'See all, sir – say nothing.'

We wouldn't want to confuse the head with details, would we? Not when you've got your ambitious little gaze set on his position. That would suit you, wouldn't it, making sure you get the glory for bagging the royalists? Another success to bolster your section, to polish your already well-honed reputation. Well, the transaction-engine chambers will run cold below your feet before I help you inflate your pension any more, you supercilious old bugger.

'Best you had Tull, and when you're finished in there, I'll introduce you to your new partner. Someone to make sure you don't get into any more mischief behind my back.'

'You can rely on me, sir.' *Just as sure as I can rely on you.*

When the clerk outside the head's office bid Dick enter, he found Algo Monoshaft bent down on the floor, the gas lamps in the room turned down low, allowing the natural light of the glass architecture to spill across hundreds of pieces of paper connected by thin crimson yarns. Daguerreotype images of faces, newspaper cuttings and scraps of paper scrawled with the steamman's own iron hands littered the floor. Algo Monoshaft had started off in the board's cipher section – no finer mind for cracking enemy codes. But that had been centuries ago, and now the steamman was well past his best years. The single stack rising from his spine trembled as his boiler heart struggled to fully power the creature of the metal's ageing systems. Where once the single steel sphere mounted to his traction unit had spun smoothly, now the unit matched Algo's state of mind, lurching and catching his falls and stumbles as he rummaged through the papers spread out before him.

'It's here,' said the head of the board. 'Can you see it?'

'I'm not sure, sir.'

'Sergeant Tull,' said Monoshaft, glancing up, the flicker of recognition on his metal skull's vision plate. 'You must be able to see it?'

'*It*, sir?'

'Treason, sergeant. Treasonists, all around us. All connected, all of them in the pattern down there, if only I could see the devils clearly enough.'

Oh Circle, one of his funny turns all right. Why me? Why couldn't it be Billy-boy in here, having to humour the old fool? 'See everything, sir.'

'We see nothing, Sergeant Tull. Nothing!'

'Well, we did see one of the royalists on the watch list, sir. Carl Redlin. Making contact with someone at the residence of Lord Chant.'

'I've read the report you sent in. The rebel helped murder Lady Florence.'

'That was a mistake, sir. My mistake. Lady Florence is very much alive.'

'No,' the steamman's voicebox trembled with agitation. 'She is dead, dead for sure and to my mind, Lord Chant is a treasonist, no doubt working in the pay of the rebels.' He tapped one of the pieces of paper, following the trail of the thread along the oak floor. Dick looked at the document. A clipping from the *Illustrated*, the bodies found drained of blood near Cripplefield, the work of the so-called vampires. Monoshaft had scrawled "*War war war*" by the margins.

'Chant is a pottery magnate, sir. One of the richest buggers in the Kingdom. I doubt that he's in the pay of anyone.'

'Oh, the royalists have all the money they need, sergeant,' said Monoshaft. 'They are being funded by the gill-necks. I have followed the paper trail and there can be no doubt, the royalist cause is now being embraced by the great underwater nation. The Advocacy mean to use our rebels to fight a proxy war against us.'

'Our conflict with the Advocacy is at sea, sir. What do the gill-necks care if it is Parliament or a royalist monarch who rules on land? It's simply a dispute over whose territory is being sailed over. Taxes and trade. Parliament will reach a settlement with the gill-necks.'

Cheaper than funding a war against them, anyway.

Monoshaft bent down, urgently rearranging the papers in a symmetry better pleasing to him. 'It's all connected, sergeant, all of it. Haven't you heard? The Kingdom's ambassador has just returned from the Advocacy. Never welcome at the best of times, she was expelled by the gill-necks over the heightening tensions between our two nations. There is a pattern here, a code, if we can just crack it. Where is the other agent who was with you, where's William Beresford?'

'Reassigned, sir.'

'What? Not by me. Not by me. Don't trust him, sergeant. If he's not here with us, he can't be trusted.'

Now we're getting somewhere. 'I don't trust him, sir. He's not one to be relied on, definitely not officer material.'

'Now, your royalist at Lord Chant's residence, Carl Redlin. See where the yarn runs. Follow his trail back to the gill-necks. We have a war to avert – we have royalists to crush. If only *they* would help us.'

'They, chief?'

'The Court of the Air, sergeant, the Court of the Air.'

'Ah.' *Bugger this, just how senile is he now?* The Court of the Air. The shadowy senior service, set up centuries ago with an endowment from the democratic leader who had emerged victorious after the civil war, Isambard Kirkhill. The Court of the Air. The court absolute, floating in judgement over the land in their high altitude aerial city, wreathed by the constant concealing clouds of their great transaction-engines, modelling – so it was rumoured – the possible futures of the Jackelian nation. *What did we use to call them? The wolftakers. Every enemy we faced just disappeared, vanished by the good shepherds protecting their flock.*

'They were destroyed, sir, during the invasion from the north,' Dick reminded the old steamman. 'Don't you remember? We found bits of wreckage from their bloody great airship city scattered for miles. Nobody has heard of one of their agents being active for years.'

'They look down on me, on us, on the board.'

Dick shrugged. 'They looked down on everyone, sir.'

The head of the service continued as if he hadn't registered the sergeant's quip. 'They treat us as a joke, badly funded amateurs dabbling in the great game, endangering their position on the board.'

'The State Protection Board?'

'The chessboard, the great game,' the steamman's voicebox quivered in agitation. Algo Monoshaft started tugging at the threads running through the mess on the floor. 'And the Court are here again, I can feel them. Just follow the connections, someone else's tugging at them too.'

'I think it is obvious that I'm going to need to tread carefully, sir.'

'You know what they call us down here, you know what the Court of the Air calls the agents of the State Protection Board?'

'The peculiar gentlemen, sir?'

'No – no! That's them out there.' The steamman's iron digits stabbed out to the sprawling civil service buildings. Then, as if revealing a great confidence, he pointed up to the crystal panes arcing above their heads, stained glass scenes of civil servants diligently performing their duties at desks, other bureaucrats bustling through the halls of parliament. 'They call us the glass men. Just like our roof. Poke, poke, and we shatter. Brittle, useless, a liability, sergeant, that's all we are to the Court of the Air.'

And now we're on our own. Just the board to safeguard the realm. Well, I've always been on my own, it's all I've bloody known anyway. Who else have I got to rely on – you, you mad old steamer? Ambitious chancers like Billy-boy? Self-seeking politicians like Walsingham? Just me. And soon enough, I won't even be a memory around here. But I want my money before I go.

Dick raised his finger to point out a particular sheet of paper, a rough daguerreotype image with his own features printed across it. Was that his service record, spooled off the turning drums of the transaction-engines below their feet?

'Why am I down there, sir?'

'This thread,' the steamman hissed in satisfaction. 'To my mind, this thread is the only one I can rely on.'

'You can always trust in me, sir.'

'You're not important enough,' mumbled the steamman. 'Not important enough to be bribed, to be turned. Never a double agent, never.'

Dick Tull nodded grimly. That was the sanest thing he'd heard from the head of the board today.

Dick shut the door to the head's office, finding Walsingham waiting for him with a short broken-nosed bruiser who looked like he belonged in the board's interrogation section.

'Well, sergeant?'

'Apparently there are treasonists everywhere, sir.'

'I rather hope not. The board is busy enough with the royalist threat.'

'Nobody has been able to tell me where Lord Chant's royalist visitor ended up last night, major.'

'I have other people trailing Carl Redlin, Tull. We wouldn't want to lose him, eh? Lose him like, say, certain silverware reported missing by Lord Chant.'

Dick attempted to look perplexed and shook his head sadly. 'And all those policemen at his house last night too.'

'This is your new partner. Corporal Cloake. Work your informants in the capital. If there are rebels in the city, then they may be spreading money among the flash mob. Find anyone looking for false papers, guns and explosives . . .'

Dick indicated the corporal. 'My informants'll get nervous if I bring along an unknown face.'

'Your informants belong to the board, not you, Tull. You make sure they are all written up and accounted for in your duty book. You'll be leaving us soon enough. They're not your private property. They better get accustomed to meeting the rest of us.'

And that day will come sooner rather than later if you have your way, won't it, you old sod?

Corporal Cloake was a taciturn bugger, which suited Dick down to the ground. If more employees of the board observed the 'say nothing' part of their motto, the service would be a far better place to work. They took the lifting room down to the armoury to pick up the pistols they had to check in when visiting Greenhall's corridors. The armourer on duty was Haggerston, a gruff old devil – showing about as much care of his guns as he did of his untidy, knotted beard, rubbing

44

his fat fingers on the leather grease-stained apron he wore as he appeared at a desk built into the equipment cage.

'Sign the chit,' barked Haggerston. 'Two pistols, five charges apiece.'

'Five?' Dick queried. 'And what happens if I run into six royalists.'

The armourer pointed to Corporal Cloake. 'Get him to shoot one of them.'

Dick checked the quality of the pistol he'd been given, working its clockwork hammer mechanism to make sure it wasn't rusted beyond use.

Skinflint. I bet he's selling our ammunition on the side, some nice little arrangement with the gun shops along Dawson Street.

'It fires fine,' said Haggerston. 'I passed it on the test range myself yesterday.'

'You ever done a real day's work in the field? You're going to get me killed one day.'

Haggerston mimicked a swift drinking motion with his chubby hand. 'That gun's better than your aim, Tull. Now jigger off.'

Corporal Cloake checked his pistol and then slid it into the concealed holster under his black frock coat, adding each charge carefully into his belt. After he pulled his stovepipe hat down he might have passed for an undertaker. But a man like Cloake made corpses, he didn't care for them.

'Your informants . . .' said Cloake.

Tull nodded. *Oh, you'll meet them today, Corporal. Every penny-ante pickpocket and counterfeiter I have ever shaken down, starting with the most useless first. Let's see how long it takes before you lose interest. We'll hide that tree among the forest and see how you sodding like it.*

Corporal Cloake, it transpired, didn't lose interest – possibly because his stubby little skull lacked the imagination to hold much of anything in the first place. It was like dragging a lump of lead pipe around, only useful to slap recalcitrant informants around the head; but Dick didn't doubt that the dour, uncommunicative little thug was carefully noting all the names and addresses of the contacts they were meeting. Hopefully he lacked the imagination to notice they weren't shaking anything noteworthy out of the mob of second-raters and riffraff that Dick was leading them around.

After half a day of such profitless encounters, Dick pointed across the street – towards a sign hanging from a building, no words, only a painting of a haunch of lamb on a roasting spit.

'Lunch?' Dick started to cross the pebbled street, but the corporal stayed where he was. 'You eat don't you?'

'Not there,' said Cloake, 'not serving slop . . .'

'That's value for money, that is,' said Dick. 'A couple of pennies for a plate and a draught. What do you want, the headwaiter at Ravelow's to plump up a cushion and drop gilded gold pear slices down your throat? If you're going to be working with me, corporal, you can break bread over the table of an ordinary.'

'See you back here in an hour, sergeant.'

Dick shrugged and cut through the lane's busy traffic, carts, milk wagons and kettle-blacks hissing steam around the hooves of shire horses. Oddly, the beasts seemed to mind the new steam-driven contraptions less than the old-style horseless carriages driven by high-tension clockwork. Always unsettled by the whine from clockwork engines, the nags were. Dick stepped out of the way of an old man under the sign of the ordinary, a face more wrinkles than skin, his clothes so tatty you could hardly tell where his original tweed began and the patching ended. Well, you didn't eat in places like this for the company. The lack of words on the sign of the establishment gave the game away that much of its custom came from the illiterate poor. And there were few apartments in the rookeries, the city's cramped slums, which possessed kitchens, or would have risked the dangers of fire even if they'd had the space. This is where the poor ended up. This is where Dick Tull ate.

Dick looked with approval at the scene inside. Rows of wooden tables and benches, cheap wooden plates with sets of iron cutlery chained to the boards of the table. A choice of – not just *one*, mind, but *two* – roasts turning on the spits at the other end of the long room, a haunch of pork and a whole side of lamb. How could you call this slop? It was value, value for money. And there were other things to be had here too, things that Dick had been counting on the corporal turning his nose up at inside an ordinary – its food and the cheap clothes of its patrons. Dick nodded back to a one-eyed man shovelling red meat through his broken teeth by the door. Then he approached the owner. The proprietor was currently ensuring the patrons only dipped their wooden cup once through the open barrel of budget beer, only carved off a single portion – and not too large with it – of meat. For some men, being thin was a matter of build, for Barnabas Sadly, it appeared a natural extension of his pinch-faced demeanour. Other men doing his job might've got fat on the greasy leftovers and natural spillage that went with the position. But not Barnabas Sadly, and this was hardly his primary source of income, either. The ordinary he minded was a gateway, a bridge between the normal life of the capital and its criminal underworld. A stroke of genius, really. Most greasers – the fixers and middlemen of the underworld – set up court in alehouse backrooms and eventually attracted the attention of the constables, no matter how dangerous the slum district. But an ordinary? Everyone needed to eat, didn't they? Among the clank of chained spoons and the rattle of wooden plates, other business was conducted here. Well away from the detectives of Ham Yard and the corporals of the board, who, however poorly paid, were never so humble they would willingly eat in a place like this.

Sadly's nose twitched like a rodent's when he saw Dick bearing down on him, nervously glancing to either side of the beer barrel in search of an obvious escape route. Dick cut him off easily, the owner barely beginning to hobble away on his twisted foot and brass-handled walking cane. Dick backed him into a storeroom where long carving knives and spit sharpeners dangled on hooks. The top of Sadly's head scarcely came up to Dick's nose.

'Anyone would think you didn't want to see me, Sadly.'

'Don't say that, Mister Tull. I was just thinking about flagging down a brewery wagon for a fresh barrel, is all.'

'Fresh?' Dick growled. 'There's not much fresh being served in here. Not unless it's what's concealed in one-eyed Osborne's bag by the door. That's probably fresh from whichever poor sod's house he took his crowbar to last night.' Dick reached out to one of the hooks and lifted a knife off, scraping it along the sharpening block dangling next to it. 'You're not keeping this sharp enough.'

'You're just like all my customers, Mister Tull. I lay your sustenance down and you carve it off, one slice at a time. No thought for me, no thought for what it costs, say I.'

'You're a bad advert for this place, Barnabas Sadly. Customers like to see their hosts jolly and round-faced, not pockmarked and as hungry as a sewer rat.' He thumped Sadly in the solar plexus and the man doubled up, Dick catching him almost gently before Sadly dropped his cane and then he pushed the informer back against the storeroom wall. 'No padding around the ribs. You think the proprietor of an alehouse would have even felt that with a decent beer gut? Royalists, Sadly, royalists . . .'

The informant's eyes darted away from Dick's. *A little too quick. What do you know?*

'Captain Twist and his noble troublemakers are back on the streets of Middlesteel, Sadly. And the board's not happy with the thought of it. Because, if Parliament gets a whiff of the royalist rebels' malarkey, we're going to get—' Dick tightened his grip on the man's shoulder until he winced with pain, '—squeezed.'

'This isn't the old game anymore,' complained the rodent-faced little man. 'Things are going on, that—'

'That?'

'They've got money this time, the royalists. Normally nobody in the flash mob would give them the time of day, you know that. Blowing things up is bad for business. Leave it to the politicals and the anarchists and the bloody Carlists, say I.'

'But Captain Twist is being flasher with the contents of his purse this time?'

'Lords-a'larkey, but I don't know what's going on, Mister Tull. There are people getting together with no cause. Foxes and hens, say I. Mousers and mice. What do you think when you see those two dancing together?'

Foxes and hens. Lord Chant and his mysterious royalist visitor, Carl Redlin. Another royalist, Symons, spying on them, snooping on his own people. *Strange days, indeed.*

Dick brushed the dandruff from Sadly's patched collar. 'And what do you think, my limping little friend?'

'I heard the board is involved, Mister Tull. Your people. And I think I should keep my head down. There're people being pulled out of the river, and not just tramps accused of being vampires, beaten to death with pipes and sticks, either. Some of the floaters are royalists.'

'I haven't heard of any royalists being fished out of the Gambleflowers?'

'There was another one this morning, Mister Tull. Third this week as I count it. Rufus Symons, a notable rogue. Raised to manhood with the royalist fleet-in-exile and dedicated to the cause.'

Rufus Symons. Sweet Circle, and if I'd followed him for a couple of hours longer, told the board and handed him over, then we would've found out who . . . Dick's ace-in-the-hole had just been swept off the card table.

'You look like you knew him, Mister Tull?'

'I know he shouldn't have died last night.' *Not until he spilled his guts to me. Not until he made me look good in front of the officer class. Who did it? You, Blacky? Did you put a bullet in his back and then roll him into the river? And now, if I tell anyone about following him out to your house in the hills, I'm going to look like the stupid jigger who messed up everything again. It's never made easy. Not for me.*

'And this time, the rebels aren't after guns and explosives. Nobody in the flash mob's been asked for them. And why is that, ask I? Because the royalists are already being supplied with weapons by the gill-necks. Looks like it could be war, Mister Tull. Us against the Advocacy, and the gill-neck leadership have found some friends among our own dispossessed, dissatisfied nobles, I say. Arm our rebels, stir them up, and set them off against us before war breaks out between the Kingdom and the underwater people.'

The same nonsense that the old steamer was spouting back in the board. *Maybe there's something to it after all, then?*

'You said you thought the board was involved in this. What makes you say the board's involved?'

Sadly tried to point back at one of the tables, his walking cane twisting in his hand. 'One of my regulars is a news sheet man for the *Garrotter's Gazette* – says the board has served his paper at least three times recently with a section thirteen notice gagging the paper. All for stories about royalists fished out of the river. He didn't complain as much as he should've done; not now there's a public disorder gag on the vampire slayings too. Nearly got hanged by a mob down the road myself yesterday.'

'I told you, you're too thin and pale by half.' Dick opened his coat and hung the two silver candlesticks up on the hooks. 'I want a good price for that pair. I can't use the pawnshop because they're on the constables' watch list. When a squat little thug with a board corporal's badge comes to ask where I am, tell him I paid for a couple of flagons of beer and stumbled out to sleep it off before he arrived.'

'And where would you be going, Mister Tull?'

'Fishing,' said Dick. 'I'm off to land me a nice fat fish.' *A duplicitous fish by the name of Commodore Black.*

Charlotte Shades stepped out of the palatial expanse of Middlesteel Museum. Her mind spun with the architect's plans for Parliament she'd been consulting, the great House of Guardians nestling in the shadows of the bell tower of Brute Julius. Of course, none of the plans detailed the security measures and mechanisms defending the crown jewels, the last sceptre of the last absolute monarch. But there was a lot you could infer from the spaces that had been left blank on the layouts. And in those voids, you just knew there was going to be trouble. Why had she ever agreed to go along with the mysterious Mister Twist? Well, there was the obscenely large amount of money being offered. And the implicit threat of violence if she didn't acquiesce. But it was

51

more than that. The challenge of it. Something she couldn't take; something far beyond her station. There was probably a breed of mouse in the world, the sort of mouse that saw a mousetrap baited with cheese, the sort of mouse that tingled with the sight of what was forbidden and dangerous. That mouse never lived too long, but there were things far worse than dying. Like boredom, being really poor and looked down upon.

And then the mouse saw the cat.

Charlotte started as the steamman lumbered up in front of her, her mind instantly clearing of Parliament's plans and levels and scales of distance. *But this isn't a steamman, is it?* None of the organic, smooth movements of the people of the metal down from the Steamman Free State. This was one of the clumsy, hulking, man-milled mechanical servants surely? But it had the head of a steamman, polished and out of place on the rest of the body, and its voicebox vibrated with the words of something clearly sentient.

'Damson Shades? Charlotte Shades? Known by the stage name of the Mistress of Mesmerism?'

Should I deny it? Nobody knows that I'm here. Not the flash mob, not even that devil Twist.

She nodded.

'I have been sent for you, Damson Shades. My name is Boxiron.'

'I'm as curious to understand how you knew where to find me as to know who sent you, old steamer.'

'Your name is being whispered by demons, Damson Shades,' said the hulking creature. 'You are marked for death.' Then, as if it had just occurred to him that she might find this ever so slightly alarming, he added. 'And I have been sent to protect you as we travel.'

'Travel?'

'Travel to church, the man I work with must speak with you. He has a warning for you . . .'

A warning of a psychotic metallic servant on the loose, perhaps?

'Church? Is your friend a vicar?'

'He used to be a parson,' said Boxiron. 'But he was thrown out by the rational synod when he started believing in gods.'

'I can see how that would be a problem.'

The Circlist order and their atheist church had no room for heretics behind the pulpit.

'And let us say I don't care for a sermon today?'

'Then regretfully,' said Boxiron, a wild clicking coming from the rotating calculation drum in his chest, 'I shall carry you the distance.'

'How delightfully direct. Then by all means, let us attend church this afternoon.'

Following the lumbering curiosity, she walked in the dust raised off the road by his two clanking claw-like foot plates and a distant memory began to rise through her mind, something told to her by one of the Cat-gibbon's enforcers, eager to impress her with his knowledge of the capital's criminal underworld.

'I seem to recall there were tales of a steamman knight whose head was transplanted onto the body of a human-milled mechanical by grave robbers after a battle. And that this steamman later worked as an enforcer for the flash mob, cracking skulls and suchlike.'

'And where did you hear that story, Damson Shades?'

'I believe it was a penny-dreadful,' Charlotte lied. '*Mayhew's Tales of Mechanical Mayhem.*'

'I can see how that would make a good story,' said Boxiron. 'But my body is that of an old butler unit – a family heirloom.'

And haven't all the bullet holes and axe dents been neatly hammered out of it.

It was an old city church that the clanking creature led her to, walls, roof and chimneys wedged between two modern buildings. So ancient that its lines appeared organic; flats and verticals given life by so many sags, curves and tilts. Charlotte almost expected to see the building breathe. Inside, round glass windows in the ceiling brought coloured light down like pillars, the formula of the church's mathematics mottling the humble olive-wood pews below. There was a middle-aged man standing in the illumination of one of the lights, a female figure hovering nervously at his side.

Charlotte indicated the metal creature pulling up behind her. 'You have a novel way of filling your congregation.'

'My apologies, Damson Shades,' said the man. 'I have found time can often be of the essence in these matters. Do you object if I use your stage name?'

'It's the only one I have, honey,' said Charlotte. 'And yours is?'

'Jethro Daunt,' he replied, then indicated the female figure. 'And my friend here is Fidelia, the Reverend Felknor, the vicar of this parish.'

Charlotte felt the pit of her stomach tighten. *Jethro Daunt.* That was a name she had heard far too many times. 'You're the consulting detective who recovered the *Twelve Works of Charity* when the painting was stolen from Middlesteel Museum?'

He seemed pleased at being recognized. 'The same. Although of course, the painting never physically left the museum. The reverse of its canvas was painted over with a new work, and then it was turned around and rehung for removal later. Are you interested in art, Damson Shades?'

She smiled. 'I can take it or leave it.' *Normally the former.* 'Your old steamer said something about my life being in danger, and some craziness about demons . . .?'

At those words, the female vicar made the sign of the circle and wrinkled her nose in distaste. 'The demons of ignorance are the ones we battle.'

Daunt rested his hand reassuringly on the cleric's shoulder. 'Boxiron still sees things through the eyes of a steamman, the ancestral spirits of his people.'

'Then how would you explain what is happening in the back room, Jethro softbody?' Boxiron asked.

'Let's start with the rational and work our way out from there,' said Daunt. He looked at Charlotte. 'It will be easier to show you, Damson Shades. If you would be so good as to accompany us to the infirmary.'

Charlotte followed the vicar and the consulting detective through a narrow brick-lined corridor, Boxiron's weight thumping behind them. Daunt talked as he went. 'I used to be a parson, Damson Shades. In fact, I studied at the seminary with Fidelia here. Knowing my esoteric interests, she asked me to help with a little problem she's having with a family here in the parish. Her problem seems to coincide with a case I am currently engaged upon.'

Charlotte's heart jumped. *Damn my luck. Not only a consulting detective, but an ex-churchman. And would your case have anything to do with the Lords Commercial I've been working this year, notorious Mister Daunt?* She had to be careful around the man. He would have been well-trained in synthetic morality by the church, equipped with a mind like a steel trap. The atheist church of Circlism venerated science and learning. Its parsons, priests and vicars were trained as scientists and philosophers, as doctors of the flesh, mind and spirit. It was said a Circlist priest could read the soul of a person as if it was a map. Healing minds wracked by faith in false gods as proficiently as they healed sick flesh. Their insights could be preternatural, almost telepathic. *And mine is one soul that I don't want read by any consulting detective. How many cases has he taken where my dirty mitts were the real hands behind the job?*

'A problem?' Charlotte said it nervously, as if just speaking would be enough for the man to pounce on her, pronounce her body language that of a criminal, and drag her to the nearest police station.

'The unknown, Damson Shades. The uncomfortably unexplainable, a walk through the darkness.' He dragged a paper bag out of his jacket pocket, rustled it and proffered it in Charlotte's direction. 'Would you care for a Bunter and Benger's aniseed drop, my dear?'

'Put those filthy opiate-riddled things back in your pocket,' complained the vicar. 'You are standing on rational grounds.'

'Scurrilous scare stories manufactured by their competitors, my precious Fidelia,' said Daunt. 'Weights and Measures would have banned the sweets long ago, if there was any truth to that title tattle. Besides, they help my mind come to clarity.'

'They *have* been banned,' the vicar muttered as the private investigator rustled the bag back out of sight. They started to climb up, an enclosed spiral staircase twisting around to the church's upper level.

'Your case, Mister Daunt?'

'The mayor and the city elders have engaged my services. The current plenitude of bodies being discovered around the capital with an absence of bodily fluids is not good for trade, and it is all about trade these days, isn't it?'

Thank the Circle for that! So you're not onto me after all. Charlotte breathed a silent sigh of relief, confusion about her role in his affairs replacing the blade of fear that had been sliding into her side. 'You don't believe in that nonsense the newssheets are printing do you? Vampires stalking the Kingdom?'

'I have little choice but to believe in the corpses being found,' said Daunt. 'Boxiron and I have become quite the regular visitors at the public mortuary, have we not? As to the cause of the deaths, well, we shall see.'

Charlotte stepped into the church's infirmary, a number of clean white-sheeted beds lying empty apart from three occupied cots at the end of the hall, a little cluster of old but functional-looking medical equipment arranged in an arc around the bunks. As she got closer, Charlotte saw each bed held an identical-seeming girl a couple of years younger than Charlotte herself, their pretty brows soaked with sweat under long flaming red curls of hair.

Triplets?

She noticed they were tied to the bedposts, hands and legs restrained by leather straps, and they seemed to be mumbling in a unison so synchronized it was uncanny.

'Who are they? What is it that they're saying?'

Daunt bent forward and wiped the sheen off the nearest girl's forehead. 'Meet the sisters Lammeter, daughters of this parish's undertaker. When they got sick, a doctor was consulted who was left quite baffled by their condition. Supernatural forces were suspected, religious infection, so their girls' parents brought them to the church to see if it could help. And as to what it is they are saying, that is rather the nub of the issue.'

'They are possessed,' said Boxiron, his metal bulk swaying slightly at rest. 'They are talking in tongues. It is as if Radius Patternkeeper is riding them, Lord of the Ravenous Fire himself.'

'Watch your words, steamman,' snapped the vicar. 'As a believer, I'm tolerating your presence here on sufferance.'

'Yes, yes,' said Daunt, raising his hands placatingly. He turned back to Charlotte. 'Where we can even identify their ramblings, the dialects and languages being spoken are very old. I've been recording the words phonetically in the hope of having them translated.'

'And what does this have to do with me?' Charlotte demanded. 'Do I look like a professor of ancient languages?'

'In truth, you're barely old enough to have matriculated, Damson Shades. But there are certain words that we do recognize. People's names being shrieked out in the dark of the night. Your name, as a matter of fact. As well as Nancy Martense's. Andrew Dunsey's. Emma Osgood's.'

Those names sounded familiar. Charlotte raised an eyebrow inquiringly.

'You'll find them all laid out on the mortuary slab, Damson Shades. All very pale, as you would expect for a body totally drained of blood. Little more than empty sacks of flesh.'

The newssheets. I've read those names in the Illustrated.

'You're the only name we've managed to trace who is still alive.'

As he stopped talking, the three girls started shaking uncontrollably, and as one they began chanting: 'Shades. Shades. Shades. Charlotte Shades. Mistress – of – Mesmerism. Mesmerism. Mesmerism. Shades. Shades. Shades.' Charlotte recoiled physically at the unholy wailing, her name passing across the lips of these three restrained banshees. As quickly as it started, the noise fell away to be replaced by a guttural alien chanting, unknown words hanging in the air like intruders in the calm sanctuary of the Circlist church.

Beneath Charlotte's dress, the gem around her neck was burning cold again, just like it had been when she had met the mysterious Mister Twist and his pet thug, Mister Cloake.

'That demon song,' said Boxiron, 'told us where we could locate you.'

'I don't suppose their rants have given you the name of the

lunatic running around Middlesteel with a taste for human blood?'

'I'm working on translating it,' said Daunt, tapping an open notebook on a bedside table, full of shorthand scribbles of the girl's mad ramblings, 'with high hopes. In the meantime, I would like you to accept the protection of Boxiron. I would not be here if it was not for my friend's rather direct methods, and I would like to offer his talents for your service also.'

A copper's bloody nark following me around while I house-break into Parliament? I don't think so.

'That would not currently be convenient, Mister Daunt. I have professional obligations to keep. After I have fulfilled them, your metal friend may burn his coal outside my bedroom door if it suits you to do so.'

'Please,' Daunt pleaded, pressing his card into her hand. 'Reconsider. The murderer –or murderers – behind this wave of slayings may be privy to your engagements. They could well be counting on you fulfilling them.'

'I've been looking after myself for a lot longer than the *Illustrated* has been scaring the city with vampire tales.'

Besides, there are plenty of thugs in the pay of the flash mob who can match any madman in town with their taste for blood, butchery and fancy knife work. Charlotte had to resist the urge to skip happily out of the room like a little girl, suppressing a sneer at the much-overestimated abilities of these church-trained meddlers. *Read me like a book, indeed. Please. My body language couldn't have been guiltier when I was hauled in here by that iron brute, and those three buffoons have nary a clue.*

Boxiron watched the young girl leave the church, his neck joins juddering intermittently as if he was inflicted by palsy. 'She is only a child – she failed to take your warnings seriously.'

'Oh, I think she took them seriously enough, old friend,' said Daunt. 'But not as seriously as she takes her living. Driven to it, wouldn't you say?'

'You read her body's cues, didn't you?' said the vicar. 'There wasn't much she said that was true.'

Daunt shrugged. 'Yes indeed, I did read her. Still, she is old enough to decide to put her living before her life, whatever that living may be.'

'You'd know all about that, Jethro.'

'That's hardly fair, Fidelia. I've been putting my mind to the best use I can, since the Inquisition revoked my parsonage and tossed me out of the rational orders.'

'Do you still hear the old gods?'

'Actually, not for some time now.' Daunt glanced back to the three sisters, their synchronized ranting rising and falling with an almost hymn-like quality. *At least, not directly. And not until I came back here.*

'Why didn't you tell her what you've already discovered, you and that filthy book of yours?'

'It's the Inquisition's bestiary,' said Daunt. 'Not mine. It's merely on loan to me.'

'Semantics won't help the sisters recover.'

Sadly, not much will. 'One thing is true, however. Damson Shades certainly believes she can handle herself. Don't put your daughter on the stage, Fidelia.'

'I am sorry?' said the vicar.

'And that is not something the Mistress of Mesmerism learned while being groped in music hall dressing rooms by over-eager stage managers,' Daunt continued, half talking to himself. He popped a sweet from the bag hidden in his pocket and rolled it around his mouth. 'It is a curious thing, but many of the grand houses that young lady has entertained have exhibited an unfortunate tendency to fall victim to housebreakers. Either during or shortly after her performances at them. Who would suspect such a young flower, eh? But then, perhaps that is the point.'

'Is it possible she's connected to the killings?' Boxiron asked.

'In this instance, I think not. Damson Shades is guilty only of being reckless and impulsive. Youth personified. Were we ever that guileless at the seminary, Fidelia?'

'Not you. You always were a queer fish,' said the vicar. 'Even before the gods sent you insane with their mad whisperings.'

'I'm recovered now,' said Daunt.

'They are sulking,' Boxiron explained to the vicar. 'Your people's ancient deities. Jethro softbody upset them.'

'I know how they feel,' sighed the vicar.

'Look after the sisters, Fidelia. No more sedatives. Tonics and herbs won't suppress what these poor girls are channelling. The Mistress of Mesmerism is my problem now.'

The vicar jerked her head towards the infirmary door. 'If Charlotte Shades is murdered, will the sisters get better?'

Jethro Daunt shook his head. 'Goodness, no. The sisters will, I suspect, only recover when we find and defeat the dark force their possession is attempting to warn us of. And as far as deaths go, I fear we haven't even begun taking a true tally yet.'

Dick removed his hand from the bell pull, the peels still echoing on the other side of the tower-like building's front door. After a minute there was a slow, heavy shuffling on the other side and the door swung open to reveal Jared Black, the bear-like man in the unbuttoned jacket of a civilian u-boat captain.

'Blacky,' said Dick. 'Answering the door yourself these days are you? Hard times is it? Where've all your metal servants got to?'

61

The submariner scratched at his unkempt forked beard and eyed his unexpected visitor with a mixture of suspicion and contempt. 'Dick Tull come visiting. Is the board out to disturb an old man's rest again? Can you not let me have any peace? I'm done with the great game and all your lies and your schemes.'

'That, we can talk about,' said Dick, entering the grand hall of the tower. Iron drones stood like sentries around the sweeping walls of the oak-panelled staircase, powered down. *Warm in here. Decadently warm. Your boiler chewing its way through a couple of normal men's salaries. Not shivering like me, are you? What have you ever done that I haven't, to end up here in this bloody grand palace of yours?* 'Your steamman friend is out of the house, then? And the writer girl who lives here? They finally got tired of your whining and complaining?'

'Coppertracks and Molly are away in the colonies. Off on an archaeological dig accompanying an old friend of mine.'

'Looking for old bones,' grinned Dick, 'while your old bones rest here. But you've been keeping busy, Blacky, haven't you? And not just on keeping the town's vintners solvent. Give me a spot of the good stuff, then. Let me drink just a little of your unexplained wealth.'

The commodore reluctantly led Dick through to the kitchen and pantry, coughing and complaining all the way.

That cough. I have heard that kind of sodding chest before. Yes, indeed.

Sitting down at a long oak table, its surface a battlefield of chopping knife scars, Dick watched the commodore's chubby fingers pouring a measure of wine into a clear crystal glass, and Dick kept his fingers raised until the glass was sloshing with the thick, ruby liquid.

'Drink up,' said the commodore. 'And I'll tell you what I told Algo Monoshaft last time I saw the old steamer. I'm done with the blessed board. I've put my carcass in the way of assassin's blades and foreign powers' bullets for the last time for you and yours. I have lied and fought and spied in foreign fields from Cassarabia and Pericur through to the black shores of Jago and I am too mortal old for the great game anymore.'

Dick sloshed the wine about the glass, watching the liquid run slowly down the sides of the crystal. *Good legs on it. Expensive.* 'You don't need a board pension, Blacky. Not sitting in this pile. And we don't give them out to royalist turncoats anyway. Here's the thing, I think you're still in the great game, but playing for whom, that is the question?'

The commodore started to cough, slugging a measure of wine to still his hacking. 'I'm out of it.'

'Is that what you told Symons when he came visiting?'

Watch his face closely now. See how he reacts to me knowing about his late night royalist visitor.

'Did you catch him, then? Poor old Rufus. How many of his fingernails did you have to remove before he blew on me?'

He's already dead, you old pirate. Did you kill him? Let's see how much you spill when you're on the defensive and shook up. Let's press my advantage. 'No more than he deserved. But you know how it is. I need your story to match Symons'. Come on, I need to know you're still on Parliament's side.'

The old man's face flushed redder still with anger. 'I've never been on Parliament's side. Your people winkled me out of hiding and strong-armed my poor carcass into your service. Anything I did, I did for the people of Jackals, not your parliament of shopkeepers and mill owners. The Lords Commercial have paid for your wicked soul, not mine.'

'What did Rufus Symons say to you last night?'

The commodore folded back into his chair, toying wistfully

with a plate of cold sliced beef sitting between them. 'There's been a split in the cause. A dividing of the ways over how the rebels should seize the Kingdom back from Parliament.'

'That we knew,' Dick lied. 'Why did Symons come to you?'

'To ask for help. And I told him the same thing I told you. I'm out of it.'

'Why would you want to help him and not the rival royalist faction?'

'Because it's my sister who's been helping the gill-necks, Tull. Gemma Dark, captain of the fleet-in-exile now and war leader of the Star Chamber.'

Sweet Circle. The underwater nation, the Advocacy. It was true then. The head's paranoid rantings. But which side had Symons been serving?

Dick felt the lines of his greying moustache. 'And how do you feel about that?'

'Well, there's a blessed good question. It makes no sense to me. The gill-necks had no time for us surface-dwellers when I skippered for the cause. The Advocacy called us pirates too, hunted our u-boats as keenly as Parliament's fleet ever did. As for helping the cause overthrow Parliament, why should we trust the gill-necks? Why should they trust us? Symons felt the same way. So did a lot of rebels. Helping the Advocacy fight the Kingdom felt a might too close to treachery to him. My sister and her new allies purged the royalist dissenters, and now they're on the run from her, you, and the gill-necks both!'

'What about your sister? Why would you—'

'Didn't they let you read my file, Tull? Gemma's a hardliner. When Parliament broke the back of the fleet-in-exile at Porto Principe, I fled for my life. As far as my sister's concerned, I'm a traitor and a coward. And that was before I got her son killed on some fool adventure and the board started blackmailing me. I'm never going to be on the same side as

64

Gemma again. Not unless it's planted in a grave four feet beneath her boots.'

Dick supped greedily at the rich wine. 'That's quite a story.'

'It's the blessed truth.'

'I know it is,' said Dick.

'Ah, poor little Rufus. I remember him as a lad on Porto Principe, always running around the corridors of the u-boat pens, always firing a thousand questions at us. How long did he last with the interrogation section?'

'I know it's the truth,' continued Dick, 'because you've got nothing left to lie for. You're dying, aren't you?'

Commodore Black coughed and refilled his glass, a tired expression crossing his face. 'Rufus didn't tell you that . . . I never told the lad I was sick.'

'I watched my mother die of black rot in her lungs. I know that cough.' *And you're just like her, aren't you? You haven't told anyone, not your friends or your family. You were planning to drag yourself away one night like a wounded animal and die alone. Exactly like she did. That's why your housemates are in the colonies and you're finishing your cellar off alone here. Just like ma did to me. They don't know about you, you old sod, do they?* 'But you've got the coins to pay for a good doctor?'

'Lying rascals with their hands in my pocket,' said the commodore. 'There's nothing the likes of them can do for me. I've seen a lot of sailors with black rot. If you spend long enough under the seas, the dust from a boat's air scrubbers always clogs you up in the end.' The old u-boat man raised his glass in a mocking toast to Dick. 'I'm due a grand long rest, and that's why the board's threat of tossing my poor bones in jail doesn't hold any water with old Blacky anymore. Because you give it a year, and bones are all you'll have left of me.'

'Any more of your old rebel friends show up, you send for me,' ordered Dick. 'The board can help them. You don't want the gill-neck fleet and your sister bombarding our harbour towns do you?'

'Fight my sister without me,' coughed the commodore. 'I'm not going to be around to save your skins anymore.'

Maybe not, but you've saved mine, you old sod, you and your breakaway royalist friends. This intelligence is going to salvage my career and give me a pension worth more than half a penny to leave with.

Dick glanced back at the illuminated clock face at the top of the tower as he walked away through the grounds of the house, steam venting into the cold air from grilles around the building's basement level. *All that money it costs to heat a tower that large. Lucky, wine-warmed bastard. He's passing away in comfort. More comfort than old ma had. More than I will.*

Corporal Cloake watched from the shadows of the trees as Dick Tull emerged from the tower opposite the house's orchard; the corporal noting the silhouette of Commodore Black at the open door spilling heat into the cold winter air. What had they discussed? Well, it really didn't matter. Another one who would have to die, along with the snitch back in that cheap slop-house of an eatery that the corporal had been watching. But that was the nice thing about being employed by the board. They had a special section that specialized in disposing of rubbish.

It was time to call in the dustmen.

Boxiron cradled the volumes in his iron hands, the books of forbidden knowledge that Jethro had asked for shaking slightly as he navigated his way across their apartment's worn red carpet. There were so many ironies here. Once he had been a proud warrior, a steamman knight of the order militant. But that body had long since been destroyed, only his skull and his soul-board salvaged by the human scavengers who arrived like crows at the aftermath of a battle. Stripping the dead steammen for parts that could be sold to the devilish human tinkers in artificial life, their Loa-cursed mechomancers. What had been left of Boxiron's body had been amateurishly joined to the defunct body of a treasured family servant, the warrior's memories suppressed and left to haunt the human-milled body like a ghost. But ghosts had a way of coming back to haunt their owners, and so it was with Boxiron, the first true memories of his reawakening returning as he stood in an inferno, his hands clutched around a can of lamp oil, the widow Aumerle's grand house burning down around his metal frame. The screams of its owner upstairs, crying for help from the ageing mechanical she had grown up with from a girl. The only thing she had truly loved in her barren, childless life. The mechanical she had spent a small fortune reanimating with stolen steamman body parts.

Boxiron had stood there in the grounds, watching her crazed silhouette flapping at the window against a backdrop of flames. *Is this hell*, he had wondered, *is this the dark realm of Radius Patternkeeper, Lord of the Ravenous Fire?* Hell had yet to find him, although he had come close to purgatory wandering the streets of Middlesteel, turned away from the temples of the people of the metal, outraged that this desecration, this walking corpse, should come to them begging succour. This metal zombie who should have deactivated himself rather than violate the perfection of the design blessed upon him by King Steam and the Hall of Architects. Was it any wonder he had drifted into the clutches of the only society who would accept him – the human capital's underworld? The flash mob, only too glad to allow their mechomancers to soup up his ill-fitting frame. Giving Boxiron power enough to break the arms and legs and skulls of those who would not pay protection money. Giving him the skill to crack locks, both physical and those rolling on the calculation drums of the race of man's primitive steam-driven thinking machines.

Oh yes, the irony. Once a proud warrior of the people of the metal and now barely able to navigate a true course across a drawing room without spilling what he carried or upending the table where Jethro Daunt was working. It was the eccentric ex-parson who had saved Boxiron from the life he'd fallen into. Allowed the soldier to reclaim some sliver of honour. It was the challenges of the cases that they undertook together that allowed Boxiron to feel a vestige of the thrill of the battlefield that had been the purpose of his old existence. That gave him direction enough to keep on going, rather than taking the path of honourable deactivation that the people of the metal's code demanded of a desecration.

Increasingly, however, Boxiron found this was not enough. His mind clear, his body so wrecked and inferior. The juxtaposition grew heavier with each year. Much how a young softbody might feel, once fit, gazing upon withered limbs made sick by a wasting disease. He hated his shaking fingers, so slow and brutish. He loathed his pistoning legs, so heavy and so inelegant. He hated his weak boiler heart, puny and pitiful and so incapable of supplying a strong, regular flow of power. He hated the way he would direct his body to action only to have it respond milliseconds too slow to react to a threat, lurching and reeling from foot to foot. *Why did it have to be like this? Why couldn't that incoming shell have destroyed my mind and left my body intact for the scavengers. Why must I be imprisoned inside this pitching, stumbling corpse? Would dying be so bad? I'm hard to kill, but not that hard. I could climb to the top of one of the city's pneumatic towers, so high that the shadow of the airships darken the air vents, leap from the roof. The impact would kill me, surely? My skull smashed. My mind at peace. My ancestors have forsaken me. My people wouldn't miss me, only—*

Daunt looked up from the table and smiled, pushing aside the volume from the inquisition's forbidden library that he was browsing. Here was another irony. The human's Circlist religion, the church that denied all gods, with all the knowledge and lore of their old ways, their superstitions, wrapped up and concealed in these goat-leather bound tomes. Devils and demons and monsters and legends. Some real, some legends. It was wise of the Inquisition to conceal them, for it was only the power of belief that could animate gods, and the distinction between what existed in truth and myth was often blurred. You couldn't always predict what people would believe in.

'These are the last of the books,' said Boxiron.

'Thank you, old steamer. The longer I look at them, the more I feel the answers we seek are elsewhere.'

'Are there any superstitions and irrationalities of your people that the Inquisition have not secreted away inside their pages?'

'What those poor possessed girls are screaming at night has its roots in history, I am convinced of it.'

'The hysteria sweeping the city grows worse,' said Boxiron. 'Our landlady took great delight in describing how a local mob chased a dog to his death under the wheels of an omnibus. It was a vampire apparently, a shape-switcher changed form, and the crowd swore they heard it beg for mercy as they beat the piteous, wounded animal.'

'Poor fools.' Daunt took his reading glasses off and rubbed his tired eyes. 'What are the vicars of their parishes doing?

69

They should be calling the people to meditation, balancing their souls. Healing their minds.'

'There is an old saying in the Steamman Free State,' said Boxiron. 'When you cease to believe in the ancestors and the Loa, you do not believe in *nothing*. You believe in *anything*.'

'We don't believe in nothing, old steamer. We believe in each other, and we believe in rationality and our own power to make things better. It is always a hard thing to ask a person, to climb the mountain alone with empty hands.'

Boxiron shrugged. 'Yet, it is not steammen who are chasing hounds through the streets with clubs and pitchforks.'

Daunt smiled kindly. 'You have no blood to suck, old friend. Maybe a little oil, but I doubt there is much sustenance in that.'

'There will be little left in you, either, Jethro softbody. If you sit there hour after hour staring at tales of garden sprites and witches' spells.'

Daunt nodded and shut the book, collecting up the notes he'd made from the possessed sisters' ramblings. 'I have to agree. I believe it time to seek help from an expert in antiquarian matters.'

'Do you wish me to return these books to the Inquisition?'

'Not yet,' said Daunt. 'I have another task in mind for you, old steamer. One a little more suited to your . . . unique talents.'

CHAPTER FOUR

Charlotte glanced around Damson Robinson's pie shop to make sure that there were no customers left inside. Then she turned the sign hanging on the door to read 'closed' and locked it shut. On the other side of the sawdust-strewn floor, Mister Twist laid out an architect's blueprint for the ground floor of the House of Guardians, all of Parliament's lintels, lunettes, elevations and eaves laid out on the ageing parchment.

'You have not explained the details of how you expect to obtain King Jude's sceptre for us?' said Twist. He looked over in annoyance at the old female proprietor of the pie shop hovering nearby. 'It would be better if you weren't here.'

'I am sure it would, dearie,' replied Damson Robinson. 'But seeing as it is the Cat-gibbon who procured Charlotte's services for you, the flash mob would like to make sure there's no business between the two of you going on under the counter.' She tapped her worktop and pushed a large chopping board out of the way.

Twist shrugged and lifted up a battered red leather case, the kind clerks and civil servants used to lug paperwork across the city. Laying it on top of the counter, Twist undid the clasp and revealed a velvet-lined interior filled with neat cord-tied columns of gold sovereigns.

Damson Robinson sighed in gentle satisfaction. 'There's a sight to warm an old bird's heart.'

Charlotte had to agree. The money always helped.

Twist closed the case and placed it between his boots. 'You'll take your share of it when I have the sceptre.' He tapped the plans, impatiently.

'Only I ever know the details of my jobs,' said Charlotte. 'A girl has to keep her secrets.'

And we wouldn't want you copying my plan and deciding to execute it without me, would we?

'Results are what count, Mister Twist,' said the shop owner. 'We don't ask, you don't ask. That way there's no recriminations about who knew what, should any detectives from Ham Yard come calling at a later stage.'

'Professional tradecraft,' said Charlotte. 'Just like I haven't asked where your friend Mister Cloake is tonight.'

'Mister Cloake and my associates will be waiting here to take possession of the sceptre when you get back,' said Twist. 'I have other business to attend to.'

How many rebels are there swarming over the city? Well, I don't need to know. Just so long as that case full of money is still here when I return.

Damson Robinson came over to give Charlotte a little hug. 'You be careful, dearie. I stepped out with a sergeant major from the house guards regiment when I wasn't much older than you. They're tough old buggers. You won't find any of them sleeping at Parliament's gate.'

'You keep my share of that money safe,' said Charlotte. 'I'll keep my soul well enough out there.'

Charlotte stepped out into the street, her mind preoccupied

with all of the dangers of the night ahead of her, the floor plans she had memorized, the challenges she would face. So immersed in her own world that she didn't notice the figure slinking back into the shadows of the alleyway on the opposite side of the road.

This was just as well, for if she had, Parliament was the last place Charlotte Shades would have visited.

Damson Robinson sighed, watching Charlotte depart with her housebreaking equipment. Then the old woman locked the door again and made them safe. *All my pigeons have flown and left. But let this one come back, come back safe with a valuable little gee-jaw stuck between her talons.*

'Roll your plan of Parliament up from the counter, young man. It's going to be a long evening and I have an order of eight pies to complete for morning's opening.'

'Disgusting,' said Twist, concealing the map beneath his frock coat.

'They're meaty enough, if you bone the partridges properly before you boil them,' said Damson Robinson.

'The way you consume food, it disgusts me, eating like cattle. Crumbs and juices pouring out of your mouths, the disgusting slurping sound you make as you crunch away at the flesh and the baked seed flowers. The foul stench as you defecate your waste back out again.'

'What are you—' Damson Robinson turned to see Twist removing a tuning fork-shaped object from under his coat, the thing shaped out of glittering crystal ruby. 'Is that a tuning fork? I don't have a piano here, dearie. Not in my shop.'

Then a strange thing happened, although the queerness of it was lost on the proprietor of the shop. The client who had commissioned tonight's pilferage disappeared, replaced by a beau from her past, young George. She was so glad to see him; it had been so many years. They had set up the shop together before he died of a bowel abscess. Passed away from her far too young. She stretched her arms out to greet him.

'Yes, a song,' said Twist, upon the old lady in two long striding steps, plunging the crystal prongs into her neck. Damson Robinson stumbled back, blood fountaining out across the counter, her greeting for George muffled by Twist's hand clamped over her face. 'A song of blood and flesh! The Mass must feed.'

Thankfully for the shop owner, the pain that should have accompanied the sight of the spinning room as her heart gave up was absent; the pressure of her rapidly vanishing blood more than her seventy-year-old body could stand. She didn't hear even Twist's last words as the blackness flowed over her. She was too busy kissing George.

'No taste, you filthy old crone. Not like the girl, she'll taste sweet for Mister Cloake, she'll taste—'

Jethro Daunt let go of the lion-shaped handle of the bell-pull, listening to the echo of the chimes inside. The ex-parson-turned-consulting-detective smiled at the sound. It put him in mind of the bells in his old parish, back in the small northern town of Hundred Locks. The locals who complained the church's campanologists set to ringing their bells with too much gusto, whatever the occasion – be it funerals, weddings, or Circle Day services. *Before I was defrocked, before . . .*

The door swung open and the bushy eyebrows of the bear-like man who'd answered rose in surprise. 'Ah now, it seems to be my week for receiving old faces back into my life.'

'I do trust I am not intruding?'

'Far happier to see your face than the last fellow, and that is the truth of it,' said the commodore, leaning forward conspiratorially. 'A government officer, full of guile and treachery he was. Where is your old steamer, that great metal lug Boxiron? Is he not working with you still?'

'He is,' smiled Daunt as Commodore Black ushered him into the great open hall of Tock House. Daunt glanced with interest around the space, noting the bulky walls that held the front door and the huge blast door hidden above, ready to smash down if the house's owner decided to trigger it. 'Even as we speak, in fact. He might turn up here later. And speaking of old friends, I suppose it is too much to hope that Professor Amelia Harsh is presently in residence within your house?'

'You have missed her by three weeks, lad,' said the commodore. 'She's off to the colonies with the rest of my friends. The miners out in Concorzia have found some rusting old ruin of a city out there, and so away my housemates have flown to poke about for relics and lost history.'

'The professor's favourite kind, as I recall,' said Daunt. He bit back his curiosity and restrained himself from asking why the commodore had not transported them to the distant shores of the colonies in his own u-boat. After all, it had been on just such a mission to the dark Isle of Jago where Daunt and the old submariner had made their acquaintance. There was, Daunt sensed, something amiss in the old sea dog's presence here all alone in the great tower.

'I turned up at the university seeking the professor's wisdom,' explained Daunt. 'They pointed me in the direction of Tock House.'

'If it is wisdom you want, you may find a blessed library full of it upstairs,' said the commodore. 'The professor and my crystal-domed steamman friend Coppertracks were inside the house plotting and planning for near a month before the expedition sailed. We have half the tomes from the school of archaeology at St. Vines here, and don't you think that

Coppertracks didn't have our shelves close to bursting with all his books before the professor turned up with a line of students carrying a mortal stationers' worth of volumes for her.'

'You can never have too much knowledge,' said Daunt. 'I would take it as a kindness if I might peruse her books inside your unusual home.'

'Unusual is it?' said the commodore. 'I've missed that canny mind of yours, Jethro Daunt. Filled with all the cleverness of the church and honed like a sabre on a whetstone on your laws of synthetic morality. What strikes you as unusual about Tock House?'

Daunt pointed up to the hall's second landing as they climbed the stairs. 'All those Gothic rose windows visible outside, illuminated with stained glass. But inside your hall, the only natural light is coming from above. The windows are fake, set in your walls' outer layer – walls made of fibre-reinforced concrete set ten feet thick. Your home was built to resemble a rich man's folly, but in fact, it is better fortified than a civil war pillbox. Kirkhill-period, constructed by a rich merchant after the unrest following Parliament's victory over the king.'

'Aye, you've the bones of it,' admitted the commodore. 'The windows from the fourth storey and above are real enough, and there is a courtyard in the centre of the tower that admits the sun. A weak spot if your foe climbs well enough.' A dark thought seemed to furrow the commodore's brow. 'What wicked business brings you here today? The Inquisition has not engaged you again? As I recall, I barely escaped from that blasted hell-island of Jago the last time I became mixed up in your business.'

'Thankfully, the patrons covering the expenses of my present case are a little more prosaic,' said Daunt. 'The burghers of the Middlesteel city council. You have, I trust, been following the hysteria outside . . . the upheavals in the city accompanying the vampire killings?'

'That foolery?' coughed the commodore, slowing on the stairs. 'Bloodsuckers don't leave drained bodies discarded like chicken bones outside food stalls at a winter's fair. They're clever and subtle and secretive. They come from the shadows to steal your body, and if your family is blessed lucky, you're never seen again, for they turn their victims into their own kind. What I have heard reported in the papers is not vampires' work, it's common slaughter, bodies butchered desert-style with all their life drained by some maniacs.'

'Slaughter perhaps, commodore, but the real force behind the murders is, I fear, far removed from the mundanity of broken minds with sharp blades and a depraved taste for blood.'

'You don't believe the papers' fool nonsense do you?' Leading them down a corridor with a polished wooden floor and oak-panelled walls, the commodore walked Daunt to a spiral staircase. 'I had you for a sharper fellow.'

'I have three sisters in the care of the church, talking in tongues, who suggest I would be wise to believe otherwise.' Daunt pulled a notepad full of jottings out of his frock coat. 'A set of triplets ranting in ancient languages, Jackelian dialects that predate the age of ice and the devastation of the cold-time.'

'Myth and the dust of forgotten ages,' sighed the commodore, leading him up the stairs and onto the next storey. 'You are in luck then. That's the professor's passion, and my friend Coppertracks has a taste for it too. Some of the old steamer's books are from the mountains of the Steamman Free State and as old as any I've seen.'

Accompanying Daunt to the library entrance, the commodore

unlocked a double pair of doors, pushing them open to reveal an extensive chamber split across two levels. Shelves lined the walls, a second-tier with hanging ladders to access the thousands of tomes racked above the room's expensive hand-woven rugs. Like the rest of the tower, the library felt comfortably warm. Daunt took off his coat and tossed it onto the back of one of the dozens of leather armchairs scattered across the room.

The commodore indicated the reading tables, still covered with papers, books and notes, as if the expedition to the colonies had only just left. 'Make yourself at home, lad. This is all the professor's on the table, as well as the books piled in the corner. Not that I have been reading any of them. My taste in printed matter bends more towards the penny-dreadfuls and rousing tales of adventure and skulduggery.'

'Yes,' said Daunt. 'Well, I believe we both had our fill of that out beyond the Fire Sea. Without the professor to help me in my translations I may need to work late here.'

'As late as you like, lad. You've got your pick of guest bedrooms on the next floor. I will be taking a roast chicken out of the range in an hour or two, and it's a shame to open good red wine without honest company to honour it.'

Jethro Daunt had, he realized, lost all sense of time in the library. He looked over to the one wall that wasn't filled with shelves. A polished bronze wall clock was mounted there above an old royalist-era oil painting, an ornamental fireplace below. There was a dumbwaiter hatch to the left of the fireplace, and judging by the enticing smell of roasting meat emanating from it, the drop no doubt went all the way down to the kitchen in the keep-disguised-as-folly. The scene in the painting was of a boar-hunting party, the hunters unsportingly larking around in the brush wearing gas masks as their lance-carrying retainers waded through the undergrowth, eyes watering above water-soaked kerchiefs tied around their faces. In the corner of a painting, a boar slyly watched the party blundering about a mist of evil-looking yellow mustard gas, unsuccessfully trying to flush it out. *Better to be the boar than the hunter, sometimes.*

Daunt stared worriedly at the clock. No sign of Boxiron yet. Daunt had told the steamman to seek him out at Tock House if he wasn't to be found at their apartment. Yet Boxiron hadn't turned up. *Does that mean things have gone well, or badly?*

It was late, and Daunt's progress in translating the possessed ramblings of the sisters Lammeter had been as slow as he had feared it would be without Professor Harsh's assistance. He was trying to match his phonetic shorthand against actual words in languages that had been largely lost to the modern world. It hadn't helped that the languages of the patchwork of tribal kingdoms that had preceded the long, dark centuries of the ice-age bore little relation to each other. He had to parse them through the descendent language of River Tongue, a trading language merchants and travellers used as a lingua franca across the continent. Surprisingly, Daunt found it easier to reference the older languages using the strange antiquarian books that the commodore's eminent scientist friend, Coppertracks, had carried down with him from the mountains of the Steamman Free State. The steamman's tomes sported engraved metal covers and pages made out of some composite material that felt like a mix of rubber and glass – as hard to tear as steel, yet as thin as tissue paper. But as peculiar as the books' form might be, the standardization of the people of the metal's writing across the ages made their treatises on pre-cold time civilisations far more accessible than humanity's volumes. The race of man's books that survived into the modern age were copies of copies of copies, changed and mutated with the progressive errors of each new generation. In contrast – much like the steamman race – the metal creatures' tomes were methodical, steady and full of a humble cleverness. The only grating thing for Daunt was their authors' continual tendency to attribute events to their ancestral spirits, the Steamo Loa. If they weren't thanking their gods, they were busy blaming, praising or censuring them. It was almost as if they had written their texts in such a way as to annoy a parson of the atheist, humanist Circlist church. *Ex-parson*, Daunt reminded himself. *But some habits die harder than others.*

Yawning, Daunt gathered up his notes and went in search of the tower's owner. He found the old submariner in the house's kitchen, a grand scullery with a door latched ajar onto the tower's central courtyard, the warmth of the range evenly matched against the freezing evening breeze blowing outside. Ducking under a wooden frame dangling with dozens of pots, pans and pitchers, Daunt dropped his work down on a rectangular table in the kitchen's centre, enough chairs to seat twelve heads at a single sitting.

'Your cook has the night off?' Daunt said to the commodore's back as the large man drained a pot of steaming vegetables.

Without turning, the commodore pointed to one of the goblin-sized metal figures standing inert against the wall. 'The month off, lad. Coppertracks' drones will be as still as statues until he returns from the colonies.'

'I fear I would never let Boxiron cook for me. His idea of a fine meal is a tenth of a coal box shovelled into his furnace injector.'

'Ah, but Coppertracks is a rare genius,' said the commodore. 'Clever enough to have read Damson Beaton's *Household*

Economies and Recipes for Sustenance and passed it onto his little metal puppets here. Did you find any of the revelations you were looking for upstairs?'

'Along with a measure of frustration, good captain. I have a little of the meaning of what the sisters have been saying, but meaning without context.'

'A map without bearings,' said the commodore opening the range and removing a tray of covered clay pots. 'Blessed hard to plot a course against that.'

'Much of what I have uncovered seems to concern a monarch who was said to have unified the tribes into the first Kingdom of Jackals before the age of ice swept the continent.'

At Daunt's words, the commodore seemed to stumble, almost spilling the pot's contents. 'That would be Queen Elizica of the Jackeni.'

'Indeed,' said Daunt. 'It is as if the Sisters Lammeter are possessed by her spirit, relaying her words from beyond the grave.'

'Elizica's whispers have been heard in our world before, lad. She took it in her wicked mind to speak through my daughter, once. Nothing good comes from possession by the spirit of the land. Elizica's like an albatross fleeing the storm front. If it's her mutterings that your poor lassies are babbling about, you had best close the storm shutters and start stacking sacks full of flood sand outside your door.'

'I don't believe in unquiet spirits,' said Daunt. 'And the only gods with us in the world are the ones we create in our mind.'

'Save your Circlist cant for the archbishop,' said the commodore. 'I know what I'm talking about, right enough. She's the voice of the bones of the land. Jackals itself. The Kingdom soaked with the souls and blood of a thousand generations of our ancestors before us.'

81

Daunt shrugged. 'A voice that talks in riddles . . . of a war within a war. And riddles that point back to an ancient conflict between the tribes and the underwater people. A time when gill-necks waded up our beaches and attempted to conquer the mainland.'

'I know a little of the legends of that time,' said the commodore. 'Though I wish I didn't.'

'The professor wrote a book on it,' said Daunt. *'The Fall of the Stag-lords*. She hypothesized that the magma fields of the Fire Sea were expanding during that age, driving the peoples of the underwater nations onto our shores. During the confusion of that period, the hold of the druids over the land was weakened, the invaders repelled and the tribes unified under the first queen.'

The commodore looked as though this was news he did not want to hear. 'Let it stay in the professor's history texts, lad. Wicked times, let them stay lost and forgotten, that is where they belong!'

'The tongues that the sisters Lammeter are speaking in would have it otherwise,' said Daunt lifting up his notes and translations. 'The meaning is obtuse, but they seem to suggest that those times are repeating, that the war we now face with the Advocacy is merely the turning of the circle. They warn of ancient prophecy.'

The commodore moaned and abandoned his range. He collapsed at one of the table's chairs. 'Damn her, damn her wicked tricks.'

'The professor?'

'Elizica, lad, the bloody ancient queen. Is there so little royal blood left running in our land that she must come tormenting me, sending visitors to my door until she drives me out of my peaceful rest? First poor Rufus, then that black-hearted secret policeman Dick Tull, and now you. Where was she when the royalist fleet-in-exile was broken at Porto Principe by Parliament's airships? Where was she when my wife died, when my daughter was killed? Where was she when we stood together, Jethro Daunt, on that terrible land of Jago and faced down the army of the ursine and the terrors of that terrible singing tomb and its fearful weapon fit for dark gods? But now, ah, there's trouble with the people of the underwater nation and poor old Blacky is meant to abandon his nice warm house and put his neck on the line again! And for what? A parliament that turned my noble ancestors out of their land and hunted me for most of my damned life. Where is the justice in that, where is the fairness in that?'

Daunt had never seen the commodore so agitated. He raised his hands placatingly. 'Peace, good captain. Please, it is Boxiron and I who've been engaged on this case by the capital's aldermen. I appreciate the hospitality of your library, but I certainly wouldn't ask you to share whatever dangers might present themselves while resolving this case.'

'You won't have to, lad.' The commodore shook his head as Daunt extended out his bag of Bunter and Benger's aniseed drops. 'She'll do for me, just you wait and see. There's never a choice with her. She's the land, and if you wait long enough the land will take everything from you, even the dust of your bones when you've sacrificed all that you have to give. It is my family's fate, and I've run from a lot of things, but fate is one beast you can never outpace.'

'We chart our own way on the Circle's turn. There are no gods worth believing in. No fate save that which *we* will into being.'

'I hear the parson left in you talking,' said Commodore Black. 'But you will see. She'll have her way.'

'Don't believe in the gods, good captain. Refuse them.'

'Too late for that, lad. For the spirit of Queen Elizica

believes in me. And now, I fear, she believes in you too!'

Daunt let the calm and the quickening of the sweet's flavour pass through his head, all the tiredness and cobwebs clearing. *They tormented me once, the old gods, Badger-headed Joseph and his kin. But now I am their master. I've come too far to swap their tyranny for that of a queen. Even if she is the queen of our land.*

'I shall hold to what is right and rational, and you must do the same.'

Getting up, the commodore returned with a dusty bottle of wine bearing what appeared to be an intricate label written in Cassarabian script. 'Well, that would be this, then. Let's drink while we are able. I shall toast my unlucky stars and you may toast your synthetic morality and whatever other inventive teachings the church saw fit to squeeze into your clever noggin before they booted your arse out of the rational orders.'

The two of them sat. And they drank.

There was a chill in Dick's room when he returned home, the kind that seeped deep into a man's bones and numbed them from the inside out. Dick Tull might only keep two rooms in the cheap second-storey tenement he rented, but even so, his single fireplace always seemed too small to put out enough heat, no matter how much coal he piled inside it.

Dick left his greatcoat on. Thin walls. Thin floors. Thin ceilings. Cheap windows with as much frost on the inside as outside. *I'll be out of here soon enough. The report I handed into the board. Proof that the royalists and the gill-necks are conniving together. Wait till the head gets to read that. His suspicions confirmed. My promotion in the bag. Able to afford rooms in a respectable district. Not too expensive, of course. That'd be a waste. But somewhere my neighbours aren't living twenty to a room. Screaming and shitting and crying and fighting. That'll show that urchin Billy-boy. That'll show that arrogant sod Walsingham.*

Dick walked across to his window. He had made the curtains himself, cheap thick cloth that had come from a pawnshop around the corner. There was a fight spilling out of the tavern opposite, scattering a patrol of the local citizen's committee. The patrol were waving kitchen knives, a few rusty sabres and one rifle that looked so old it'd be hard pressed to loose a single charge before it needed to be stripped and cleaned. *Good hunting, lads. You meet a vampire tonight, you had better hope it dies from a laughing fit.*

Dick glanced at his cold fireplace and the rusty quarter-full bucket of coal nestled against the grate, shook his head, then walked into his bedroom to swap his greatcoat for the soft indoor coat he kept hanging on the back of the door's hook. Fear froze him far colder than the apartment's chill, and it wasn't the wintry bedroom that stopped his heart – it was the corpse sprawled across his bed, so much dried blood staining Dick's cheap grey woollen covers that you'd think the blankets had been dyed brown. William Beresford's throat had been neatly slit open, and the young agent had been tossed down with a knife stuck in the middle of his chest.

That looks familiar. Dick's hand reached for the blade sheaf hidden at the back of his belt. Empty! *My blade. My lodgings. Sodding hell.* Dick had seen enough set-ups – arranged more than a few of his own – to know when he was being hung out to dry. There was no trail of blood across the room, so like as not, the agent had been lured here and murdered in situ. *Shit me, Billy-boy, you had to let them stick you here. In the chest too. And you knew the bugger that did it, to let them get that close. My lodgings, you stupid, young—*

Dick heard the poorly nailed floorboards of the staircase

outside squeaking with the weight of people climbing up the stairs. He'd left the board's pistol back with the office's hoary old armourer, which meant he'd have to use his own ammunition tonight. *How careful were the jiggers that did this, how well did they search my place?*

Not thoroughly enough. Dick pulled at the bedroom's loose skirting board, eaten away with woodworm, and dipped his hand into the empty space behind the wood, pulling out a short-barrelled blunderbuss from the gap between the bricks. He'd taken it from the carriage of a dead hansom cab driver who had been supplying a little more than rides to the Cassarabian ambassador. It wasn't a neat gun; whatever you said about it, the weapon could never be described as that. But then, it was designed to be pushed against drunk, flailing, violent passengers in close confines, with most of the assailants' bulk blown away by the impact of the charge. It was a terror weapon really, no range to speak of. Anyone who didn't shit themselves just looking at it probably needed to be split in half to be stopped. There was a saying in the Jackelian regiments that it took a man's weight in lead to stop a charging soldier. Well, here it was, a man's weight in buckshot loaded into its flared iron barrel, and Dick reached back again for the bandoleer holding ten more charges. He slung the bandoleer over his waistcoat before concealing in under his coat.

'Tull!' It was his landlady's voice. Damson Pegler, the grasping old cow. 'Coal man's been. How much of the black stuff are you going to take?'

'Save it!' called Dick, using the cover of the bellow to click back the hammer on the blunderbuss's clockwork firing mechanism. 'I've still got a quarter bucket inside here.'

'Special price today,' said the old crone. 'Half full gets you a second half free.'

Special price. And you're passing the money onto me, rather than keeping it for yourself, you cheap old cow. Almost as improbable as finding his ex-partner a corpse stretched out across his bed.

Dick raised his voice. 'All right then, I'm coming.' The latch on his window snapped open beneath the shout.

'Damson Pegler.'

'Yes?'

'Get your sodding head down.'

The blunderbuss bucked even as Dick dropped out of the window, sending a cloud of shot through the cheap door and the flimsy walls, the brief satisfaction of hearing yells and screams outside his lodgings by way of reply. Hurling himself at the ladder on the fire escape, he kicked the ladder's latch out and rode it all the way down to the street outside.

'Vampires!' Dick screamed at the patrol of the local citizen's committee, dozens of heads turning to see where the commotion was originating. He flung his hand towards the entrance hall of his tenement building. 'Sweet Circle, man, there's bloody vampires inside the building, they're slaughtering everyone. It's a sodding massacre in there.'

Give them that much, there was only a moment of hesitation on the mob's part, then, as one, they surged towards Damson Pegler's building, their numbers swelled by the drunk brawlers who'd been fighting outside the alehouse. They were game for it and looking for trouble. Inside, they'd find it. Dick was reloading as a head poked out of his window, a black rubber stench-mask fixed to the face. *Sod me, it's the dustmen.*

Dick fired the blunderbuss towards the head, cracking the window's glass and throwing out a cloud of splinters from the rotting wooden walls of his building. Furious cries sounded from inside the entry corridor. *The mob won't last long against the dustmen, not waving pitchforks and sabres against a cadre of trained assassins.*

Cracking open his gun as he sprinted down the street, Dick ejected the spent charge and pushed a fresh one inside before snapping the weapon shut. Bellows sounded behind him, getting louder, people coming down the street blundering out of his way as they noticed the gun in his hands and the wild look on his gasping face. *Never get away from them now.*

Dick almost slipped as the kettle-black careered around the corner, only just managing to halt short of the massive iron wheels crunching past his boots. He raised his blunderbuss towards the driver's step at the front and stopped himself from firing as Barnabas Sadly's rat-like features twitched down towards him. 'Onto the cart, Mister Tull.'

Dick leapt for the ladder on the side, hauling himself onto the driver's perch even as the vehicle swung around, the massive boiler and barrel-laden flatbed on the back interspersed between them and the first shots whistling down the street, bullets clanging off the heavy iron of the carriage.

'Your people came for me, Mister Tull. The dustmen came for me when I was in my cellar, killed the brewery delivery man and two of my customers, they did.'

Dick stood on his toes and risked a glance behind the kettle-black's single stack pumping steam out into the evening air. Three men in dark coats and rubber stench masks were sprinting after them, but falling back as they lost ground to the powerful engines of the cart. *And they set me up too. What was it you said, Sadly? Foxes and hounds, mousers and mice, all dancing together.*

'Why, Mister Tull? Lords-a'larkey, what have I ever done against the board? Haven't I always given you the truth of it, at considerable risk to my own life?'

'Damned if I know,' said Dick. *And damned for certain if*

we don't find out. The dustmen. Sod it. How dead does that make us?

Retirement had finally been forced on Dick, a retirement less comfortable than even he had imagined.

In the tall, cold chambers of the State Protection Board, its head, Algo Monoshaft, whistled in anger and frustration as the steamman tried to find a place for his latest report on the paper-strewn floor of his office.

Corporal Tull's report that detailed how Dick Tull had been accepting large bribes in exchange for turning a blind eye to the royalist rebels' activities inside the capital. The report that made clear how the sergeant had murdered his own partner when he had been found out, but only after tossing his royalist contact's dead body into the river to ensure his treachery remained undiscovered.

Algo Monoshaft maniacally pulled at the crimson threads criss-crossing the paper fragments. *Where does this go? WHERE DOES THIS GO?*

There were hordes of staff working within Parliament's walls, cleaners and caterers and the hundreds of personnel who waddled through its warrens wearing antiquated cloaks and powdered wigs. But none climbed so high or worked so cold as the bell-men who tended the intricate clockwork mechanism of Brute Julius, the massive bell tower that emerged like a brick spear from the gothic architecture of the debating chamber.

Once an hour its twenty bells chimed their resounding call across the roofs of the capital, ringing loud and clear over Middlesteel's towers and warehouses and slums. Walking through the oak-panelled corridor of Parliament, the master of the bell's boots echoed across the largely empty corridors and staircases, walls hung with political cartoons from the *Middlesteel Illustrated Times* and its rival newssheets. Strangely, the boots of the master's apprentice made a great deal less noise, even though she was carrying a heavy toolbox. It took practice to be that stealthy.

The master of the bells pulled out a pocket watch chained to his waistcoat. 'Nearly time for eleven-chime.'

'No,' said the apprentice. 'They've already sounded. It's time for the nightshift to begin.'

'Yes,' said the master. 'Time to hand over to the nightshift.'

His apprentice passed over the toolbox to the old man. 'Time to go to the *Ship and Shovel* for a drink. I'll see you there.'

'Time to go to the *Ship and Shovel*,' said the master. 'See you there?'

'Of course,' said the apprentice. Charlotte watched the old man walk to the red-coated sentry at the door at the end of the corridor, King Jude's sceptre concealed inside his long toolbox, along with all the equipment she'd needed to tease open the vaults' clever locks.

It was quite a piece, that sceptre, symbolic value aside. Discounting the intricately carved solid gold rod that made up most of its three feet of length, King Jude's sceptre was banded by rubies with large amethysts and an egg-sized sapphire inlaid in its handle. If that wasn't enough to get any thief salivating, the sceptre's spear-like head was mounted by seven platinum leaves crafted like a bulb, and contained the largest diamond Charlotte had ever seen – an octahedral-shaped beauty larger than a big man's fist. It managed to be both beautiful and strangely deadly at the same time, a spear crafted in rare metals for a warrior queen. *I can almost see why Twist is willing to pay me so much money for it.*

It hadn't been simple either, getting into the vault. Even

with the Master of Bells operating under the misconception that Charlotte had been his apprentice for the last three years, even with the burning weight of the jewel between her breasts to mesmerize all the guards and the attendants. The locks and tumblers set to protect the crown jewels across five vaulted passages hadn't bent to the Eye of Fate's hypnotic power. No, those brutes had required every ounce of Charlotte's proficiency with tumblers and the safe-cracking equipment she was lugging along, they'd taken every drop of sweat she'd shed defusing the poison gas injectors and capture cages concealed in the false ceiling. The traps that most definitely had *not* been detailed on the floor plans or deactivated by the pass cards supplied by her mysterious patron. *Well, if it had been easy, the royalists would have done it themselves.*

A momentary sadness struck Charlotte. It would be hard to top this job. All the safes and vault rooms and cunning tripwires and ingenious traps she had faced in her career, they could all be relegated to experience now. Merely the practice she'd needed to hone her craft to the level necessary to break into Parliament and spirit away its most valuable symbol of power. Things wouldn't be the same in a couple of months, after she'd lain low long enough for the hue and cry the newssheets would raise over this crime to fade away. Where would the fun be in facing down the run-of-the-mill protections guarding a merchant lord's antiquities after this? It would be like a master painter reduced to setting up an easel opposite the capital's national gallery and capturing the likeness of tourists in charcoal for thruppence a caricature. Well, at least she would always carry the warmth of her memories of having humbugged every one of the honourable members of the House of Guardians. The outrage of this crime a slap in the face to every one of the smug, superior aristocrats . . .

the gallants who in a rightful world would have been Charlotte's equal in station.

And she could use the time to lay low to avoid the fate the mad ex-parson Jethro Daunt and his hulking, malfunctioning half-steamman friend seemed to think was lurking around the corner, waiting to befall her. Money would help. Money always did. It was amazing how being rich could cushion you from the worst the world had to throw it to you. Charlotte could speak with authority on that. Her shameful memory of having been so hungry as an abandoned child that she had been reduced to eating grass and leaves. Grubby and crawling on her knees, cramps slicing across her stomach like a hundred knives being plunged into her. Bile rising in her throat as she tried to chew down on coarse grass. Real hunger, not just being ready for dinner. That had been close to the time when *she* had first found Charlotte, taken pity on her . . . another stab of shame, more deserved this time. The gypsy woman. The gypsy.

Money? No, money wasn't a family's love, but it was as much a comfort as Charlotte required. So much money she'd taken over the years. Then, in a fit of irony, she'd spread it out across all of the capital's major banks and counting houses, just in case there was a run on one of them and Charlotte lost her savings. *Security.* With enough money she would have security; she would know peace. If she got ill, she could afford to pay for doctors and medicine. If she got hungry, she could pay for food to still the pain of hunger. If one of the people she cared for ran into hard times, then she could help them to survive too. Charlotte just needed a large enough amount of money and then she would be protected, for now and forever. It was strange, how she could fill her accounts with silver and gold and notes of the realm, the amount on deposit curiously swelling on its own account as interest was applied.

But it could never grow larger than the fear of what might happen to a young woman all alone in the world. The fear always expanded faster than the money. Perhaps that was the nature of fear. Or perhaps it was the nature of money. Still, having money always helped. There was no doubt about that.

Charlotte's reverie was broken by the intrusion of the red-coated sentry as she approached the end of the corridor where the Master of Bells had passed a minute earlier.

'You, I don't know,' said the soldier, a ham-sized fist stretching out to halt her.

'I'm one of the new grease monkeys working on the Bell Tower,' said Charlotte.

'Young for it,' said the soldier, his eyes narrowing suspiciously. 'Staff in the tower are mutton, not lamb. Letters after their name, with apprenticeships to their machines and a way with cogs. Now you, you look like lamb to me.'

Charlotte sighed. She was tired. Using the jewel, the Eye of Fate, so frequently in such a short space of time was a terrible drain on her, but it couldn't be helped. Usually she embraced its touch. She became a different person when she used the jewel on the stage. More confident. The fears and worries of life a distant, fleeting thing. Her jealousies and ambitions and fears of failure and loneliness melting away. But too much use and the jewel grew heavy . . . ice spreading out across her blood as she shifted her blouse, the soft blue nimbus from the crystal reaching out from her chest and drifting towards the sentry as though the fog were the softest of cigar smokes.

'Look into the light,' Charlotte urged. 'There's no lambs inside the light, no mutton, no apprenticeships or cogs.'

Blinking furiously, the soldier stumbled back, the light splitting into a forest of fractal branches as it caressed the cheeks around his sideburns

'You have a brother or a sister with children?' Charlotte asked, trying not to grimace as the cold spread through her veins, sapping away at her strength.

'A brother,' mumbled the soldier, 'with six little ones.'

'Then you recognize your niece.' Charlotte tried to smile, even as the pressure of the jewel pressed down against her lungs. 'The niece who you've been showing around the debating chamber now that Parliament is shut for the night.'

'Yes,' the soldier returned her smile without any of the pain that Charlotte felt, 'I know my niece, my Alice.'

'We need to go,' said Charlotte. 'You had better get me out into the square before the colonel of the House Guards finds out that you have been larking about on duty with your family.'

'Bloody Nora, lass, you're going to cost me my corporal's stripes,' moaned the soldier. 'Let's go!'

'Yes,' said Charlotte, pushing the jewel out of sight once more. 'Let's.'

'Thank you for showing me around, uncle,' said Charlotte as the soldier unlocked a sentry door in the high spear-headed railings that surrounded Parliament. 'I won't say a thing. I don't want to get you into trouble.'

'Off with you, girl,' said the corporal, nervously glancing behind him to make sure they were unobserved. 'Don't say a thing to your ma. You'll get me into right trouble, you will.'

Charlotte winked at him and slipped away into the night. The force of her mesmerism was similar to a waking dream. Give it a couple of days and the soldier would be hard-pressed to tell if his niece's visit had been real or a fancy he'd imagined. He was in good company. There would be plenty of parliamentary staff who would be experiencing the same sense of confusion over the next couple of days. But there was one man for whom the glamour she had cast would hopefully last at least a few hours more. She had made sure it was a strong one. The Master of the Bells was sitting in a nearby tavern waiting for his apprentice to join him for a last drink before he wound his way home. And Charlotte did not want to disappoint him. Not with the sceptre of the last king of Jackals wrapped up in rags inside the master's tool case. That, surely, was worth raising a cup of ale to. She rubbed her arms as she crossed the street, dodging into the shadows of one of the tailor shops that specialized in the robes, wigs, and finery of the myriad positions filled by Parliament's masters and servants. A warm hansom cab ride to the tavern? No, Charlotte hardly had the strength left to wipe the cabbie's memory of the journey, and she had come too far to leave a careless trail from Parliament's railings back to her home. Even the dullards in Ham Yard might get lucky once, and by tomorrow they would be a legion of constables and inspectors crawling over the streets desperate for witnesses. *There's a cheery thought.*

Charlotte's arm was beginning to ache from the weight of the long toolbox and the sceptre concealed within. Just another worker winding her way home through Middlesteel's streets and lanes after a full day's graft, nothing out of the ordinary to be remembered by the townspeople trudging their way back from mills and clerks' rooms. Damson Robinson's establishment still seemed to be working late, oil lamps visible through the cracks of closed blinds. *Of all the things I can depend on, Damson Robinson's waiting up to take receipt of our crime lord's share of tonight's bounty is pretty high on the list.*

Charlotte rattled the door handle and finding it open, entered the pie shop's front. Inside, contrary to Charlotte's expectations, there was no sign of Damson Robinson, or indeed Captain Twist. His malevolent little toad of an assistant – Mister Cloake – was there, though, as promised along with two other men. She marked them as dustmen from the look of their dark simple-clothes and the stench masks dangling from their necks. Except that refuge collectors shouldn't hang there so still and dangerous, like blades hovering for a belly to gut. Apart from her friend, what was also markedly absent was the case containing the gold coins that had encouraged Charlotte out of the shop earlier.

'Are we emptying our bins early tonight, honey?' Charlotte asked.

'An object as valuable as King Jude's sceptre cannot have too much protection. I trust you have it with you?' said Cloake.

'If I didn't, I'd be lying gassed inside a vault under Parliament and being prodded by the guards' bayonets, not standing here. Where's my money and where's Damson Robinson?'

'Both out back,' said Cloake. 'Pass me over the sceptre. I need to verify its provenance.'

Out back, eh? Because you're so very generous, you'd let her take a bath of gold guineas while the three of you wait out front for my return.

As Charlotte glanced to the kitchen door she caught the acrid smell of pastry turned to cinders.

'Here it is, honey,' said Charlotte, bending down and undoing the clasps along her long toolbox's side. She lifted up the sceptre, still wrapped and swaddled with grease rags. 'It's heavy.'

Without a word, the two dustmen stepped forward to take the sceptre. Pretending to stumble, Charlotte closed the distance between them in a step and then continued to swing, pounding the gold handle into the first man's navel. As he was doubling up, she rammed its diamond head into the second bruiser's face, connecting with the nose and sending him stumbling back, the stench mask swinging wildly as the pain of a broken bone percolated through his stunned mind. 'Damson Robinson never burnt a pie in her life, you royalist bastards.'

Cloake was advancing on her, pulling a weapon out from under the back of his coat – a wicked double-pronged thing, like a crystal tuning fork. It might be sharp, but she still had the advantage of range with the sceptre's length.

'I am going to lay you next to her corpse in the oven,' Cloake leered. 'After I have drained the last of your juices. The Mass must feed.'

Charlotte raised the still swaddled sceptre, holding it up as a lance to impale the treacherous little thug. He turned his strange weapon in his hand, the crystal throbbing and pulsing with red light. As it sparked, the jewel beneath Charlotte's blouse flared hot against her skin, all the cold of her weary, exhausting night's labour mesmerizing the staff of Parliament banished in a moment. *Hot. It's never burned hot before, only cold!* Two feet from her, Cloake had collapsed onto his knees, howling like a banshee. Cracking in the air, the crimson energies from his strange blade wrapped around the man, whipping and burning his skin. Charlotte was in no position to focus on his agonies. She was folding to her own knees, the blood of her body burning, running like acid inside her.

Blue light from the crystal pendant peeled away from her chest, reaching out towards Cloake's weapon, where its crimson sparks hissed and coiled angrily towards the Eye of Fate's blue light, a dance of duelling vipers in the air between them.

'Kill her!' Cloake yelled through gritted teeth.

Confused by the strange ethereal duel of energies in the air, the dustman Charlotte had winded was getting to his feet.

Charlotte couldn't move. Her body was paralysed, supplying the life force the jewel was draining, channelling. Cloake cursed and yelled again, and this time his words seemed to percolate through his henchman's bewildered brain.

Drawing a hunting blade almost as long as a forearm from his belt, the dustman carefully avoided the coiling lashing energies striking across the air and darted forward. He pulled his arm back to slash down on Charlotte neck and near decapitate her.

'This is it, Mister Tull,' said Sadly, sounding impressed that Dick knew someone who lived in so grand a residence on the outskirts of town.

'Big it may be, but the coin that paid for this pile is as dodgy as its owner,' said Dick as Sadly threw the lever to release pressure from the kettle-black's traction mechanism. Their great iron carriage slowed up outside the wall.

Dick glanced around the open stretch of the duck pond and the crescent of hilltop houses opposite. *No sign of the dustmen, but that doesn't mean they're not coming here. Young Billy-boy carved up like a slaughtered pig on my bed, Rufus Symons' corpse found fished out of the river. Everyone who's touched this affair is being cleaned up. Careful, I have to be careful, before my last surviving lead is tidied out of existence.*

Sadly stood up on the driver's step, gazing down on the gaslights of the capital, the length of Middlesteel spread out beneath a full moon. 'That is a sight, that is, Mister Tull. Must be nice having that at the end of your drive, says I. They won't be coming here, will they, the dustmen? The board doesn't mess with the quality, do they? Not the folk with money, not carriage folk?'

Dick thought of the murder of Lady Florence Chant that

young William had reported. It had been shortly after that that his old partner had been reassigned, then murdered. Maybe Dick has been too quick to dismiss the story of the killing as a prank by the boy to land him in trouble with the board's officers. Dick shrugged. 'It'll take more than a few notes from Lords Bank to buy off the board's band of killers.'

The little rat-faced man seemed unnerved by the prospect of being pursued inside. 'Let us be away then, Mister Tull. We don't need to be bottled up inside that old place. The steam is still up on the carriage. Roll the weight of the barrels off the back and we can make it across two counties on the coke left inside our coal box.'

'Running blind, that's running to your death,' said Dick, checking his blunderbuss had a fresh charge resting in its breach. 'Old Blacky inside there has answers. And if you're right about the gill-necks being involved in this mess, then we are going to need a u-boat to follow their trail.'

'Lords-a'larkey,' coughed Sadly, beating his chest. 'He's not a submariner, is he? I'm no good on the water, Mister Tull. I gets sick taking a wherry to cross the river, I does.'

'I need you alive to testify for me,' said Dick, 'and I'll take you seasick and without a bullet in your back over the reverse. Don't you worry, when it comes to piloting the seas, old Blacky is as slippery as they come. He was born with a smuggler's soul and a privateer's silver cutlass under his royalist cot. That's what the board has mostly been using him for, running cargo no one else would touch. You'll like him – he's a snitch and a turncoat, just like you.'

'That, Mister Tull, right offends me. I just work the middle and I've always been true to you.'

'The middle doesn't get to be offended,' said Dick. 'And I think we've both fallen off the fence now.'

Well off and hanging over the ledge, that's what we sodding are.

Wrapped in the fire of her jewel, joined in agony with Cloake by the snaking energies that connected the thug to the Eye of Fate, Charlotte could hardly muster the strength to raise her eyes towards the assassin about to plunge his long-bladed knife into her neck.

Even with the pain, Charlotte's ears still worked well enough to be near deafened by the sudden splintering explosion of the pie shop's front door. If Damson Robinson had been alive she'd be spitting blood. As it was, enough of that splattered over the sawdust as Boxiron continued his lurching charge through the entrance. The steamman connected with the first of Cloake's thugs, the surprise that was no doubt on the man's eyes hidden by his stench-mask as Boxiron ploughed through where he was standing. The assassin was lifted into the air as if he had been upended by the horns of a charging bull. The blade that had been seconds away from slicing through Charlotte's neck somersaulted upwards and embedded itself in the ceiling's oak beam. There was no scream. There was no time.

Kneeling, Charlotte just managed to use her hands to stop herself falling forward and colliding with the floor. It was gone – the interweaved bridge of coiling, lashing energies joining her in suffering to Cloake. Her jewel had turned cold almost the instant that the spinning body sent flying by the steamman collided with Cloake. He'd dropped his double-bladed knife, but Cloake wasn't out of the fight. He didn't so much move as scuttle, like a spider or a crab, his body scurrying across the sawdust-strewn floor, seizing the crystal blade and speeding towards the door into the bakery room. There was something ill about the way he moved so strangely, so quickly. Something sickening. *The backdoor. The yard. Bastard.* Maybe it was the shock of being disconnected from the surging force, but Charlotte worked hard to hold down the vomit.

He was quick, the second thug, Charlotte gave him that. Even with the sight of the steamman bearing down on him like a loosed crossbow bolt, he maintained his poise and pulled out a pistol concealed behind his back. It sported a long black barrel with a serrated knife fixed underneath, but whether there was a charge loaded into its breach or not was a moot point, as the steamman slowed not a jot, simply running the killer down like a charging war-horse flattening a victim on the battlefield. He spun with the impact, the thug, and a spray of blood painted the floor followed by a sickening thump of cracking bones as Cloake's man barrelled back into the far wall. It wasn't so much a fight at a demonstration of the laws of physics. Half a ton or more of unstoppable force murderously impacting with a skin-covered sack of flesh, blood and bones. A strange, low whine like an annoyed cat came from the body. *No man would die like that, surely?*

Charlotte shivered to her feet, still clutching the sceptre. *I have it. No buyer, no patron, no case full of gold coins, but I still have King Jude's bloody sceptre.*

'Help me!' The first noise to sound from the steamman beyond the initial explosion of physical violence, his voicebox quivering with a plaintive, pleading quality. Boxiron was flailing his brick-sized fists at the counter, smashing chunks out of the worktop, little clouds of masonry and flour spraying into the air. 'My gears have slipped.'

As Charlotte got closer she saw there was a lever on the back of the steamman's smoke stack, a plate cut with gear positions. The little engraved brass plate placed there by the manufacturer read 'idle' at its lowest position, but Boxiron's previous employers had scratched a line through the script and painted it over with the words 'slightly less-murderous'. Right now the lever was quivering energetically in five, locked in top gear. She threw the lever down, twisting it around to 'idle'.

There was a gasp of wheezing smoke from Boxiron's stack as he shuddered back down to stillness. 'Curse this human-milled, coal-choked malfunction of a body.'

'I would say bless it, for I would be dead for sure without you,' said Charlotte. 'Although I do seem to remember telling you that I didn't need your protection.'

'Yes,' said Boxiron. 'As I was standing outside I could hear you were doing a superior job of managing to protect yourself. I merely entered to see how it should be done.'

'Bugger you and your parson's prophecies,' Charlotte threw back.

'Jethro Daunt tries hard not to believe in prophecies. I, on the other hand, have no such compulsion. The spirits are riding the sisters Lammeter and it's still your name spilling out of their lips.'

Prophecy? This isn't a prophecy. This is just business. Those Royalist twisters tried to double-cross me, is all. Keep their money, keep the sceptre too. So, the rebels want their ancient symbol of authority back, do they? Now it would cost that cheating dog Mister Twist three times what he'd offered her before, for even a sniff of this jewel-tipped beauty. Charlotte recalled the eerie way that Cloake had fled while escaping their duel of lightning-like energies. Moving like nothing human has a right to. Her jewel had saved her. The Eye of Fate had known. *No, I'm imagining it. This was a royalist double-cross, no more, no less.*

She kicked at the corpse of one of her would-be murderers on the way to the bakery. The back yard was open, cold air blowing across the room, the oven door standing ajar. Against her better judgment, she opened it wide and peered inside, having to choke back the vomit still riding her belly. Damson Robinson. What was left of her. *Just like the killings in the papers. Drained of all her blood. But not a pair of fangs to be seen among these bastards.* Charlotte had to stop herself from reaching out and touching the remains stuffed inside the oven. To feel the confirmation that here had been a human life, someone she had known, someone she had joked with. Damson Robinson had looked after all of her thieves. It might've been the kind of care that a highwaymen showed for a useful brace of pistols, oiling and cleaning and greasing them, but Charlotte hadn't had such a great surfeit of friends in her life before that she noticed or minded the difference.

She heard the clanking legs of the steamman following her inside the bakery room. 'There was a third man.'

Charlotte glanced outside and finding no sign of Cloake, shut the door, locking it. 'He was on his toes fast enough after you flattened his two bruisers, the dirty jigger. And you, you followed me to the shop . . .'

Boxiron tapped his shiny vision plate. 'My head is my original and I still have the sight of a steamman knight. That, at least, is not degraded. Give me line of vision and I can track you across the city from a mile away, day or night.'

'That must come in useful.'

'So, I have found it. But I didn't require magnification optics to observe the Loa-cursed energies flowing between you and the leader of the ambush.'

'I have no explanation for that,' said Charlotte. 'The force just appeared, crippling both of us when Cloake tried to strike me down with that queer-looking crystal blade of his.'

Boxiron reached out to rest a thick iron finger on the cloth-wrapped sceptre Charlotte was carrying. 'And did this also appear to you in a burst of mysterious energies? Jethro soft-body requested that you keep a low profile, yet you have in your possession something that looks suspiciously like it's been removed from the Parliamentary treasury.'

'What, this little thing?'

'It's many years since Jethro softbody reclaimed me from my employ as an enforcer for the flash mob,' Boxiron wearily explained, 'but even back in those days, it was well-known that you did not interfere or demand protection from Damson Robinson's pie shop. Or was she no longer acting as a fence for the Cat-gibbon and her criminal faction in the under-world?'

So, it's true. I knew you were crooked once, old steamer. 'First time I visited the shop, honey. I just developed a hankering for an ale and beef pie, is all.'

Boxiron looked inside the oven, the wreckage of the body stuffed into the space, then fixed Charlotte with a steely stare. 'I would suggest you switch your patronage to an alternative supplier.'

CHAPTER FIVE

There were a lot of scenes that Dick Tull might have imagined discovering on the other side of the door when Commodore Black opened it to him and Sadly. The sight of a gorilla-sized steamman ruffian and a beak-nosed fellow sprawled across the floor of Tock House's entrance hall pinning down a woman was not one of them. She looked young, and whoever the girl was, she was writhing on the tiles spitting out fever-mangled sentences as she twisted and turned.

'A wicked storm crow, riding two minutes forward of the darkness,' the commodore practically hissed at Dick. Without another word, the old u-boat man fished into Dick's coat and came out with his hip flask. Leaving the door open, the commodore rushed back to the struggling woman, grabbing something out of a paper bag the other man was proffering towards Blacky, crushed it, mixed it with Dick's fire water, then poured it down the girl's throat.

Her thrashing lessened, and the commodore ordered the brutish steamman and his beak-nosed friend through to his kitchen table.

'You and me,' Dick called to the commodore. 'Words, now!'

'The board can bloody wait,' the commodore called back as he disappeared down the corridor. 'Lock the door behind you.'

That is what you think, Blacky. What's coming after us ain't going to wait, not for a second.

'Are you sure we've come to the right place, Mister Tull?' asked Sadly, disbelief wrinkling his disagreeable features.

'Don't you mind old Blacky, he was raised with the fleet-in-exile. Manners of a pirate, he has.'

Sadly was bending down on the floor where the girl had been seconds before, examining a long cloth-wrapped object left there. 'Oh my giddy aunt. See here, Mister Tull. Lords-a'larkey—' he flourished King Jude's sceptre. 'Oh my pretty, is this . . .?'

'It's the rope outside Bonegate jail,' said Dick, snatching the sceptre off Sadly. 'For anyone caught with it, if it's real. Get your thieving hands off.'

Dick went after the commodore, the informant hustling after him, still seemingly mesmerized by the sceptre. 'We need to be on our heels, Mister Tull. Low profile is the thing, not every Ham Yard crusher and redcoat in the regiments beating the bushes with their sabres looking for that.'

That's Blacky all right, never a dull moment. Where did the board think he got his fortune from? Running grain ship-ments across the sea?

The steamman and his friend were lifting the girl onto the kitchen table while the commodore cleared it of a leftover meal by the simple expedient of sweeping the contents crashing onto the floor. She was speaking like a madwoman, her words incomp-rehensible, coming out garbled in a rapid continuous stream.

'What language is that?' Dick asked.

Before anybody could answer, her trembling hand thrust out towards Dick. 'The spear-carrier, the spear-carrier has arrived.'

Dick glanced to at the sceptre still in his hands, the hulking steamman noting the rod in the agent's possession and snatching it back off him. *Not much of a spear.* Then the girl returned to vomiting alien nonsense once more.

'She is being ridden by the Loa,' said the steamman. 'She speaks the language of the spirits, the dead.'

'Damson Shades,' said the steamman's friend, restricting the girl. 'Peace. Keep still. You are going to bite your tongue off.'

'Poor lass,' said the commodore. 'She has it bad, she does. Pass me another one of your foul little sweets Jethro, so I can mix it with a drop of the hard stuff.'

Dick saw the bag of Bunter and Benger's aniseed drops about to exchange hands and he grabbed the commodore's arm before the old u-boat man could accept it. 'No more of those for her.'

'Are you the doctor we sent for?' asked the man.

'Doctor my arse. He's the wicked rascal I told you about,' said the commodore. 'Dick Tull, a filthy government officer come along to disturb my quiet.'

'I know enough about drugging a body and keeping 'em alive enough to answer questions at the end of it,' said Dick. 'You give the girl another dose of whiskey and opiates and she'll die on you. The booze jolted her out of her fit, give the opiates another five minutes to pass through her blood and stop her whispering that nonsense.'

'I can assure you there are no opiates in any Bunter and Benger's aniseed drops,' said the beak-nosed man. 'That is merely a scurrilous rumour spread by their competitors inside the trade.'

Dick shook his head in annoyance. 'Who are these two damn jokers, Blacky? A music hall act?'

'I am Jethro Daunt,' said the man proudly, as if he was

announcing he was a prince among men. 'And along with my colleague Boxiron, we're protecting the young Damson Shades here. She is in the care of our agency for private resolutions.'

Private resolutions . . . a consulting detective with delusions of grandeur. How sodding fine.

'Then I suggest you care for her elsewhere, Daunt. Amateur hour is over. Blacky, you and I have business to discuss.'

'Hang your business,' said the commodore. 'I told you before; I'm finished with the board.'

'Truer than you know,' said Tull. 'Whatever mess you've got yourself into with your old royalist friends, it's put you on the murder list. The board tossed Rufus Symons' corpse into the river, and they tried to top me just for reporting that pack of lies you passed on to me.'

'Been disavowed have you?' laughed Commodore Black. 'Your badge melted for scrap. All the shit you've done in your life, how can you even tell where the smell's coming from?'

Dick yanked out the blunderbuss from under his greatcoat, grabbed the commodore's lapels and shoved him against the kitchen wall, the barrel pushed under his throat. Boxiron lurched forward towards them, but Sadly had a tiny sleeve-pistol out and pointing at Jethro Daunt's head. 'Not another step, see. I have got your back, Mister Tull.'

The head of the spring-loaded arm hidden up his sleeve quivered as the little rat-faced man kept the trembling pistol pointed at Blacky's friend. *Bloody Nora. Never knew Sadly kept a sleeve gun. Never knew he had a gun at all for that matter. Never realized he had the balls for it.*

'Your friend Rufus Symons is dead. My old partner is lying back on my bed sliced up like a side of pork belly on a butcher's slab. The board tried to kill my little acquaintance Sadly here just because I talked with him. Everyone who's had anything to do with your royalist accomplices has been left for a corpse. I should be one! You think because you're dying that you've got nothing left to live for? Let's put it to the test. I'll do you now before the board comes for you. I'll put a charge's worth of lead shot through your fat, thick, wealthy head and decorate the expensive tiles of your nice warm kitchen with a new pattern. Blacky red. It could be a new style. What do you say?'

'Trigger your weapon,' Boxiron threatened, 'and you join him in death a second later.'

'This is not a rational course,' protested Daunt from the other side of the table. 'From what you have said I believe our causes are linked.'

'Shut your cake-hole, amateur. I'm looking for the reason why I've been placed on a death list. I've not been engaged by a rich widow to track down her bloody missing cat.'

'Missing pets and errant spouses do not engage my professional interest. Missing citizens who are absent of blood are another matter,' said Daunt.

The vampire slayings. That's what the head said, too, the mad old steamer.

'Lower your wicked gun,' wheezed the commodore. 'I wouldn't insult my gravestone by having it recorded that my life ended at the hands of a two-penny ruffian like Dick Tull.'

You think? Dick pulled back the hammer on the clockwork of firing lock as if he was going to shoot, and then pushed the safety forward. *Many would say that would be a fitting end to your life.*

As Dick lowered his gun, a loud bell started filling the kitchen with its clamour. 'You got another houseguest inside here Blacky, sending down to the kitchen for their soup?'

'Perimeter alarm,' said the commodore. 'Someone's jumped my wall and is coming through the woods.'

There was a series of thumps throughout the house, the

109

kitchen floor shaking as a heavy metal blast door dropped out of a slot within the wall, sealing off the inner courtyard. *They're locked out, or we're locked in, depending on your point of view.*

'It's the board, Mister Tull.' Sadly looked panicked. 'They've come for us.'

'Surely it could be a fox, good captain,' said Daunt. 'A false alarm?'

Another thump, louder, the distant rain of falling rubble following it.

'Wouldn't be heavy enough to set off my minefield,' said the commodore.

'Bloody hell.' Sadly looked at the tiny pistol in his hand, as if he was realising this was all he had to stop the dustmen. 'Mines.'

'This isn't my first ride at this carnival, lad,' said the commodore, opening the door to his pantry and fiddling with something hidden under the shelves inside. 'I've grown mortal tired of receiving the wrong sort of visitor at Tock House. Boxiron, lend me the weight of your shoulder plates here.'

Boxiron and the old u-boat man pushed at the shelves and they swung to one side, revealing a concealed room on the other side, iron railings surrounding a well-like opening in the middle of the floor – spiral stairs leading downwards from the pantry.

A hidden strong room. 'Where's your treasure, then?'

'Is the preservation of your miserable life not booty enough for you, Dick Tull?' The commodore waved them inside the room, lighting its gas lamps with a spark switch while the steamman and his consulting detective friend carried in the murmuring girl. Once inside, Dick helped the commodore push shut the concealed door. No wonder it was so heavy.

Five inches of reinforced metal on the other side of the shelves, riding large rollers across the flagstones.

Sadly was sweating. 'This isn't right. We're as tight as rats in a pipe here. Just like when the dustmen came for me in my cellar.'

'Tight as the sweet decks of a boat,' said the commodore. 'Down the stairs and let's see if we can't make a little mischief for them.'

There was another room below, larger, windowless and with a series of doors leading off that that might've belonged on a submersible, solid riveted iron with wheel locks to open them. Racks had been built into the walls between the doors, canned food, barrels of water, guns, charges and equipment piled from floor to ceiling. Dick ran his finger along one of the shelves. *Not much dust. Less than a couple of years old down here.*

'You are well appointed for a siege,' said Daunt.

'Life gives you what you expect,' said the commodore, lifting a dustsheet off a bank of equipment. 'And well glad I am for my preparations, too, we'll give them a few licks before we go down.'

'That's the spirit, good captain,' said Daunt. 'There's no bad weather, only bad clothes.'

With the commodore pulling and tugging at the control panel that stood revealed, a screen came to life showing the exterior of Tock House and the tower's grounds. There were figures moving about in front of the tree line, but the colours of the monitor seemed all wrong, the whole scene coloured in a green tinge, while the lights thrown by the house shone like flares.

'This equipment was constructed by the people of the metal,' said Boxiron, helping Daunt lay down the girl's body.

'So it was,' agreed the commodore. 'A little project for my

111

friend Coppertracks. Something more practical than his usual fancies and forays into high science.' He fiddled with a lever and the speaker a voicebox mounted above the screen crackled into life.

'—want the sceptre. We know you have it. You have five minutes to surrender it and then we'll burn you out of there.'

I recognize that voice. Dick lent forward to look at the figure standing in front of the house. *Bugger the lot of them. It was him.* 'That's Walsingham, one of the State Protection Board's section heads.'

'Oh, law,' Sadly squeaked. 'We're dead down here, says I.'

'That's not the name he was using earlier today,' said Boxiron.

Dick turned to look at the steamman.

'That man is the leader of the gang that set the ambush for Charlotte softbody. His fighters called him Captain Twist.'

Dick swore under his breath. 'You're sure?'

Boxiron tapped his hearing manifolds. 'Perfectly. I was using my voicebox to reflect a low-frequency carrier wave off the shop window he and his soldiers were hiding in. It is an old steamman artifice to eavesdrop at short range.' Boxiron indicated one of the other figures on the screen. 'And that's the fighter he left in charge of the ambush after he departed. His name is Cloake. He is lucky to be alive after facing my fury.'

Dick looked closer, noting the stocky short-arsed figure standing by Walsingham's side. 'Sweet Circle.' *Corporal Cloake.*

'They're your people . . .?' said the commodore.

Dick nodded.

'Captain Twist is a pseudonym,' said Daunt. 'A royalist figure of legend who led Parliament on a merry dance centuries ago.'

'I know that, lad,' said the commodore. 'And more recently

112

than that, too. Didn't I wear the proud title once in my youth?'

On the screen another figure emerged from the tree line, his voice carrying over to Tock House.

'King Jude's sceptre is not just another bauble for you to pawn, commodore. You will hand it over, by order of the Star Chamber!'

'Carl Redlin,' spat Dick.

The miserable royalist bastard who started all of this. If only I hadn't been on duty that night, waiting for Redlin to turn up at Lord Chant's mansion. None of this would have happened, or at least it would have happened to some other poor sod of an officer. How fine would that be?

'I told you Mister Tull,' moaned Sadly. 'Foxes and hens dancing together. Royalists and the board, both working hand in glove. It doesn't make any sense to me.'

The commodore angrily pulled a speaking pipe out of the console, his voice carrying over the garden from behind the intruders, silhouetted figures jumping as his voice boomed from hidden speakers inside the wood. 'I know you well enough, Carl Redlin. A lickspittle of a skipper who wouldn't raise a periscope without first sending for sealed orders from the Star Chamber. Has the blood of the cause run so thin that you're letting a dirty secret policeman wander around calling himself Captain Twist? Did you murder poor young Rufus, or did you let your new board friends do it for the sport?'

Redlin looked furious. 'I'll take no lessons from you, you cowardly turncoat bastard. We will have the sceptre from you now!'

'Found a backbone, have you Carl Redlin? Now that your pockets have been stuffed full of gill-neck gold? Here's your answer and it's good for you, my wicked sister, the gill-necks and your State Protection Board bully-boys, all.' He threw a switch and there was a cackle of rifle fire from the top of Tock House, the figures on the screen diving for cover among the trees.

'Won't hit a blessed one of them,' sighed the commodore. 'The guns in the rifle slits need Coppertracks' drones to man them. We're firing blind, but it will keep their thick heads down until they realize we're not upstairs.'

Daunt held up the sceptre, regarding it with a mixture of dismay and reverence. 'So this is the real article then, after all. King Jude's sceptre. I fear my deductions about the nature of Damson Shades' true vocation are proved correct. I take no pleasure in it.'

Dick looked at the girl, still comatose and muttering in tongues. 'She's a bloody good thief to have lifted the sceptre out of the House of Guardians. How did she end up like that?'

'She collapsed as she was walking through the grounds towards the house,' said Daunt. 'Boxiron had only just carried her inside before you arrived.'

The hulking steamman nodded. 'Charlotte softbody was injured in the ambush, but she suffered no normal wound, no physical injuries. She and the man called Mister Cloake appeared to be fighting with dark powers, unnatural energies flung and exchanged between them.'

Dick snorted. 'Him? Corporal Cloake would stick a blade between your ribs as soon as look at you. There isn't any more to him than that. He is one of Walsingham's knifemen, that's all.'

Commodore Black lifted the sceptre out of Daunt's hands. 'I'll be keeping hold of this.'

'The sceptre is more than a symbol,' warned Daunt.

'It is duty seeking me out,' said the commodore. 'The land has had her wicked way again, forcing me out of my rest and

114

pushing me down the hard path. I told you, lad, did I not warn you that it would be this way? No choice in the matter for poor old Blacky. There never is. Always me. Always me alone.'

'You are not alone,' said Daunt. 'We stand by you in this.'

The commodore stalked to one of the iron doors, seized the lock, and spun the metal weight around. 'You stand by me, do you? No time for standing around, boys, let's be out of here before those killers outside realize there's nothing more upstairs than a few rusty old guns pointing out with not a defender behind their sights.'

On the other side of the door, a narrow corridor of raw rock face curved around to terminate by the waist-high gates of a lifting room. The lift looked ominously ramshackle, waiting to be activated by them.

'Another new addition to the place, Blacky?' Dick asked.

'That's the thing about living on top of the hill,' said the commodore, 'it always occurred to me that there should be a quicker way to reach the bottom. And since I must make the journey, it only seemed equitable for me to purchase the tavern in the village below whose cellars we shall emerge in. That way, when I entertain in an ale house, I'm not pouring my money into some other rogue's pockets.'

How much money had the old sea dog blown on building a backdoor to his pile? Well, not so much blown, Dick thought to himself. *No, definitely not wasted this time.*

It was a tight squeeze inside the lifting room's cage, just enough space to shut the gate behind the party after they carried the girl thief inside. As the gate clicked shut there was a lurch while the lift's counterweights attempted to match the overloaded state of the cage, and then they were moving down, faster and faster. Dick hoped the commodore had not short-changed the builders who'd installed his escape route.

It would be an ironic end to all the murderous missions he had undertaken for the State Protection Board if Walsingham and his killers broke into the tower only to discover six bodies lying mangled at the bottom of a hidden shaft.

'Unless this tunnel drops all the way to the other side of the world,' said Dick, clutching on tight to the railing, 'we're only going to be putting off pursuit for half an hour.'

The commodore appeared happy enough with that. 'Well now, there's luck for us. Just long enough to get to the airship fields north of the city.'

'You have got to be joking me,' said Dick. 'The board is going to have their people watching the loading ramps of every 'stat in the merchant marine. You won't even get past the ticket desk before Walsingham's people are step-marching you outside with a pistol shoved against your back.'

Daunt appeared concerned too. 'And there is the small matter of Damson Shades here, good captain. I doubt there will be many airship officers who would be willing to embark a young lady in Charlotte's condition without demanding that a surgeon be sent for.'

Commodore Black just winked back at them. 'Well now, there you might be surprised.'

The dustmen moved cautiously into the unlit room left exposed behind the kitchen's hidden wall. A lot more cautiously since two of their number had slid down a chute in the great hall to be impaled on one foot-high steel spikes. This cursed house held a lot of tricks. What Walsingham was fairly sure it didn't contain anymore, was Charlotte Shades, Dick Tull, the commodore and his damnable friends. In front of him, a dustman rolled dirt gas grenades down the spiral staircase, the assassins waiting a couple of seconds for the room beneath to fill with choking, cloying poison, before storming the lower-level in a disciplined formation. A line of killers filed down with carbine rifles raised, each man covering the next, their rubber nose hoses swaying under their brass goggles.

'They've taken the sceptre with them,' whined Redlin, the royalist making sure he was positioned well beyond any gunfire that might break out inside the hidden chamber.

'If they had any doubt of its value,' said Walsingham, a tone of weariness permeating his voice, 'your clever demands for its surrender disabused them of that notion.'

'I am going to suck the marrow out of that bitch Shades when I catch her,' said Corporal Cloake, rubbing the bruise on his ribs where he had been bowled over during the fight at the shop.

'It is a pity matters must be kept tidy,' said Walsingham. 'If we had only paid her off and let her live, we would have the sceptre by now.'

'No, that bastard Jared Black knows what he is about,' said Redlin. 'Why else would the commodore set his steamman friend to protecting Charlotte Shades? Your clever little thief girl planned this all along, they were working together from the start.'

'I don't think so,' Walsingham. 'They are fleeing blind. They have no idea what we require the sceptre for. It is this damned land. Her soul is set against us. She senses us here and is moving against us in subtle ways.'

'This land,' said Redlin angrily, 'is *ours*. It belongs to the cause. Do not forget it. When that dirty parliament of shop-keepers has being turned out and the last guardian is left hanging from a street lamp, boots twitching in the air, then the nation will rest happy enough.'

Walsingham shrugged and smiled knowingly. 'Yes, the Baron of Lexham, aren't you? Well, if you and all your exiled royalist friends want to play at being lord of the manor again, you had better get me that sceptre back.' Walsingham turned to look as one of the dustmen entered the kitchen from the main corridor, clutching a box of books. 'These were open upstairs in the library, sir. The reading lights are still on inside the room.'

Walsingham picked out the top book, *The Fall of the Stag-lords*, and opened it to where it had been bookmarked. His breath sucked in as he saw what the inhabitants of the house had been reading. 'Curious, lucky and dangerous. That is an unfortunate combination for us.'

'You still believe they don't know anything?' asked Corporal Cloake.

'Not quite enough. Not yet.' Walsingham rubbed his chin thoughtfully. 'Double the watch on the State Protection Board, search out anybody who is an asset and contact of Dick Tull. Not a piece of paper or a person is to get close to Algo Monoshaft's office that we have not first checked, cleared and frisked for any warnings, coded or otherwise.'

'That senile old mechanical,' said Cloake. 'I would love to push him out of his window and watch his cables scatter across the civil service's front yard.'

'He is not Lady Florence or Lord Chant,' warned Walsingham. 'Such a pity we cannot handle his kind using the old ways.'

'That coward Blacky won't stay around to try and warn anyone in the board, he'll run,' said Redlin. 'It's what he does best.'

Walsingham shrugged languidly, as if that should have been obvious, peering down the staircase. 'Of course he will. He knows as well as Dick Tull that if he stays inside the Kingdom, the board will hunt him down in quick order. Unfortunately, the commodore has run business for the State Protection Board in Concorzia, Pericur, Quatérshift, Jago, Cassarabia, the

Catosian City-states . . . well, it would be far easier to list the countries he does not have friends and contacts in.' Coming to a decision, Walsingham pointed to the intelligencer who'd been watching Tock House before the dustmen arrived. 'Send descriptions back to the board of the visitor to the house and his steamman bodyguard. I want to know who that pair is within the hour. As far as the rest of Tull's renegades are concerned, have posters of them hanging at every coastal port and airfield, every coaching inn, every canal lock house, every police station, every tollbooth and regimental barracks from the uplands to the northern border.'

'Taken alive or dead?' asked the intelligencer.

Before Walsingham could comment, the tower shook with the force of a vicious explosion, a lick of fire and rubble exploding out of the spiral staircase inside the concealed chamber.

Walsingham picked himself up from the floor, strips of rubber from the dead assassins' masks floating out of the smoke, twisting and burning in the air.

'I told you to be careful!' Corporal Cloake shouted into the smoke. But he was slaking his anger against corpses and rubble.

'The former if you please,' said Walsingham brushing the explosion's dust off his breaches. *Yes. It was hard to interrogate corpses if they were dead before the torture began.*

CHAPTER SIX

Jethro Daunt pulled the greatcoat in tight against the cold of the night air. It still had the epaulets of the Royal Aerostatical Navy on its shoulders.

If it wasn't for Boxiron carrying the semiconscious form of Charlotte Shades across the cliff-top fields, any late-night drinkers leaving the tavern on the other side of the hill might have spied the group under the blue moonlight and mistaken them for a group of Jack Cloudies on leave. Even Dick Tull and his complaining rat-faced informant friend wore RAN-issue great coats, Barnabas Sadly nervously glancing down at the waves of the sea breaking against the bottom of the coves below.

Perhaps it shouldn't have surprised Daunt that the commodore had friends in the Royal Aerostatical Navy, welcoming him like a conquering hero – peculiarly under the impression that he was called John Oldcastle and held an officer's rank in the high fleet. A nudge and a wink and a tap on the side of the nose and the mere mention of State Protection Board business enough to secure them passage across half the Kingdom. The one thing you could say about being transported by a military airship like the RAN *Iron Partridge* – apart from the warmth of its jackets against the cold – it was a most effective way to circumvent the checks on their identity papers that a flight with merchant carriers would have entailed. There was little about the commodore that dumbfounded Daunt, apart from perhaps one thing, and there would be time enough to talk about that later. Behind them, the tavern's sign was swaying in the wind, the creaking carrying across the damp grass a counterpoint to the gentle lapping of the waves below and the distant murmur of voices from the ale room.

'An unusual location for a rendezvous with your boat, good captain,' noted Daunt. 'No docks, no jetties.'

'I've a mortal aversion to paying harbourmaster's fees.'

'No doubt,' said Daunt. *And a similar one to paying the revenue service's duties on cargoes, I wager.*

They followed a rocky path down from the cliffs curving around to the shale-covered beach of the cove below. Waiting for them was a handful of locals, oiled leather coats marking them as fishermen. Although it clearly wasn't local fishing boats one of their number was signalling as he pulled the lid off a covered lantern and waved it aloft. There was an answering light from the darkness of the waves, lost beyond the crashing surf. Bright and high. Just where a conning tower would be if a u-boat was lurking out beyond the margins of the coast.

Daunt looked across to Boxiron, and the steamman nodded. 'It is the *Purity Queen*,' he confirmed, voicebox set low, as if he didn't want to trouble the bundled body of Charlotte Shades folded over his iron arms. The steamman's vision plate could see almost as well at night as during the day, and a lot further than any mere ex-parson from the race of man. And he had known the commodore's craft well before the two of

121

them had taken passage on the u-boat a couple of years earlier, heading for the dark isle of Jago. Daunt smiled to himself. The usual thought of most men in his current predicament would be *simpler days*, but their time on the island had proved anything but. Embroiled with the schemes of the Inquisition and the local ruler and a pantheon of the ancient gods besides.

Daunt smelt the approaching flotilla of longboats from the *Purity Queen* before he saw them, a bad egg reek from the small gas-driven paddle wheels carried ahead on the sea wind. Almost silently, four tiny craft pushed up onto the beach close to the man with the signal lantern. Without conversation, the group of locals standing around Daunt began to haul the boats out of the reach of the surf, sailors inside pushing out loading ramps and commencing the decanting of cargo. Whatever the contraband – brandy, mumbleweed, wine – barrels rolled down rapidly into the cove. Each wooden cylinder was small enough that it could be hefted up with built-in straps and tied to the back of a labourer before disappearing into a dark cut in the cliffs behind. Where did that cave end up, Daunt wondered? The cellar of the local tavern? Somewhere far out of sight of any riding officers from the revenue service, of that much the ex-parson was certain. For a royalist scoundrel like the commodore, the avoidance of Parliament's taxes was a duty as much as an income stream, a warm glow of satisfaction supplied with each pint of cheap alcohol and discounted ounce of weed that made its way into the hands of a grateful populace.

The commodore indicated his longboats with a generous sweep of his arm. 'There we are then. The board can watch every port from now until winter, but they can't spy on every cove along the coast.'

Sadly was moaning about having to take to the water, until Dick Tull gave him a shove in the direction of the small boats.

The little rat-like fellow limped unhappily forward on his cane.

'So this is how you pay for your fine living, Blacky?' asked Tull.

The commodore shrugged. 'The board isn't so mortal fussy about the *Purity Queen*'s schedule when it comes to dropping off agents on foreign shores, nor running sealed message bags and crates of rifles sent to those it supports.'

'I wouldn't know,' said Tull. 'I only ever got to nobble people on our own shores.'

Using the sceptre like a walking stick, the commodore boarded a craft now emptied of barrels. 'Then lucky you are for it. Nobody would hang you for spying in the Kingdom's green and pleasant fields. Not when it's your people with their hand on the lever of the gallows' trap door.'

'Not until sodding now,' said Tull. And quite unhappy he sounded about the matter to the ex-parson's ears.

Boxiron laid Charlotte Shades' body carefully in the aft of the flat-bottomed craft. 'I do not like running away, Jethro softbody.'

Jethro Daunt patted the steamman's hulking back reassuringly. 'Would that we were, old friend.'

No. I fear that we are heading for the heart of this affair. May the Circle turn us to the centre of this evil in time to stop an all-out war between the gill-necks and our people.

Charlotte could hear breathing coming from the dark between the trees; hard, rhythmic rasps, as the branches scratched and scraped at her while she forced a passage between the boughs. There was a smell of salt in the air like the sea, but how could that be when she was crashing through the night and a forest? She could sense the hunting party, flashes of distant light – from lanterns, or the pursuing creatures' eyes. Charlotte was completely sodden, but she couldn't remember getting wet. Had she waded through a stream to escape? The slippery mud beneath her bare feet was wet enough that there must have been a recent rainstorm sweeping through the woodland. Beating down on the roof of the one place where she could be guaranteed a warm dry bed for the night. There it was! Madame Leeda's gypsy caravan, the two connected burgundy-coloured carriages pulled up in a glade, an antique high-tension clockwork engine in the rear carriage being wound tight by a small portable steam engine set up like a tripod on the adjacent ground. Rainwater had cleaned the gaudily colourful sign hanging on the side of the front cabin. *Madam Leeda's Cures and Potions.* Each word in a different font, every letter in a different colour. A rainbow splash of ornament in the moonlit glade. Much like its owner, covered in a thick blanket-like hooded robe, swaying, despite her age, in a tuneless dance on wooden steps lowered from the carriage's side.

'Madam Leeda,' Charlotte shouted, nearly stumbling over the partially exposed roots of a nearby oak tree. 'It's me, Charlotte!' If Charlotte didn't say anything, perhaps the old gypsy woman wouldn't notice the state her visitor was in, clothes torn from the pursuit through the woods.

'I see you,' called the old gypsy, turning on the steps and peering out beyond the fire-pit she'd dug in front of the caravan, brushing the long silver hair out of her face. 'Is that my Lotty come back to me?'

'It is.'

Why wasn't Madam Leeda asking Charlotte about where she had been all these years? Then Charlotte glanced down at her cold hands. Tiny, child-sized and her clothes – the same dress she'd been wearing when the family she had thought was her own had thrown her out. Just another failed crop on their farm after the payments from Charlotte's mother to her adopted family had dried up. Charlotte's only parting gift from them, the knowledge that she wasn't their child . . . just an illegitimate bastard from an affair between Lady Mary and the scandalous lord commercial, Abraham Quest.

No wonder Charlotte had been so slow running through those woods; barely ten years old, a diet of berries and grass and leaves for week after week. She was inside the caravan, its main room crowded with cupboards, small wooden drawers by the hundred. Things to sell. Potions that could cure or curse, depending on who was buying, how much they paid, and what degree of respect they showed to the old gypsy woman selling them. The smell of herbs drying, mushrooms being cured, and a hare hanging up over a porcelain wash-basin, bloodied and skinned. With so many amulets and charms, more fake than real; the belief of buyers usually all that was needed to provide the push for true love or the courage to face up to some local difficulty.

'You may go into any of these drawers in this room,' instructed Madam Leeda. 'But not the ones through there.' She indicated the slim rubberised lock that connected the lead carriage to the rear. 'There are dangerous things inside there. Not for any child. Not for anyone not of the *Shena*, who has not mastered the old arts and the true gaze of knowing.'

'I promise,' said Charlotte solemnly. Though she couldn't help but notice the intricately carved oaken box that would be removed from the second carriage's drawers shortly before Madam Leeda was about to conduct any important piece of business. A particularly significant seance or card reading, hiring an engineer for a vital repair to the caravan's clockwork engine, or maybe smoothing the superstitious hackles of an irate Circlist priest or a local dignitary. The well-oiled hard-wood box with the carvings of ancient runes that the gypsy people called *sly-talk*. Not just a charm, the jewel inside, the

125

Eye of Fate. Not when the crystal seemed able to bend the will of those in its presence to the inclinations of its owner. The jewel so bright, shining and calling to Charlotte, singing to her blood. Promising her a life of opulence and luxury far from the tight confines of a tiny travelling show. A life where the jewel could be worn among the high society Charlotte had been born to traverse. Not locked up, used to convince yokels that the fair price for a sack of grain was half of what it should be. If only she could have—'taken it!' shrieked Madam Leeda. 'You've taken it.'

'I haven't,' swore Charlotte, feeling towards her neck where the jewel's chain lay, making a lie of her words.

'I fed you,' bellowed Madam Leeda, the outrage turning the pallid lines of her face an unsightly purple. 'I took you in and raised you as one of the people! This is how you repay me? You were good for nothing before! Nothing but sucking on dried-up bush leaves and milking peasants' goats. I taught you the sly arts and you've broken the only rule I set. You never steal from your own people!'

'I haven't stolen the Eye of Fate,' pleaded Charlotte. 'I've only borrowed it a little while.'

'A while!' Madam Leeda wailed. 'You think I have longer than "a little while" left to my old bones? Sneaking off in the middle of the night with my living about your pretty young neck. What does that make you?' She lunged for Charlotte tearing the jewel away from her.

'A thief,' yelled Charlotte, trying to snatch back the jewel from Madam Leeda's clawing hands. 'A common gypsy woman, like you, a dirty *roamer*, just like they shout at us in every village we pass through.'

Finally catching back hold of the Eye of Fate, Charlotte threw herself out of the carriage, but she wasn't in the forest glade anymore, she was on the doorstep of her true mother,

Lady Mary. Or rather, the house of her new husband. And there she stood, Lady Mary, holding the door of the townhouse firm against Charlotte, two of her household staff behind her, brandishing the canes they used to see away beggars and vagabonds.

'I do not know you,' said her ladyship, her tone superior and distant. 'I have no daughters, only sons. Now be off with you before Lord Kane returns home and has you arrested for trespassing on his property.'

Charlotte opened her mouth to beg to stay, but she was being pulled back by Madam Leeda, the old gypsy woman's bony fingers around the back of her neck like a collar. 'The Eye has limits, Lotty. It can cast many a glamour, but it can't move the heart. It can't make a mother love her daughter, that's one thing it can never do. Love, you must first deserve, and then it comes naturally.'

Charlotte tried to protect the jewel, but other hands were reaching for her. Mister Twist and his bludger Cloake, the pair of them turning her, jabbing her, trying to cut the Eye of Fate away from her breast.

'Give it to me,' Cloake demanded, 'let me have the Eye.'

Twist's hands locked around her neck, tightening ever closer and closer.

'No! It's the sceptre you want, not the Eye, King Jude's sceptre.'

'Don't you see,' laughed Twist, spit from his mouth spraying across her face, 'they're both the same.'

'I'll give it to you!'

'You'll give us everything,' laughed Cloake, his hands grabbing the back of Twist's head, pulling at the man's hair. Ripping the skin off, scalp and the flesh falling away like flaking candle wax. Underneath the peeling skin, something black and wet and scaly swelled out, distending and growing larger. A hideous fanged

127

face took shape; part-lizard, part-snake, part-fish, its wet scales licked by a forked tongue and its bulbous mutated head pierced by two crimson eyes that glowed like twin wells sunk into a dark, dark place. Having split Twist's face off, Cloake's fingers dug into the skin around his own nose and began scratching and clawing, a similar monstrosity bulging out of his own torn flesh, a hairless scaly forehead rising and rising, knobbly and pitted, a tall helmet of bone above gleaming hellish eyes.

'Oh, that's handsome,' said Madam Leeda, shoving Charlotte towards the hideous pair. Charlotte was backing away from them, her mother's townhouse replaced by the stalagmites of a dripping cave, pools of stagnant dark water enveloping the old gypsy woman's feet. 'They'll take everything, all right. Nothing left of little Lotty, only a husk. See what it's cost you, now, girl? Your big life in the city trying to be like the quality, aping their stupid, superior ways, trying to be like them that don't even want you. You should've stayed in the woods with me, rolling through the villages in the sun and the snow. That's the life for us. For a dirty little roamer girl.'

'Save me, please—!'

In answer to Charlotte's pleas there was a sudden explosion of light and the monsters were sent scrabbling like spiders back towards the darkness of the distant shadows. Out of the darkness emerged a silhouette, the figure of a woman, a nimbus of light at her back.

'Madam Leeda, are you out there? Have you come to take me back?'

'I am not your gypsy,' said a female voice. It whispered all around her, a breeze filtering through the leaves of an ancient forest. Charlotte raised a hand to cover her eyes as she tried to gaze on the figure. 'Mother?'

'Mother of us all,' hissed the reply. 'The blood of a thousand generations squared, baked and frozen into the soil of Jackals. The memories of your ancestors' dreams and the echoes of souls too free to fade into the shared sea of consciousness.' As her words faded, Charlotte caught the distant repetition of the words whispering in a thousand lost languages. So many tongues, just like the church back in the capital. Charlotte remembered the fevered dreams of the three sisters; Jethro Daunt set on her trail with his strange clanking steamman friend.

'I am Elizica of the Jackeni,' the voice hardened, spinning around Charlotte. 'The resonance of my soul still sings through the bones of the land, flowing through its quartz and granite. Joined with all of those who followed me, all those who preceded me.'

'What do you want from me?'

'I have been here before you. You must follow in my footsteps.'

'I'm no queen,' Charlotte protested. 'No royal blood flows through my veins.'

'The daughter of your mother . . . can you be so sure? It matters not. I was the first queen of Jackals. Was I born noble? No, I was born of the land and that is all that matters. You are Jackelian and the land abides.'

'I can't help you, please don't ask me.'

'You have everything you need. Remember, you walk in my footsteps.'

'No!'

Light was fading, the shadows growing, darkness returning while monsters circled and awaited the departure of Charlotte's protector.

'What do you need from me?' Charlotte cried at the woman's ebbing shape.

A faint whisper came from the vanishing point of light. 'What I always ask for. A sacrifice.'

Mister Twist was upon her again, the jewel from her chain clutched in his black, clawed, scaly hands – the Eye of Fate transforming in a shimmer of light, turning red and pointed. After it had transmuted into a two-pronged blade, Twist plunged the thing into her neck, the touch of the blade burning like acid. Charlotte was impaled and falling to the cave's flooded floor. She watched the water run red with blood, *her blood*, as the two creatures dropped and feasted on her body. Poor. Little. Roamer.

CHAPTER SEVEN

'Poor lass,' said Commodore Black, watching while Daunt tipped the potion he had concocted from the contents of the u-boat's medical cabinet down Charlotte Shades' throat. 'Is her fever fading yet?'

'Getting worse if anything,' said Daunt. 'But it must break soon.' His words sounded hollow, even to him. *If it was any normal fever. Not this cursed illness. Her body lying wracked by an unearthly presence, just like the poor sisters.*

'I heard a noise from her berth in here, a wicked whistling and rattling as if her cabin's air scrubbers were about to overload,' said the commodore.

'She was speaking in tongues,' noted Boxiron. 'But this language was an ancient steamman dialect, sung in raw binary.'

'An unholy racket, whatever,' said the commodore.

'It would sound better emanating from the voiceboxes of my people,' said Boxiron, 'but not by much.'

'Everyone else is in the ready room,' said the commodore. 'Waiting on your frightful intellect to descend and solve all of life's little mysteries.'

'I will settle for getting to the heart of our current affair, good captain.'

Commodore Black spun the wheel on the iron door of the u-boat cabin, opening it onto the passage outside. White sodium light soaked the interior of the craft, lending everything a fine, harsh cast. Even the brown wood panels that should have softened the passage appeared bright and severe, every knot of oak throbbing under the artificial illumination. Inside the *Purity Queen*'s stout hull, the u-boat hadn't changed a jot since Daunt and Boxiron had sailed with the commodore to the Isle of Jago all those years ago. The ex-parson had noticed the changes outside, though, as they were ferried across to the submarine. Small interlocking plates, thousands of them, welded over the surface of the catamaran-shaped u-boat's twin hulls. It was as though a smith had decided to turn the submersible's hull into a piece of sculpture, plate upon plate, all crusted green with the embrace of the sea. In places the angles at which they joined the hull seemed random; in other spots the plates took on a swirling pattern, a fresco cut in steel. The reworking of the *Purity Queen* might have been mistaken for an attempt to sculpt on the scales of a fish, an organic texture to soften the warlike lines of the ex-fleet sea arm vessel, although there could be no masking of the double-prowed submarine's torpedo tubes. It transpired that the remodelling hadn't resulted from the artistic inclinations of an insane blacksmith. According to the commodore, the alterations were state-of-the-art theorisings of a naval architect who had been handsomely paid to ensure that the old u-boatman's vessel could set to sea with an experimental hull able to wrap sonar waves around her length. Fold them so gently the *Purity Queen* might as well have been a ghost slipping through the depths.

Daunt followed the commodore through the narrow corridors, squeezing past the stripe-shirted crew going about their duties – as roguish and varied an assortment of sailors as befitted Blacky's unorthodox cargoes and smuggler's landings.

'Well, this much I can tell you, lad. If my sister Gemma is involved, there'll be a good bit of dying to be done after we've set a tack across her wind.'

Daunt entered the ready room with Boxiron behind him; the steamman's clanking legs startling the boat's cat, the surprised feline a black streak as she shot between the commodore's legs in search of a less crowded cabin.

Dick Tull and his informant, Sadly, were waiting at the long room's oval table, a polished wooden surface inlaid with scenes from Jackelian naval history, suiting the u-boat's previous status as a war-horse of the state. Kingdom dreadnoughts clashed with Cassarabian paddle galleys, submersible flotillas exchanged torpedoes above an underwater mountain range, athletic u-boat men struck heroic positions of defiance on a bridge as their captain hung vigilantly onto a lowered periscope. It seemed to Daunt that the surface would be more appropriately decorated now with views of smugglers concealed beneath bushes from revenue service riders and redcoated soldiers. Although even with fresh artwork, the table would still look out of place being set, not with food, but the crown jewels of the last absolute monarch to rule over Jackals.

'Oh, this is a rich biscuit, say I,' moaned Sadly, his face a greenish pallor – and not just from the shade of the ocean outside the room's armoured porthole. Even sitting down and resting his clubfoot, he clung to his cane like it was his sole handhold on the world. 'A fortune in nicked jewels and precious metals laid out in front of me, and I'd get a fast blade in my back if I dared to set foot back home to fence it off.'

'You've already got a walking stick, lad. You don't need

my mortal sceptre for a cane,' noted the commodore, sitting himself down at the head of the table. 'And this belonged to the royalists long before the House of Guardians laid their grubby hands on it, or the poor lass back in my cabin.'

'She's still not come around?' asked Tull.

'It's not a physical injury,' said Daunt. 'At least, not as the vessel's doctor understands it.' *Beyond any of the healing techniques I mastered in the church, too.*

'Pity,' said Tull. 'The girl must know something about why Walsingham is nobbing around the capital, pretending to be a royalist and helping the rebels make off with King Jude's sceptre.'

'I doubt, good sergeant, if Damson Shades knows any more than whatever tale she was fed to get her to steal the jewels.'

'Your metal friend reckons that they tried to kill her. She must be good for something.'

'Mere thoroughness on their part,' said Daunt. 'The Mistress of Mesmerism may not even have known that the royalists were involved, let alone the State Protection Board.'

'Why?' Tull laughed. 'Because of that yarn you spun me earlier about some sisters babbling the same kind of nonsense on their sickbed that the girl's spouting?'

'Are you a good Circlist, Mister Tull? Holding to what is right and rational. Rejecting superstition?'

'Do I look like I go to church regularly, amateur? I know it takes more than some ancient mumbo-jumbo to turn a ruthless sod like Walsingham. If the major's skulking around the capital holding hands with royalist rebels, there's more in it for him than the whisperings of shades and ghosts.'

'Is he a good traitor?' asked Daunt.

Dick Tull started to say something, then stopped himself. He was about to speak again when Daunt warned him: 'Your first thoughts, if you please. What initially jumped into your mind when I asked you the question?'

'That Walsingham isn't the sort,' said Dick, playing thoughtfully with the edges of his greying moustache. 'Oh, he's ambitious all right, and not carrying too much weight in the way of scruples when it comes to getting his way – inside the board or out. But selling the country down the river to the rebels? And to the gill-necks to boot, if they're financing the royalist cause? I'd never have pegged Walsingham as good for that.'

Daunt stroked the sceptre. 'Not even for a king's weight in gold?'

Dick Tull snorted and turned to Sadly. 'Could you fence that piece?'

'Lever the jewels off and melt down the rest for gold, is more the way of it, Mister Tull. Who would buy that fancy piece intact, says I? Who would have the money to do the deed or the nerve to hold onto it? Maybe the caliph down in Cassarabia. He might hang it in his palace as one in the eye for the infidel northerners, but he's about the only one.'

'Exactly,' said Daunt. 'Its value, its true value is a symbol. To the caliph, or—' he pointed at the commodore, '—to you, or to any royalist. But, Mister Tull, your old employer is not of a royalist bent, as you so clearly pointed out. So what is the true value of the sceptre to him?' He turned to Boxiron. 'I saw the way you were examining the jewel on the end of the sceptre. It seems to me, in the same manner you were inspecting the jewel around the neck of our Damson Shades.'

'Both gems share much the same composition,' said Boxiron. 'Close to the reflective index of diamond, but not quite.'

'And, as you witnessed, the jewel around her neck appeared to ward off unnatural energies from Mister Cloake's blade which are the most likely cause of her collapse and her subsequent coma. I wonder if the sisters Lammeter were urging us to find Charlotte Shades, or the thing she wears around her neck?' It was to his chagrin that he hadn't been able to save the other names the sisters had been chanting. He would *not* fail Charlotte. Daunt lifted the sceptre up and offered it to Boxiron, the weight of the thing such that he could barely manage to pass it while sitting down.

'Examine it closely, old friend. Set your vision plate to its maximum resolution.'

Boxiron leant in close towards the sceptre, the red dot pulsing in the centre of his visor-like vision plate narrowing in size until the light was barely visible. 'Yes, there is something inside the jewel – a pattern, finely etched. So fine I can barely distinguish it at my optic's maximum resolution, and on that setting, the side of a hair appears like the contours of a mountain.'

'Is it an image perhaps, or cursive script?'

'No,' said Boxiron. 'It's circuitry, I'm sure of it. But on a granular scale unlike anything I have heard of. The crystal boards designed by the architects of my people are as cave paintings compared to the sophistication responsible for this.'

'The sceptre's a bloody antique,' said Tull. 'How can that be?'

'Ah, this is a dark business,' said the commodore. 'All the rightful queens and kings who have held that sceptre over the millennia, wielded it in good faith, and you are telling me it is etched full of wicked sorcery?'

Daunt scratched his chin. 'Yes, all those hands. All the way back to the Queen Elizica, before the cold time and glaciers covered the world. All the way back to the first war between the tribes of the Jackeni and the gill-necks. A war then, and a war now.'

'Let's not be digging up old history,' said the commodore. 'No blessed good can come of it. You remember the trouble we got into on the black isle of Jago when we started disturbing dark ruins.'

'I believe it was the professor who told me that those who don't understand history are doomed to repeat it,' said Daunt.

'History books won't bleeding keep us alive,' said Tull. 'What's this mess got to do with yourself and the old steamer anyway? You're meant to be tracking down a nest of bloodsuckers for the town's alderman, not prancing about taking on bent board officials and royalists backed by the Advocacy.'

'I believe the victims of the vampire slayings are collateral damage, good sergeant,' said Daunt. 'A few poor souls good for the pot. Those who knew too much, or perhaps too little. Much like yourself. And from what you said, it was what you and your fellow intelligencer saw on the night of your surveillance at Lord Chant's residence that got your partner killed and would have seen you assassinated too. And as for the rest, yes. The pieces are starting to fall in place.' Daunt rummaged around in his pocket for a Bunter and Benger's aniseed drop, then offered the bag in the direction of Dick Tull.

'You've got to be joking me, amateur. Those things'll rot your teeth and your mind.'

'Lubrication of my mental processes, harmless stimulation only,' said Daunt. He sucked on the sweet and looked over at Commodore Black. 'There wasn't much in the books at Tock House about the modern gill-necks, good captain. Beyond the fact that the Advocacy's ancestors were once driven onto our shores by changes in the magma currents of the Fire Sea, and the tribes living on our land united to drive them away.'

'Nor will you find such learnings in the university's dusty towers,' said the commodore, tapping his skull. 'It's all up

137

here. In the heads of a few honest skippers, in the noggins of adventurers like me who brave the sea.'

'It is said that the Advocacy are an insular people.'

'Ah, a little beyond that. The gill-necks of the Advocacy live their lives by a book of rituals and law called the Misleash – and according to its teachings, there is an eternal cycle of life where mankind abandons the sea and returns to the land, before returning to the sea again. Their words for home, universe and sea are one and the same, and if that doesn't tell you all you mortal need to understand about how they think, then I'll add that their word for land has another meaning which is "torment". There's blessed little the Advocacy need from us to live below the waters – they only tax the shipping that passes over their territory to discourage visitors.'

'But they're an evolutionary offshoot of the race of man,' said Daunt. 'Just like the graspers or the craynarbians.'

'Aye, not that you would know it to look at them, stubby muzzles and skin like sharks. The proof of the pudding is that the gill-necks can interbreed with us, although such misbegotten babes as result only gives truth to the notion of us surface dwellers as accursed. A mewling, twisted babe ill-suited to land or sea, that's the sad result of any union between man and gill-neck. Your Circlist friends should be pleased by them; they don't have any gods, just the sea as their great mother.'

'A noble race, then,' said Daunt. 'Ruled by law, and no heaven or hell.'

'Ah, well, they have a measure of hell. They believe that the dark of the abyss sends devils to punish them when they abuse the seas.'

'Even more intriguing. But I see why you are uneasy about the idea of an alliance between the royalist rebels and the gill-necks.'

138

'There is no royalist rebellion, lad,' said the commodore. 'Not anymore. Parliament's airships broke the fleet-in-exile when they took Porto Principe. All that survived of the cause are a few submarines whose crews turned to slavery and privateering. The gill-necks are meant to be breathing life back into the cause all these years later? Why? The Advocacy doesn't give a fig who rules the land, not when they call the sea their realm. The ocean's magma fields are in retreat now, not expanding, there's no trouble to drive the gill-necks in desperation towards our shores.'

'They have a king, don't they?' said Tull. 'Maybe the gill-necks decided they'll be safer in their land with a friendly monarch sitting on the throne of Jackals again.'

'Pah, that's parliamentary propaganda, you old rascal,' said the commodore. 'What you call a king, the gill-necks call the Judge Sovereign. They're not ruled by a royal court, but a court of law. A supreme mucky-muck selected from the bench of the four Princes Intercessor, the Bench of Four, appointed by their societies of ritual. The bench interprets their laws and set out the rituals and ceremonies that every guild and clan must abide by. The Advocacy know as little of our affairs as you do of theirs – or at least that was the way it used to be. How my sister got in tight with them is beyond my tired old noggin. And that Parliament has let a trade dispute escalate close to war is wicked foolery even the idiots in the House of Guardians should be ashamed of. Like watching a squid and an albatross fighting over whether the squid should live in the sky and the bird under the water.'

Daunt nodded his head sadly. 'Bob my soul, so here we are. Teetering close to a war with no cause and no real prize for its victor.' The ex-parson ran his hand along King Jude's sceptre. *And this is the glue that binds the mystery together. Are you what this conflict is being fought for, or the key to*

139

halting it? If we're ever to return to the Kingdom, if we're to stop this senseless war, we need to find out. 'The gill-necks have no fondness towards surface dwellers?'

'They have a mortal aversion to our people, which is a pity for us, as the Advocacy experiences more than its fair share of surface-dwelling fortune hunters trespassing across their territory.'

'What does the Advocacy have that's so valuable?' Sadly asked, his interest perking up at the mention of fortunes.

'Their engineering's based on crystals. They grow what they need near high-pressure fissures on the seabed. Gems like diamonds and as big as boulders. Common to them, but rare enough to us to bring a constant stream of fool lubbers trying to sneak into the gill-necks' waters, thinking how easy it'll be to pillage their crystal fields.'

'I take it that those they capture are not treated with leniency, good captain?' said Daunt.

'Never seen again, is what they are,' said the commodore. 'The gill-necks and the people of the underwater nations are born to the sea. This is their realm. Visitors to it are all we will ever be, and blessed unwelcome ones when we trespass into their territory.'

'Crystals,' hummed Daunt. 'Interesting.'

'Your sister is going to tell us what's going on then, Blacky?' said Tull. 'We just sail up to her and she'll spill her guts out about why Walsingham and the gill-necks have suddenly taken it to mind to support the rebel cause?'

'There'll be doubts,' said the commodore. 'In the royalist ranks, people like Rufus Symons. Tossing out a parliament of thieving tradesmen is one thing, collaborating with a foreign occupation of Jackals is another kettle of fish.' The commodore unfolded a chart across the table and laid a finger in the ocean. 'This is the muster point for the convoys to the colonies that are passing across the disputed waters. We can join one as a free trader, then slip away from the convoy and sneak out into the heart of the Advocacy waters.'

'Won't we be a little conspicuous sailing into their territory, good captain?' said Daunt.

'Right enough,' said the commodore, 'but we won't be going in as surface traders.' He pointed to an adjacent area on the charts. 'This is the territory of the seanore . . . ocean nomads. Some of them are close enough to the gill-necks in form and tolerated as ocean dwellers; a multiracial society like the Kingdom – even a few of the race of man who've embraced a life on the seabed among their numbers. Humans known by the moniker of wetbacks by us salty sea-dog types. I've had dealings with the seanore before. If we can get in tight with the nomads, then we can travel into a gill-neck city without raising too many hackles.' He looked over at Boxiron. 'Apart from you, old steamer.'

'I can travel underwater,' protested Boxiron. 'All I need is a respirator for my stacks and a buoyancy tank.'

'That you may,' said the commodore, 'but while a seanore clan might count three or four of the underwater races among their number, one species you will never find among them is a steamman. The gill-necks will tolerate the odd wetback among the seanore as some poor unfortunate surface dweller trying to do the natural thing and return back to the sea-essence, but if they spy your metal hull bobbing along above their coral, they'll rumble our game in a blessed minute. My sister Gemma isn't exactly the trusting type, and we'll have enough trouble trying to find a friendly face among the royalists without Gemma spotting me first. With a steamman by my side, I might as well swim into the gill-neck capital dragging the lion and portcullis of the House of Guardians on a standard behind me.'

Daunt's heart sank. Boxiron shook angrily – a mixture of anger and shame at being left out of the fray. The ex-parson had only just managed to get his steamman friend engaged with the case; occupied enough to set aside his increasingly maudlin broodings about the reduced state of his body. Boxiron had little enough to live for as it was. A once-proud steamman knight, reduced into the frame of a semi human-milled monstrosity, crude and malfunctioning.

How can I abandon Boxiron on the Purity Queen, grieving about his exile from his people? His so-called duty to suicide? What will he do without me?

But when it came to it leaving his friend behind, when push turned to shove, Daunt would have no choice. The stakes were too high to do anything else.

After the others had gone, Dick noticed the commodore was watching him. The spy ran his fingers over King Jude's sceptre, a calculating look on his face as he estimated how much he could get from melting it down and stripping it of its jewels.

'Your people have already stolen the blessed thing once from its true owners,' accused the commodore.

Dick reached for his hip flask and took a quick hit of its warm contents. 'And what will you be doing with it, Blacky, when all of this is done? You got the Jackelian crown squirreled away somewhere too? An ermine-lined souvenir for you to keep your brainbox warm? Settle yourself down in your favourite easychair back in the big house, wrap your fingers around the sceptre and dream of the good old days when your ancestors got to lord it over mine?'

'When this is all over, lad, I'm figuring I'll be too. I'm on my way out, but where I'll be going, you won't be so far behind me.'

'There you're wrong, Blacky. I'm planning on a long, happy retirement.' He glanced at the richly appointed sceptre. A fortune waiting to be smelted into a form no policeman would be able to trace. *I just need a little more money, a little more luck. Maybe I'll take my share of yours, you old pirate. Someone's got to come out of this ahead.*

'A cosy cottage on the cliffs above the sea? Nosing out a previously undiscovered knack for tending roses? Men like you and me, Dick Tull, we're good for lying and scheming and killing and trickery. Playing the great game all our lives, you think you can take your eyes off the board? It's too late for us. This is all we know and all we're fit for. You think you're going to find a wife now, raise a family to replace the ones who died off or were scared off? There's no sight as sad as a rusty old sabre trying to turn itself a garden trowel.'

'You're talking about yourself, not me,' said Dick. *But we're not, are we? All the lies of our trade. Can we fool ourselves too?*

The commodore reached out and tugged at Dick's jacket. 'Cheap cloth. Taking your meals at an ordinary and telling yourself it's where your informants are, living your cheap life. How much money do you think you need to leave the State Protection Board behind? Ten guineas a year, a hundred, a thousand? It'll never buy you what it takes to leave.'

'Says the man living in a grand tower with a private orchard to do his bloody philosophising in.'

'We are what we are,' coughed the commodore. 'And we're it under a roof with one room or seventy.'

'You're wrong,' said Dick, his confidence wavering. 'The board's just a job, and I won't miss one hour of this life when I'm done with it.

Liar, something deep within him whispered. *How often*

143

have you dreamed of what you're going to do outside of the board? Where are your hopes of another life? A man who wanted out would have a dream, wouldn't he, a plan, something?

'What happened to you, lad?' asked the commodore. 'We've done enough business together over the years, you and I. You could have been one of the great ones, but here you are at the end of the game, huddled like a miser counting coals in front of his fire.'

'Give it a bloody rest. The only cause you've ever really worked for is yourself. You try doing it for parliament and country all your life. Not as some quality, not as officer class, but as a mere humble bloody ranker. For the last forty years I've done the job as fine as anyone, and watched well-connected carriage folk take the credit for every one of my successful operations while sliding me a plate of shit to eat on the failures. If my father had been an industrial lord or a bishop, I'd be a colonel in the board by now. Instead, I'm counting a ranker's pension and nicking candlesticks to put a pair of new shoes on my tired old feet.' Dick made to tip his hip flask to his mouth again, but Blacky stopped him.

'I need the man you were, you rascal, the man you still can be. I need an ironclad Protection Board bastard by my side. Not some sot two drinks from the grave.'

'Then I hope your u-boat can travel in time as well as in water,' said Dick, 'because that man ain't here anymore. Just me. That's who you've got. And that man's going to take a cosy cottage on the cliffs above the sea just as soon as it becomes available and leave the great game to someone else. The board's officers can find another cow to milk for their successes and bugger the lot of them.'

'Well, there's one consolation for you,' said the commodore, thumping him on the back. 'Poor old Blacky won't be around to say *I told you so*.'

When Jethro Daunt entered the wardroom, the only other occupant was the rat-like informant. Barnabas Sadly was standing over a table riveted to the floor, leaning on his cane, a large sea chart spread out across the table.

'Can you interpret a navigation course, Mister Sadly?'

'Lords-a'larkey, not the likes of I. But it makes me feel a little better, knowing that someone on this tub has an idea of how to sail through all of that out there. Have you glanced out the porthole? Valleys and mountains and forests of seaweed and fish like birds in the sky. Just the sight of it set my stomach off into a right queasy turn.'

'No,' said Daunt. 'There can't have been many lessons on matters nautical in your poorhouse classes.'

'Poorhouse?' said Sadly, a tone of indignation creeping into his voice. 'I'm no poorhouse foundling. My father was a cobbler along Velvet Street.' He tapped his boot with his cane. 'Couldn't take over the trade, could I? Customers would come in and take one look at my bad foot and say, well, that one don't know anything about making a good pair of shoes. We'll move our business down the lane.'

'Of course,' said Daunt. 'My mistake. There must be nearly fifty cobblers' shops and stalls along Velvet Street.'

'But customers still needs to eat, and them that come into an ordinary don't care much about the person serving them, as long as the beer ain't stale and the meat overcooked like dry old shoe soles.'

Daunt nodded. Blackening the meat was a favourite trick when it came to disguising rancid cheaper cuts. 'I hope you don't lose too much custom back home while you're on board the *Purity Queen*.'

'Mister Tull won't have thought about that,' said Sadly. 'Not once. Any more than his masters at the board gave it a thought when they sent the dustmen over to my place to cut my liver out for what I might have told Mister Tull. I'm useful to the board, they toss me a few bones, but when it suits—' he drew a finger across his throat, '—that's the way it is with the little people. Nobody thinks about us, nobody cares if that which we've built is trampled underfoot by the grand schemes of the quality and the carriage folk.'

'All of life is flow, Mister Sadly,' said Daunt. 'You can only find serenity when you accept the course of the river, rather than trying to build a home of sticks in the centre of the flow and worrying that it will one day be swept away.'

'It's true then,' said Sadly. 'You're a churchman as well as a thieftaker.'

'Unfortunately, the church does not permit parsons in the Circlist order to believe in gods.' Daunt held up his hands. 'Defrocked. They are sticklers in such matters. Abandoned, but still occasionally useful to the inquisition. Perhaps that makes both of us little people.'

'Not you, says I,' Sadly insisted, his voice lowering in awe. 'Your name's whispered in fear among the bad sorts back in the city. When Jethro Daunt is engaged, the villain of the piece had better scarper for the hills, for if they don't, they'll end up dangling in the noose outside Bonegate jail. Don't even think of nobbling him, or that metal ogre of his will drop you off a building with your skull crushed in.'

Daunt ran a finger across the contour lines of the chart. *Feared by the underworld, abandoned by the church. Is this what my life has come to?* The increasingly faint stimulation of pitting his wits against the most vicious and devious masterminds in the slums of Middlesteel. Crime spread like algae in the stagnant pools of the poor. As soon as one case was solved, there was always another. Their clients, mostly the outraged rich who could afford to pay Daunt and Boxiron's bills; commercial lords affronted by the down and desperates' efforts to relieve the rich of some of their wealth. Was it any wonder that Boxiron was growing suicidal with his life, crippled and crammed inside his malfunctioning frame? Any wonder the steamman felt that way when even Daunt – hale and healthy – worried that they chased ever-greater risks in the cases they accepted, just to feel the tingle of being alive. To distract them both from the truth: that for neither of them, was this the appropriate channel their short time in the world had been destined to flow down. What would Daunt's father have thought of him now, if his bones hadn't been long buried? His father had been disappointed enough that his son had turned his talents and intelligence towards the seminary, rather than following him into the law. But the life of an articled clerk in the middle court, even rising to be a judge – his father's dream, never his – had held little appeal. No, it never did to dwell on the might-have-beens. If Jethro Daunt had been stuck in his father's dusty office, stamping legal summons and reviewing court proceedings, then he would never have been able to rescue Boxiron from his previous life as an enforcer for the lords of the underworld. How many murderers would've gone free to kill more innocents?

And if I weren't here, who would minister to Damson Shades? Certainly not the drunken sop who passed for a surgeon on the *Purity Queen*. Dose her up with laudanum and reach for the bone saw to carve off a mangled limb. *Such methods won't keep the poor girl alive. To doubt is human, but I need a clear mind and a focused soul if I'm to get to the heart of this matter. I fear the blood of many thousands will be on my hands, should I fail.*

Daunt was reaching for the comforting round sphere of a

Bunter and Benger's aniseed drop when the commodore entered the room. 'With me, lad! The girl's fever has taken a turn for the worst!'

The commodore stepped out of the way while Daunt felt Charlotte Shades' forehead and then took her pulse. Her skin was soaked with sweat while her possessed ramblings had dropped away to a faint murmur. 'Her fever is not getting worse, Jared. Quite the contrary, it is breaking. She is on the mend.'

'Are you sure, lad?' He allowed himself a burst of relief.

The consulting detective nodded. 'I know my previous occupation concerned itself with the state of my parishioners' minds and souls first and foremost, but the third component of the natural trinity is the body. And I'm happy to say that young Charlotte Shades' flesh is returning to balance.'

Seeing Charlotte stretched out on the cot in front of him put Jared Black in mind of another woman, another time. The commodore sighed. One of the strange things about surviving long enough to see your own death swimming up in the water towards you was that the events of your early life often seemed more real and immediate than the occurrences that had happened just the day before. Maybe the brain preferred to remember the body as it had been, hale and fit and with a whole life of possibilities stretched out in front of it, denuded of disappointments. Not crumbling, a casual victim of entropy – eroded by the natural course of life and its sicknesses. *Ah, it's a tricksy thing, a man's mind.* There had been many women, of course, wives who had died and borne him children, but the first love was always the fondest remembered. *Maeva, are you still alive? Still out here with the nomads of the sea?* He had been in love with her from the first moment he had seen her. *And who wouldn't be? So full of fire. Calling you in like a moth to her light.* What he'd felt for Maeva wasn't just a function of the fact that she had saved his life. Pulling him from the wreckage of a broken u-boat like a fisherman levered winkles from the rocks of the shoreline. There were tales of mermaids who did that, who rescued drowning submariners, but Maeva had been entirely human. And like all the finest women, she had made him feel more human too. After the royalist-in-exiles' hidden island base had finally been located and destroyed by parliament, Maeva had given Jared Black the thing he had needed most: a reason to go on living.

Was our first meeting so many years ago? It feels like yesterday. There had been a blackness in the wrecked conning tower, the kind of complete, utter blackness that could only come from the sea flooding in and even the flicker of light from the instrument panels sparking out as her power drained. Legs trapped under a collapsed hull plate, he had watched as a bobbing fairy light in front of him had grown to the glow of a diving helmet's face plate, looked on Maeva's ethereal porcelain beauty, snowy-white like only a life lived under the sea could make a woman. *How old was I, twenty, twenty-one? My first command shot out from underneath me. Everyone else, my friends and family in the crew, a corpse.*

She had prodded him, checking he was as dead as all the other u-boat privateers, drawing back as she saw his mouth grimace in pain. Connecting her suit to his with a communication line. 'You're a u-boat pirate, I presume? Not a captive held for ransom by the marauders.'

'Privateer, lass, never a pirate. Licensed to take back what's ours by right. And you, I presume, must be one of those murderous underwater savages that roam the oceans, a seanore.'

'I understand that the self-proclaimed nobles who wrote

149

your dubious licenses of brigandage are much like this vessel, now. Dead in the water.'

'So then, news travels fast.'

'There are probably clans on the other side of the world who were woken by the sounds of the depth charges striking your u-boat pens.'

'War's a right noisy business. Not much quietness in it.' He'd watched her pick up her lance. 'Make it quick for me, lass, before you strip my boat.'

She'd jabbed him, experimentally in the chest. 'You're a very unsuccessful pirate. Not a single chest of treasure I can find on board.'

'Privateer, please. And I was a more successful rebel than I ever was a liberator of cargoes.'

'Not very clever, either. Silks and spices always have a market. Causes are cheap. Almost everyone can invent one for free.'

'I'd thank you kindly to murder me before the lecture, rather than after.'

She raised the lance, but rather than spearing him with the deadly crystal blade, she had pushed it under the hull plate trapping his legs and begun to lever it up. 'The price on your head makes you the most valuable thing in this wreck, surface-dweller.'

'Too valuable to sell, if the truth be told.'

'You're every bit as arrogant as your people are said to be. Why would I want to keep a filthy surface-dwelling rascal around?'

'So I can look at you, lass. So I can just look at you.'

How many years did we have together? No more than two, as I remember it. Jared Black felt a brief stab of pain. He'd vowed to Maeva he would never leave her. He had vowed to himself that he would never flee from parliament again. But when he had been recognized by a trader, sold out to parliament's agents for the price on his rebellious head, then he had abandoned her. For how could he bear to witness what had befallen his family and comrades-in-arms happen a second time to the simple nomads of the sea? Bombed and ruthlessly hunted for harbouring a notorious royalist captain? No, that was never going to happen. The commodore had cut and run from their gloriously uncomplicated existence together. He had run and he had kept on running, and perhaps he had never really stopped. Changing identities like other men changed overcoats. There were many prices that fate demanded of a man. None so painful as a life he had never had a chance to live.

The hammock Charlotte Shades was lying in rocked as the *Purity Queen's* hull shifted, bringing the commodore back to the present with a jolt as the floor's angle shifted to an incline then jarringly righted itself.

'We've surfaced,' said the commodore. 'Time to signal the ships out there we've a mind to join their convoy.'

'A mind for one last voyage, Jared?'

'What's that, lad?'

'I heard what our friend from the State Protection Board said when he had you pinned against the wall at Tock House with a gun in your chest. Before he even said it, I had noticed that you were down a couple of pounds in weight. Your lungs are broken; I can hear it every time you cough.'

'Is that why my mortal trousers no longer fit me?'

'It's a serious matter.'

'No, Jethro Daunt, it is not. Dying comes to us all, sooner or later. You cannot cheat it. The life I've had foisted on me, I should've been dead a dozen times over. I should've died with the fleet-in-exile at Porto Principe; I should've died in the dark halls of Jago or the sand dunes of Cassarabia or the

151

foreign fields of a dozen other rotten countries. You can't choose not to die, only where you stand when you blessed do. It's my time, and even the land has seen fit to turn me out of my rest, to see out my last days with a sabre in one hand and a pistol in the other.'

'There are medicines that could be tried.'

'And my ill-gotten gains have paid for them all, lad. You'd be better off turning back to those old gods who haunted you out of your parsonage. Put in a word with them for poor old Blacky.'

'After what you and I did to them on Jago, even they have deserted me now.'

'Ah then, matters of death I shall leave to the church and the graveyard diggers. Life I understand well enough, and this I know to be true. With my unlucky stars I was never fated to die peacefully curled up underneath a warm blanket with my wife and daughter sitting by my side. I'll go like I lived and sell myself dear with it.'

Daunt seemed concerned by Jared's evident lack of care in this matter. The Circlist church would have it that after the commodore's death, his soul would be tipped out and poured into the one sea of consciousness, mingled with all that was, is, and was yet to be, before being poured back out into all the myriad lives still to be born. But somehow, the commodore couldn't imagine that fate suiting the audacious, coarse trajectory of his life. It was the most basic Circlist teaching that all that was living was joined, the same, indivisible. Jared Black's life felt too dark to be diluted and combined with the rest of humanity. Yet, the end had to come eventually. Nobody could capture the river. Every time you knelt by the stream and cupped your hand in it, all you could ever come out with was water. Not the river. The river was flow and movement, just like the life they had been given.

In the hammock, Charlotte Shades' eyes flickered open and she moaned and moved a shaky hand out to cover her eyes from the light. Her other hand, the commodore noticed, went to the chest to check the jewel on her chain was still there. She did it barely consciously. A reflex; but an instinctive touch that spoke of its value to her.

'Where am I?'

'Safe, Damson Shades,' said Daunt.

'There are monsters here, I have seen them. Their skin's peeling off. The monsters.'

'Not yet, lass,' said the commodore. 'But we will be sailing towards them. You can count on my poor unlucky stars to guarantee that.'

There was a silence on the bridge as the commodore explained the nature of the message he'd received from one of the navy convoy's surface vessels. Flashed across by the light of a gas lantern as the *Purity Queen* crashed through the waves topside, conserving her air and fuel supplies.

'It is normal practice, good captain?' asked Daunt. 'For a convoy commander to invite the masters of the vessels under his charge to dine on board the flagship?'

'I would have to say no, lad,' said the commodore. 'Usually, the fleet sea arm treats trader convoys with all the love and affection a drover shows towards his geese, the flat of his boot and the sharp of his stick to keep them together while driving them to market.' The old u-boat commander tugged on his big silver beard thoughtfully. 'But then, normal convoys don't sail so large. This convoy's been named *Operation Pedestal*, as I've been signalled it by our navy friends. Forty tramp freighters, six paddle liners and close to a dozen seadrinker boats like our own, not to mention the navy iron-clads, support ships and coalers running by our sides. With such a fleet, the House of Guardians is making a statement to the Advocacy about who controls the blessed oceans. Yes, I would say the vice-admiral is sailing under parliamentary orders, keeping the shipmasters sweet and sucking up to his shopkeeper masters in the ruling party. You don't climb so high up the greasy mast without learning whose arse to kiss.'

'Best you trim your beard then, Blacky, before the flagship's launch comes to pick you up,' said Dick Tull. 'You don't want to be embarrassing us all when you're nibbling on the vice-admiral's plump partridge breasts.'

'I wouldn't be getting as far as the captain's table if I accepted his invite,' said the commodore. 'Vice-admiral Cockburn used to be plain speaking Captain Cockburn, and the last time we met it was the at the end of a round of depth charges after he'd spent near fourteen months chasing me across the world's oceans, trying to stretch my neck for a privateer. Fortunately for us, our little contretemps was in my previous boat, the *Sprite of the Lake*, or we might have found our place in the convoy occupied by a spread of mines!' The commodore swept his large fingers to take in the bridge crew, the sailors hunched over their boards and navigation panels. 'While the half of my crew that didn't once sail for the cause are known to a mite too many ports and courts as smugglers, privateers, mutineers and deserters.'

Daunt raised an eyebrow. 'Will the absence of the *Purity Queen*'s officers from the vice-admiral's table not create a few suspicions?'

Commodore Black tossed his skipper's cap at Daunt. 'Well, that I don't believe it will, *Captain* Daunt!'

Daunt placed both hands on the boat's rail, the deck heaving with the roll of the waves. Apart from the jouncing of their launch in the dark waters, the sight of the convoy on the sea might have been Middlesteel viewed at night, so tight were conning towers, masts and superstructures packed in, hundreds of portholes and wheelhouses aglitter under the stars. Of course, if it had been the capital they were travelling towards, Barnabas Sadly wouldn't be moaning and retching over the side. The oiled seaman's coats they had borrowed seemed scant protection against the crashing waves. They had developed a false perspective of the sea travelling on the u-boat. It was only when you were tipping up the crest of waters as tall as a hill and sliding down the other side that you caught a glimpse of all its dangers and immensity. *Not even the darkness can hide how vast it is.*

Daunt might only have been masquerading as a skipper, but he had no trouble in identifying the convoy's flagship, *The Zealous*, an ironclad with a radical new design the newssheets had termed a 'wheelship'. A platform weighted down with mighty guns and a citadel-like superstructure, she was pierced with six slots that held a series of twinned hundred-foot high spherical wheels on either side. Turning and churning the sea, her six wheels provided both buoyancy and propulsion. Rotated by powerful steam engines pouring smoke into the sky, balance in the water was provided by a series of hydrofoils on either side. Launches that had made their rounds among the convoy waited in the shadow of lifting cranes, escaping the thunderous waves as they were winched up into the docking cradles of a boat bay under the flagship's platform. Larger shadows hovered over the bow of the flagship, pocket airships returning from patrol to seek out the safety of the vessel's hangars. Unconventional and ugly, *The Zealous* was said to be the lion of the waves, unmatchable by the men-o'war of any other nation's fleets. She reared out of the waters as she powered forward, her guns given a stronghold's commanding view over the ocean, contemptuous of the waves below. *Unsinkable.*

Boxiron moved to stand by Daunt's side. 'I fear I make almost as unconvincing a seaman as Barnabas Sadly.'

'With this many vessels in the convoy commander's care, I trust the vice-admiral will have too many guests to hone in on our nautical deficiencies,' said Daunt. 'Besides, the commodore's crew appear to my eye as varied an assortment of chancers and rogues as our own company.' He glanced back at Barnabas vomiting over the side. 'And as the good captain assured me before we departed, some of the greatest naval commanders in history have suffered from a "mortal spot of seasickness".' *Although, I will admit, not with quite so much gusto as Barnabas.* Daunt adjusted a peaked cap slipped over the steamman's head, a faded badge in its centre with the arms of an anchor and seahorse on the cap's crown. *And at least we look the part.*

'When a steamman starts to wear clothes,' said Boxiron, touching his cap, 'it is usually taken as a sign of mental illness.'

Daunt indicated the exploding waves. 'Chased out of home by an unlikely alliance between royalists rebels and the secret police, with us heading into the heart of a war waiting to be declared, I thought that might be taken as a given.'

'It should prove to be quite a distraction.'

'I'm not sure I follow you, old steamer?'

'My body may be the ramshackle product of your people,' said Boxiron, 'but only below my neck. My vision plate is still fully functional. I am not yet blind or insensible to what is going on. We have had many offers of work this year, yet you only accept the most dangerous and challenging of cases.'

Daunt shrugged. 'They pay the most.'

'We do not need the money. You are seeking to distract me from my predicament – the mind of a magnificent steamman knight inexpertly fused to this stumbling monstrosity of a body.'

Daunt tapped the hulking creature's chest plate, just above the squeaking transaction-engine drum rotating in his centre. 'But it is our mind that makes us who we are, old friend. Our memories, not this. All flesh is dust.'

'In my case,' said Boxiron, 'I believe all flesh is rust. There are those among your race who suffer from wasting diseases, and they sometimes count it as a kindness when family and friends cut short their thread on the great pattern.'

Daunt sighed. He knew that steammen who had their design violated, corrupted outside of the pattern laid down by King Steam and his Hall of Architects in the Steamman Free State were expected to seek suicide. It was a hard code, but one a warrior of the commando militant was expected to adhere to. 'You might be diminished, but you are by no means a cripple. You share some of the memories of the human-milled automatic whose body your head was grafted onto. You are a unique being in your own right. Hardly perfect, but which of us can say such a thing?'

'I am neither one thing nor the other,' said Boxiron. 'I am stuck in an existence I did not ask for.'

'Yes, I believe I know how you feel.' *Is that it?* Daunt mused. *Are you merely the steamman reflection of myself? Poor Jethro Daunt. Cast out of the church, seeking redemption where he can find it? No, there must be more to it than that. We've come so far together since I found you working as a hulking enforcer for the flash mob; too far for it to end like this.*

'Have I ever thanked you for saving me?' asked Boxiron.

'I believe we've saved each other,' said Daunt. 'Many times in fact, over the years.' He looked at the steamman. Daunt knew his friend well enough to know what he was thinking.

How easy it would be to fall over the side, allow the fury of the waves and the depths of the seas to claim his walking corpse of a body.

One day, this won't be enough.

For Dick Tull, having a believable alias was second nature in his line of work. Second officer of a u-boat or an anarchist with a taste for sedition and assassinating parliamentarians, you observed the traits and tricks of the type, then you mirrored them right back. When you were dealing with amateurs like the ex-parson and his metal mate, you had to work with what you'd been given. A brief, tight cover story that was easy to hold onto and remember under duress. Jethro Daunt was now masquerading as a wealthy eccentric who had decided to sink the greater part of his fortune in a shipping concern, transporting high value caffeel beans and tea powder between the colony plantations and the Kingdom. A part that the churchman played to perfection with his strange habits: humming nonsense ballads and limericks to himself; the way he would drift off into a daydream and start pointing and wagging his finger as if he was conducting a debate against an invisible opponent, lecturing unseen students. Meanwhile, the steamman's cover story was that he was the brute of a first mate whose clinking metal fist kept the unruly crewmen in order. Barnabas Sadly was the general officer who kept the stores, ran the books and oversaw the galley. There was one thing none of the party from the *Purity Queen* had to fake. All the u-boat crewmen in the gathering carried the same untidy, dishevelled air compared to the officers from the convoy's surface freighters, paddle ships and liners. Living cheek by jowl in the cramped, sweaty confines of a submersible had that effect on a sailor, and even a cursory attempt to scrub up for an engagement couldn't quite remove the impression.

Four of us hard-pressed to tell stem from stern. It's a good thing the convoy's brass seem more interested in the spread of food than the conversation.

'It don't seem right, Mister Tull,' Sadly whispered by Dick's side. 'All this food laid out and nobody with a care to charge by the plate.'

Dick found it hard to contradict his informant. The main mess of *The Zealous* had been arranged with linen-covered tables and a sizeable buffet set across its surface. Sailors in white dress uniforms and enough braid to befit an admiral served behind the tables, lifting silver domes to reveal slices of lamb and beef roasted to perfection, meats swimming in their own juices. There were plates with cheeses from every county in Jackals, others overflowing with oranges, grapes and exotic fruit that Dick couldn't even put a name to. The crew on the ship wouldn't get to eat like this normally, that was a given. Probably not the officers, either.

All the money it costs for the state to mollycoddle a few rich merchants on this tub, and they'll still make me scrabble like a swine in muck for a decent pension.

Every few minutes the distant sound of whining stabilisers swelled above the rumble of chattering guests, the flagship's platform adjusting its angle to match the pitch of the seas she was cutting across. Officers from *The Zealous* were circulating through the hundred or so guests, making polite conversation with hands steadied on dress cutlasses hanging from their belts. *Braying arses.* They moved with an easy confidence, as if they were born to command. And in a sense they were. Mill-owners' sons, wealthy quality, carrying the clout to launch them into an officer's career in the fleet sea arm. *How many of them've had to start as a common sailor and work their way up the ranks? How many of them've had to pull an honest day's duties on board this tub? This is what my ancestors fought on Parliament's sodding side for? To swap one bunch of masters for another?* That was Dick Tull all right. Always the tenant, never the landlord. *But your ancestors weren't sitting on a comfortable saddle behind the lines waving an expensive sabre in the air*, needled an envious little voice inside him. His ancestors? Just muddy-fingered citizen soldiers, clutching a pike or balancing an old heavy rifle on a tripod as they faced their mirror image across a field. Peasants who happened to be in the pay of gentlemen factory owners rather than gentlemen farmers when the war started.

There was a loud clinking on a glass as one of the officers called for silence. 'Ladies and gentlemen, honoured guests of *The Zealous*. Pray silence for Vice-admiral Cockburn.'

Stepping forward, the vice-admiral looked more like a pugilist than a navy officer. Short and stocky, he had shoulders wide enough for his crew to build seats above his lapels and place a sailor on either side to mount the vessel's watch. Hard, ruthless eyes swept across the convoy's visiting officers and Dick had no problem imagining his tenacious pursuit of old Blacky across half the world's seas. The old sod resembled a pitbull, and once a pitbull sank its teeth into your flesh, it never let go until it'd claimed a healthy-sized chunk of meat.

'Good evening, ladies and gentlemen of *Operation Pedestal*. I trust you are finding the wardroom's hospitality as abundantly in your service tonight as our guns are in your vessels' safe passage. The majority of you standing here today are merchants, and you do not need reminding that the prosperity of our nation has been built on free trade. That prosperity depends on the free passage of our vessels. But it seems there are some who need to be reminded that we will not suffer its impediment lightly. We lay no claim to what is under the waves. We cast no nets for fish here. We send down no divers to explore for minerals. However, where the Fire Sea has withdrawn, opening up a passage free of the need of fire-breakers, we will allow no nation to extend its territorial limits and then demand a bandit's toll priced in threats for transgressing open waters. We braved these currents when they were threatened by volcanoes and fire, and any enemy who seeks to close them to us now will find that we carry with us fire of our own. Fire enough for all foes foolish enough to play the privateer against *our* people!'

Polite applause echoed around the mess hall and the vice-admiral circulated through the crowd, shaking hands with a firm grip and making reassuring noises to the commercial masters. *Spoken like a reliable little politician on the make.*

Jethro Daunt's beak-like nose appeared to be twitching in distaste. 'There is something amiss here,' he whispered.

'You're not wrong, amateur. It's my tax brass being used to fatten up a mob of merchants who don't need a crumb of it.'

'No,' said Daunt, sotto voce. 'It's the vice-admiral. He's a blank to me – his body language, all of the tells that should be in his gestures and his voice, none of them are present. According to my finer intuition, it is as if he doesn't exist.'

'You might be having a bad day with that mumbo jumbo you're taught in the church, but he looks solid enough to me.' *Solid enough to thump a shark unconscious with one hand and make a soup out if it with the other.*

'Synthetic morality is hardly mumbo jumbo,' protested Daunt. 'My skills in these matters have never failed me before.'

'Maybe you've eaten a bad prawn,' said Dick, toying with his greying moustache. He was enjoying needling the ex-churchman.

Sadly clung to his cane, waving away a sailor circling the room with a tray of drinks. 'I don't blame you, Mister Daunt.

All that pitching and rolling in the launch to get across here. It's enough to muck up anyone's plumbing.'

Daunt peered across the room. 'But it's only the vice-admiral. Everyone else I've observed at the function is reading normally by my faculties. I wonder? I think it's time that the master of the *Purity Queen* was introduced to our host for the evening.'

Dick groaned. They were meant to be keeping a low profile on the warship. Just enough for their absence not to be noticed and the *Purity Queen*'s position in the convoy fall under suspicion. Having the ex-parson bearding the commanding officer in his own lair just because the amateur's church senses were running spiky was hardly part of the plan. It wouldn't take much for Daunt's ignorance of the smooth running of a u-boat to be called into question, the kind of conversation that would be expected to pass between two nautical masters. Dick was desperately casting for a way for a first officer to divert his skipper without arousing additional suspicions when the ship's siren sounded and did the job for him.

A voice followed the alarm, reverberating around the room from wall-mounted speakers. 'General Quarters! All hands, all hands man your battle stations!'

Saved by the bell, except I don't think this indicates any improvement in my sodding fortunes.

Two officers came running into the mess deck, out of dress uniform, a seriousness of purpose as they whispered to the vice-admiral. He nodded grimly and then departed with one of the pair trotting after him, leaving the task of explaining the situation to the remaining lieutenant. Even the vessel's stabilisers couldn't disguise the fact that the warship was picking up speed, the mess slanting upward as the ship rose higher on her aquaplanes. Outside her portholes the spray of stars in the sky flitted past as the flagship pressed on faster, the sounds of water churning under her monstrous propulsion wheels swelling to a crescendo. The assemblage fell into a hush for an explanation. As the strident wail of the alarm dropped away, the silence that replaced it hung heavy enough in the air for the *Purity Queen*'s screws to carve slices out of it.

'Quiet, please. We've picked up the sonar signature of Advocacy war craft ahead of the convoy. When we attempted to alter course to bypass them, other elements of the gill-neck fleet rose to the surface to our bow and stern, blocking our safe passage.'

Sounds of panic started to rise among the merchant crewmen.

'They mean to extract their toll,' noted Boxiron. It sounded as if the brute was relishing the chance for battle.

'Send us back to our ship,' someone shouted. The cry was picked up and began to echo out among the milling merchants and trader officers.

'We are manoeuvring too fast to drop our launches,' called the lieutenant. 'You'll need to stay confined to the wardroom until we've outrun the gill-necks.'

Angry shouts came from the guests, demands to slow down and sail them back to the vessels where their responsibilities lay. Used to unquestioning command on their own ships, hard men who could command coarse sailors, this wasn't, Dick considered, the kind of crowd you wanted to turn ugly on you.

Dick watched the sailors who had been acting as stewards and hosts vanishing purposefully into the bowels of the ship, called to their battle stations. Not sprinting, but hardly slouching either. *Well trained. Cogs in a machine that's been greased by practice.* 'We need to get back to the boat bay.'

'I concur,' said Daunt, his gaze flitting between the angry

163

faces of the convoy's shipmasters. 'It's only a matter of time before someone on the bridge thinks to assign a company of marines to ensure the safety of their guests – not to mention our compliance.'

Sadly groaned and extradited himself from the comfort of a chair where he had sunk. 'I'm not one to shy away from a little aggro, Mister Tull, but does it have to kick off at sea?'

'I won't let you die,' said Dick, pushing his informant towards the door they had used to enter the mess hall. 'I still need you to testify for me, don't I?'

'My word won't count for much, says I.'

'It'll count for a lot less if I let Walsingham's assassins toss your corpse in an alley back home.' *And it's not as if I've got that many friends left alive, is it?*

Boxiron closed the door behind them. The four of them were standing in the open on a deck gantry, the ship's aft lanterns running behind them. Dick stared out between the flagship's churning wheels. *Nothing.* How could you hope to spot anything out there? Just dark crashing waves, the night sky's canopy only set apart from the sea by stars. No sign of the gill-necks. No sign of a war brewing.

'They haven't tried to stop a convoy before, have they?' Sadly asked.

'Harried only,' said Boxiron. 'I believe this counts as an escalation in tensions.'

It's never made easy. Not for me. But it was more than that. Something about tonight felt wrong, and it wasn't only the ex-parson's odd reaction to the vice-admiral. The gill-neck force just happened to have chosen the precise time to corral the convoy when the masters of the convoy were off their bridges and on the flagship. Even at the best of times, moving a convoy was more akin to a drover driving his flock to market. With the captains gathered here, it wasn't so much a convoy, as a seaborne shooting gallery. And as used as Dick was to bad luck, this felt too much like it was straying from coincidence into the realm he specialized in. *Treason.*

CHAPTER EIGHT

'The escort ships are pulling out of line and forming up as an independent flotilla,' announced the sailor on the *Purity Queen*'s sonar station, two greasy hands clasped to his earphones with his eyes shut, as if he could picture in his mind the ironclads taking position.

'A grand disposition for cutting through the gill-necks' ranks,' said the commodore. 'But it leaves our line of civilian tubs as ripe for picking as plums on a warm summer's day. They're not going to be happy out there.'

Charlotte knew how the merchant vessels' crews felt. Waking up groggy and disoriented and with bizarre memories of a pursuit by monsters was bad enough. But waking up to find herself pressed into the crew of this strange submersible craft; its roguish company with their insular manners and sailor's slang – an alien tongue of binnacle lists, drift counts and parbuckling – a miniature kingdom of cramped corridors and cabins and unfamiliar equipment. And everywhere Charlotte wandered the same odour of burnt oil and uniforms sweated by near-tropical heat while running submerged. She might still have King Jude's sceptre, but the price she was paying for its possession was growing higher by the day. Sometimes, it was hard to tell where reality started and her delirium-haunted dreams had halted.

Charlotte piped up. 'What about our people on the flagship?'

Our people. Well, the steamman had saved her life, so she supposed she owed him, not to mention the eccentric ex-churchman who seemed determined to warn her of supernatural threats to her life. Feeling gratitude to people wasn't something Charlotte was used to, or a situation she felt at ease with. Especially because she wouldn't complain if the commodore decided to turn his u-boat around and head right back for the solid land of home. *I'd take my chances in the rookeries and disappear into the underworld.* There was only so far the reach of a bunch of evil royalists and crooked secret police could extend, wasn't there?

'*The Zealous* is turning to meet the enemy vessels,' said the commodore. 'They're moving at a rate of knots now, too fast to lower their launches safely. Jethro and that sly old bugger Dick Tull will be confined on board, though not willingly, I'll wager, if Boxiron slips his gears.' He scratched his beard thoughtfully. 'Fire up our fish-scales outside – let's see if the money I paid that brainy wretch in the naval yards is any more useful than a scraping of barnacles growing on my new hull. Prepare to bring us around, helm.'

'Stealth plating receiving charge,' reported the crewman. There was the slightest of vibrations from outside the hull, as if a tiny mosquito had come awake and was doing circuits of their cramped control room. 'Acoustic profile is approaching optimum.'

The commodore checked a bank of machinery that looked more recently installed than most of the rusting, heavily greased equipment on board. 'As slippery as an eel and hopefully as hard to seize too, to the phones of every boat in the water. Down-plane two degrees, helm, slip us out of the convoy and turn us around. Run us into the wake of *The Zealous.*'

'We're taking pings,' sounded the phones man. 'No back-echo. We're displacing all incoming noise!'

'One number short on the convoy's list, then.' said the commodore, his voice satisfied. 'We've got two hours or so before we have to rest the stealth plates, or the mortal things will burn themselves out. After *The Zealous,* now. If I know Jethro and the rest of our friends, they'll be pushing off the warship before long. We'll pick them up and let Vice-admiral Cockburn and the gill-necks dance the sea waltz together while we set a course for the heart of the Advocacy.'

'Fish in the water!' warned the sailor on the phones station. 'Multiple launches running hot. Depth charge spreads descending too.'

His words were borne out by a distant reverberation, the *Purity Queen's* hull quivering at the faraway detonations.

'Who fired first?' the commodore demanded.

'Simultaneous exchange of fire, skipper,' said the sailor. 'Damned if both fleets didn't open up on each other at the same time!'

'Bloody fools. This is meant to be a convoy, not a wicked sea duel. Cockburn's orders should have been to avoid trouble, not provoke it.'

Another volley of depth charge explosions shook the u-boat.

'Are they shooting at *us*?' asked Charlotte.

'They can't even see the *Purity Queen* now, lass,' said the commodore. 'No, those are our fleet's depth charges, and meant for the blessed Advocacy's boats. The gill-necks don't have surface vessels as such – though their fleet's thick with submersibles. Take us up to periscope depth, pilot, I need to take a peek at what those blockheads are doing up there.'

A minute later and the old u-boat man had pulled a steel tube down out of the ceiling, using two grips on its side to twist the periscope around.

'Skipper,' warned the sailor on the sonar desk. 'I'm picking up the sound of gyroscope rings being rotated.'

'I see them, phones,' said the commodore. 'Starfish surfacing in the water, at least three of the terrible things.'

Charlotte had to resist grabbing the scope from the vessel's skipper. 'Starfish?'

'Nothing good for our convoy, lass. The gill-necks have come armed for the hunt. Look at the terrible things getting ready to go into operation. That's it for Jethro and our friends. They belong to the gill-necks now!'

'What is that thing?' shouted Dick. On their starboard, a metallic dome rising out of the waves started rotating, sea water pouring off five massive metal arms spinning around its head. There seemed to be nodules running across the arms, hundreds of them, giving the appendages the appearance of octopus tentacles.

Boxiron ran to the railing on the ship's gantry, his vision plate emitting clicking sounds as his head jutted out over the edge. Whatever tricks Boxiron's skull was playing with the sight of the bizarre carousel-like machine out there, the steamman recoiled back as if he had been physically struck. 'A boarding device! The capsules in the arms are packed full of soldiers.'

Multiple detonations sounded, dozens of capsules exploding out from each arm. As sharp as a steel needle at their business end, the capsules rammed through the hull-platform of *The Zealous*, the vessel shaking as they pounded into her. On a normal ship the capsules would have struck just above the

169

waterline, but on the wheel-ship they sank into the flat hull of the platform riding high above the waves, metal splinters shattering where each of the boarding devices hit. It was only then that Dick noticed a ring holding a large steel cable built into the flat rear of each capsule, the lines still connected to the dome-like thing surfaced off their side. With a hideous squealing sound, the dome began to rotate, rewinding the multiple steel lines it had cast out back into a groove around its base. As the cables wound, the wheel-ship started to list badly, the hydrofoils on the opposite side of *The Zealous* rising out of the water. *It's towing us towards it!*

On the ship's gantry, Dick, Jethro, Boxiron and Sadly were thrown across the deck as though they were little more than ants on a capsizing toy boat. Dick's hand lurched, catching hold of a depth charge platform and hanging on for dear life as their ship was dragged across the waves. Boxiron's firm grip lashed out onto the depth charge loader, clutching hard onto Jethro Daunt with the other, while Sadly swung in turn on the ex-parson's hand, attempting to jam his cane into something solid enough to support his weight. Sailors unluckier than the four of them were sent tumbling off the superstructure and decks, shaken into the sea below and swallowed without a trace by the peaking waves. Beyond *The Zealous*, all was confusion. The long line of the convoy had broken, ship's lights scattering across the sea, thunder sounding from warships' guns, explosions and fires flowering in the darkness. *But this ship, they want intact.* As *The Zealous* was drawn in against the boarding machine, the angle of her deck righted, Dick tossed back from the edge into a wall behind. Boxiron spun into a porthole, smashing the toughened glass into a shower of shards as his arm shot out to stabilize himself.

With *The Zealous* reeled in alongside the Advocacy's machine, a flurry of magnetic cables lashed out from a ring of holes at the apex of the siege craft, flying over the top of *The Zealous* and securing the gill-neck's catch. A tangle of lines impaled the soft skin of one of the vessel's pocket airships, the 'stat three-quarters reversed out of the hangar at the stern of the flagship as the projectiles struck. Capture cables tightened and the impaled airship crashed towards the launch deck, her command bridge and engine cars smashing down into the wheel-ship. A series of explosions rocked the vessel, a propeller cartwheeling across the deck in a cloud of debris as the airship's expansion-engine gas ignited. Smoke gushed out from an open swinging door behind Dick, cries of alarm and orders drifting across the superstructure as a crew of sailors struggled past, unravelling a fire hose between them while Dick and the others picked themselves up. Tellingly, the guns of *The Zealous* had fallen silent.

'This is a pretty picture,' moaned Sadly, brushing broken glass off his clothes. 'Pride of the bleeding fleet sea arm and we're stuck here, a fly in the gill-neck's web.'

'They want the ship as a prize,' said Dick.

'Her capture would make a powerful propaganda coup for the Advocacy,' said Daunt. 'That much is certain.'

Dick and Boxiron leant over the vessel's railing. In front of them the vast wheels were churning uselessly; behind them a wheel had stopped turning altogether, tangled by the cable shots of the underwater nation's strange vessel.

'Too far to jump. Even with a buoyancy vest, the fall would break your softbody necks.' Boxiron glanced over at Daunt. 'Not mine though.'

'Let us hope that our boat bays are still in friendly hands, then, old steamer.'

'Survive the fall, maybe, but you'll float as good as a sinking rock,' said Dick.

'That is a common misconception,' said Daunt. 'In fact,

Boxiron will float like a sealed drum and fare rather better, I fear, than we will.'

'Well, good for him, amateur. How about you float home on him? Me, I'll choose Blacky's old tub again.'

Small arms fire chattered within the vessel, boarding parties clashing with Jackelian marines. *How many gill-neck soldiers were shot across in each of those capsules? Sweet Circle, it's never made easy. Not for me.*

'How are we going to get out of here?' complained Sadly.

'I possess perfect positional bearings,' said Boxiron, the tone of superiority positively leaking from his voicebox. 'I can place our location inside the ship, including our point of entry on this vessel, within two feet.'

'Just take us back to the boat bay,' growled Dick.

'Follow me. I shall lead the way.'

Taking Boxiron at his word, the party plunged inside, allowing the steamman to take the lead. Whatever havoc the gill-neck boarding parties were creating inside the vessel, their handiwork had done significant damage so far. Gas lamps set into corridor walls flickered intermittently, throwing areas of the vessel into darkness – a gloom broken by the bobbing hand lamps of crewmen scurrying about on action stations. Worse still, the stabilizers that balanced the platform above the ugly propulsion wheels had been damaged. Previously stable enough in choppy waters that Dick had been able to rest a glass on a mess table, the drink's contents as still as a mill pond on a summer's afternoon, now the ship's passages lurched and shifted with each swell of the waves below. Unlike a normal vessel, the wheel-ship didn't possess the natural stability in the water that a keel's weight would have given her.

Staggering like drunken sailors, the four of them navigated by Boxiron's supposedly infallible sense of direction, clambering down steep ladders with ridiculously thin treads, as if the naval architects had deliberately been trying to create injuries from falling. At times, Dick thought he recognized some of the corridors from their escorted journey up from the boat bay. Mostly, he was navigating a narrow-passaged purgatory of unfamiliar shifting iron walls, slippery floors and intermittently hissing gaslights. They blundered through the strong smell of sea water, machine oil and the acrid tinge of smoke and gun cordite. If there was any consolation, it was that Sadly appeared to be sharing Dick's tribulations in magnified misery, the green-tinged informant's mouth intermittently opening to make gurgling noises as if he was going to vomit. His cane tapped out when their illumination failed, knocking at the sides of the corridor, grunting as he hauled his weight along on his clubfoot. Jethro Daunt, by contrast, seemed serenely untroubled by the confusion and carnage they were passing. Unbothered by the sound of running boots, shouts, the distant firecracker rattle of weapons fire, sweaty faces of red-coated marines looming up like devils in the half-light as they came pushing past towards the fray. There was, though, a quizzical look on the ex-parson's face. As if he didn't quite understand why they should be here, on *The Zealous*, at this time. As if their involvement was a puzzle with a definitive answer that could be teased out. What they found instead was a corridor full of gill-necks below. On the opposite side of a two-storey chamber, long-barrelled rifles were raised against a handful of marines, fire spurting from slots in the weapons' muzzles as they exchanged fire with the crew. Snout-shaped silver war masks hid the soldiers' faces, while their elongated skulls bobbed with a cone of frilled-ridges capped by a fin-like slash of bone. Roughly of human height, the heavily muscled scales of the attackers' wet skin shone in the half-light – not much of it on show beneath carapace-like

173

chestplates. Armour that might have been ripped off crabs, shell plates covering metallic mesh that shimmered with oil rainbows in the flickering lamplight. Used to being able to cut rapidly through the deep waters of the ocean, the underwater warriors moved with sinuous speed in the unnaturally thin environment of the air. The gill-necks betrayed their origins as a branch of mankind's evolutionary tree . . . vestigial surface lungs that could allow them to exist briefly out of the water fluttering weakly below their chests, a reverse rebreather mask connected into their masks to allow them to suck at the precious sea water they craved. The Advocacy soldiers' weapons gave off snake-hisses as they fired, the outnumbered human sailors facing them answering back with the oak splintering crackle of their sea pattern rifles. With the initial volley depleted, each side charged at each other, bayonet stabbing against bayonet, although the gill-necks' blades were more like crystal-edged spears running underneath the long length of their weapons' barrels.

So, this is what we're bleeding fighting? We're no match for their strength.

'They're blocking the way to the boat bay,' roared Boxiron. 'I fight in five!'

Behind Boxiron, Daunt gripped the rusting gear lever of the hulking steamman and dragged it slowly through its network of grooves until it came to a rest in the slot where someone had scrawled 'murderous' on the plate. Tilting a piercing spear of steam towards the ceiling, Boxiron vaulted the rail and hurled himself down towards the floor of the circular chamber and the two sides locked in a mêlée. A cry echoed up from his voicebox as he plummeted, a metallic steamman landslide. 'Top gear!'

He fights in five.

Coming hard and fast, the gill-necks threw themselves onto

Boxiron, the crystal blades of their weapons bouncing off his hull plates, scraping and scratching his already dented surface. Two iron fists lashed back, cracking carapace armour, bones and flesh, sending broken bodies flying into bulkheads. No more sidestepping his true nature, attempting to temper his clumsy malfunctioning body. No more trying to dampen down his servos so that he didn't inadvertently crack floors, dent walls, snap the toe bones of those standing too close to him. This is what Boxiron was for. Damage. Indiscriminate. Clanking. Raw. Damage. His legs lashed, his arms flailed, his head butted. Steam was spent and blood was shed.

Taking advantage of the confusion, Dick, Jethro and Sadly slipped down the spiral stair gantry to the chamber's floor level, circling to the side of the fight, the few human sailors left alive demoted to the battle's periphery. For its centre, its core, was now the throb of a boiler heart, Boxiron a wild hurricane of metal whipping through the disordered ranks of the enemy's warriors.

Dick scooped up a rifle from one of the fallen soldiers, pulling off the corpse's pack of shells. By his side, Sadly triggered his sleeve gun, the small single-shot pistol thudding into his open hand.

'I told you not to bring that peashooter. We're meant to be u-boat traders.'

'Sailors shoot each other, don't they, Mister Tull?'

'Against those gill-necks, you're more likely to annoy them.'

There was a corridor ahead of their chamber, the passage that led down to the boat bays – now filled with gill-neck warriors falling back under the fury of Boxiron's onslaught. Bodies lay littered in the steamman's wake, some broken and as still as death, others writhing in agony on the floor. Dick added to it, the butt of his rifle cracking down into the skull of one of the warriors trying to pull himself back onto his feet. There was a satisfying crack as the gill-neck slumped back down.

'That was hardly sporting,' protested Daunt.

Said the man who's unleashed a metal demon onto the enemy. 'What, you think there's rules for this, amateur?'

'He was trying to surrender.'

'He was going to take a bite out of your leg!'

The force of the impact had dislodged the gill-neck's silver mask, revealing humanoid features that were proudly defined by a burnished lightly scaled skin. Fierce and proud, even beaten unconscious. Its teeth were sharp and white, though, Dick had got that much right. They were famous for their bites weren't they? At least, so the colourful stories of the penny-dreadfuls would have it – the Kingdom's drowning mariners murdered by the savages of the sea before being dragged down to drown in their submerged palaces.

Dick felt the breeze ahead. They were close to the boat bay at the bottom of the vessel. He could almost taste his freedom. Dozens of runabouts and launches suspended on crane lines waiting to be lowered down to the choppy surface of the sea below. One of the little beauties had his name on it, waiting to take him back to the *Purity Queen*.

'Coronation Market rules, Mister Tull?' said Sadly.

Coronation Market. Middlesteel's worst slum district. *Guaranteed to leave its streets with a knife in your back and a bad disease between your legs.* 'They're the only rules that count.'

As they pushed out into the open space of the boat bay, the party was assailed by gill-necks on either side of the boarding gantries, strong, muscled arms holding drum-headed weapons. The enemy soldiers opened up and weighted nets spun out from the strange guns, slapping into the steamman from both directions. Boxiron began to pull the netting off, tearing at it even before its lead-weighted ends had finished wrapping around him, but as he clawed at the material, Dick noticed the netting was still connected to the weapons by dangling cables. Cables that jolted as the charge they were carrying struck Boxiron, the steamman making a very organic sounding yelp as the mesh glimmered with the devastating force of the power electric. A deafening crash echoed around the boat bay as Boxiron tumbled onto the deck, his netting dancing with sparks.

Dick hardly had a moment to take in the sight of the felled steamman twitching on the floor before he was smashed in the back. Slammed to the floor just in time to see the bare webbed feet of a fresh boarding party of gill-neck fighters pistol-whipping Sadly and Daunt down to the deck with a flurry of blows. The rifle was kicked out of Dick's hand and sent spinning over the edge of the boat bay into the waiting sea. Vanishing, along with any hope of an escape back to the u-boat.

A swift kick in his side turned Dick over. He was greeted by the sight of a dozen gill-neck weapons pointing at him, blades under their barrels balanced inches away from his bruised face.

'Trespassing surface dweller vermin,' hissed the sibilant voice of the nearest warrior, the frill of gills in his neck vibrating as he talked. 'Let us see how long you have left.'

'Left before what?' coughed Dick.

'Before your death, surface dweller. Before *that*.'

'She's dead in the water,' said the commodore, banging the side of the periscope in frustration. 'Damn their evil starfish, they have *The Zealous*. Wrapped like a kitten in yarn.'

'Jethro and Boxiron?' asked Charlotte.

'No boats have launched,' says the commodore. 'Ah, the

poor unlucky fools. The best we can hope for is that our friends are still on the ship and not among the poor wretches treading water underneath *The Zealous*.'

'We can't get them off?'

'Not with a starfish wrapped around *The Zealous*, lass. Those iron beasts are troop carriers – nautical siege engines. That vessel will be swarming with boarding parties. If there's one crumb of comfort for our friends, it's that the gill-necks must be looking to take prisoners and prizes. Hostages to bargain with, and a prize vessel to embarrass Parliament into negotiating.'

He surrendered the periscope for Charlotte to gaze out for a moment onto the carnage. It was as if an octopus had clambered over the dark silhouette of *The Zealous*, two vessels locked in a death struggle which the Jackelians had already lost. With *The Zealous's* propulsion wheels stilled, fires were left burning across her decks, lights in her portholes flickering. Sailors who had fallen off or abandoned the flagship were visible as small as bugs under her beam, struggling in the water.

'Phones,' said the commodore. 'Any sign that the gill-necks are aware that we're here?'

'No pings being received, skipper,' answered the sailor. 'They're too busy chasing the rest of the convoy off.'

'They've still got eyes, though,' said the commodore half to himself. 'We are taking a mortal risk, sitting here. We just need a single gill-neck swimming close enough to lay their peepers on the *Purity Queen*.'

Charlotte sighed. What had she been thinking? That they would just sail up to *The Zealous* while Jethro Daunt and the steamman tossed themselves off the deck and landed in front of the u-boat? This was the reality of war in the periscope's sweep . . . confusion and murder and darkness and men drowning in the water or burning in the oily debris set afire, two vessels locked together while marines tried to hunt down the opposition. A world shrunk no larger than a corridor down a gun sight and the comrade minding their rear from ambush.

'What do we do now?'

'We wait and we watch, lass. For a boat to launch with our friends, or for the cables of the starfish to disengage from the hull of *The Zealous*, or for our clever stealth skin to wear out. Either way, we get to leave.'

'What will the cables disengaging mean?'

'That the wicked gill-necks have taken the ship. That all resistance on board has been beaten down.'

Charlotte could tell from the strained lines on the faces of the crew how dangerous staying here was. An oppressive silence spread amongst the men and women waiting on the bridge, fingers nervously wiping the same oily spot on an air scrubber, the red knuckles of hands clutching onto the sides of seat stations. All of them with ears cocked to the distant sounds filtering through the hull of the u-boat. Never was a silence so loud. They clung to the hush expectantly, waiting for a sudden sound, anything that would indicate their discovery. But what would that be? A torpedo detonating against their hull, a sudden inrush of water followed by the screams of dying men struggling to seal off bulkheads?

At last, the commodore folded the handles on the periscope and sent it retracting down into the floor with a clatter as it locked into place. 'The starfish is disengaging and making for a dive. How long have we got left on our stealth cells?'

'Ten minutes, skipper.'

'Time enough to clear these wicked waters. Down-bubble two degrees. Slip us past the Advocacy flotilla. We'll hug the boils of the Fire Sea until we're close to the seanore hunting grounds.'

Charlotte wiped the sweat dripping into her eyes away. She realized her clothes were soaking with it. 'Are we going on?'

'Only forward, lass. There's nothing behind for us, not until we get the answer of what my sister is up to with the gill-necks and those rascals who paid you to steal King Jude's sceptre. Between the cover of the magma flows and the *Purity Queen* on silent running, we'll show the gill-necks they are not the only masters of the ocean. There are a few lessons in seamanship they've sill got to learn from old Blacky.'

Charlotte nodded grimly. *Why do I get the feeling that it's not an answer that any of us are going to like?* Half the people who had tried to help her plucked by fate and captured by the gill-necks, or worse, as dead on the flagship as poor old Damson Robinson in her pie shop. *I'm not a lucky person to be around.*

Charlotte woke with a jolt, eyes opening to the sight of her cabin's porthole; the same circle of armoured glass where she had just been dreaming of monstrous faces pressed up against the window. The oily, scaled skin of their distended heads banging and whacking to gain entry, break through the u-boat's hull and feast on her blood.

As Charlotte struggled to separate the reality from the dream, she realized that the Eye of Fate was leaking a blue light. A mist of illumination spread across the metal floor, shapes similar to those she'd been dreaming breaking up as if the first sunshine of morning was dispersing it. What was happening to her? This had never happened before. Ever since that thug, Cloake, had tried to kill her back in the Kingdom, nothing had been the same since. She touched the jewel nervously as she kicked off the blanket from her cot. *You protected me back in the capital. Is this your price, now? Driving me half-insane with these impossible visions?* Except that part of Charlotte knew that maybe they weren't so impossible after all. Distracted, she realized that the tapping from her dream had returned. Someone was knocking on the door of her cabin. Charlotte got out of the cot and reflexively reached out to touch King Jude's sceptre laid out on the top bunk. All the money she had saved up from her robberies, squirreled away in the Kingdom's banks and counting houses. What use was it to her now? As good as exiled, on the run with her so-called patrons waiting to murder her if she ever showed her face again at home. No, she couldn't think like that. She still had a small fortune here in the sceptre. She just had to find a way to parlay the stupid antique into its true wealth. *Find the leverage, and the rest will follow. The money always helped.*

It was Jared Black standing outside her cabin, the old u-boat man carrying a long metal object that had the look of a weapon about it.

She raised her hands, mockingly. 'Stand and deliver?'

Black shook the long device. 'An old friend. The same mortal weapon the nomads of the sea use underwater. A shock-spear. It fires a directed current accurate up to thirty feet below the waves.'

'That doesn't sound like much of a range?'

'For anything further away, they use a rotor-spear, cast like a handheld torpedo with an internal motor to carry it towards its target. You see one of those heading for you, lass, you swim out of the way as fast as you can.'

'Time to leave the *Purity Queen*?' Charlotte felt a frisson of fear.

'We're in the seanore hunting grounds,' confirmed the commodore. He led her through the u-boat's corridors, down

181

a ladder and into a chamber surrounded by diving suits, a central well of an airlock set in the middle of the suiting area.

'Let's see if the rough rascals remember me kindly.'

'Honey, why would they remember you at all?'

'I spent a little time with them in my youth. After the fleet-in-exile was broken at Porto Principe, there weren't many friendly ports for an ex-royalist officer with no money and the stench of defeat clinging to his uniform. Losing myself with the nomads of the sea was a blessed relief. It's a simple way of life, following schools of fish and hunting for the day without a thought for tomorrow. You can forget yourself and relinquish your mortal cares.'

She recognized the almost wistful tone in the old man's voice. Right now escaping her past seemed a good idea, to Charlotte. Two sailors arrived to help her and the commodore suit up. The diving suits were made of a soft brown canvas that felt as if someone had spent many long nights oiling them, their rebreather tanks and helmets bronzed metal cast with a variety of seashell and ocean creature mouldings. As the helmet was locked down onto her shoulders, she was sealed in; the last owner's scent blended with a faint mustiness at the suit being kept too long racked. One of the sailors attached a thin cable between Charlotte and the commodore's belt and his voice echoed in her helmet.

'Keep the voice line attached, lass, unless there's an emergency and we have to break away from each other.'

'What qualifies as an emergency?'

'If it happens, you'll know it.'

After Charlotte had been given the thumbs up by the crewmen checking her suit, the commodore removed a cigar box-sized metal device from the racks and clipped it onto the front of her suit, pulling a rubber cable out from the device and connecting it to her helmet. She noticed that the commodore had a similar arrangement on his own diving suit. 'The voice line allows us to speak direct-like to each other without anyone earwigging in on our conversation. This box, though, will allow you to hear what the seanore are saying in the water and project your voice back out. When you talk, hold your hand over your heart, so people know it's your voice coming over the phones. You forget to do that, the seanore will think you're lying or trying to hide something. It shows your hand is away from your knife and the trigger of a shock-spear.'

'Seanores can speak our language?'

'Those from the race of man among the nomads can; the others, when it suits. Anything you hear that sounds like words, the nomads call babble-tongue. If you hear singing over your box, that's what they call far-voice. Sounds produced by pushing an air stream in different directions within their respiratory track. I can understand much of it, but I sound like a blessed whistling kettle when I try to speak it. If you hear far-voice, they're calling to each other over a grand old distance.'

He handed Charlotte a slightly shorter version of his own shock-spear while the crewmen poked and probed her diving suit to check she was airtight and shipshape. The weapon had a half moon curl of a trigger, enough space for even her gloved hand to slip around it. 'I've never used one of these before.'

'Act as if you have and you won't have to. That rebreather pack of yours is seanore, handed down the generations. Remember this, treat it as if it's the most valuable thing you own, and that the only way someone should get you out of it is to cut your corpse off it.'

Charlotte nodded, ignoring the twinge of guilt stabbing at her. The life he was describing sounded uncomfortably similar to gypsy society. Proud and independent and distrustful of outsiders, wild and free. And one she had already forsaken for the comforts of the capital. The Eye of Fate throbbed between her breasts, reminding her that it had prior owners. *Not my first theft. Not my last.*

Following Commodore Black's lead, Charlotte slipped into the airlock pool in the middle of the floor. Once inside, she watched the iron door closing over her head, before a similar one opened by her feet. The commodore checked the buoyancy adjuster on her belt and they exited together, accompanied by a fizzing along the sides of their rebreather packs. Whatever alchemy the device's innards was working, separating oxygen from the surrounding water, it seemed to activate on contact with the ocean.

If the slope of rock the *Purity Queen* was drifting over was a hill, the plain below them lay covered by an underwater forest, fronds of red, orange and green kelp climbing as high as twenty feet amidst clumps of hydrophyic plants attached to flotation sacs, coral reefs snaking through it all like veins. Only shoals of orange fish darting above the wavering forest indicated that the vista was submerged, not a scene from the valleys of home. The two of them swam over the forest, slanting rays of light from the surface illuminating the brass of their tanks. To Charlotte, connected to the commodore by the umbilical-like cord of the voice line, this felt like flying, moving solely through the gentle motion of the rubber flippers on her feet. Curious fish wheeled in to watch her before vanishing as her hand reached out towards them. The water was warm too. A reminder that the magma of the Fire Sea wasn't so far off to the north. Before long, the slope where the double-hulled catamaran-shaped silhouette of the *Purity Queen* was floating disappeared out of sight, and only the submerged forest was left stretching out in all directions.

It almost seemed a sacrilege to break the spell of the place by speaking, but Charlotte, spooked by the alien immensity of the scenery, felt a need to fill the silence. 'How do you know the seanore are close?'

'Look down there, lass . . .'

She followed the thrust of his diving glove. Rising out of the kelp arched a dome composed of white bones lashed together by seaweed chord.

'It's the remains of a whale hunted down by a clan.'

'Was that the site of their camp?'

'The seanore leave them behind as a frame for coral to settle around; keeps the forests fresh and growing. Nothing is wasted down here. What can't be used is returned.'

Similar to the care Madam Leeda used to take removing all signs of their presence in the woods before moving her gypsy caravan on. Or had that been self-preservation to make sure she and Charlotte weren't followed? There was no mistaking the seanore camp when the two of them came across it, visible in the distance as a series of shadows swaying above the kelp heads. As they swam closer, Charlotte saw the shapes were a series of spherical nets anchored to the forest by lines of kelp rope, nets teeming with large silvery fish and minded by dolphins circling the catch as though they were shepherds' dogs. Beneath the nets the forest had been felled, the seabed anchoring a varied collection of structures that could best be described as air-filled tents, canvas bubbles tied together by ropes and webbing. In their lee were other structures set into the seabed. Not air-filled, but canvas stretched over frameworks that might have been made of bamboo-like material harvested from the underwater forest. Moving around the assorted structures were hundreds of swimmers, and from their shapes, Charlotte could see that the commodore's description of the sea nomads as a society as multiracial as Jackals' own was no exaggeration.

185

As well as human-shaped figures weighed down by helmets and rebreathers, there were figures that had to be related to gill-necks, although a lot less ferocious-looking than their images from the lewd works of popular fiction suggested. Swimming through their midst were some of the other races that the commodore had described back on board the *Purity Queen*. Sea lion-shaped creatures beating their way through the camp with a powerful mermaid-like tail and arms that seemed too thin to be holding the objects they carried. Heavy, clumsy things that resembled six-legged salamanders, their arms webbed with wing-like skins and working on repairing the fish nets with a surprising level of dexterity. Other beasts that might have been goblinized gill-necks, pointed snout, large eyes, hooked teeth and an oversized proboscis that covered the smooth hairless skin of their lips.

The pair didn't have to signal the nomad camp, their presence was noticed almost immediately, the tame fish-keeping dolphins arrowing in towards the two intruders. Followed by sudden flurries of activity inside the camp as they realized the intruders might be scouts from an approaching rival clan.

'Stay still now,' the commodore whispered to Charlotte, the hushed tones unnecessary since they were still connected by the voice line. Charlotte noticed that the commodore was already covering his heart with his right hand when he talked. 'Keep your hands away from your shock-spear when they approach.'

The dolphins approached, making loops around Charlotte, the speed of their movement pushing her down towards the kelp forest – her chest-mounted speaker box supplying a series of rapid clicking noises from the creatures. Others were approaching from the camp, seanore armed with shock-spears that looked identical to the weapons the commodore and Charlotte carried slung across their backs.

Charlotte's sound box picked up their voices passed up to her helmet. 'Pah, it is not the Clan Coudama, they are surface dwellers.'

'U-boat traders from the world above.'

'We do not trade. What belongs to the sea stays in the sea.'

'We are not from the Clan Coudama,' spoke the commodore, 'or any other clan. Nor do we come as traders. If you have not the eyes to recognize Jared Black then take me to Poerava.'

'Poerava no longer rules the Clan Raldama,' came the voice of one of the seanore.

'Is that so? Then we'll settle for whoever sits as chief of the clan.'

A song-like wailing came over the sound box and the commodore answered with a similar burst of sound.

'There are children who speak with a better accent,' said the gill-neck. 'You who claim to be seanore and issue commands as though you issue edicts.'

'I speak with my heart, clansman. Now, you just see before you an old white beard and a young girl. If your new chief scares easy enough to be shy of us, then just be saying it and we'll be on our way.'

'It's obvious you haven't been around the Clan Raldama for a long time, white-haired surface dweller. Come in – but let us see if you thank me for the invite later.'

Seanore hung in the water around them as Charlotte and the commodore made their way into a clearing inside the kelp forest. She noted that some of the tethered buildings had air inside, swelled out, as though the nomads had decided to stake a series of balloons in their midst. The buildings constructed on the seabed, though, were obviously for the nomads' gills-bearing members – white whalebone frames stretched over with elasticized fabric and shielded with

187

interlocking shells laid over the framework. The shells were a rainbow, mottled and ringed with dancing colours. As Charlotte looked closer, she saw they'd belonged to crustaceans, repurposed for the camp and hung as shields on the surface of the collapsible constructions.

A group of nomads emerged from one of these larger buildings – two gill-necks and one human swimmer in a suit similar to Charlotte and the commodore's, except that the newcomer had a mohican-like wedge of spiny bush attached to the back of her helmet's brass skull. A female face was visible under the clear crystal of the helmet. The first of the gill-necks was a large male, green-scaled-shoulders as broad as a weight-lifter's, his mail-like tunic clinging to an expansive, muscled chest. The other gill-neck was a female, her face hidden by a golden mask, a forehead covered by swirls of curling tentacles moulded into the metal for hair.

'*Them.* Well, this is starting out grand,' Charlotte heard the commodore whisper over the voice line. So, he recognized the clan's new leaders.

'I wondered if it was you,' said the old female, 'when they said a surface dweller was asking for Poerava.'

'Poerava passed seasons ago,' said the large male gill-neck. 'I lead the clan now.'

'And a tale in the telling that must be, Vane. You were a wild young buck in my day, always sailing close to being banished by Poerava.'

'She was old and tired even back then. Too confused to see what a liar and a dark-heart you were.'

'Who is this Vane?' whispered Charlotte over the voice line. 'He sounds like he hates you.'

'As he should,' replied the commodore. 'His father died out hunting with me. We were cut off and became prey ourselves when a pack of tiger crabs turned up.'

'Do not whisper to each other like thieves,' Vane's voice boomed over the speakers. 'You have come here to speak to the clan leader, you shall speak to me.'

'Hear him out,' urged the female gill-neck. 'He was of the clan once.'

'Thank you, Tera,' said the commodore. 'As surprised as I am to see Vane with the chieftain's trident, it surprises me not a jot to find you as the clan's wise-woman.'

'Wise enough to remember my predecessor's warnings about your honeyed tongue, Jared silver-beard.'

'I could've told you that,' said the human woman.

'Wasn't it you who said to me that our life underneath the waves was never fêted to be, Maeva? Too much air in my veins, you said.'

'Saying goodbye might have been an expected courtesy,' said Maeva. There was a resigned tone in the old woman's voice, as if she'd expected no better. 'It was I that fished you out of the broken hull of your ravaged u-boat. I that ministered you back to life. Did I not deserve better?'

'Always better than me, lass,' said the commodore.

'You owe her a life debt,' said Vane, the muscled arms of the leader bunching in anger. 'You owe my family one, also. How many others among the Clan Raldama?'

'I had trouble following in my wake,' said the commodore. 'I had to flee to Cassarabia. One of the wicked surface traders who'd come among us recognized me as a royalist rebel. If I had stayed, I would have an ocean full of life debts, and a corpse is only good for paying back carrion.'

The wise-woman, Tera, danced from side to side in the water. 'Do you not have trouble following you now, Jared silver-beard? I can scent it on you like blood leaking from your pores, calling every shark and tiger crab in the territory to us.'

189

'It's brewing up a storm, Tera. But I fear it's coming your way whether you heed my warnings or not.'

'Enough!' cried Vane, jabbing out with the clan leader's trident. 'Go now, back to your iron vessel, full of surface air and surface dwelling scum. I smell the gas from its engines fouling our forest's waters.'

The commodore shook his head. 'I claim the right of admittance to the clan as one who was once seanore, and protection for me and the girl.'

Maeva's voice spat over the speaker. 'Take your old carcass and your fancy piece's back to the surface. Your time among us ended long ago.'

'I claim the right of admittance,' insisted the commodore. He pointed at Tera. 'Is that within clan law?'

'It is.'

'Then I shall take my life debt from you,' said Vane. 'Your claim is accepted.'

'What does he mean?' Charlotte asked.

'A duel, lass,' the commodore said over the voice line. Then he switched to the public speaker. 'Name your champion.'

'I will not fight with a champion,' laughed Vane. 'And neither will you two. You shall *both* fight, you and your young surface dweller here.'

'This is between you and me, Vane. Leave the lass out of it.'

'Two seek admittance to the clan, two shall fight!'

'Just my old bones for the clan, then, Vane. Charlotte, make your way back to the *Purity Queen*.'

At the clan leader's gesture, the seanores' shock spears lowered, a circle of bristling violence being thrust towards the pair. 'The claim's validity has been accepted, you vile dark-heart. Both must fight, both must win.'

'Do I look like a seanore warrior to you?' protested Charlotte.

'No,' said Vane. 'You look like bait for the hunt. But then, death always did follow the silver-beard like a shadow. Today it shall be yours.'

Jethro Daunt groaned as the vision returned to his head, the sound of scraping ground bumping below him. He was lying on a makeshift stretcher, a thick sheet of canvas lashed between two iron pipes, the litter being dragged by Boxiron. They were part of a trudging line, prisoners from the convoy by the damp, bedraggled appearance of the sailors – fleet sea arm as well as merchant seamen. In front of the steamman was Barnabas Sadly, limping along on his cane and the State Protection Board agent, Dick Tull. The latter had his leg in a temporary splint and was hobbling too, a pair of invalids among many. The Jackelians carried a resigned air of defeat with them as palpable baggage. *But carried, where?* Hearing him moan, Boxiron turned around and Daunt noted the addition of a new metal device over the steamman's chest, hiding his rotating transaction-engine drum. It lent the steamman the bizarre appearance of a metal cleavage, all he needed was a dress and he could've been performing in a panto as an old widow.

'Have you been repairing yourself in the field, old steamer?'

'This further foul violation of my architecture,' said Boxiron, tapping the device's front plate with one of his hands and nearly spilling Daunt out of his stretcher, 'is our captors' idea of a leash for my race. It is an inhibitor for my boiler heart. I hardly have the strength to pull you along, let alone make a break for freedom.'

Daunt lifted up his arm and the steamman bent down to help put him up. 'No need, I can stand, I think.' He let the sudden sensation of dizziness pass, his nose filling with the lush, rich scent of wherever they had ended up. The line was

191

marching along a well-worn track, grasses as high as a man's knee off the path. Ten feet further on either side stood thick rain forests dripping after a recent rainfall, steaming mist rising among the clammy, tropical heat of the place. Eschewing the path for the grass, a gill-neck came along, his golden mask hooked up on either side by two rubber pipes feeding into a tank-like backpack. *A diving suit in reverse. But why? Wouldn't we be more secure as prisoners if we were held in cells in one of their cities under the waves, at a depth where any attempt to escape would mean drowning?*

'If you no longer wish your metal servant to drag your useless carcass along the ground, surface dweller, then march.' He thumped Daunt in the ribs with the butt of his weapon. Urged on by the guard, Daunt stumbled alongside Boxiron, the steamman supporting him with an iron arm, the stretcher left abandoned in the grass.

'Where are we?'

'An island, Jethro softbody. We were on an Advocacy transport submarine for a couple of days after we were taken prisoner. That places us in the heart of the gill-neck kingdom.'

'An area of the atlas left disappointingly vague by the Advocacy's refusal to allow foreign surface craft to traverse their territory, old steamer.'

'It is called Ko'marn, Mister Daunt,' called Sadly hobbling in front of the steamman. 'One of the gill-necks said I was welcome to the place when he pushed me off their u-boat's gangway.'

'Perhaps that's their word for hell,' Daunt mused. 'Offered by way of irony. After all, by the lights of their thinking, only the cursed and misbegotten snub the sea for dry land.'

'I'm wagering it ain't their word for hotel, amateur,' snarled Dick Tull, pulling his injured leg along. 'I've never seen a prisoner of war camp that I wanted to stay in.'

Daunt bit his tongue. He had a feeling there was more to this place than a camp for holding captured surface dwellers. 'What a pity. I was hoping we might get to see one of our captors' legendary crystal cities. If I recall correctly from the commodore's anecdotes, the gill-neck capital is called Lishtiken, and the few who have visited it speak of it as one of the wonders of the ocean.'

Daunt gazed at the gill-neck guards walking either side of the line of shuffling captives. The Advocacy soldiers were dripping from the heat as much as any among their prisoners of war. Their body language positively cried out with discomfort and displeasure at this duty. He noted the way their heads moved, jerking around. They were close enough to the race of man for him to be able to read them, and they betrayed their dislike for this realm with every gesture. How must the island appear to them? The claustrophobia of only being able to move in limited dimensions. No up, no down. The restrictiveness of this environment combined with the almost infinite expanse of the sky, sight-lines stretching to the horizon, rather than the restricted visibility underwater. *They don't like this*, he realized. *Bob my soul, but they don't like this at all. This is a hardship posting for them. Short duration and frequent rotations of duty to stop them developing, what shall we call it, land sickness, perhaps?* He murmured thoughtfully to himself. 'There once was a gill-neck from the sea, which on the land he had to be. When he took in the air he was sick, and he could only last out of water a bit, so home he swam in time for tea.'

Daunt patted his pockets and sighed in appreciation as he discovered his aniseed balls were still in his pocket. 'They didn't take them?'

'I told them it was your medicine,' said Boxiron. 'It didn't seem like a lie.' The steamman gloomily tapped his power

193

limiter. 'My might they had already tasted, however, and the fastblood devils were quick enough to steal that.'

'And my sleeve gun,' complained Sadly. 'The blighters had that away fast enough.'

'Ah well,' said Daunt. 'At least they left you your cane to march with.'

'Wouldn't get too far without it, Mister Daunt, my bad foot and me. Not sure how much longer I can keep up with this, truth to tell. March, march, march, all day. No water in this heat. You'd think the gill-necks would appreciate the wisdom of staying hydrated, says I.'

'Maybe they'll let you open up a food stall when we get to where we're going,' sneered Tull.

'Quieten your incessant ramblings, you diseased surface dweller vermin,' hissed one of the guards. He removed his mask for a couple of seconds, rubbing the chafing scales of his green skin, and spat out a stream of water at the inform-ant's feet. 'There is your water. Now keep moving, you shall stop for more of it later.'

The later in question became evident with the guard's sibi-lant laughter when the trail through the rainforest gave way to a stinking stretch of everglades. The water around their feet started out barely lapping around their shoe leather, but rapidly rose deeper, soaking their knees before stopping at their hips. Still the prisoners marched on, a gloomy silence fallen upon the exhausted sailors, throats dry and croaking. But however thirsty Daunt grew, he was never once tempted by the thick, badly reeking water of the everglades. Insects skimming across the surface in enough variety to have kept a Jackelian entomologist engaged for years, the majority of the bugs only too happy to add a faltering column of soft-skinned Jackelians to their diet. *Would that I had an entomologist's netted hat, gloves, and sealed linen suit.* Only

Boxiron was immune from these biting, annoying swarms; clouds of them bothersome enough that Daunt began to swat at his skin with every tear of rolling sweat, mistaking perspiration for bloodsucking needles.

After an hour of slogging through the glades, the trees fell away and an island of raised land appeared surrounded by tall reeds, a rough path sawn through the ground and paved by something like bamboo. The exhausted prisoners were herded up a ramp and onto the path, reeds eventually falling away to reveal a camp built across cleared land. Simple barracks of white bamboo-like material, a fence just shy of the height of a man's head. *Not much to stop a prisoner from escaping.* But then, the barricade wasn't the barrier. That would be surviving for long enough to escape off the island and then navigate across hundreds of nautical miles of an ocean that was the sole dominion of the gill-necks. Not totally unguarded though. Guard towers rose out of the fence every hundred yards or so, simple wooden platforms with roofs of thatched palm trees, the silhouettes of lounging guards and their long rifles. *A camp where the guards' rifles point out, not in. What, I wonder, is out there to engage their attention in such a manner?* On the far side of the camp stood a series of larger, more permanent-looking metal structures; a small forest of cranes rising beyond that. There was a distant hammering of steam engines carried by the weak febrile wind, the drumbeat of a slave galley for the emaciated figures of captives moving around the camp, pushing carts along rails or staggering under the weight of heavy hemp sacks. *Not a prisoner of war camp then, but a work camp. And these aren't mere make-work labours to busy minds and bodies so hard they can no longer think of escape, either. I detect the whiff of serious industry on the air. Interesting. A camp where the guards are as uncomfortable as the inmates, literally fish out*

195

of water. This has a purpose to it. I wonder what I would find inside those sacks the prisoners are lugging?

Turning left at the main gate of the camp, the columns of captives were marched towards a long shed-like structure, two bamboo doors swinging open. Inside was a wheezing machine that Daunt recognized from the Kingdom. A blood-code machine, the slowly rotating transaction-engine drums of its central control panel poorly oiled and squeaking in the humid atmosphere. The sailors in front of Daunt and his friends were led before the machine in turn, their arms pushed into a rubberised hollow, the grimace on their faces indicating the moment a needle was extended to sample their blood. For Boxiron, they didn't even need the machine, a flurry of activity among the gill-neck engineers administering the tests. One of them fluttered a white card with the unmistakable black silhouette of the steamman's unique form.

'This is bloody wrong,' said Dick Tull.

Daunt reached into his pocket and palmed an aniseed ball before popping it into his mouth, half-melted and sticky. 'I agree, good sergeant. The Advocacy shouldn't have access to such a machine, let alone our citizen records swirling about its memory.'

Our identity details should be kept jealously guarded by the civil service's bureaucrats back in the capital's engine rooms, not freely floating around an enemy power.

'This is much more than that crooked sod Walsingham and his cronies selling us out,' said Tull.

Daunt nodded. 'I rather fear it is.'

Extra guards arrived, along with a high-ranking officer, judging by the ornate gilding of his helmet. They cut Boxiron from the line, their raised rifles somewhat superfluous given the power-limiter they had fitted on the steamman's body. With Barnabas Sadly, Dick Tull and Daunt passed through the blood-code machine and their identities confirmed, the four of them were marched under guard out of the building and taken towards the more permanent set-up at the rear of the camp. Shoved rudely inside one of the mill-like structures, they were led through iron passages that could have passed as the interior of the *Purity Queen*, until they reached a chamber lined with empty windowless cells, unpadded bunks its only furniture. Rusting metal bars slid into the ceiling at the bidding of a gill-neck soldier standing at the end of the corridor. Daunt was shoved inside alongside the others. Then the bar sank deep into pits set into the floor as the guards departed.

'Lords-a'larkey, they know who we are, don't they?' groaned Sadly.

'It would seem we are now wanted in two states,' said Boxiron.

'Your corrupt friends on the State Protection Board are to be congratulated,' said Jethro to Dick. 'Fast work indeed, to uncover who we are and circulate our descriptions so widely and rapidly.' He placed a hand on Boxiron's shoulder. 'I rather fear it was your involvement, old steamer, which allowed the board to identify us. Your unique physiology featured rather prominently in the police files once upon a time.'

'Whereas Sergeant Tull and his little rodent stool pigeon's were rather easier to come by,' announced a voice.

Daunt looked around. A middle-aged woman and a nondescript looking man. *Ah, the man from outside Tock House. Walsingham, alias Mister Twist.*

'No salute for me, Sergeant?'

'Piss off, traitor,' growled Tull. 'How much are the gill-necks paying you to sell us out?'

'Let us say a comfortable accommodation has been reached,' smiled Walsingham. 'A little something for everyone involved, including my friend here, who—'

'—is Gemma Dark,' said Daunt. 'Otherwise known as the younger sister of Jared Black.'

She inclined her head in acknowledgement of the fact. 'Yes, I was told you used to be a Circlist priest. A clever fellow, full of tricks.'

'You share more than a passing resemblance. Chin, voice, physical mannerisms.'

She stroked the bars playfully. 'A clever man like you, you must already know why I'm here.'

'You were hunting us, obviously,' said Daunt, matter-of-factly. 'These two—' he indicated the State Protection Board agent and his informant, '—to ensure their silence. Myself and Boxiron to discover our involvement and the extent of our knowledge of your little royalist conspiracy. The commodore, because you hate him more than anyone else in the world, and Damson Shades, well, the young lady most of all. Because she has King Jude's sceptre.'

'Where is the girl?' Walsingham demanded. 'Where is my sceptre?'

'Probably out in the colonies by now,' shrugged Daunt. 'We split up. The commodore and Damson Shades sneaked a berth on a RAN airship across to Concorzia. We took the slow route by liner.'

Gemma Dark shook her head in disappointment. 'How easily the lies trip off your tongue. There is a missing u-boat from the convoy's logs, one that bears a suspicious resemblance to the lines of my brother's current craft.'

'Mere coincidence.'

'He's a slippery fish, my brother, an eel covered in grease. I've been trying to kill him for years, but he runs and hides so well. You know that Jared Black isn't his real name? He was born Samson Solomon Dark, a duke's blood in the cause he betrayed.'

'I know a little of his history,' said Daunt. 'Betrayal is rather strong a word. I think perhaps he just outgrew you and your royalist friends' need for revenge.'

'Outgrew!' the woman shrieked. 'This is who we *are*. Our history – our land, everything stolen from us by Parliament's thieving shopkeepers. The cause is not a waistcoat you grow too fat for and discard. He ran when he should have fought. A coward and a traitor.'

'But not always,' said Daunt. 'Sometimes he fought when he should've run. Like the time when he had your son released from Bonegate jail. A convicted river slaver offered parole in return for acting as a pilot, and that was a voyage he didn't return from.'

'You snivelling pious bastard,' she screamed. 'You dare call him a slaver? Treat us like outlaws and how do you—?'

'Hold your tongue,' advised Walsingham. 'The churchman is manipulating you. He wants to use your anger to goad you into filling in the copious gaps in his knowledge.'

Daunt shrugged behind the bars. 'I should take that as a compliment coming from you, Mister Walsingham, alias Captain Twist. Who would've imagined, such a high-ranking secret policeman assuming the mantle of a royalist bogeyman? What complicated webs we do weave.'

'It's not a compliment,' spat Dick Tull angrily gripping the bars between his hands. 'A traitor to all he believes in. It's a sodding insult.'

'That rather depends on what he believed in to start with. A little like the good commander of our convoy, Vice-admiral Cockburn. I believe he was a friend of yours?'

Tull sank wearily onto one of the bunks. 'What are you talking about, amateur?'

'You should listen to your friend, sergeant,' said Walsingham. 'He's a clever man indeed. Dangerously clever, in fact.'

'You want him, then?' asked the commodore's sister.

'A defrocked parson of the Circlist church?' Walsingham mused. 'Such an obtuse organization with no real power in the Kingdom. When you believe in nothing, you believe in anything. Still, waste not, want not. Take him out of the cells. We shall kill two birds with one stone.'

She indicated Dick Tull and Sadly. 'These two?'

'A blunt knife and his diseased lapdog. I think not. Cannon fodder. They can die in the camp.'

Tull lunged through the bars, but Walsingham stepped back.

'I'm still sharp enough to snap your neck, Walsingham.'

'You *have* surprised me, sergeant. The duties I set you were specifically allocated on the basis of your complete lack of utility and possession of the scruples of a sewer rat. In the end, you've proved just good enough at your job to get yourself killed. It won't be fast for you, but I guarantee you will make yourself useful before you waste away. Give him a beating for his insolence. Remind him of the proper forms that should be observed between master and servant.'

As the wall of bars retracted up into the ceiling, Boxiron moved in front of Daunt as the gill-neck soldiers swarmed in. 'Do not touch him!'

Gemma Dark laughed as the guards easily restrained the steamman while others laid into Dick Tull. 'You're just strong enough to slave for us in the camp, old steamer, but your days of cracking skulls are over.'

Daunt leant in to the steamman and whispered words of reassurance before the gill-necks seized his arms and dragged him out.

'Where are you taking him?' Boxiron demanded.

'I need to gauge just how clever your ex-parson actually is,' Walsingham said.

'I imagine the process will be quite painful,' sighed Daunt as he was bundled out.

Walsingham followed with the commodore's sister fast behind him. 'Torture usually is.'

CHAPTER NINE

Voices were crackling so rapidly from Charlotte's speaker box that the device was having problems interpreting the cacophony of shouts and calls; the box collapsing into an intermittent rack-rack-rack noise as it was overwhelmed by the seanores' cries. There was no point trying to work out which of the nomads was signalling, the crowd encircling tall seabed impaled rotor-spears, seanores beating their chests as they hollered and whooped. Their spears were arranged in a field-sized semicircle along the rocky seafloor, the sketched out arena bounded by the chasm of a supposedly bottomless trench. If the proximity of the trench was meant to add an additional frisson of danger to their trial of admittance into the seanore's ranks, then Charlotte considered the choice of venue largely superfluous. It wasn't as if she was going to last longer than a couple of minutes against a mass of deadly muscle such as the clan's chieftain, Vane.

'This stands against all the blessed forms,' the commodore protested, close enough to sound loud and clear over the jeering assembly. 'It's old Blacky who should be fighting you first.'

The clan leader shook his head, 'It was you that sought admittance, silver-beard, not I that offered it. And I say your surface dwelling fancy piece shall fight me first.' He glanced meaningfully towards Charlotte, then back at the commodore. 'You shall know loss before I meet you in the arena.'

'Ah, Vane. I've known loss since I left the clan. I lost the woman who would have been my wife and seen my own daughter perish. I've lost friends by the dozen and my mortal pride by the pound as I've scurried and run from my enemies. But this lass is not my blood, there is no need for you to involve her in our vendetta.'

'Then you will not mind greatly when I slice her apart in front of you before tossing her carcass down into the darkness.'

'The forms do not require that this be a death match,' said Tera, the clan's wise woman bobbing behind the chieftain.

'Nor do they forbid it!' He beckoned to Maeva and the old woman came forward bearing a case embedded with polished crab shells. Opening it, she revealed two short spears topped by jagged blades of diamond.

'No rotor-spears in this trial,' Vane said to Charlotte. 'You must be close enough to look into my eyes when you come at me. To seek admittance to the clan you must understand us, know your blood and ours.'

No rotor-spears, but Charlotte had something else. She touched her diving suit below her neck, the Eye of Fate nestled reassuringly beneath the thick canvas. *Will the amulet work underwater, beneath the suit? If I can throw him off for a second, paralyse him, then maybe I can live through this after all?*

'I've known more than a few bastards in my time,' said Charlotte. 'I don't need to be close enough to you, honey, to smell your stink.'

He laughed. 'A little spirit from you at last. I may hope for a show after all.'

They moved through a gap in the weapons and inside the semicircle of spears.

Vane traced a line in front of the rotor-spears. 'Stay inside this space during the trial of admittance. Pass no further than fifty feet above the seabed. Flee our circle before the trial ends and we will slaughter you.'

The commodore moved in to disconnect their voice line, whispering over the private line as he did. 'Vane will toy with you first, lass. He wants to draw the wicked game out to make me squirm and please the clan. Before he finishes you, he'll swim behind and sever your rebreather's air hose. Wait for that moment and jab behind. Go for his neck. His scales are weakest there, for flexibility. Until then, just play the damsel in distress.'

Play? This is one act I won't have to study for. 'All right.' Charlotte was trying to fight down the rising feeling of panic, not helped by the cold currents from the trench playing across her diving suit. *As cold as hell*, a voice inside her whispered. Somehow, she knew that this was the reason they were fighting here. The nomads believed that the trench was the opening to the underworld.

Someone in the ring of surrounding seanore – it might have been Tera – held a crystal aloft on the end of a staff, triggering a short sunburst from the gem. Vane didn't need any further urging; the chieftain launched himself above her head, short powerful thrusts of his legs powering him through the water. It was all Charlotte could do to spin around trying to fix his continually shifting position. If the clan leader had been minded to, he could have torn the spine of her suit open on the way past. *Bastard. He's playing with me.* The roar of the crowd transmitted to her speaker box diminished to a distant surf as she raised the short glittering head of her spear against Vane – but the nomad wasn't where she thought he would be. *Where?*

'Over here,' hissed Vane, a shadow moving off her side. 'Has the silver-beard not trained you better than this? Can't you even swim, surface dweller?'

She contorted around and jabbed out, but the chieftain was moving too fast, a sinuous twisting shape beating an undulating passage through the waves as though he was a merman.

'What would you do among the seanore, what good would you be?' he laughed. 'I would not trust you to clean the seaweed off our nets.'

Vane darted in and stabbed her in the right thigh, a quick piercing pain burning her muscles. *So fast.* She yelled in anger and tried to thrust back, but he was already gone, an underwater whiplash retreating. The water around her leg was misting with blood, her blood. *I don't have that much to spare to begin with.* At this rate she wasn't going to last until Vane came at her from behind to sever her rebreather's air pipes. Charlotte willed the Eye of Fate into life, but instead of the tug of power that usually filled her when the jewel leaked its hypnotic radiation, her head flared with an aching light. A panicked breath as she mistook this new spinning lance of pain for the ground falling away under her feet.

'Foolish girl,' something whispered. 'Duelling with a lowly nomad of the depths.' The words were coming out of Charlotte's lips, but not at the bidding of her mind!

Not my voice! That's—

'Elizica. I told you, girl-child, you walk in my footsteps.'

Vane slashed at Charlotte's arm with the jagged gem-bladed shaft, but she had already turned and kicked herself away. A slight, spare movement, but the inch of distance between Charlotte and the spear might as well have been a mile. The clan leader hissed in frustration as he realized she had avoided his blow.

'And now, my footsteps walk in you,' whispered Elizica.

'What are you babbling about, surface dweller?' snarled Vane.

'That a clan chief should be more careful who he chooses to fight.'

The gem nestled between Charlotte's breasts weighed down as heavy as a block of lead, absorbing all of her mass, the rest of her left so light, buoyant and quicksilver fast. The jewel's energies were not entering Vane, casting a glamour over him. They were entering Charlotte, binding her, changing her. *What is this?*

'The Eye of Fate has had many owners over the ages. Even I was not the first of them, although I had a hand in refashioning the eye's original purpose. I wore it once, my soul imprinted across its angles when I walked where you walked,' said Elizica.

Charlotte had worn the Eye of Fate for so long, how had she failed to see? All these years, had she been using the amulet or had the jewel been using her? Preparing Charlotte until the shock of her confrontation in the pie shop reawakened the gem's true purpose.

As Charlotte spoke a dead queen's words, her left hand fiddled with the controls on the chest-mounted speaker box, her right turning the spear, tracing a deadly pattern through the water. Slowly, the constant roar of the crowd died away to be replaced by a different sound . . . a low-pitched whistling rising and falling. The modulation of the box was changing with the sinuous movement of Vane circling Charlotte, the clan leader trying to unsettle her into dizziness. *You've changed the range and frequency of the box. I can track him!*

'That's all sound is underwater . . . sonar.'

'The sounds of your death scream!' cried Vane, arrowing in with his spear to impale Charlotte. She bent herself into a ball, before unfolding on the charging clan leader's flank, cutting out with her spear's blade like a sword. Vane connected with its lethal edge along his ribs, an explosion of blood clouding above the seabed.

'You bleed red blood, gill-neck, just the same as me. Why is that, I wonder?'

Vane moaned, clutching his side and no doubt re-evaluating his options now that Charlotte was proving to be an opponent worthy of the challenge.

'I think it's because your ancestors were outcasts who slunk into the sea because they were too lazy to survive on the surface. They were sitting in a bath for weeks and discovered they enjoyed it too much to ever go back to the hunt. And look at you, the mighty Vane, unable even to defeat the young fancy-piece of the man that got your father killed,' laughed Charlotte. 'I can taste your blood in the water, Vane, and it runs true. Your father was probably sitting on his fat arse when the tiger crabs turned up for him.'

Vane yelled in fury, closing with her. Rather than avoiding him, Charlotte stepped in, her body matching his in a supple grip of angles and joint-locks, twisting him about, stealing his momentum, thieving his considerable strength. There was a groan as Vane hit the rocky seabed, a shower of sand rising up from the slam. Charlotte had him pinned beneath her boot, the blade of her spear pushed a fraction of an inch underneath the green scales of his bare neck, ready to be hammered through his thyroid cartilage if he so much as quivered.

'The silver-beard tricked me,' moaned Vane. 'You're not what you appear to be.'

'Which of us is, leader of the Clan Raldama?' Her fingers fumbled with the speaker box, adjusting it back to its normal

207

range and she called out. 'Do I hold his life before my blade?'

Cries of confirmation returned from the seanore, uncertain at first, then louder and clearer as the magnitude of the turnaround in the arena became apparent to the clan.

'Finish me,' demanded Vane.

'But I am not finished with you,' said Charlotte. 'I have need of you.' She pushed her palm out. 'I have need of you all!'

Tera had entered the arena through the space in the fence of rotor-spears, the wise woman swimming in above the pinned leader and the challenge's victor. 'Who are you, creature? What is your true name?'

'Would you know me better if I carried a silver trident down from the surface? Would you know me better if I entered the ocean from a beach, two lions walking by my side? Lions that swam alongside me?'

Tera fell back, shocked.

Charlotte nodded. 'It is good that you still sing the songs from the time before the sides of the sea froze. I am returned.'

'What else, what else has returned?'

'You know the prophecy of the shadowed sea.'

Tera cowered above the rocks. 'A thief shall walk among us. A thief to fight the greater thieves, the thieves of life!'

Dick groaned as the two guards dragged his beaten body out into the light, throwing him onto the ground in front of Boxiron and Sadly. The two of them were helping him out of the dirt when the silhouette of a gill-neck loomed in front of Dick's vision, light from the high, hot sun glinting off his metallic vest. Dick didn't need to note the creature's finery, his jewelled insect swatter or the entourage hanging back from him. The swagger of the gill-neck was easy to read. *Another bloody officer.*

'You have missed my welcoming speech to the other surface dwellers,' said the gill-neck officer, as if the fact of their imprisonment in the camp cells had been an act of provocation on their part. 'I am On'esse, the camp commandant. I only ask two things of my prisoners. First, you do what any gill-neck orders you to do. Second, you work until you die. There are only two punishments for breaking these rules. One is death. The other will make you wish for it.'

'Begging your pardon, sir,' said Sadly. 'But what is this work, I ask?'

'A pertinent question,' said the gill-neck. He moved forward and kicked the cane out of Sadly's hand, sending him falling to the floor; then he lashed into the informant's stomach with his boot, Sadly rolling away in agony. 'But I am not here to answer your questions. Anything you need to know, you diseased surface-dwelling scum, you will be told when we require it. Anything else, you can beg or steal from the other inmates here.' He clicked his fingers and a prisoner ran forward, her tattered uniform laden down with a silver tank. She hosed the officer with a thin mist of water and his face bobbed in pleasure as he absorbed the moisture. 'Barely tolerable, much like life here. I loathe this place as all my people do. But I am a notorious sadist and I find its discomforts counterbalanced by the opportunities to inflict suffering on your outcast hides. To serve me is life, to fail to serve me is to fail to live.' He paused, as if inviting comment, but none of the three of them were foolish enough to rise to the bait this time.

'Better. You seem to have come to the attention of our royalist allies. It is not good to draw attention to yourself here. I have you marked as troublemakers.' He examined the three of them as he swaggered past. He prodded Boxiron with his jewelled insect swatter. 'Two years.' Then Dick. 'Fourteen

209

months.' Then Sadly, still struggling up on his cane from the dirt. 'Six months for the runt.'

'Our sentences?' Dick queried.

The gill-neck commandant swivelled and punched Dick in the gut, doubling him up, and then pushed him down into the dirt. 'A slow learner and insolent with it. That is how long I expect you to last here. Your rations are not what anyone would call generous, but I do have to account for them in my supply plans somehow.' He knelt down next to Dick and hissed in his ear low enough that only Dick could hear. 'Do you like this as much as I do? I have more to give you than you can take, Fourteen Months.' Without a backward glance, the camp commandant and his retinue moved off, a human prisoner on either side spraying the officer with moisture.

'Why did you goad him?' Boxiron asked. 'A broken body will not help you to survive here.'

'Shit like that I take from the State Protection Board,' said Dick. 'Damned if I'll take it from a sodding gill-neck.'

'Your soul has pride,' said Boxiron. 'I used to have a measure of that myself.'

'What happened to it?'

'I believe it leaked away from this clumsy body I'm trapped in. I used to have raw strength too, but the gill-necks have sapped even that from me. What good am I now?'

'Alive as a cripple is better than dead, as my ma used to say,' said Sadly.

The light behind the steamman's vision plate pulsed with what might have been dejection. 'You confuse existence with living.'

'Pragmatists often do,' said Dick. His eyes glanced around the prisoners shuffling about the camp, the clothes of most the captives hanging as tattered rags. No prison uniforms.

They would rot away in the heat and the damp. The prisoners wore what they had, until they didn't; the state of decomposition in their clothes like counting the rings on a felled tree. *And this place looks to be full of sodding pragmatists.*

There was a hideous wailing from deep inside the gill-necks' processing complex.

'Oh, Lore,' said Sadly. 'What was that?'

'The sounds of torture,' said Boxiron. 'The sounds of Jethro softbody.'

'What did the amateur say to you, back in the cell before they dragged him off?' Dick asked.

'That to the fish about to bite a hook, its bait looks a lot like supper.'

Dick listened to the piercing yells sounding again. *But who is bloody eating who?* If this was some sort of plan by the ex-parson, then it had gone badly wrong.

Gemma Dark watched Jethro Daunt's twitching body strapped seated inside the machine, a dozen crystal rings circling the man and exchanging waves of ugly green energy between each hoop, lending the ex-parson's semiconscious form the distorted appearance of being viewed through a heat haze. The screaming had stopped ten minutes ago. Daunt had lasted a little longer inside the lashing energies than most before he surrendered to the inevitable, but not much. Not as long as Gemma had anticipated. Weren't Circlist priests meant to have minds of steel? The teachings of their much vaunted synthetic morality giving them an almost supernatural ability to stare into the souls of their parishioners. There hadn't been many priests among the royalists in the fleet-in-exile, not when the rebels' work was privateering and whatever it took to survive. *Circlist priests. Milksops and faint hearts.* They didn't have the guts to survive in the royalists' cruelly altered realm, a world where

211

the rightful heirs of the Kingdom had seen their birthright stolen by thieves and murderers. Forced into a game of hit and run for weary centuries, the royalist hegemony bleeding away, until they finally devolved into a tattered ragbag collection of pirates and slavers, antique u-boats and noble titles that weren't worth the ink on the ancient velum of their charters.

The machine the ex-parson was confined in was connected by twisting root-like crystal cables, winding organically around each other, until they linked up with a similar machine visible behind the first. For a moment, Gemma Dark was glad that the climbing waves of energy were hiding the shape of the form inside the second machine. Her luck, her famous luck. Allies at last to turn around the declining fortunes of cause that had so nearly been lost. *And if this is the price, then it is a small thing indeed.*

'Do you have his memories?' asked Walsingham from behind Gemma.

A voice answered from within the burning cage of the second machine. 'I do.'

'Solomon Samson Dark,' snarled Gemma, surprising herself by the loathing engendered simply speaking the traitor's name. Her cursed *brother*. 'Also known as Jared Black. Where is the dog and does he have my sceptre?'

'The sceptre is still in his possession, along with the girl thief, Charlotte Shades. They were on board the Jackelian submersible, the *Purity Queen*, until the Kingdom's convoy was attacked. Jethro Daunt does not know their location after that point in time.'

'I knew it,' laughed Gemma in triumph. 'But the sea won't swallow you this time, my treacherous jigger of a brother. Not with the entire gill-neck navy at my disposal.'

'His submarine has a stealth hull designed to disperse sonar waves,' warned the shadow inside the second machine.

'Then it is time we committed some of *our* ships to the hunt. Rest,' Walsingham commanded the thing inside the device. 'Give the ex-parson's memories time to settle into you. Meanwhile, we shall discover if the commodore's rudimentary submersible also has a way of disguising its mass from our sensors.'

There was a hideous screeching noise from the cage, like a fox baying, the talons of a scaled hand reaching out towards the semiconscious form of Jethro Daunt. *No, you couldn't always choose your allies.*

Walsingham listened to the screeching, a frown crossing his face. 'Speak only in Jackelian from now on. Use your new memories.'

The thing inside the device obeyed. 'The priest-man can sense our presence. He realized that the vice-admiral on the convoy was one of the Mass.'

'What is it that Daunt can detect?' Walsingham snapped, looking as troubled as Gemma had ever seen him.

'It is what he cannot. There are signs of the body, subtle cues that he could not detect when he was standing close to the vice-admiral. The Circlist church trained him in this art. Their absence gives us away.'

'That is not a problem,' said Walsingham. 'Now that we know about his profession's skill, we can focus our attention on any priests we encounter and fill in the signals they are expecting.'

The baying sounded again, louder and more insistent.

'He is not yours to consume,' Walsingham commanded angrily. 'We must keep Jethro Daunt alive in the camp for a little while longer. You may need his mind and his memories again.'

'Not for too long,' said Gemma. 'Not if events go as they should.'

'Hope for the best, plan for the worst,' said Walsingham.

They were meant to be words of reassurance, but as Gemma considered where they had probably been dredged from, her blood ran cold. *The Mass must feed.*

If there was ever a reassuring face to wake up to from the burning clasp of feverish unconsciousness, then Boxiron's silvery vision plate was hard to trump. Less so, the miserly pinched expression of Dick Tull. With one arm apiece, the two of them hauled Daunt upright. 'How do you feel, Jethro softbody?'

'Drained, quite literally.'

'A day,' said Tull. 'That's how long we were taught by the board to hold out under interrogation. Long enough for your side to realize you've been taken and compromised. Any longer and you're broken beyond use anyway, if your captors are serious about it.'

'They were serious, but it wasn't that kind of interrogation.'

Dick Tull lifted the ex-parson's arm, no doubt counting his fingernails. 'What kind was it?'

'They have a machine that rips out your memories, that allows them to crawl inside your mind.' Daunt glanced around. He was in one of the prison camp's barrack buildings, sitting on a crude bunk lashed together out of bamboo poles.

Sadly was on the bunk opposite, resting his chin on the top of his cane. He had kicked one of his shoes off, his clubfoot swollen larger than the shoe leather in the close heat. 'That sounds right effective, Mister Daunt.'

'Surprisingly so.' *Although not quite as effective as they think.*

'What were they after?'

'They want King Jude's sceptre back. And the commodore's

214

sister would like her brother's head on a platter for betraying the royalists, not to mention getting her son killed. They also wanted to know all about my life.'

Tull grunted. 'Of course, you're so interesting.'

Daunt smiled. 'Again, surprisingly so, but they forgot one thing.'

'What is that, amateur?'

'There is an old adage of the church. Well, actually something of a warning. Be careful when staring into the darkness, for the darkness also stares into you. What they have forgotten is that oft times, the converse can also be true.'

'What have you found out, you devious fastblood?' asked Boxiron.

Daunt raised his hand. 'Have you spoken to the other prisoners about the camp and why we're here?'

'We are to start work later today,' said Boxiron. 'The camp's task is to harvest a purple fruit from the jungle that the Advocacy calls gillwort. The juice is used to help suppress a common sickness among the gill-necks . . . hyperplasia. The disease attacks their respiratory system, eventually causing death by suffocation.'

'And let me guess, our new island home is the only place where this cure grows.'

'Correct.'

'The guards need us here,' said Tull. 'They can't stay out of the sea for more than a couple of weeks at a time without doing their nut in.'

'The exception being the camp commandant, On'esse,' said Boxiron. 'It is said that he never takes any leave.'

'And he's as barmy as a bucket full of badgers for it,' said Dick. 'His guards are terrified of him, let alone the prisoners.'

'Sometimes the job chooses the man,' said Daunt. 'Or should that be evolutionary offshoot of man? No matter, I am sure the beatings will continue until morale improves. There is a graveyard inside the camp?'

Boxiron raised a heavy hand towards one of the walls. 'A sizeable one in the Northeast corner. Dysentery, malnutrition and overwork are to be our bedfellows.'

'I rather think rust, in your case.' Daunt stood up. 'I suspect there hasn't been a churchman here for years, even a defrocked and sadly wayward one such as myself. Time to pay my respects to the departed.'

'You'll be joining their ranks sharpish if you're not here when the next work party is due to leave,' warned Dick.

'I'm sure there'll be time aplenty to discover my humanity in simple labour.' Daunt remembered the guard towers along the walls, the rifles and focus behind them directed outwards. *A set time to go out implies a schedule. But not a timetable, methinks, for our convenience.*

It wasn't much to look at, the camp's graveyard. Not much to mark the passing of so many lives. Hundreds of mounds crowded in with single spikes of bamboo, ranks of them crudely carved with the name of the passed and the date of their removal from the camp's rolls. A few of the more recent graves had tiny scrolls of paper pushed into the bamboo's hollow centre. Daunt squatted down and removed a couple, reading the messages before folding them back into place. Simple memories and farewells from friends in the camp. Standing in the far corner were the oldest graves, their bamboo markers splintered and weathered to near destruction by the passage of time. If there had been paper farewells pushed inside these, they had crumbled into dust long ago; food and nesting material for the ants crawling over the dirt.

As Daunt had anticipated, there were noble titles carved on some of the oldest markers. *Only to be expected.* The royalist fleet-in-exile had been trying to survive in the gill-necks' realm, frictions were bound to erupt between the rebels and the Advocacy. It hadn't just been Parliament trying to call time on the glorious counter-revolution. Who were the others . . . adventurers and interlopers? The treasure hunters the commodore had spoken of back on the *Purity Queen*, driven by visions of gems as large as boulders? This was their final resting-place, then. There were no gill-necks buried here, but that didn't surprise Daunt. With the gill-necks' worldview, the Advocacy doubtless conducted ceremonies that saw their remains scattered into the sea. Returned to the watery universe from which they came.

Daunt pulled himself up and moved along the line of graves, tracing the oldest dates back to the more recent burials. From the graveyard he could see the corner of the camp behind the gill-necks' processing complex and beyond to the sea. There was no wall there. The camp ended in a steep cliff, jagged rocks – a sheer drop hundreds of feet to the ocean below. A constant lashing of waves on the rocks, neither the cliff nor the sea willing to compromise – the maelstrom below the result. Cranes on the cliff top were lowering barrels of gillwort juice towards the open hold of a gill-neck submersible freighter being tossed side to side by the wild sea. The processing centre looked to be a camp within a camp, only gill-necks permitted beyond the internal fence. *Too steep to climb, too far to dive without snapping a neck.* And even if you survived the trip down, Daunt had a sneaking suspicion escapees wouldn't care for what was swimming around those waters – not if the presence of the guard towers bespoke what he suspected. But then, these cliffs weren't the way Daunt was planning to leave – not if the more recent grave markers bore out his theory.

He allowed a smile to soften his face as he discovered one of the graves he had been expecting, quickly followed by a second among the more recent burials. He removed one of the markers to inspect the message.

'I so rather hoped I would be proved wrong this time,' he murmured to himself.

A crunching in the dirt made Daunt turn. Boxiron had come to stand by the ramshackle fence separating the graveyard's rise from the rest of the camp.

'What have you learned from the dead?' Boxiron called across to the ex-parson.

'That it is better to be among the living, old steamer.'

'It is time. Our work party has been called and is assembling by the gate.'

'Of course. One note of caution, old friend. The gill-neck soldiers escorting us out are not to stop us escaping, but rather for our protection.'

'You have been speaking with the other prisoners, Jethro softbody?'

'Not yet. What have they told you about our labours outside the camp?'

'Tiger crabs,' said Boxiron. 'The waters around here are infested with the creatures. They frequently crawl up from the shoreline into the everglades to hunt. It is why no one has ever escaped from the island to tell of this cursed place.'

'Land is only ever cursed if you are a gill-neck,' said Daunt. 'Have heart.'

The steamman clanged the device welded to his chest in frustration. 'I have not enough of it, my boiler bled dry by this foul limiter. How much more reduced beyond my life as a steamman knight does the great pattern intend to see me degraded? For all the gross inferiority of my human-milled monstrosity of a body, I still had raw power . . . I could fight in top gear! Look at me now. I am no stronger than that wretch Barnabas Sadly. If only my ancestors had not forsaken me, I would call upon the Loa to give me the strength to rip this evil contraption out of my chest plate.'

'We'll find a way yet.'

'I should be able to protect you. That I cannot is beyond shameful. Is that not why our association has proved so successful? You supply the intellect and I supply the muscle.'

'Not just the muscle,' said Daunt. 'You have the boiler heart of a champion, and I have relied on the compass of your soul as much as I have relied on anything.'

The steamman did not seem convinced.

'Listen to me, old steamer, I need you yet. We have a battle or two left before us. I glimpsed such terrible things in the interrogation machine, in the dreams and shadows of their infernal contraption. We cannot afford to lose. We cannot afford to let ourselves die in captivity here.'

'What did you see, Jethro softbody?'

'I believe I saw the same things that have been haunting the dreams of the Sisters Lammeter, the same things that have been tormenting Charlotte Shades.'

'Vampires?'

Daunt joylessly shook his head. 'Not as the florid fictioneers of the penny-dreadfuls describe them. The true enemy is something else. We have to escape, old friend, we have to locate the commodore and carry the sceptre to safety.'

Boxiron indicated the sea beyond the cliff. 'Where will be safe? We are hunted in the Kingdom of Jackals, my people in the Steamman Free State will not help me. Where can we go in this world that will be safe?'

'I think there might be a place, and the person who can help us is closer than you think.'

'Is this another ploy to engage my interest?'

'No ploy, old friend.' *But bob my soul, how I wish this all was just an entertainment for your distraction.*

I'll never complain again about working for the bleeding board, Dick promised himself, swinging his machete against the clusters of leathery purple fruit hanging in beards around the tree. Every weary bite of his blade released an unpleasantly bitter smell, thin fronds attaching the fruit to the trunk seemingly as tough as steel.

Immediately below Dick, another prisoner was sawing off low-hanging fruit while Sadly, Boxiron and the ex-parson stood in the water and caught the gillworts, piling pear-shaped fruit in their shallow-bottomed boat. Not that the craft was there for their comfort and transportation through the humid flooded world of the everglades. No, it was only with them to keep the fruit from being soaked and spoiled. Shortly after a gillwort made contact with water it flowered as it bobbed on the surface, releasing a pungent smell to attract lizard-like fish to disperse its seeds; making quick work of the fruit, not to mention trying to take chunks out of any convict pickers' legs.

It was an old lag, Roald Morris, who had been assigned to convert the newcomers into an effective component of the camp's harvesting machine. Only too glad to stick to the sides of the boat and issue advice, he had at least warned them to enter the everglades only wearing their breeches. After all, their clothes would be reduced to rags soon enough and they didn't need any extra layers to perspire like pigs out here. Only Jethro Daunt refused the advice, the eccentric ex-parson pushing their harvesting raft in his full tweeds, sweat rolling off his forehead like a waterfall. A life where the State Protection Board paid a man to stand outside suspected treasonists' lodgings and watch through the long night hours seemed a world away from the fatiguing labours the Advocacy demanded of its captives.

Morris had lasted in the camp for six years. Supposedly a pearl diver who had lost his compass during a storm and ended up deep inside gill-neck waters, Dick could tell that the man's story sounded as flimsy to his ears as it no doubt had to the gill-necks who'd discovered Morris's little ship bobbing in their territory. He had admitted he had once served as a corporal in the regiments back home, and his presence here on the island probably meant he had been a deserter before drifting into smuggling and developing a taste for the gill-necks' crystals. But Morris had endured out here and had the knowledge of how to live in this hell, which made him someone worth listening to. Surviving had taken its cost, though: Morris's skin worn as brown and wrinkled as leather from working in the sun every day of the week. He had been fat once, too. Dick could see it in the way skin hung in jowls down the man's neck. If the sister he talked of so mournfully saw Morris now, she wouldn't recognize him. She'd walk right past without a hint of recognition. *At least he has someone who cares. Who will remember me? Who's there to miss Dick Tull when he's gone? Only Damson Pegler in her slum for the last week's rent he never paid.*

Circular platforms were built into the side of a handful of the semi-submerged forest's trees, gill-neck guards squatting languidly outside of the water with their rifles by their side. It didn't seem right, them with their affinity for the life aquatic staying out of the water while prisoners from the race of man waded through the everglades with slop up to their waists. But then, the brackish green subtropical wetland smelled bad enough to Dick halfway up a gillwort tree, and *he* wasn't even attempting to breathe the stuff.

'Let yourself hang back in the harness,' Morris called up.

'You'll take easier swings at the fruit. And cut down, not up, gillworts resist less that way.'

'You can always send the steamman up here,' Dick said.

'You'll all get a chance, that you will.'

'It is your race that is believed to possess simian ancestry,' said Boxiron, 'not mine.'

The steamman got his turn soon enough. Wading through the thick water up to his waist, Morris located a second tree with ripe fruit nearby. Boxiron was dispatched to climb up its trunk while Sadly and Daunt manoeuvred the harvesting raft halfway between the two trees, a couple of convicts sent across to catch the fruit the steamman began slicing off. Even with the strength-sapping device welded onto Boxiron's chest, the steamman made a faster job of harvesting gillworts than Dick, pneumatic servos beating his tired old muscles, cramping from sweat and heat. After half an hour more of swinging the machete, Dick's labours were interrupted by the sound of a small gas-driven engine. He glanced over his shoulder, sweat rolling off the tip of his itchy nose and falling towards the swampy surface below. It was On'esse. The camp commandant lounged under a shaded stretch of canvas in the middle of a shallow draft boat, a gill-neck guard at the front of the boat leaning into a tripod-mounted gun while another sat at the back, directing the small motor's rudder and steering its passage through the everglade forest.

'Work, you surface-dwelling scum,' the commandant called from his shade. 'We are two tonnes behind quota for my next shipment. Fall behind, and I'll take every tenth man from this gang of slackers and peel your backs with my whip.'

If there was any sign of irony on the part of the gill-neck commander, urging them to labour harder from the comfort of his personal launch, the old sod was hiding it well.

A minute after his boat passed, zigzagging its way through

the trees, panicked shouts began to sound from the workers in the water behind Dick, yells growing more urgent as the convicts scattered, some wading though the waters towards the guards' platform, others heading for the harvesting rafts and the trees. Down below, Morris was shinning up the gill-wort tree's trunk, throwing a harvesting strap around the tree as he climbed.

'Bloody On'esse,' snarled Morris as he stopped under Dick's position, five foot up from the water. 'He knows the noise of his boat's engine sounds like their challenge call.'

Dick looked down at the skeletal prisoner. 'Whose?'

'*Theirs!*' The convict pointed towards thin bone-like wands cutting though the water with the deadly intent of sharks' fins. 'Snorkel spiders. Get out the water, all of you!' he yelled down at the prisoners below.

Sodding hell. Sadly and Daunt and the two sailors below were casting around, trying to locate the cause of the commotion and work out their response. *Too slow.* The harvesting party behind – other sailors captured from the convoy – screamed out as bony snorkels lifted out of the everglades to reveal nests of mandibles stabbing in front of evil blanched skulls. Seconds later the human prey collapsed into the water under the leaping weight of these living thrashing machines. Now the newcomers knew what to do! Yelling in terror, prisoners desperately waded for safety, heading for the guard platforms, trees and the harvesting rafts. Underneath Dick, one of the sailors was trying to climb their tree trunk, but soaked and panicked and lacking climbing strap and hooks, he was barely able to scale a couple of inches above the waterline.

'My hand!' shouted Morris, reaching down, but the gap between him and the other prisoner was too wide. A frenzied storm of clicking mandibles lashed out, impaling the man in the spine and pulling him back screaming. Vanishing under the water, he left an outrush of bubbles and a slowly growing slick of blood as the only trace of his presence.

The other sailor in their party had dragged himself aboard the harvesting raft and was trying to pull Daunt out of the water. Behind the ex-parson, Sadly was wading towards the raft, using his cane like a punt to speed his limping passage forward. A bone-white snorkel was arrowing in on the informant and Dick could see the inevitable outcome of their relative speeds. Sadly would be snapped up before he got to the protection of the raft. As it closed on the informant, the creature's bony skull began to surface, thrashing mandibles extending for the man. Dick hefted the machete he had been using and hurled it with all his strength. It windmilled around, sailing down, impaling itself in the back of the snorkel spider. *Not enough.* The snorkel spider slowed slightly, the thrashing of its mandibles growing ever more frenzied, leaping towards Sadly as the informant reached a hand's gap from the raft. Both the sailor and Daunt were straining back out to the surface to catch Sadly, but he turned and dived under the water. *He wasn't pulled, he went under on purpose!* Landing where Sadly had just been standing, the monstrous thing disappeared, the water churning. Then its snorkel bone flashed up and down. More thrashing, and Sadly exploded out of the murky liquid, one hand on his cane as he pushed it into the dying, jolting creature in front of him. He was using his cane as a lance, manoeuvring it between the bony plates of his attacker and ramming it into the soft vulnerable flesh. Pulling out the cane as though Sadly was a duellist withdrawing a foil from a skewered opponent, he flopped around and caught the others' hands, Daunt and the sailor hauling his soaked, bloody form into the raft.

'Sharply done,' whispered Dick in surprise. *I guess there's a survivor in everyone, if you just prod 'em hard enough.*

From the Deep of the Dark

'Too much blood in the water,' moaned Morris.

At least the pool of blood underneath them belonged to the snorkel spiders, not their fellow prisoners. An angry rattling that sounded like the motor on the commandant's boat filled the everglades. The commandant's launch had turned around and was coming back to survey the damage to his operation, dozens of snorkel spiders in the water roaring counter challenges at the clattering engine.

'Who has permitted this to happen?' yelled On'esse, standing up at last, roused from his torpor under the shadow of the shade. 'Why are you cowards not harvesting?'

From one of the guard platforms, a gill-neck called out in the commandant's native tongue, indicating the snorkel bones hunting across the now empty waters.

On'esse dismissed the excuses with a stream of angry curses and pointed at Daunt, the sailor and Sadly on the raft. 'You are standing on top of my harvest, you lazy fools! Spoiling today's crop. Why are you not collecting fruit?'

'There are bleeding monsters in the water!' called the sailor.

On'esse strode to the front of his craft. 'Am I blind? Am I unaware of this? Why do you think it is you pulling gillworts from this swamp and not I?' He pushed the soldier on the tripod gun to one side, swivelled the weapon towards the convict labourer and triggered the gun. There was a shock of recoil through the commandant's launch, the Jackelian sailor struck in his chest and thrown back off the harvesting raft. Three snorkel spiders thrashed against each other as they competed to claim the corpse. 'Only those on the highest harvesting strap may stay in the trees. Everyone else, in the water, NOW! There are only seven beasts that I can see and half of those have been fed. We may lose a few of you untrained surface dwelling scum, and then everyone will work a double shift to make up for this debacle.' He rocked the gun towards

225

Daunt and Sadly. 'You two first, climb off my precious fruit and down into the swamp with you.'

There was an almost approving rattle of mandibles from the snorkel spiders circling Sadly and Daunt's raft.

As Charlotte sat inside the dome, she could almost see its structure extending. Each new clan of seanore that arrived at the tribal gathering brought their own plates cut from crab shells, adding them to the interlocking structure in new and innovative ways. The communal space had been transformed from the open hall of a single clan into a rambling warren of interconnected chambers, a few even filled with air and separated by transparent permeable membranes. It was hard to imagine that Charlotte was responsible for all of this, her recitations of ancient prophecies, her victory in the arena over Vane. Except it hadn't been her triumph, it had been the spirit of Elizica of the Jackeni's, the ancient queen's thoughts and memories so intermingled with Charlotte's own now it was hard to recall there had been a time when she had just been simple Charlotte Shades, Mistress of Mesmerism. Born to nobility, raised by a gypsy, and inclined to the removal of valuable objects that didn't belong to her.

As the ancient monarch had grown in power, she was no longer content to seep through Charlotte's blood and bones, whispering inside her mind. Now Elizica was appearing as a translucent blurred silhouette composed of shifting planes of light. Nobody else could see Charlotte's ancient visitation, of course. The seanore coming into the hall walked right though the apparition, no more than a mirage.

Will you stop haunting me if I give away the Eye of Fate?

'When you went to so much trouble to obtain it?' said Elizica, her voice veined with mischief.

Charlotte guiltily remembered pilfering the gem from

Madam Leeda. A burst of shame for stealing from the one person who had looked after her, indelibly mixed with the sadness of the first time she had used the amulet on her mother's doorstep. That was the only time the Eye of Fate had failed her.

'Its power is limited,' said Elizica, speaking of the amulet. 'You can make people believe in trivial things, you can make them see things that aren't there. But you can no more make them love you than you can compel them to leap into a chasm and kill themselves, for that matter.'

I wasn't thinking of hypnotising you into jumping into a chasm, Charlotte lied.

'It would make no difference if you did,' said Elizica. 'We leave our mark on the world as we pass through the years: in the lives of others, the action of our lives, in the reactions of the world. The children we have and the children we don't. I'm just an echo, Charlotte, burnt into the Eye of Fate and the bones of the land. You can't push an echo into a chasm.'

I bloody well can if I throw the Eye of Fate over the edge.

'You cannot, girl-child. You have been using the Eye of Fate for too long. It's bonded to you now, as you are to it. Do you remember how sick you were during your last days in Jackals and on board the u-boat? That wasn't a reaction to being attacked in the pie shop; it was a reaction to the crystal activating. When the Eye of Fate shielded you from Cloake's strike, it reset to its true purpose. As your body is locked to the crystal, the changes are mirrored in your flesh.'

No!

'You should have listened to Madam Leeda,' said Elizica. 'She suspected the truth. Why do you think she kept the Eye of Fate locked away in the back of her caravan and removed the gem only when she had real cause to make use of it? She knew enough to use the amulet, rather than the other way around.'

I don't want this. Charlotte looked around the water-filled chamber. Jared Black and the old woman Maeva stood with other air-breathing nomads in one of the membrane-sealed annexes, arguing over some matter. The cavernous space of the dome filled with clan leaders and tribal wise-women, dozens of the underwater races represented. Charlotte sat on a bench of polished stone against the wall, the others like Vane and Tera keeping a respectful distance from her. Why? This was as much their fault as hers. Vane's for letting himself be bested in the arena, Tera flapping around like fox-frightened poultry at the words of a prophecy the wise women were guardians for. What kind of fools were they? Charlotte could have stolen knowledge of the prophecy from one of them, couldn't she? She could have used the Eye of Fate to do that easily enough. Now seanore tribes were flocking to the grand assembly. What a caper this could have been. *There we go, honey. Just swim over to the Advocacy and raid their crystal fields for me. That's all the chosen one wants from you, a nice pile of boulder-sized diamonds. What do I need them for? Oh, I'll think of something.* It wouldn't be so wrong, would it? *The money helps, it always helps.*

'Not this time,' said Elizica, intruding on her thoughts.

If you want to do something useful, go and possess the commodore and Vane and the others. Get them to stop tiptoeing around me as if I'm the angel of death.

'For the seanore, I'm afraid that's more or less exactly what you are. The herald of dark tidings is always to be feared. And as for the commodore, well, the last time he heard my words was through his daughter, and she gave her life saving the Kingdom. It cannot be easy for him to feel my presence again.'

His daughter died? I thought you said you couldn't mesmerize someone into hurting themselves?

'Her choice,' said Elizica, with a mixture of pride and sorrow. 'Not my enchantment.'

Charlotte sighed and looked up. She could see the *Purity Queen* anchored above through one of the net-covered gaps in the dome that allowed the sea water to circulate. *I'm not going to get myself killed for you. Don't you think I will for a moment.*

'I am glad to hear it. A corpse isn't going to be much use in helping me fulfil the prophecy of the shadowed sea.'

Charlotte glanced around the chamber. The gems that the seanore traded from the Advocacy were put to good use among the nomads, whittled by diamond drill-bits into intricate gemstone carvings of cephalopods and dolphins mounted on chains hanging around the nomads' chests. There was nothing to match that level of artistry and craft back in Jackals, and each of the pieces would be worth a small fortune based on its uniqueness alone. This was Charlotte's preferred class of pilferage – small, transportable and practically begging to be sliced off its chains during a chance collision in a crowd. She looked over again to where Maeva and the commodore were talking. *They seem to be arguing.*

'I can channel what they are saying to you, if it will help you understand the people you fight alongside.'

All right, then. Let me hear them.

'You should have said something before you left,' Maeva was complaining.

The commodore shrugged. 'I couldn't and that's all of it.'

'Why not? You never seemed to have a problem with speaking honey before you disappeared. You loved to hear yourself speak. It was a problem ever getting you to stop.'

'I couldn't, Maeva,' said the commodore, 'because if I had

229

seen you one last time, I never could have left you. I wouldn't have had the heart for it. And then you and all your people would have died trying to protect me.'

'You were one of our clan. That's what we do. Then. Now.'

'Ah, not for me, never for me. I've enough on my conscience. That particular hold is full.'

'You could have taken me with you. I would have left the seanore with you.'

'For what, a life on the run, on the surface, away from your family and friends and everything you loved in the sea? I ended up in Cassarabia with other survivors of the royalist cause. Sucking up to the caliph there in return for the guns we needed to fight on. That's no country for you. Heat like a furnace, sands that'll sup the sweat from you with a vampire's thirst, nothing but enemies and plotting and sorcery as evil as any you're ever likely to see in this world. None of the countries and intrigues that followed after were any better. Just death and treachery and a cause that was lost long before I was even born. Taking you away from the oceans would have been dragging an angel down into hell.'

Maeva frowned. 'It's not a choice you should have got to make alone. I'm not some weak-willed surface-dwelling maiden. I am a warrior-born, free and unbound. It was *my* decision to make, not yours.'

'I'm a pirate, remember? I stole it from you. And that was my decision.'

'I thought I had made a seanore of you. Well, damn you for a pirate. Damn you for a *privateer*.'

Enough. Charlotte felt guilty she had even agreed to the royal spectre's suggestion.

The shape was beginning to fade away, the planes of light glowing translucent as they seeped into the water. 'As you wish. We have more important matters to focus on than the life they lost together. We have more important things to worry about than the weight of your purse.'

More important things won't put food on my plate when I get back home. Charlotte didn't need to sound the silent *if* in that train of thought.

'I grow tired. I've slept for so long. I will return when you have need for me.'

Come back, I need you for this now.

'For this jabbering mass? No, I have you for that.' Elizica's laughter faded into the chamber. 'So many of the underwater races here, yet so much hot air beneath the waves.'

Underneath the shell plates, interior surfaces daubed with frescos of legends and battles and creatures of the sea, Tera stepped forward and raised her arms. The wise-woman's voice carried loud in Charlotte's helmet speakers. 'It is time for the grand congress of the seanore to convene.'

Many floating in the water took their seats on the simple stone benches, as did the commodore and the air-breathing nomads behind the membrane. Those of the assembly without legs angled their bodies at neutral buoyancy, tails and fins holding them at anchor, waiting with expectant faces. One of the visiting nomads had stayed on his webbed feet, half his body armoured, the other half bare muscle with a gladiator's physique. 'Why are we here, Tera of the Clan Raldama? Why do you waste my time and all the chiefs of the water by bringing us here to a grand congress to stand before this—' his hand jabbed towards Charlotte, '—surface dweller?'

Tera grew incensed. 'You are here, Korda of the Clan Coudama, because your wise-woman reminded you of your obligations under the songs of the shadowed sea.'

'Where is the prophecy *here*? I do not see it?' The angry clan chief indicated the *Purity Queen* drifting outside the

231

tribal hall. 'Only a crew of surface-dwellers, the gas from the outcasts' engines fouling the great forests.'

'The signs and currents flow true,' said Tera. 'Are we not arrived at a time when the people of the water are at the throats of the surface dwellers? The time of madness is close, when demons shall emerge from the scars of the world and claim us all in the confusion.'

'Demons from the deep of the dark,' Korda sneered. 'The only devils I see are these surface dwellers. Is this the time of the shadowed sea? I think not. The Advocacy is habitually in dispute with trespassing surface dwellers.' The clan chief pointed at the commodore standing behind the membrane. 'And that one is the worst of all. A u-boat privateer notorious for his avariciousness. Do you not know him? You sheltered the silver-beard once, and here he is back again, full of tricks and lies and false words.'

Vane joined the wise-woman in facing down the rival clan chief. 'There are more than words at work here. This girl beat me in the ceremony of admittance and then sang words from the songs of prophecy.'

'Pah!' Korda's contempt filtered through Charlotte's helmet. 'Words can be stolen as easily as crystals. You stupid weakling, you let the commodore's fancy-piece best you in combat and now you seek to cover up your embarrassment by placing credence in ancient lore that Jared Black has pirated from us and whispered in her ear.'

Another clan leader stood up as Vane stepped forward, boiling to challenge his guest to combat. 'The peace of the grand congress be upon you both. Let us hear what this girl has to say. Speak, surface dweller. Were you the bearer of the lion trident in ancient times?'

Charlotte looked at them all uncertainly. *Now would be time for you to speak through me.* Nothing, empty silence within her, the Eye of Fate as inert as a useless piece of coal.

Korda's sarcastic laughter filled the water. 'For this I have dragged hundreds of the Clan Coudama's finest warriors away from our territory, away from the hunt and the gathering. And what are we fed with here? The confidence tricks of surface dwellers.'

'The one who gave you your prophecy has spoken through me,' said Charlotte, 'although by the Circle, I wish it was otherwise.'

'On your wishes, we can at least agree,' said Korda. 'Speak now, then, surface-dweller. Sing the secrets songs of the prophecy. Let the grand congress echo with your wisdom.'

'I am not a dancing monkey to caper to your whims, honey. I only know what I've seen and heard to bring me here,' said Charlotte. 'There are royalist rebels from my nation scheming with the Advocacy alongside highly placed officials inside the Kingdom, and the whole filthy conspiracy is swirling like a whirlpool around the twisted monsters appearing in my dreams.'

'Bad dreams have carried you here? Not just you, surface dweller girl, your foolishness has called thousands of seanores to stand in this congress.'

'I think the monsters in my dreams are the chasm-demons of your prophecy.'

'You *think*—'

The commodore's voice interrupted the clan leader's outburst. 'You want proof, lad, then here it is!' Charlotte turned. The commodore was clutching King Jude's sceptre, unfurling the staff from a stretch of canvas where he had concealed it. 'This is what the dark-hearts chasing us are really after.'

'And she shall return with a staff of gold and a crystal from outside the world,' pronounced Tera.

'A bauble made to order by you, Jared Black,' accused Korda.

Commodore Black pointed at the wise-woman. 'Tera only told me of your prophecy yesterday. I knew blessed little of until then, though I recognized the description of the sceptre well enough when I heard it.'

'Am I a fool? You've ordered that gaudy rod manufactured to lend credence to your schemes. I don't know what you are here for, but I do know it will cost seanore blood spilled in the water if we listen to you. Let the squabbling surface dwelling factions and the Advocacy murder and war and plot against each other, but let it *not* involve us.' He struck his way out of the waters, turning his back on Charlotte. There were murmurs of agreement echoing throughout the clan leaders' assembly hall, many rising from the stone seats and ready to begin following the Clan Coudama out of the grand congress.

The nomads' outrush was interrupted by a company of rotor-spear wielding sentries urgently pushing against the surge of leaving leaders. 'They are coming!'

Vane shouted down the crowd to hear his warriors. 'Who is coming?'

'Darkships, we have seen darkships approaching over the forest.'

'How many?' asked Vane.

'Two.'

'You fools!' Tera yelled across the clan leaders. 'You wanted proof of the songs of prophecy, here it is. Did the old silverbeard manufacture the darkships, too?'

Before the words had sunk into Charlotte, there was a rush of panicked nomads speeding for the exits out onto the seabed, a flurry of hidden weapons – forbidden at the congress – emerging in nomad hands.

Elizica's disembodied words whispered in Charlotte's ears. 'I think you will be glad I rested, girl-child.'

What are darkships?

'What the prophecy was intended to warn against, girl-child. Demon chariots, the chasm's seed.'

Charlotte didn't need to ask what they had come for. They had come for the sceptre. And they had come for her.

CHAPTER TEN

'Are you deaf?' bellowed On'esse as Sadly and Daunt hesitated in climbing off the harvesting raft, snorkel spiders circling the boat with an eager, hungry intent.

'This is inhuman,' Daunt called out. 'I must protest.'

'Protest all you like,' laughed On'esse, 'but protest from the water. You have just as long as it takes my soldier here to reload his gun. All of you, restart your cropping!'

'Cracked old arsehole,' cursed Morris, now moving down the tree, but as slowly as he could. Obviously hoping someone else would get to the water first and attract the remaining snorkel spiders' attention. 'He'll do for us all.'

Dick Tull could only agree. He'd had the luck to be on the tree strap, cutting down fruit when the attack started, otherwise he'd be taking part in this slow-motion race to see who would survive. *Just so long as On'esse doesn't notice I'm no longer holding my machete and orders me down too.* Commandant On'esse had lost his patience waiting for his raft's big tripod mounted gun to be reloaded with a fresh shell. He pulled out his pistol and waved it threateningly towards the nearest guard station. 'You there, push the surface dwellers off your platform – those stands are for us, not these vermin.'

Something moved behind the commandant's launch. At first, Dick thought that what he was watching was one of the snorkel spiders attracted to the commandant's still humming engine, but the shape kept on rising and rising. Not a flurry of mandibles, but an orange-coloured carapace mottled with camouflaged yellow stripes, a long flat curve of armour wider than the commandant's launch and balanced by two huge serrated claws.

'Tiger crab!' warned Dick.

'Not just any tiger crab,' muttered Morris, abandoning any pretence to be heading back into the water. 'It's Old Death-shell back again.'

Now Dick saw what the heavy bore weapon on the front of On'esse's boat was for. Unfortunately for the camp commandant, he'd already wasted its shell on a hapless Jackelian victim. Desperately trying to reload, the soldier on the bow was near decapitated when Old Death-shell brought down its two claws onto the boat. Struck amidships and stern at the same time, the boat crumpled into three pieces under the tiger crab's touch, On'esse discharging his pistol as he was flung back by the collapsing craft and the impact of the man-sized claws. His pistol shot rebounded off the shell close to Old Death-shell's eyestalks, a new black scar of explosive residue joining a hundred others. Old Death-shell wore its previous encounters with the guards and their prisoners of war like medals on its armour, a constellation of scratches and lacerations speaking of how hard it was to kill. Trampling the boat, fair dancing across it in triumph, the tiger crab's eight legs carried it over the debris and towards the thrashing form of On'esse. Old Death-shell's left claw lazily swung around into an upper cut, smashing the commandant and sending him flying out of the surface before landing with a splash and a thump towards the bottom of Dick's tree. Rifle fire from the soldiers on the guard stations raked the tiger crab from behind, and it swivelled around, slamming both claws into a wooden platform and cracking it asunder. The gill-necks that weren't flattened by the claws tumbled off with the cowering prisoners of war who had reached the trunk's elusive safety. All around the trees, the guards and convict labour were scattering – perhaps the snorkel spiders too, as Dick couldn't see any sign of their previous attackers' bony periscopes. All fear of the water was gone now among the harvesting party. There wasn't an inch of sentient flesh in the Everglades who didn't know what to fear now . . . the most vicious armoured predator on the island had come to dine, and there wasn't any creature that was off the menu. Old Death-shell danced towards Dick's tree, trampling over Sadly and Daunt's raft as if the flatboat was nothing more than a waterlily, the two of them leaping out into the water before the raft splintered into pieces, hundreds of gillwort fruit sent flying.

Sadly and the ex-parson waded backwards as Old Death-shell advanced on their tree, the semi-conscious form of the commandant bobbing in front. Both of them ducked behind the tree, the tiger crab's claws prodding forward, clacking, each pinching movement enough to cut a bull in half. One of its claws came cutting up, slicing the strap off Morris and sending the howling prisoner falling out of the tree towards the surface. Down below, Sadly and Daunt were shouting in terror as Old Death-shell scuttled forward, closing the gap between them to a couple of feet. Dick was desperately swinging himself around the tree trunk to avoid the claw swishing through the air when a whistling battle cry pierced the swamp. On the tree behind, Boxiron had sliced his climbing strap off, plummeting down towards the tiger crab beneath with his machete raised.

'No!' Daunt called from below as he stumbled backwards. 'Old steamer, you're not able to shift gears with that limiter welded onto you.'

Boxiron's strength might have been throttled down, but his fury at the creature threatening his friend was undiminished. Dick took advantage of the steamman's diversion and released his own belt to fall towards the surface, hitting the warm water and coming up alongside Sadly and Morris.

'Your friend's got a death wish, see,' spluttered Morris.

On top of the tiger crab's carapace, Boxiron had one metal hand digging into its shell, the other hacking down, trying to force its way into the flesh beyond the carapace joins. Old Death-shell was not reacting well to having a rider, making a furious chirping noise, rubbing its legs together as it was bucking, its claws trying to angle back to sweep this metal parasite off its back.

'This is my fault,' moaned Daunt, as he dragged the wounded commandant's body clear of the lashing tiger crab's assault. 'Boxiron shouldn't be here.'

Dick tried to shove Jethro Daunt away from the gill-neck. 'Let me strangle the murdering sod.'

Morris grabbed Dick from behind. 'I would be right behind you, matey. But if we do for him like he deserves, the gill-necks will make everyone in the camp pay.'

With the commandant pulled back onto the tree's roots, Daunt grabbed one of the raft's punts floating past and charged the flailing tiger crab, jabbing at the eye stalks. Breaking free, Dick snatched the machete off Morris and ran forward to stand by the amateur's side, pushing his blade out at the enraged creature. Old Death-shell was not used to this. Prey ran. It did not fight back. It did not attack! Confused, its

239

attention divided between the three of them, Old Death-shell's left claw withdrew from trying to dislodge Boxiron and snapped out at Daunt. The amateur had waded out of range, but his punt was sliced in half. Dick ran forward, slashing at the black feathery fronds growing like a beard around the bottom of the tiger crab's shell, then darted back as the creature shuddered in pain.

Daunt scooped up the half of his punt fallen in the water and tossed it up towards Boxiron. 'Old steamer, give me a lever long enough and I shall move the world.' The Circlist koan of the blessed fulcrum.

Boxiron seized the punt and rammed it into the gap in the carapace he'd been trying to cut open, driving a metal foot down onto the pole. Lifting up the armour with a terrible ripping sound that sent the tiger crab into a fit of shaking fury, the tear was not much, but enough to expose the soft flesh of its fibrous brain casing underneath. Boxiron lifted a victorious spear of steam into the air from his stack and he cried in triumph, driving the machete down with both hands. Limited in strength, but never in soul.

Chirping in agony, Old Death-shell's eight legs buckled, its wide carapace collapsing into the everglade's surface, and there it lay, trembling and shaking as its life leaked away.

'Were you trying to die?' demanded Daunt as the steamman slid off the mottled orange and yellow shell.

'No, Jethro softbody, I was trying to live.'

There was another scream of fury, not the dying tiger crab this time. 'You dirty surface-dwelling vermin!' On'esse staggered in front of the tree, snapping shut the pistol he had just reloaded. 'You dare to save me! To lay hands on me as if I am one of your dirty herd, as if my life is in your hands!' As he raised his pistol towards the famous consulting detective, Dick threw the machete, its blade rotating once and hitting

On'esse in the chest, slamming him back and pinning him to the tree trunk. There was a brief look of astonishment on the commandant's face as the shock of his death sank in.

'And that's my way of saying *thank you*, you murdering old sod.'

On'esse slipped forward on the blade, croaking, trembling. Then the commandant's shuddering increased, becoming more than just the last dying tremors of a gill-neck, his body shaking, fast and faster, blurring in the air, his form being replaced by something else. Something more or less the same size as On'esse, but with a terrible distended head, wrinkled skin that gleamed slimy, foul and as dark as night.

Boxiron stepped forward to examine the corpse. 'By the beard of Zaka of the Cylinders, what is this thing?'

Daunt reached out to stop the steamman, grabbing his arm. 'Stand back!' As he was speaking there was a burst of light from the corpse's chest and a spiral of fierce red energy wrapped the commandant's body. By the time Dick had blinked the tears and afterimage of the explosion out of his eyes, there was nothing but charred ashes left sinking into the water. A shadow had been burnt into the tree trunk, the now half-melted machete still sunk into the smoking wood.

'Lords-a'larkey,' whispered Sadly. 'I've seen a few things, say I, but that, that—'

'Let's see if I am right,' said Daunt, advancing on the sinking mound of blackened residue. He dipped a hand down, searching for something under the water, then came back up with a jewel. 'Does this look familiar? Rather like the gem that Damson Shades wears around her neck, don't you think?'

'What's happened to him?' Dick demanded. 'Did that crystal do that?'

'I believe it might be expedient if I saved your answers until we have reached the safety of the beach. The guards who fled will doubtless be back soon with larger guns.'

Dick waded through the water, retrieving a rifle and a satchel of soaked shells from the remains of the commandant's broken boat.

'There's no safety on the beach,' cried Morris, his dripping arms windmilling around the humid air. 'You think we haven't tried to escape, man? Every year some green arseholes steal a harvesting raft and make for the sea.' He jabbed a finger towards the gently shaking carapace of Old Death-shell. 'There are hundreds just like that beast in the waters around the island. What do you think Ko'marn Island means in the gill-neck tongue? It's "Death-by-claw Island"! This is one of the islands where tiger crabs lay eggs every summer.'

Daunt smiled, looking meaningfully at Barnabas Sadly. 'Oh, I think we can do better than a shallow-beamed harvesting raft, a sail made out of tattered shirts and an old punt, don't you?'

'What, the cripple? You think he's got a private sloop tucked up his shirt-tails?' Morris scoffed.

'Not a sloop, but a trick up his sleeve. Or rather, inside his cane. How about it, Barnabas?'

Sadly nodded thoughtfully. 'Your reputation is well deserved, Mister Daunt. How did you work it out?'

'Many signals, but two matters stood out rather glaringly. Firstly, your clubfoot. Those born with *congenital talipes equinovarus* in a single limb always learn to compensate with their other foot by the time they reach adulthood, leaving the heel of the good shoe worn away. Someone who came from a family of cobblers should know that. Whereas for you, sir, your good shoe's heel stands as flat as a mill-pond. I can thereby deduct that you weren't born with what is solely a congenital disease. A womb-mage's alteration of the flesh, I expect? I doubt if that's the face you were born with, either.'

Sadly nodded in approval. 'And the second thing?'

'You told me you hadn't been born in a poorhouse. There is a good reason why Sadly is such a common surname in the slums of the capital. It is because it is the name automatically entered in the rolls by a workhouse when a male baby is abandoned at a church and handed over to the board of the poor. If you had been an abandoned baby girl, you would have been called Templar, after temple, while Sadly comes from the *Ballad of Franklin Sadly, the Saint of the Workhouse*.' Daunt began to hum the tune. 'In a long and hungry line, the paupers sit at their tables, for this is the hour they dine, with poor Franklin Sadly.'

'A guinea for you to stop bleeding singing. You are quite a fount of useless trivia, Mister Daunt.'

'I would say there's no such thing as a piece of useless information.'

'And what amongst your vast store of ephemera makes you think I'm going to take you with me?'

'Us,' said Daunt, indicating the group. 'And I think you'll take us with you because I know the answers to what is really going on here.'

'Who are you?' Dick snarled at the informant, the flush of anger rising within him as the truth of the matter started to dawn. 'Have you played me for a mug, Sadly?'

'Not a mug, good sergeant,' said Daunt. 'And he's treated you no differently from the rest of us. That's the purpose of bait, isn't it? To be impaled on a hook and dragged through the water to see what bites. Well, your mission has been successfully completed. You've caught quite a whopper, and now you're going to make sure that we're the ones that got away.'

243

'I'm going to need a taste of that fish,' said Sadly. 'Just to make sure you're telling the truth.'

'I would expect nothing less from a trade that deals in lies and deceits.' Daunt reached under his breeches and removed a bamboo rod that had been tied to his leg. He tossed it to Sadly. 'From the graveyard here. Read the name engraved on the marker.'

Sadly did so, a worried frown creasing his rodent-like features. Then he pitched it back to the ex-parson. 'All right then, consider that your ticket out of here.'

Dick stuck his hand out. 'Let me see it.'

Daunt passed it across and Dick scanned the name on the grave marker, then looked at the date of the burial. The feeling of confusion swelled within the sergeant. 'How can that be?'

'A riddle, indeed,' said Daunt. He passed the marker across to the obviously curious steamman. 'What do you think, Boxiron? How can Walsingham have been buried in the camp's graveyard two years past, when the good sergeant's employer was only just interrogating me? Quite a curiosity, and enough to stump even—' Daunt pointed to Sadly, '—an agent of the Court of the Air.'

Daunt pushed back the undergrowth in his way as they cut a passage through the everglades, the harvesting machetes put to a use their gill-neck captors would not have approved of. Sadly was not limping quite so badly now, the act of his cover identity abandoned for expediency's sake as they slashed their way to freedom.

Boxiron was hacking in front, Dick Tull and Morris behind the steamman, the State Protection Board agent surly and uncommunicative towards the man he'd believed was his informant. It was not an easy thing, to flip from predator to prey with such speed, and the sergeant's professional pride was clearly wounded worse than anything his capture by the gill-necks had inflicted upon him. Boxiron released the exhaust of his labours from his stacks in brief, short bursts, nothing to draw attention of the pursuit by the camp's soldiers that had to be underway by now. If the State Protection Board officer's pride had taken a beating, Daunt hoped that Boxiron's had been restored by his victory over Old Death-shell. Even limited by the gill-necks' device, he was still a steamman knight. *I just hope he knows it, and that his plunge towards the tiger crab was to save me, not a suicide attempt.*

'Walsingham wasn't the only one in the graveyard, was he?' Sadly said, cutting at the bush with his cane.

'No. It was a veritable notables' list of Jackelian quality – admirals, vice-admirals, generals, industrialists, mill owners, members of the House of Guardians, and those were just the names I recognized.'

'The Court of the Air will need them all,' said Sadly. 'Along with everything else you know about how they got there.'

Daunt fished in his pocket, withdrawing with a Bunter and Benger's aniseed drop. He looked at the sticky mess in disappointment then replaced it back again. *Inedible.* Perhaps it would dry out later? 'First things first, good agent. We need to locate the commodore, Charlotte Shades and King Jude's sceptre before the commodore's sister and the gill-necks do. Otherwise there won't be much of a Kingdom left to save.'

'You've a cheek, Mister Daunt. We're not your bleeding private carriage service.'

'I know what the Court of the Air is for,' said Daunt. 'You must have suspected that your dealings over the centuries have come to the attention of the Inquisition?'

'What do you know of the Court?'

'When Isambard Kirkhill seized power in Parliament's name after the civil war, he had only one fear left – and that was the throne. The army wanted Kirkhill to become king. Old Isambard had to fight them off with a sabre to stop them crowning him the new monarch. Then there were our royalists-in-exile plotting a counter-revolution and restoration. Kirkhill knew that if Parliament's rule was to last, it would have to resist both the plots without and the ambitions of its own politicians. So Kirkhill established a court sinister as the last line of defence, a body that was to act as a supreme authority and ultimate guarantor of the people's rule. But it was to be a court invisible. While the House of Guardians knew the Court existed, they knew nothing of its location, its staff, its methods and its workings. If any politician were to start looking at the throne restored with envious eyes, the existence of the Court would give them pause to think.'

'There's such a thing as being too clever for your own good,' warned Sadly.

'So people keep on telling me. However, in this matter I think you will find your mission and my own perfectly aligned.'

'Are you an Inquisition officer, Mister Daunt?'

'Perish the thought,' said Daunt. 'The church wouldn't have defrocked me so readily if I had been. They're under the misapprehension that they employ my services every so often, and it only seems like fair play to draw upon their resources in turn. The commodore's sister made the same mistake when she linked me up to their machine to sift through my memories.'

'And now you're asking the Court to repeat the error? You're not very reassuring, says I.'

'Oh, I'm sure the Court of the Air is far too devious for me to play you along.'

The everglades' bush was thinning out, the orange dunes of a beach ahead and the crashing sea beyond. The danger of the place was underlined by hundreds of abandoned carapaces lying in the sand, outgrown by generations of maturing tiger crabs. *And how many tiger crabs are scuttling about out there with their shells still on, I wonder?*

'And what's your explanation for the camp commandant burning up when he died?'

'Patience, good agent. What exactly do you have concealed inside your cane? Not a flag rolled up with the word "help" sown on, I trust?'

'An isotope,' said Sadly. 'Its signature can be followed from half an ocean away.'

Daunt glanced at the bottom of the man's cane. It was leaking the last of a foul-looking green liquid onto the sand.

'You've flushed it into the swamp . . .?'

'Water nullifies it.'

'And the signal stopping is the sign for your extraction,' said Daunt, satisfied with himself. 'I trust your colleagues have stayed near.'

'You never know when you're going to outwear your welcome.'

Any self-satisfaction vanished with the whistling of bullets past Daunt's left ear, close enough to shave his sideburn.

'Camp guards,' yelled Morris, sprinting for the reedy dunes in front of them and throwing himself over the ridge. Jethro, Boxiron, Sadly and Dick Tull were fast behind the wiry convict, spurts of sand chasing their passage as they hurled themselves towards the sparse cover of the beach. *There was something about the footsteps they had left in the sand, but what?* Daunt didn't have time to ponder. A cloud of gull-like lizards exploded into the air as the party of escapees landed close to their nests in the dune grass, bullets flitting over their heads with the buzz of roused hornets. Dick Tull pushed a shell into the stolen rifle and fired back, the gill-necks keeping cover, hunkering down along the edge of the everglades in response

247

to this solitary, lonely voice of opposition. Geysers of sand erupted as the guards concentrated their volleys on the muzzle flash of Dick's rifle.

'There's too sodding many of them over there,' said Dick.

'We just need to hold them off for a few minutes more,' called Sadly. 'Look!'

Out at sea, a u-boat was surfacing, but not any design that Daunt was familiar with . . . a bulbous, almost organic-shaped hull with a rotating stern composed of large metal tentacles that gave the craft something of the appearance of a steel squid. With a conning tower set as low and angular as a shark's fin, a hatch in her lee was opening to release a pair of low metal surface boats. Both boats angled out heading towards the shore. Sailors stood on the prows with capacitor packs cabled up to tridents, the men releasing bursts of wild energy at the tiger crabs surfacing around the submarine. Old Death-shell's kin appeared incensed at this strange metal interloper intruding upon their realm. The creatures weren't the only ones to spot the rescue craft. More guards emerged in front of the jungle, throwing themselves down and sighting on the dunes.

'If we try for the sea, they'll cut us down before we make five yards,' said Boxiron.

'You go old steamer,' urged Daunt. 'The gill-necks might have dialled down your strength near to mine, but they haven't yet exchanged your hull for flesh. Wade out there and find Commodore Black, tell him to place King Jude's sceptre under the protection of the Court of the Air.'

'They must have recovered the commandant's corpse, see,' moaned Morris. 'We're dead men now, whatever we do.'

As if in agreement with the convict's prediction, the drone of the fusillade over their heads was swapped for a strident cannon-like booming, explosions of sand in front of the dunes swelling, showering them with beach debris.

'They have brought up the heavy guns used to do business with the tiger crabs. Pass me your machete,' Boxiron ordered Morris, feeling its heft in his left hand as the convict did as he was bid, its weight balancing the other blade gripped tight in the steamman's right fist.

'Boxiron,' Daunt pleaded, 'do not do this.'

'What else am I for, old friend?' asked Boxiron. He rose to his full height from behind the dunes and charged, a lumbering zigzagging assault caused as much by a lack of motor control as any desire to dodge the guards' bullets. Shots cracked around him as he pounded through the sand, the gill-necks adjusting their range to home in on him. A couple of guards were thrown back by Dick Tull using the distraction to increase his rate of fire, reloading from his satchel of charges like a demon. Out at sea, the boats were closing on the beach, seconds away from landing. The crewmen inside were kneeling now, riding in on the jouncing waves. The tiger crabs had temporally withdrawn out of range of the sailors' capacitor packs, bobbing around the submersible and awaiting for their food to return. It wouldn't take long for the camp guards to redirect their fire towards the rescue boats. And if the boats were struck by something that could discourage a tiger crab, they would be in trouble.

Dick Tull rose, firing the rifle from the hip. 'Leg it for the water.'

Boxiron had reached the line of guards, a few gill-necks standing up just in time to face his machetes, twin windmills of death as he cut and slashed about him. He was staggering back from the blasts at short range. Not even the armour the criminal underworld had fitted their hulking ex-possession with was proof against this level of abuse.

'Move!' called Sadly, dragging Daunt back. 'Right now, your noggin's the most valuable thing on this island.'

Only to everyone at home. To Daunt, the most valuable thing on the island was the steamman about to throw his life away against the ranks of their gill-neck pursuers.

When Charlotte saw the two darkships, the only part of their description that covered what she had been expecting to see was their colour: a shining, oily darkness rippling along their featureless hulls. Nothing else about them resembled any submarine she had heard of. Pear-shaped and driving forward on the sharp of their noses, the crafts couldn't have been more than forty feet long. Their approach was soundless. There was no sign of a means of propulsion, no portholes, no torpedo slits, no hydroplanes, no conning tower, no ventilation intakes, no rudders for steering. It didn't take much to believe this evil pair had escaped from Elizica's prophecy and the legends of the seanore. Demon chariots, the chasm's seed, their skins sucked the light out of the ocean, surfaces made a rippling absence of matter, organic teardrops of devilry solidified into twin darts and sliding with pernicious intent towards the nomads' grand congress.

Where the outskirts of the underwater forest gave way to the encampment, dozens of warriors rose from sentry positions in the wavering kelp, casting rotor-spears at the ebony teardrops accelerating towards the assembly. At least seven explosive-headed rods were heading straight for the bows of the two craft, white trails of bubbles fuming behind rotors built into their shafts, the darkships suddenly banking contemptuously into the swarm, detonating the spears. Both darkships powered forward, even faster now while the warriors below had drawn their shock spears, angling the discharge of electric bolts towards the belly of the two ships. The twin craft overshot the warriors. As they passed, the seanore underneath doubled up in agony, clutching their ears and left writhing above the wavering forest of kelp. Just being in the proximity of the darkships was enough to drive the nomads into waves of agony.

Elizica's words resonated inside Charlotte's mind. 'Sound – the enemy is using sound as a shield. The seanore's eardrums exploded when the darkships passed, ruptured like the triggers on the rotor-spears' warheads, detonating before they hit the hull.'

How do we fight them?

'There is a way. Head for the weapons the nomads left outside the congress.'

Charlotte swam though the panicked nomads packed inside the expanded camp of the Clan Raldama. Thousands of seanore warriors had been waiting to hear the results of the tribal elders' deliberations. Now they had been reduced into an undisciplined mass desperately seeking the commands of their chiefs, most of whom were tightly mixed with the ranks of their rivals and neighbours. Behind Charlotte, the darkships had rammed the line of spherical nets holding the nomads' schools of fish, kelp-rope lattices bursting apart as waves of silvery fish burned in the interlopers' dark energies, floating dead towards the surface. When the teardrop-shaped darkships passed over the encampment, their shape seemed to change, flattening, taking on a manta ray configuration. They had jettisoned something in their wake, an inky mist spreading though the ocean, heavier than the sea water and sinking towards the dozens of domes raised on the seabed. Hitting the interlocking plates of the structures, a devil-dust crackling fizzed over Charlotte's helmet speakers, a fierce popping. Collapsing as if they were decaying flesh, the chambers began to crumble inwards, unlucky nomads who had not yet evacuated eaten away wherever the black mist touched them. A froth of disintegrating bone and flesh bubbled out along every point of contact with the wicked wave of pollution that had been unleashed.

'The chasm-demon's breath,' whispered Elizica as Charlotte hesitated. She had been swimming straight for that evil substance. 'I would sleep away another age if it meant not waking to see that filthy weapon afresh.'

A strange blurring in the water beyond her visor caught Charlotte's eye. It was the *Purity Queen*, the catamaran-hulled submarine had fired up the stealth plates along her hull and they were vibrating like the polyps on a reef's Dead Man's Fingers. Her bow was slanting down, rising on an explosion of air from her ballast tanks, a beast rearing in the water to challenge the two newcomers. She was positioning herself for a perfect firing solution against the two darkships.

The commodore must be back on board.

'They'll go gentle with the u-boat,' said Elizica. 'They've tracked the submarine and will sense the sceptre is within her decks.'

Four torpedoes powered away from the *Purity Queen*'s forward firing tubes, a pair sent streaming from each bow towards the darkships. Neither of the enemy vessels altered course, rather, their bows flowed out into needle-like lances, quick flashes of burning light – but black light, like the negative on a daguerreotype plate – pulses hitting each of the propelling torpedoes and sending them spinning towards the seabed. Inert lumps of slagged steel with their chemical warheads burnt into a cloud of yellow particles chasing the torpedoes' wake down.

The two darkships passed either side of the *Purity Queen*, lances forming along the side of their waxy skin as the pair released an underwater broadside at the u-boat. As they struck, Charlotte's sight vanished with the explosion of light across her retina. The fireworks departed and her vision returned.

Charlotte saw the *Purity Queen*'s hull had been left with dozens of steaming, melted holes, the new crevices in her hull leaking air as though it were blood. The u-boat's proud conning tower had been singled out and left a ruin of melted metal, her forward and aft hydroplanes sheared off. In that single pass, the once proud vessel, ex of the Jackelian fleet sea arm, had been left a filleted wreck. One of her two propellers was still active and she nosed down towards the seabed, crashing into the kelp forest and ploughing it up. Then her stern rose, keeping the *Purity Queen* vertical for a second, a strange metal tower implanted on the seabed, before she tipped forward under the propulsion of her remaining screw. The remains of the submarine's mangled conning tower impaled the vegetation and there she lay, stretched out on her belly, rivulets of oxygen streaming upwards from multiple hull ruptures.

Go gentle with her, my left foot!

'For the chasm-seed, that was a light touch. Quick, girl-child, that way! Swim for those rotor-spears.'

Circling the *Purity Queen*'s upended hull in vulture loops, the darkships had lost interest in the seanore, stunned into a near-rout by the appearance of these deadly auguries of destruction in their waters.

'They are scanning the wreck for the sceptre, for the crystal in its orb,' warned Elizica.

Charlotte was close to the centre of a clearing in the kelp forest. Corpses caught in the current floated past above rotor-spears and shock-spears piled against each other in cones of weaponry, the nomad mob jostling as they snatched wildly at the arms laid aside during their grand congress.

'Take the Eye of Fate off your chest,' ordered Elizica. 'Press it against the warheads of the rotor-spears.'

Charlotte did as she was bid, spotting Vane amid the mob of

scrambling nomads, trying to restore order among the warriors. 'Vane, have them stand aside, I need to get to these weapons.'

'Back, clansmen!' Vane threw punches at the clawing warriors, holding the line against the panicked mass. 'Do you have a plan, surface dweller?'

Charlotte rubbed the Eye of Fate against each first rotor-spear, a green light radiating from the amulet briefly rendering the weapon's mechanism transparent. 'You know how it is, Vane, a bit of that old-time prophecy juice.'

I hope this is good.

Elizica's voice slipped through her mind. 'I'm burning out the rotor-spears' detonation triggers so there will be nothing for the darkships' perimeter sonics to detonate early when they pass through their shields.'

I'm no engineer, but if you do that, just how in the Circle's name are they going to explode when they hit?

'Contact force,' said Elizica. 'They'll need to be thrown from no further than twenty feet for them to have enough velocity to detonate.'

That sounds like suicide.

'Let's compromise and call it the act of a champion, girl-child. When I was your age I'd already jumped a bull and strangled a lion unconscious in an arena's sands.'

You reached my age? Charlotte finished with the last of the cluster of rotor-spears, looping the Eye of Fate around her chest again. Picking up the nearest rotor-spear, she passed it to Vane. 'These will do the job now, if there are seanore here courageous enough to swim close enough to the enemy to stand in a darkship's shadow.'

Vane examined the rotor-spear, running a finger along its warhead as if he expected it to tingle now. 'I fear shadows less than I fear your enchantments. I hope your witchery will be enough.'

Charlotte located the two darkships, their black mass hovering above the wrecked Jackelian u-boat. Weapon horns had formed along their bows, smaller this time, focused cutting beams slicing out and opening up the broken vessel's hull. Someone was swimming towards the submarine from the camp – a solitary figure. Maeva? What did the old woman think she was doing over there? The third member of the Clan Raldama's council hadn't been spotted yet. The two interlopers were still too busy carving up their prize in their search for King Jude's Sceptre. *My sceptre, you bastards.*

'It'll be enough.' The nomads were hanging back uncertainly, Vane and his warriors, Korda too, the rival nomad chief's skull covered by a silver war mask he had yet to push forward to cover his face. 'You might need to find your balls first.' Charlotte tugged one of the rotor-spears out of the seabed and pushed off for the wreck of the submarine.

Just tell me that the commodore is still alive inside there?

'He may be.' Elizica's words slid through her head.

I'm not doing this for you or your dammed prophecy. I owe Jared my life and that sceptre is mine. I stole it . . . I get to sell it.

'Yes, you get to sell it.'

Seanore were overtaking her now, the nomads shamed into action, their powerful webbed feet powering them ahead of her. Soon enough Charlotte was only swimming alongside wetbacks like her, the clans' human members weighed down with rebreathers and diving suits. There were more warriors by her side than the numbers of rotor-spears she had altered – many were rushing towards their deaths with weapons that would prove useless against the intruders. Some of the nomads were already releasing rotor-spears, engine bulges propelling the spears forward in a flurry of bubbles, seanore war cries echoing inside Charlotte's helmet as disembodied as Elizica's voice. 'Too far away.'

I don't think that discipline is their strong point.

A flurry of warheads detonated before they had even reached the darkships' ebony surface, others bouncing uselessly off the hulls, their velocity too spent to explode on impact.

I hope they don't notice the duds bouncing off their ships.

'They will release their demon's breath again when they have recharged their tanks. This is our only chance, girl-child. Close with them, ATTACK!'

Charlotte had covered half the distance to the *Purity Queen*'s wreckage, the seanores nearer still, close enough for the initial acceleration of their rotor-spears to detonate on impact now. The nearest of the darkships above the dead Jackelian submarine juddered with a wave of flowering explosions, the wash of shockwaves rattling Charlotte's helmet and throwing her back in the water. Damage had been taken along the closest darkship, although it was nothing like the destruction the two craft had visited on the *Purity Queen*. Black folds fluttered along the invader's ebony surface as though in torment, oily globules vomiting out of the rips. Its hull flexed and writhed close to the impact strikes.

Charlotte had difficulty concentrating this close to the darkships, the throb of pain in her head intensifying with every foot she swam nearer. Not just the pain, their proximity was setting her nerves on edge, an almost superstitious dread tunnelling into her deepest, darkest fears. Every iota of Charlotte's being screamed at her to flee, to swim away from these underwater terrors and keep on going. She was breathing hard, the visor of her diving helmet misting up on the inside. Her bones vibrated with panic, shaking in terror.

'The darkships sing their own song,' Elizica's voice warned. 'They seek out the frequency of fear within your heart.'

Both darkships had returned to their pear-like configuration and pulled up from the *Purity Queen*'s belly, the craft further away lifting and using the hull of the damaged darkship as a shield. From one of the rents near the *Purity Queen*'s amidships a figure emerged pulling another, both in diving suits. One of them was Maeva. The prone form; the commodore's. But was he alive? No sign of King Jude's sceptre; that must still be inside the wreck.

These cursed things; these were part of the conspiracy that had set Charlotte up to steal the sceptre, before coldly attempting to slaughter her as they had murdered poor old Damson Robinson. They had hounded her from her home and were hunting her still, hungry for retribution. With a yell Charlotte cast the rotor-spear, the rush of water activating the gas charge inside the staff, its small motor accelerating the projectile towards the damaged darkship. It struck exactly where she'd aimed, the top of the craft's bulbous bow, the intuition – supplied by the ancient spirit haunting her mind – that this was where the pilot was succoured by the foul black substance. Her shaft's explosion was one of many. The seanore didn't need to follow Charlotte's example to press home their advantage against an obviously wounded party. The damaged darkship reversed erratically, its surface breaking up and threading away as if it were a lump of lard melting in the pan. Tilting forward, the surviving craft had learnt the danger of ignoring these attackers, its bow reforming into a lance. With a flash of strangely dark light, the cutting force of the craft was unleashed against the attacking seanores. To Charlotte's right, one of the human nomads was cleaved from head to groin in a broiling second, his two halves split and simultaneously cauterized into a bloodless death, drifting apart in a frozen rictus agony. There seemed no limit of range to the weapon; when it fired, the sea boiled and everything in its path was carved into slices.

Charlotte yelled in alarm as the beam punched past her, the sound echoing in the confines of her helmet, flinging her down towards the seabed. Close enough to sear the skin beneath her diving suit. A handful of seanore were swimming in above the kelp forest, using their rotor-spears set low to carry them in before launching the weapons – literally riding the projectiles down onto their foe. The undamaged darkship pivoted, the cutting beam moving with it, ploughing through the forest – ground erupting like the fault line of an earthquake with its violence – before bursting through the raiding party.

Charlotte crawled through the kelp towards the broken hull of the *Purity Queen*. Maeva was in the lee of a rent, oxygen from the crippled craft streaming out behind her as she held onto the prostrate form of Commodore Black. The surface of the old u-boat man's suit appeared burnt and there was no way to tell if she was cradling a corpse or not.

'Just like when we first met,' Maeva's murmurs carried across to Charlotte's helmet. 'Always pulling you out of the wreckage of your mishaps.'

'Leave them, girl-child. Find the sceptre,' ordered Elizica.

'Shut up.' Charlotte banged her helmet's side as if that was enough to silence the bodiless ghost.

There was a crackle of exploding speaker boxes behind her. The darkship was looping back, passing over the human nomads of the seanore, felling them with the proximity of its ear-bursting shields. The seanore didn't have any rotor-spears left, all their projectiles spent in the initial attack. A couple of shock-spears fired licks of energy at the darkship, too far away, their foe moving too fast. Close enough to hit it with

258

their hand weapons was near enough to be cooked by its mere proximity.

In front of the ship, a party of five seanores emerged from ambush among the underwater forest's fronds, flinging themselves towards the darkship in a suicidal frontal assault. Korda was among them. The leader of the Clan Coudama diving forward with a crystal-bladed harpoon, raising it to impale the supernatural vessel. They rushed the enemy vessel despite the agony they must be undergoing, its hymn of fear rupturing their eardrums, but the darkship and whatever agency propelled it into battle cared not a fig for their bravery. The evil craft accelerated through the war party, running them down, its surface briefly spiking out into a thousand small spines like a bloating pufferfish, a terrible cloud of floating limbs and skewered pieces of the fighters left behind.

Ignoring the roar of static from her speaker box, Charlotte fell back as the darkship's central weapon extended and carved the *Purity Queen*'s remains in half, riding through the boiling, bubbling water of the discharge. The darkship closed on her position. Charlotte's helmet phones squealed with all the distress of a swine feeling its throat slit, her helmet's machinery overloading under the fury of the vessel's dark radiations.

Daunt broke away from Sadly's grip as the first of the shallow-draft boats hit the beach, sprinting around a tiger crab's abandoned shell and vaulting the boat's gunwale. He was seizing one of the spare capacitor packs in the stern as Sadly and Morris caught up with him.

'We need that to return to the submarine,' one of the sailors in the rescue party yelled at Daunt. 'My battery's almost spent.'

Pulling the pack onto his back, Daunt twisted the trident off a side-clip connected to egg-scented chemical batteries by a dangling cable. 'Don't worry good fellow, I have an intuition that the tiger crabs won't be in the water on our return journey.'

Dick Tull was retreating backward, firing his rifle and reloading from the satchel of charges, bursts of sands and spouts of sea water all around him as the camp guards divided their fire between Boxiron's suicidal assault and the escaping prisoners. Sadly blocked Daunt's way, the Court of the Air agent's face incredulous as he saw the ex-parson trying to delay their departure. 'Are you cracked? You can't fight half the bleeding camp's guards with that!'

'There's too many of 'em, amateur.' Dick agreed.

'I don't intend to fight the gill-necks,' Daunt said, slipping past the hobbling agent. 'But I don't intend to leave Boxiron behind either.'

Not today. Not ever.

Sadly cursed the ex-parson, the cane that had contained the tracking isotope suddenly pressed into service to push him after Daunt's retreating form. He turned to the sailor in the prow of the first rescue boat as the second craft slid in under fire. 'Get these two men to safety. Tell the sub commander to hold steady.' He pointed at a sailor on the front of the second boat. 'You, wait for me.'

Using the cover of the abandoned shells, Daunt circled around the heart of the skirmish. Daunt gained the top of the grassy bank just as Sadly caught up with him. Hiding in the line of the everglades, the camp guards had realized their small-bore rifles were having minimal effect against the steamman. Now they were concentrating their fire on Boxiron with their heavy guns. The steamman's chest armour had been torn up, gaping holes in the iron revealing his innards, coiled pipes and crystal boards crudely cobbled together in the human mills that turned out artificial servants. Unfortunately for his attackers, their heavy weapons had also chewed chunks out of the power limiter they had fitted to his boiler heart. Its original function had been reduced to so much scrap metal, and now Boxiron was powering up, the warrior's stacks pouring ugly black spears of smoke into the air above him as he slipped through his gears. Boxiron lurched through their midst, fighting at close quarters, his twin machetes a dervish dance of death, lumbering, brutal, hacking and chopping. Breaking gill-neck bones with every contact of his body. If the guards had been concentrated in a single formation, Boxiron might have been able to overcome the gill-necks in the mêlée, but they were scattered up and down the beach. Their heavy guns boomed straight through their own ranks as they recognized that this was the only way to bring the steamman down. Before he turned his fury on them too. Boxiron's chest crumpled under the volley of fire, the plating he'd been fitted out with by the Kingdom's criminal under-world no match for the armour piercing shells loosed against him. Boxiron's right arm blew away in the assault, the steamman staggering and nearly slipping, briefly recovering, his left arm lashing out with a blade and catching a gill-neck in the face – or what was left of it after that terrible impact.

Daunt tore his gaze away from his friend's last stand. Down the slope was a line of rock pools, sand turning marshy where it joined the start of the undergrowth.

'You know why tiger crabs have adapted to the land almost as well as the sea?' Daunt said to Sadly, lowering his trident towards the beach. He didn't wait for the court's agent to answer. 'It's because this is where they lay their eggs, out of reach of their fellow predators of the ocean.' Daunt opened up with the trident, the sparking discharge of the power electric hitting the water and scattering across the damp breach, lightning chasing along the ground. There was a furious popping and whistling beneath the marshy sand, soft pieces of shell exploding out of the water. Daunt walked along the beach, squeezing the trigger under the trident's insulated handle, power forking out and causing the beach to erupt. 'Forgive me,' whispered Daunt.

'Beg that from their mothers, says I!' Sadly shouted.

Behind the two Jackelians there was an angry clicking as dozens of chirruping tiger crabs surfaced out of the sea, the cries and stench of their smoking young pulling in the adults.

Daunt sprinted across the marshy dune grass, down the slope towards the steamman, firing to his right as he ran, leaving a distinct trail for the furious trilling tiger crabs emerging out of the water to follow. 'Bob my soul, but now the camp guards will have something a little more pressing to aim at.'

Disoriented young crabs – megalops – each the size of a dinner plate, emerged from the blackened sand and broke through the sugar-like crust of slagged sand left by his capacitor's trident. Daunt zigzagged as he sprinted, but it was becoming increasing obvious that the camp guards had bigger fish to fry now – quite literally.

Salvos from the guards' rifles grew erratic, their fire redirected. The sight of dozens of angry tiger crabs lumbering up the beach and heading for them enough to turn any gill-neck's thoughts to self-preservation.

Sadly limped behind Daunt's trail, his cane now being used as a mere support, the boot of his good foot lashing out to overturn a snapping juvenile version of the monsters rising out of the sea behind them. 'That's what I love about this job, always something new.'

Daunt reached Boxiron, the steamman on his knees surrounded by a pile of dead gill-necks, any challengers either dead or retreating to cover in the tree line. The steamman was nearly sliced in two, half his chest blown away by the guards' heavy weaponry, exposed pipes ruptured and fountaining hydraulic liquid over his broken human-milled machinery. With only one arm left, he was flailing about, trying to stab the ground with his remaining machete. Daunt didn't know if there was purpose to the movements, or if the pain of his wounds had overwhelmed the steamman. *Thank the Circle, his precious steamman skull looks undamaged. At least, no more dented than normal.*

Boxiron's words fell out distorted from his shattered voicebox. 'I am finished here. Finished here.'

'Help me!' Daunt begged Sadly, the rat-faced agent moving in to support Boxiron's gashed open side where his right arm had been sheered off. Daunt took the weight of the semi-functioning steamman under the remaining shoulder, jagged rents in his friend's clavicle plate cutting through the cloth of Daunt's shoulder as he attempted to spur the steamman forward.

'You've got your strength back, old friend,' said Daunt, rubbing the area above the steamman's rotating calculation drum where the power limiter had been welded. *Please, just enough strength to see us to the boat.*

Boxiron's legs wheezed steam from his joints as he blundered forward, his knee gimbals buckling as they headed for the remaining rescue boat. Daunt could see the lick of energy from the sailors' capacitors as they held back the roused tiger crabs crawling ashore.

'What gear – am – I – in?' Boxiron's voicebox fluttered weakly.

Daunt glanced behind him. The gearbox on his spine wasn't even there anymore, a wreck of holed iron in its place, crystal boards sparking in anger underneath. 'You're in top gear, old steamer.'

''Ware the left,' warned Sadly.

Daunt's spare hand twisted the trident around and he triggered a burst of energy at the tiger crabs pincering towards them. The creatures stopped twenty feet away as the blast crackled around their carapaces, waving their claws towards him in an almost human gesture of defiance. Daunt grunted and hauled his friend forward. Moving with the steamman was like trying to walk with a house's weight in bricks stuffed inside a rucksack. If Boxiron's failing power gave out on them now, nothing short of a crane was going to get the old steamer to the rescue boat.

Just up this dune and across the sands to the water. We can do that. His tattered boots dug into the dunes, sand spilling into his shoes. *So heavy. Just a little further.* Daunt considered dumping the weight of the capacitor pack, but abandoned the idea as he saw the ring of tiger crabs closing in on the beached rescue craft.

'Clever perishers,' hissed Sadly, sweating as he dug his way up the slope with his cane. He was glancing behind them. The tiger crabs had formed into a line to attack the gill-necks in the tree line, an almost orderly queue, which meant the guards' heavy guns could only be bought to bear on the lead creature. 'Always had a taste for lobsters, says I. Never realized they were so bleeding smart, Mister Daunt.'

'Lobsters are a different genus from tiger crabs,' said Daunt. 'The nephropidae family. I'll wager you never served them in your ordinary.'

'Too many pennies for the great unwashed,' said Sadly as they reached the top of the dune.

There was a strange fizzing noise from within Boxiron's exposed chest, as if some chemistry was at work, an acidic green cloud merging from the torn rents, burnt rubber and a toast-like stench. Before the fleeting tendrils of smoke evaporated they seemed to coalesce into images of steamman faces, angular and proud and angry, the sea breeze catching the mist and rubbing them out as they formed.

'The Steamo Loa,' hissed Boxiron. 'Have I – earned a – warrior's end?'

Were the ancestral spirits of his people here to help or hinder? Here to claim a noble spirit and drag him into the deep layers of code in their Hall of Ancestors?

Daunt lurched forward, swatting the smoke with the tip of his trident. 'Away with you! You're not even proper gods. Just fireflies pestering his corpse. Your kind never helped him in life, only I did. All these years, you never came to help him.'

Tiger crabs scuttled away from the circle blockading the boat, advancing towards the exhausted Jackelians and their wounded comrade. Daunt lashed out with bolts of energy, driving them unwillingly off, reluctant to back down now. 'I deny you!' shouted Daunt. 'And so does Boxiron.'

The tiger crabs could almost taste their revenge against these interlopers who had dared make a battleground of their ancient hatching ground, but the lick of the power electric was a pain that even their toughened carapaces proved no defence against. Daunt and Sadly pushed through the gap in their ranks, the ex-parson's trident swinging left and right, with the capacitor pack whining in complaint to be run down so rapidly, fire flung to either side

At last, in front of the rescue boat, the three of them collapsed exhausted. Sailors in simple striped shirts and black canvas breeches leapt out to their aid as Sadly ordered the steamman to be hauled on board.

Boxiron's silver skull rested in the sand as the sailors found their purchase below his wrecked body. 'Always – my friend.'

'Preserve your strength,' urged Daunt.

Half the sailors waded into the water to refloat the rescue boat, electrical fire from the remaining crewmen licking port and starboard, the noise of the reversing screws blended in with an unholy snapping emanating from Boxiron's exposed innards.

CHAPTER ELEVEN

Charlotte looked in horror as a party of the *Purity Queen*'s surviving crewmen emerged disoriented from the u-boat's wreckage. They were crawling out of an airlock in her keel; once designed to drop submariners onto the seabed from the vessel above, but now part of the upended craft's topside. They emerged straight into the approaching darkship's field of view, the cutting beam from its bow spine slicing out and separating the crewmen's legs from their torsos. Maeva still had her back against the wrecked u-boat's hull, lying on flattened kelp fronds, a bed for her and the unconscious commodore nestled between her legs.

'Go, girl,' Maeva urged Charlotte. 'Swim away. You've no rotor-spears left and firing a shock-spear against that darkship would be like tossing seashells against a shark.'

'My bloody sceptre is still inside the *Purity Queen*, I'm not going anywhere.'

'A royalist antique won't be any good to a corpse. There's no glory in dying for it here.'

Damn the glory, it's the money I want.

It was growing hard to focus on Maeva's words, waves of

267

pain from the nearing proximity of the enemy vessel burrowing into her skull. Charlotte wasn't the only one feeling it. Maeva's teeth were gritted tight behind her diving helmet's visor.

Charlotte knelt to feel the commodore's suit for tears. 'How is he? Can you get him out of here?'

'He's sleeping and I think I'll join him. I'm too tired to run, too tired to want to live in a world where darkships have returned. Not like you. The prophecy rests with you. You're young enough to live through this. Go, leave us.'

Out above the kelp forest the darkship had returned to its task of cutting King Jude's sceptre out from the wreckage of the *Purity Queen*. Its weapons carved the Jackelian craft into slices, pockets of trapped air streaming out as the submersible was sliced into pieces as though she were a roll of cured sausage. One of the beams boiled the sea six feet away from where the survivors were sprawled out, superheated water scalding Charlotte's left side, her skin turning numb beneath her diving suit's canvas. She just caught sight of the darkship angling in for another strike, condensation misting up the surface of her helmet's visor. The next shot from the darkship would burst through the three of them, meeting as much resistance as heated cannon shot passing through rice paper. Her hands fumbled for the Eye of Fate.

Any advice?

'You're not alone.' Elizica's words formed inside her mind.

But she was. The commodore's u-boat was cut to pieces, any seanores minded to put up a fight were either dead or heading in the opposite direction. It didn't seem fair.

Charlotte blinked warm tears of condensation out of her eyes. *I was hoping for something a little more substantial, like "duck".*

The pear-shaped darkship was manoeuvring to open up on her when a shadow whisked overhead. For a second Charlotte thought it was the second darkship, but then she realized she could still hear a faint whining noise from her speaker box, both her eardrums intact and definitely not leaking blood down her ears.

'You're not alone! Your friends have returned with Jethro Daunt, and like any good churchman, he has come to drive away the devils.'

Charlotte had thought the darkships strange, but this submersible was even stranger: a rapidly moving silvery stretch of steel propelled by a spinning nest of metal tentacles at her stern, the mysterious u-boat's conning tower a low angular slash like a shark's fin. She had no visible portholes along her hull or plate lines and rivets, but the submersible did possess a cluster of torpedo tubes circling her dome-shaped bow, and a salvo of four torpedoes hissed in anger as she angled past the ambushed darkship. As seemingly surprised by the appearance of this late addition to the conflict as Charlotte, the darkship's lance belatedly blazed out. Dark bolts of ebony lightning ignited three of the four incoming projectiles, each lost in a flowering explosion upending Charlotte and slapping her back into the *Purity Queen*'s torn length. As Charlotte collapsed forward, she saw the darkship had acted too slowly to catch the fourth torpedo, the projectile's nose cone splitting away and shedding peels of metal, releasing a cloud of tiny warheads as though it had just given birth in the water. The fleeting school of miniature projectiles buzzed in against their quarry from a dozen directions, looping and striking the darkship as hungry and mean as a school of piranhas.

There was no immediate detonation forthcoming, and for a second Charlotte thought that the enemy's shield had neutralised the strike; then she realized the warheads had actually burrowed deep under its inky skin. With no shockwave Charlotte could feel, the darkship jolted as it absorbed the internal detonation, a dozen violent geysers of black substance spewing out. The darkship simply fell out of the currents, drifting down towards the seabed and dissolving into inky fronds as it dropped.

Rotating like a victorious dolphin, the submarine turned elegantly above the forest and angled back over the seanore camp, before the strange interloper returned towards the broken, beached hull of the *Purity Queen*.

Behind Charlotte, the second darkship, already badly damaged by the rotor-spear strike she had slipped beneath its defences, turned in the ocean and vanished at speed.

'Those who stand together are rarely beaten by evil.' Elizica's words slipped across her mind. 'Evil relies on its victims acting as selfishly and supinely as it must to prosper.'

But there are always losers. Charlotte looked down at the commodore sprawled at the foot of his ravaged submarine, dozens of seanore bodies floating past mutilated, corpses held in the embrace of the currents. Did carrion care which side won or lost after they passed along the Circle, or was there just the empty void where their life had been? A gap in the lives of all those who had known and loved them?

I'm going inside the wreck to get my sceptre.

'Be quick, girl-child. The enemy know you have fought here, they will return to this camp with equipment sensitive enough to pick up and track the trail of the sceptre's radiations.'

There are more of those things?

'The darkships will return with the gill-neck fleet, with everything they hold in their power, if it allows them to seize the sceptre.'

Gemma Dark prowled behind the chair at the head of the table, growing increasingly irritated at the petty sniping between the nobles sitting at the dozen seats dotted along its oblong length. Like much of the furniture in the gill-neck capital, the table was moulded from a single piece of transparent crystal, allowing her to observe the nervous twitches of the exiled royalist lords' hands and legs as they argued back and forth. There had always been a Star Chamber in the centuries since Parliament had seized power inside the Kingdom, maintaining the increasingly slim fiction that it was the true Jackelian government, ruling in proxy for a long-deposed line of kings and queens. Had the Star Chamber always bickered and fought as fiercely as this? It was no wonder the fleet-in-exile had eventually been broken and defeated when these chinless wonders had been leading it.

'It's simply not on,' pronounced Boris Jola, the present Baron of Ranfshire. 'We are only two weeks away from beginning the raids on Jackals' harbour towns, and now the entire Advocacy fleet is being sent away? Does that fellow Walsingham understand the first thing about war? To defeat your enemy, you must first engage him. Not go charging off, chasing after some damnable will-o'-the-wisp.'

'He has his reasons,' said Gemma. 'I did not detect any reluctance to go along with Walsingham's plans when he offered you and your crew a way out of the prison camp on the Island of Ko'marn. But perhaps you prefer picking gillwort fruit to fighting Parliament? Perhaps you prefer having the Advocacy hunt you down as pirates, rather than helping you sink Parliament's wheel-ships?'

'I always said it was dangerous to put our trust in Walsingham. Fellow's a turncoat, only after his own ends. No blue blood in that fellow, no breeding, I'm sure of it.'

Angry calls to concentrate on the invasion of Jackals came back at Gemma. When Gemma had come in here, she had arrived cheered by the news that her brother's precious submarine had been left a holed wreck on the seabed in the seanore hunting grounds. That traitorous dog Jared, that stain on their family's name, possibly dead – well, she would only believe it when she saw his corpse – but now her good mood was slowly being sapped by the inane prattle of these titled fools. Everything they had, they owed to Gemma and her allies, to *her* luck. And here they were, banging the diamond surface of the council table they sat at solely through *her* cunning and artfulness. Talking about unilaterally moving the forces of their allies, partners who only suffered the royalist cause through Gemma's contrivances. If ever there was a proof of absolute monarchy's worth, these twittering blowhards were it. The Jackelian throne had waited an age for a true queen to sit on it once more, an authentic queen, not Parliament's amputated puppet. When Gemma assumed her rightful seat, this council would be as much a thing of the past as that prattling chamber of robbing industrialists who occupied the House of Guardians. Parliament would never be swapped for this council of fools, not while she drew breath. *But for now, I need them.*

'The retrieval of the last surviving crown jewel would be a powerful totem I agree,' said the Countess of Stokesay, usually one of the more reasonable members of the Star Chamber. 'But worthy of the complete diversion of the Advocacy war machine, surely not? I'm still waiting to hear news that Parliament had declared war against the Advocacy in retaliation for the sinking of their convoy and the blockade of the new sea route.'

More than a totem, countess. But Walsingham's power is my power. Sometimes it was harder to remember that fact than it should be.

'Surely we can try to convince the rulers of the Advocacy that is in our mutual interest to defeat the Kingdom first?'

The countess asked, her voice full of prudence and reason. 'When we reign again, we can flush out the sceptre and take our pick of any of the old relics Parliament stole from our ancestors.'

'Enough!' Gemma jabbed a finger at the council. 'The gill-necks' laws only allow them to assist a legitimate regime, and we need the sceptre as a token of that.' How easily the lies tripped off her tongue, she really had been associating with Walsingham and his friends for far too long.

'A different interpretation of the law can be arrived at, perhaps?' said the countess. 'Isn't that why the Advocacy have a council of four princes, so they may consider different points of view?'

'My Countess Stokesay,' snarled Gemma. 'When I found you, you and your retainers were growing barley under assumed names in the colonies, barely better than indentured labour. And you, Lord Moray, a slaver for hire trying to scrape enough coins together to refuel your u-boat and feed your crew in a Cassarabian port. You, Baron Knighton, a jobbing privateer for the God-Emperor of Kikkosico, reduced to begging for licences of marque at a foreign court. All of you were finished without me, without the assistance I have been able to secure. I brought the cause back from the brink of extinction. Me! By my will and my luck. You were all raised, like me, by our parents with stories of what was stolen from us, from our ancestors. If you want your birthright to become anymore than fancies you whisper in turn to your children, then you will let our allies do what they must do, and in return they will bring us back everything we have lost!'

There was a silence as the impact of her words settled in. Gemma turned towards the transparent panel in the flat ruby-like stretch of wall in the tower so they wouldn't see the tears in her eye. Most of them still had sons and daughters to pass their dwindling inheritance onto. Hers lay dead in a foreign grave, killed by her jigger of a brother, freed from prison to die for Parliament's shilling and the greedy machination of the great Jared Black. Her brother had betrayed the cause. He had abandoned his life and his true name and his title and his family, living as a coward rather than dying as a hero. But Gemma wouldn't. Never. *It isn't as if I've been left with anything else to live for, is it?*

After the Star Chamber cleared of nobles, a door at the other end of the room irised open, Walsingham entering. It was easier thinking of him as Walsingham rather than one of the Mass. Deceptions were always easier to maintain when it suited you to believe in what you saw.

'You suffer their prattle with an ease I can only admire,' said Walsingham.

'I am their leader; they are my people. It is my duty to listen to their concerns.'

'Unquestioning obedience suits my temperament better, but to each their own.'

'I brought you to this point,' Gemma reminded him. 'I found you and released you.'

'An accommodation still exists between us,' said Walsingham. 'After all, we are so alike. Both clawing our way back from the brink, both seeking to help our people.'

'Do you really understand me, or are they just words of reassurance you believe I need to hear?'

'Oh, I understand you perfectly. You seek dominion over your people and your land. It is the way of all things, the most natural of all the universe's processes. Only that which is strong survives. All else whithers and is consumed.'

'It is not just my rightful dominions I want restored,' demanded Gemma.

'Quite. When we are victorious, I will give you the blessings of the Mass,' said Walsingham. 'That is our agreement. You will have a life as near immortal as makes no difference. Your youth will be restored.'

'My youth be damned, sir,' said Gemma. 'I need my womb functioning again.'

'I can only imagine how hard it is to lose an only child,' smiled Walsingham, coldly. There was very little empathy in that quick flash of white teeth. 'After all, I have so very many of them.'

'That's what I *need* to have.'

'And have it, you shall. An eternity to fill this world with your progeny. Every nation ruled by your children. Filled by them, too. You need only keep as many others alive as you need to feed the Mass and maintain a viable breeding pool. Queen of a new world; *mother* to it, as well.'

'Yes,' said Gemma, the flush of excitement hard to keep from her voice. 'That is how it will be. The countess was correct. We should set aside the matter of retrieving the sceptre for the moment. We've pushed the Advocacy and the Kingdom to the brink of war. Nudge them across the threshold and let them fight to the finish. In their ashes we will both prosper.'

Walsingham gave a facsimile of a smile. 'Our accommodation only stretches so far. It is not for the hunting hound to tell the shooting party what to take for supper. Leave the larger picture to us. You may still keep the scraps from the table.'

Gemma took Walsingham's own advice on unquestioning obedience, or at least the appearance of it, and said no more. Certainly not rising to the slight that to rule the Kingdom of Jackals could be considered mere table scraps. It was a dangerous thing to tie yourself to a shark. Sever the bonds of the saddle too soon and you might end up looking less like its rider and far more like its next meal. But Gemma's luck had brought her this close to victory; she had to trust it to carry her the rest of the distance.

Charlotte looked up as Jethro Daunt entered the control room of the Court of the Air's extraordinary u-boat. While the submersible's exterior was windowless, the craft's bridge was appointed with strangely translucent viewing ports. They appeared as if you could reach out and touch the ocean, feel water streaming past your fingers. These curious portholes were fringed by light from red glowing strips that illuminated the ex-parson's face, returning some colour to his pallid features. Between tending the ruins of Boxiron's once proud frame in the vessel's small surgical bay, Daunt had been wandering the u-boat looking increasingly washed out. Their surgical bay was growing cramped. Boxiron lay alongside Commodore Black, the old u-boat man tended by Maeva, who wouldn't shift from his side. With the rest of the seanore gathering their forces for war, the grand congress's survivors having tasted the bitter fruit of their ancient prophecy first-hand, Maeva's presence here was tantamount to abandoning her position among the Clan Raldama. Charlotte doubted the commodore would approve when – if – he regained his facilities. She could almost hear his scornful tones now. *There's no love so foolish, as old love.*

Dick Tull stood up from his seat by the small chart table and Sadly turned around from the planesmen's position at the front of the bridge, two pilots lying down on control couches as they guided and nudged the nest of control sticks and wheels at the fore of the vessel.

'Has the steamman been stabilized?' Sadly asked.

'There's little of him left to stabilize,' sighed Daunt. 'But I hope he will at least last until we reach the Court proper and put him in the care of your surgeons.'

'You still haven't paid for your passage, Mister Daunt,' said Sadly.

An uncharacteristic flash of anger crossed the ex-parson's face. 'I would say that Boxiron and the commodore have both paid plenty.'

Charlotte realized she was standing ramrod straight like a sentry, clutching King Jude's sceptre as though she held a rotor-spear outside a nomad's seabed dwelling. She got the feeling it wasn't going to be easy to relax here.

'The great game is always played ruthlessly, says I. Bait's meant to attract a nibble or two. You have my sympathy and more importantly, you currently have the surgical resources of my u-boat at the disposal of your friends. A little reciprocation if you please . . .'

'Just tell him what you found out, amateur,' said Dick. 'It's not as if I don't want to know why my own people are trying to top me.'

'That's rather the nub of the issue,' said Daunt. 'They're not your people anymore, sergeant. Walsingham and the commander of the convoy shared a curious trait with the prison camp commandant. None of the three gave off any of the tells which a Circlist priest would use to read their souls. They were blank of emotions, or rather, they were walking about as a rather hollow facsimile of the real thing.'

'The graveyard back at the camp . . .' said Sadly.

Daunt nodded. 'Filled with the corpses of Jackelian notables. The machine Walsingham and the commodore's sister used on me back on the island wasn't just designed as an interrogation device, it was designed to rip memories out of my brain and implant them in something ensconced inside in a similar machine. I don't doubt there's now an enemy walking the streets of Middlesteel which is perceived as identical to me, a creature that carries enough of my memories to fool

Stephen Hunt

most of the good people of my acquaintance.' He pointed at
Dick Tull. 'It was your story of the events at the mansion of
Lord Chant that first saw my suspicions tickled. Your partner
did see Lady Florence's murder. Doubtless she had questioned
some form of behaviour on the part of the thing she believed
was her husband that seemed out of character. She was
murdered, a facsimile of her ladyship inserted in time to make
you, good sergeant, appear like a fool. Your young partner
was murdered to cover the affair up, while you made the
perfect scapegoat to frame for the crime and be executed as
an enemy of the state.'

'Why not just replace me with one of them?' said Dick.

'I rather think our enemy is limited in number. That is how
you make sense of this absurd war brewing between Jackals
and the Advocacy. The most powerful state beneath the waves
set against the most powerful nation on the continent. Who
stands to benefit? Only a third party which wishes to soften
up both sides. Simple enough to arrange, I would imagine, if
you have infiltrated the government and military of both sides
and—' he indicated Dick, '—the secret police.'

Sadly's brow narrowed. 'Who is the enemy then, asks I?'

'Not who the Court believes is responsible, good agent,'
said Daunt. 'Cast your mind back to when the camp commandant's corpse changed and then spontaneously combusted
back on the island.' He smiled at Charlotte. 'In his ashes I
found this.' He produced a crystal from a side pocket in his
tattered waistcoat.

Charlotte reached out to confirm the Eye of Fate hung
around her neck. It was still there, yet the ex-parson was
holding the amulet's identical twin between his fingers.

'I am willing to wager, good agent, that up to now the
Court of the Air had been assuming the infiltrators are
Cassarabian spies? A logical deduction, given the caliph's

womb-mages are reputed to be able to warp their spies' blood code and give them the ability to change their features. And of course, the Kingdom has been trading shells and sabre parries with the empire along the southern frontier for years now.'

'They're always good for a spot of mischief, are the caliph's boys,' admitted Sadly.

'Quite,' said Daunt. 'But a Cassarabian shape-switcher wearing my face would still give away all the subtle tells of the race of man. The reason why there are infiltrators walking around like living blanks is that they *haven't* assumed the shape of the victims they replaced.' He tapped the side of his head. 'It is our *perception* they have stolen. A trick that Charlotte Shades, Mistress of Mesmerism is also renowned for. That gem around your neck aids the mesmeric process I assume? The enemy walks around as they are, but we see only what they want us to see.'

'It's mine, honey,' said Charlotte, touching her gem protectively.

'Not exactly,' said Daunt. 'Rather, let us agree that you're presently holding onto it for the spirit of the land and those who are to follow us, are you not? Please, damson, don't bother to dissemble. No one knows better than I how uncomfortable it is to be haunted by ancient things best forgotten. The church was willing to forgive much about me, but believing in gods was one heresy more than even they were prepared to tolerate. I have caught a few glimpses of what our enemy is, but you, or rather the spirit moving you around the land like a chessboard piece, has faced this threat before. There were hints in the history texts back at Tock House. An earlier war between the gill-necks and the Jackelians long before the last ice age. The way your gem defended you when you were attacked, your fever afterwards. The manner in which the seanore were practically falling down on their knees and worshipping you when we picked you up from the clans' gathering. You're not who you once were, your body language betrays you. It's as if you are two people sharing a single frame.'

Elizica's voice echoed in Charlotte's mind. 'It is time. Have them place their hands on the gem at the top of the sceptre.'

What are you going to do?

'The sceptre's gem carries echoes of its old purpose. Do as I have told you, girl-child.'

The party did as Charlotte bid them, the sceptre's jewel pulsing under her palm, the warmth of the others' bodies mingling with hers. Charlotte felt a dizzying sensation, but she didn't fall. It was as if she was becoming the sceptre, joining with what the gem on its cap had seen, the jewel's history unravelling in reverse order before her mind's eye.

The sceptre secure in the mausoleum beneath the speaker's chair in Parliament's chamber. Being polished by the Keeper of the Vault, an ancient title but little more than a janitor now in the great functions of state.

A retainer running with the sceptre wrapped up and concealed in rags, trying to sneak it across the border into Quatérshift. But Parliament's forces captured him. Hung him from a tree before they carried their prize back to the House of Guardians. Charlotte caught glimpses of royal history in the centuries before Parliament overthrew the last true king. Being carried by royals for coronations and the opening of Parliament – the Guardians little more than favoured poodles told when to bark and bite.

Centuries of cold and chill biting winds from the north. Then the sceptre was being locked away in a barrow mound, buried by a dying monarch as the Jackeni tribes dwindled, their numbers denuded at the beginning of the age of ice.

Earlier, earlier, and then the gem was being installed, hidden in plain sight on the newly created sceptre of a newly minted Kingdom. Before that it had served as far more than a mere ornament. Charlotte gasped soundlessly, held in the sceptre's spell. In the service of its *true* masters. Creatures that Queen Elizica had battled and known as the *sea-bishops*, the same hideously wizened and fanged monsters haunting Charlotte's dreams. Charlotte could see where the nickname had come from – sea-bishops – the monsters' distended brain cases, rising out of their skulls in offensive imitation of a bishop's mitre. The sea-bishops had been members of the race of man once, but on another Earth, one of millions stretched out on the thread of creation, a single pearl on a necklace containing infinite variants of itself, endlessly repeated reflections in a mirror. Mankind had abused this world, drained it with their vampire hunger, becoming ever more dependent on their machines, their bodies withering away even as their brains grew and swelled until their heads became the mitre-tall monstrosities that Elizica had named them for. The sea-bishops' minds developed to be powerful enough to amplify their will with crystal devices, compel the creatures of the world they shared to surrender their life-force to these terrible man-things evolved so far from their humanity. Cattle that would walk towards their death convinced they were approaching their own kind. Charlotte flinched as she realized that it was one of these trickster devices she wore around her neck. Every sea-bishop carried a duplicate of her amulet. A multifaceted tool: communication device, calculating machine, weapon and mesmeric camouflage apparatus combined. Eventually, nothing was left on the sea-bishops' Earth. No food, no vegetation, no fish in the ocean, no metals left to strip-mine, no coal to burn, no sunlight capable of penetrating the dark polluted clouds that choked and swirled around their home. With their land heated to hellish temperatures, the sea-bishops retreated to the dwindling oceans, changing their bodies to live underwater in the foul acid-ridden lakes that remained and cultivated the crystal machines that sustained them. With dwindling resources, they constructed their final piece of technological art – a vast diamond cannon that could punch a tunnel through the very wall of creation itself and hurl their seed sideways into new realities on which to feed. They expended incredible amounts of power to scatter their seed this way, but the sea-bishops' investment was repaid. Those that survived the journey and prospered would grow a huge crystal gate that could open a two-way connection between the reality they'd reached and their own dead, dark, mirror reflection of Earth. A terrible gate that could only be anchored at more than one thousand times the standard atmospheric pressure of sea level. This was why the sea-bishops' seed-cities inevitably settled on the deepest part of a host world's ocean; trenches that scarred the world, darkness that nestled and protected their hidden work until they were ready. Balanced by coequal quantum pressure on both sides, their portal could open with minimal energy expenditure, and through that doorway would swarm the never-ending Mass of sea-bishops from the victim world's dark twin. This was the seanores' legend of the deep hell. Demon locusts come to feed on the native population.

The jewel in King Jude's sceptre had captured echoes of a hundred such invasions before it arrived on Charlotte's Earth. Billions of victims, some human, many different in a myriad subtle ways, but all the children of Earth, and all consumed in great orgies of destruction. Wars were sparked, revolutions fomented by the sea-bishops' tricks, the host populations softened up before invasion. And only then did the demon hordes come. Children running towards people they thought

282

were their parents just to be impaled on deadly crystal blades and their life force consumed, husks discarded. Mothers desperately trying to find their offspring only to have their children reach out and stab them through the neck. Slaughter after slaughter, race after race, nation after nation, world after world. Feeding greed without end and hunger without limit. Worlds pissed on and polluted and raped. Charlotte tried to scream and cry and turn her sight away from these hellish visions, but Elizica held her tight, Charlotte's palm bonded to the sceptre like glue.

And the sceptre's jewel, the jewel tormenting Charlotte with these visions, it served as a key and a map combined. A key jealously guarded by the commander of each seed-city launched towards an unknown reality. For on some of the shadowy mirror worlds, creatures of greater power than the sea-bishops lurked – other sea-bishops more technologically advanced, or human analogues raised to near god-hood by the fruits of super-science. The sea-bishops were paranoid that their world would in turn become prey to some variant of humanity more powerful than themselves. The sceptre's gem held the secret co-ordinates of the sea-bishop's reality and it would only to be activated by the seed-city commander if a prey-world was judged susceptible to the sea-bishop's forces. Elizica had frustrated the sea-bishops' original plans, uncovering the plot during their first attempt to spark a war between the Jackelian tribes and the gill-necks. She'd worked to steal their precious key. Elizica had liberated the Eye of Fate and with the help of a great mechomancer, she had altered it along with six other amulets stolen from the corpses of dead sea-bishops. Changed the gems to allow humans to change their appearance. Seven heroes had infiltrated the seed-city of the sea-bishops, led by Elizica, stealing the key-gem and preventing the enemy from opening the gateway to their hellish home.

Before they had escaped, the heroes had plundered part of the seed-city's engine works, a shield that had protected the sea-bishops from the hideous destructive forces of being flung across the barrier of reality. Machinery which could create a bubble of space-time sitting outside of existence, the only shield capable of surviving the crossing. Elizica and the two surviving members of the raiding party had buried the device in the walls of the underwater trench and activated the shield, trapping the seed-city in a trap of time, sealing the enemy inside eternity's cold grip.

Daunt moaned opposite Charlotte and she felt Elizica siphoning his memories, the ones the ex-parson had glimpsed during his interrogation by the sea-bishops. Elizica drew them out and gave them context and meaning. Charlotte saw what the sea-bishops had seen, returning back to the world after the shield engine crystal had been dislodged by a landslide brought about by depth charges and Gemma Dark's blundering vessel. A desperate pirate trying to escape the Kingdom's navy. The sea-bishops had nearly fed on Gemma and her crew until they had realized that here were allies. That was the sea-bishop way. Powerful as they were, the scouts of the seed-ship were limited in number. They used trickery to sow dissent and weaken the host races of the mirror world they landed on, preparing them for an effortless conquest. The Advocacy had been targeted first, the gill-necks' Judge Sovereign and the Bench of Four an easy mark, a moribund society constrained to follow ancient laws, unquestioning of new rulings once issued. Then, helped by Gemma Dark and her rump of royalist survivors, the Kingdom of Jackals next, the most powerful nation on the continent, key members of its government and the House of Guardians subverted, followed by the generals at House Guards and the admirals of the RAN, the fleet sea arm, the secret police, and the editors of the most important newssheets. Slowly, slowly the two sides were pushed towards mutually assured destruction. And finally, with two nations subverted, the sea-bishops tracked down the lost key to their world-crossing gate, hidden centuries before by Elizica's descendants inside the royal sceptre of the Jackelian state. Protected by the whole apparatus of the House of Guardians and dozens of automated sentry systems. Too many people to murder and replace. But not a difficult problem to solve. Charlotte winced as she saw how easily the sea-bishops had drawn her into their web of corruption – the most infamous cat burglar in the Kingdom, always pushing her luck. Ripe to be baited into stealing the sceptre, then murdered and her corpse offered up as the thief who had stolen it. *And the sceptre? Oh, undoubtedly fenced and stripped and melted by now, but look, we caught the sly, wicked woman behind the theft. No need to search for the perpetrators of the crime now.* Charlotte felt herself drawn deeper into the sceptre's gem, layer upon layer of information etched into its crystalline structure, encryption so dense it would take the great transaction-engines of the civil service thousands of years to crack it. But for the sea-bishops, only a minute, the time it would take to slot it into their seed-city's machines and open up a bridge. Those seconds, the death sentence for every creature on Earth. The sceptre grew hotter, the warmth of Charlotte's contact with it burning, igniting her soul. With a screech of pain she broke the connection, lurching back and seeing the spell broken for Dick, Sadly and Daunt, the men panting with their faces as pale as alabaster and stamped with horror.

We have to destroy it, smash the crystal, Charlotte told Elizica.

'You don't think I tried girl-child? I hawked that gem around the nations of the world, looking for alchemical sorceries strong enough to destroy it. No blades, however sharp, can

285

cut it, no drills scratch it, no projectiles shatter it, no weights crush it, no energy disintegrate it. I spent twenty years after the exile of the sea-bishops neglecting my Kingdom and trying to destroy the key-gem. In the end, I could only hide it somewhere I trusted future generations would protect it.'

The royal sceptre of Jackals.

'The first of the sea-bishops, the seed-city commander, the one you call Walsingham. It is said he has a way of changing the key-gem's composition and rendering it breakable. But he would only use it if he thought we posed any kind of threat to the sea-bishop's home. And that I fear, we do not. Even in my age, we only managed to wall the enemy away. Temporarily, as it transpired.'

Dick Tull rubbed his unshaven cheeks. 'I know when they must have replaced Walsingham. He was operating out in the colonies, running the State Protection Board's operations against Pericur. When Walsingham came back it was as if he was a changed man. He rose to the top of the board like a meteor, second only to the head. It was unnatural how fast it happened.'

'Unnatural indeed, good sergeant. But in hindsight, quite understandable,' said Daunt.

'It's mine,' said Charlotte, lifting up King Jude's sceptre. 'The sceptre is mine and those stovepipe hat-headed jiggers are not laying one scaly claw on it.'

'In that little matter, you'll have the support of the Court,' promised Sadly. 'We'll try to keep it out of the sea-bishops' hands.'

'Try?' said Dick. 'You better do more than sodding try. You saw what's waiting for us if those monsters get the key-gem. They'll finish off everyone in the world.'

'It's not like the old days,' said Sadly. 'The Court of the Air isn't what it used to be. You'll see.'

CHAPTER TWELVE

When Commodore Black came onto the bridge of the submersible, Daunt noticed it was with the support of a cane and trailed by Maeva, the old u-boat man shushing the woman and protesting her attentions, accusing her of being a 'blessed clucking hen'.

Daunt was glad to see that the commodore had healed relatively rapidly, but the sight of him back on his feet was a painful remainder that Boxiron was nowhere close to a similar recovery. Quite the opposite, in fact. Every day at sea seemed to bring a fresh challenge in keeping the steamman clinging onto life. It wasn't the fault of the small surgical bay – it had been equipped to deal with patients from the race of man, not a failing citizen of the Steamman Free State. The logical part of Daunt's mind knew that a single person's life was an insignificant matter in the balance of the great game they had been caught up in. But his friend's dwindling reserves of energy and increasingly tenuous hold on the great pattern somehow seemed far more concrete than the prospect of the sea-bishops opening up a gateway back to their infernal home.

'So here we are again, good captain,' Daunt greeted the

commodore. 'Wedged between that rock and a hard place. How is—?'

'Boxiron's a tough old bird,' said the commodore. 'And this boat's surgeon is game for a challenge. He got my creaking old bones back on their feet.' He waved Maeva away. 'Stop fussing, lass. There's plenty that's lining up to kill old Blacky, but it won't be a spot of exercise that does for me.' He hobbled over to the chart table and traced the headings mapped out on the table. 'What's this – this heading can't be right?'

Daunt peered to where the commodore's attention lay. The ex-parson wasn't an expert, but to his eyes the temperature gradients of the chart seemed to be running significantly hot. They were aiming for the margins of the Fire Sea. 'You've navigated us through worse than that before, surely?'

'No, lad, I haven't. This—' he stabbed his finger on the centre of the bearing. 'This is the Isla Furia. No sane sailor crosses that part of the Fire Sea.'

'The island doesn't appear to be located far inside the magma fields?'

'There's no need for it to be positioned any deeper, Jethro Daunt, for a sensible skipper to avoid it. There's an underwater vent in the region mortal fiery enough to cook out even the best u-boat's cooling system. The Isla Furia has a volcano that's the devil's own cauldron; you sail past that island and you're liable to find molten boulders as large as houses raining down on you. And should its rocks miss your hull, the terrible place spews out choking clouds of poison gas.'

'You've seen this with your own eyes?'

The commodore tapped the charts. 'From seventy miles away, that I have. As close as I ever wanted to get. We're almost on the Isla Furia's doorstep, so you'll have the sight in front of your eyes soon enough.'

That he did. Daunt saw what the commodore was afraid

of through the bridge's oddly transparent portholes. They were passing over an underwater plain of superheated water, the boils that fringed the magma fields of the Fire Sea, a basalt surface littered with the wreck of vessels, craft from dozens of nations and as many centuries. Paddle steamers and clippers, galleons and fire-breakers, u-boats and liners, debris overgrown with strange organic sculptures of fire coral.

'This wreckage grows thicker the closer you get,' said the commodore. 'Those poor devils are just the surface craft whose crews were overcome with gas and holed lightly enough for them drift out a-ways before sinking on the margins of the Isla Furia.' He turned to find Sadly, the court's agent standing behind the two horizontal pilot positions. 'Did you lose a grip on your marbles, lad, in that terrible prison camp you were locked up in? Have you taken a bump on your noggin while escaping? You're heading for super-heated vents – that's the Isla Furia on the horizon!'

'We're not a conventional craft,' said Sadly. 'We're rated for where we're heading.'

'And are you rated for being hit by a squall of molten depth charges as large as carts, lad? For that's what waiting for you on this course. I know the Fire Sea. No one has penetrated as deep as old Blacky into this foul place. Turn north-north-west twenty degrees and head for the Abbadon boils. Better choppy waters than suicidal ones.'

'I'm feeling lucky, says I.'

Daunt reached out to steady the commodore, the u-boat man shaking with incredulous anger and his remaining fever. 'Peace, good captain. I believe the Court of the Air prefers the sort of luck it can manufacture, rather than relying on fate's random charity.'

'I've just had my precious *Purity Queen* filleted by a pack of black-hearted demons and now you want me to risk my neck on this exotic tub of the Court's? Poor old Blacky, sick and in his dotage, chased out of his home by traitors and devils set on his tail by his wicked sister, hounded across the seas . . . and now his unlucky stars are calling for a chance to toss boiling boulders at him? It's a happy thing I won't be around for much longer, Jethro Daunt. A happy thing fate won't have these miserable bones to torment!'

Daunt said nothing and waited. Up ahead, the underwater plain was littered with the graveyard of vessels, ships laying on ships, moulded together by thick fire coral, a floor of unwise mariners and submariners forming their own geological strata. Beyond the hills of coral, a curtain of steaming water from the broken vents of the seabed shimmered. So thick with fury that nothing was visible beyond its violent turmoil. Undaunted, the Court's vessel passed over the carpet of destroyed craft, heading right for the centre of the maelstrom.

'Tell me, Barnabas,' the commodore moaned, 'Tell me the name of this strange craft of yours so I know on what boat my end is to come?'

'The Court doesn't name its vessels,' said Sadly. 'We're travelling on U-boat 414.'

The commodore flinched. 'No, lad, no! You talk to me of your blessed luck, then you tell me you're challenging all the forces of the sea by daring to sail on a vessel with no name?'

Sadly just smiled 'The *Purity Queen* carried a name. How long did you last against that pair of darkships?'

As Jared Black moaned, Daunt gazed at the raging wall coming up at them. In his frail state, the commodore might be better sleeping his exhaustion off next to Charlotte's cabin, or playing cards with Dick Tull and the surviving crewmen of the *Purity Queen* in the hold. True to Sadly's word, the submersible hit the wall of superheated water and passed through it with none of the creaks and complaints that would have sounded from the hull of a normal Jackelian submersible. The temperature on the bridge stayed at the same comfortable level, the gentle ticking from fans inside the airvents continuing as untroubled as if they were cruising off the green waters of the Kingdom's coast. Seconds after they had breached the curtain, its boiling frenzy evaporated leaving them travelling down a clear corridor of sea water. The furious underwater boils walled them in port and starboard, with spherical objects half-visible through the turbulence, a chain of iron orbs tied to the sea floor by cables. *Sea mines.*

'By Lord Tridentscale's beard, what's this?' the commodore cursed.

'The Court's luck,' said Daunt. 'Is that not so, good agent?'

Sadly said nothing, but he didn't need to.

Daunt pointed outside. 'These vents aren't natural, they're an artificial thermal barrier. Machines under the seabed cooking the water, with mines to sink anyone that tries to push through the shield. There must be something of considerable value on the Isla Furia to warrant all of this.'

'I think you'll find we will be able to protect your sceptre,' said Sadly.

'Bob my soul, but I hope so.'

The thermal barrier must have been protecting the island for the Court for centuries, designed by the mad, bad and dangerous to know. The graveyard of vessels stretching for miles beyond its curtain spoke volumes for its lethal efficiency. It took a minute to clear the corridor through the curtain of heat, walls sealing behind them as they passed, but whatever Daunt had been expecting on the other side, it wasn't what he found himself facing.

Beyond the thermal barrier stretched the submerged ruins of a city. Much of it looked like blackened termite mounds,

291

thousands of buildings towering and ruined and slagged. So ancient, that its structures had decayed into featureless underwater spires, only the occasional areas of surviving symmetry or flat surfaces to indicate that something sentient had once had a hand in these crags' formation. But among the lofty termite mounds, hundreds of storeys high, were scattered other buildings – better preserved, signs of stone carvings and ornamentation visible on smooth surfaces, pitted by hundreds of oblong holes. Windows once, now glassless doorways for schools of fish to dart through, the surface light slanting down onto a grid of uneven, half-silted streets.

'Bob my soul,' said Daunt. 'I have never seen its like.'

'I have,' said the commodore. 'A far ways off from here, though. The ruins of the city of Lost Angels on the seabed. One of the world's wonders.'

Sadly stood by the main view screen at the front of the bridge. 'Ironically, our scientists believe the better-preserved buildings down there are actually the oldest. They were probably sprayed with a substance that resists age. The anthills were the last buildings to be built. They're little more than dirt and dust held together by kelp now.'

Even the commodore seemed impressed. 'Compared to those sunken behemoths, the tallest tower in Middlesteel would stand like a blessed blade of grass next to a sunflower. What manner of creature lived out there?'

'You'll meet their descendants on the island,' said Sadly.

The Isla Furia's underwater rock face loomed ahead, a jagged rise of dark volcanic stone holed by caves. The Court's submersible headed for one of the openings, lanterns inside the tunnel activating as the craft entered, the vessel's own bow lights switching off. She passed confidently through a smooth arrow-straight cavern, before passing out into another stretch of water, this revealed as an inland lake when U-boat

414 surfaced. Ahead of the bridge's pilot screen a walled town was visible, concrete u-boat pens upon the shore waiting to receive their vessel. There wasn't much to see of the town beyond its high fortifications. Whatever lay beyond the wall, it obviously wasn't a land-locked counterpart of the ruined spires under the sea. They docked in the shadow of the volcano. It was a beast all right, the commodore had been right about that. Towering twelve thousand feet high, clouds of thick white smoke poured out of its throat. Current discharges aside, there seemed little sign of the violence and magma the old u-boat man claimed to have witnessed. In fact, as they docked, Daunt could see the Isla Furia's slopes were covered with terraces growing crops, a series of metal pylons driven into the incline bearing cable cars up and down into the city below.

Daunt scratched his chin. 'This is the Court's?'

'More or less,' said Sadly. 'We landed on the Isla Furia centuries ago, looking for a secluded ground base to support our operations. The islanders we found here are called the Nuyokians. Like all the tribes on the Fire Sea islands, they'd been locked inside the magma and boils of the ocean and trapped here. The natives were in a sorry state, dependent on the rain season for their crops on the slopes, blood sacrifices to hold off the steam storms. Over the centuries they've worked for us, intermarried with our staff. Agents that survive our calling often as not come here to retire.'

'And now,' said Daunt, 'this is all that remains of the Court of the Air?'

'What do you think we've been doing since the great war with the Army of Shadows, sitting on our arses and gossiping about the good old days?' said Sadly. 'We're rebuilding the Court in the marshalling yards beyond the city, making ready to refloat a new aerial city. Recruiting agents, finding the wolftakers that were scattered across the continent and bringing them back into the fold.'

'Did you ever think that the Kingdom doesn't need you anymore?' said the commodore. 'All your tricks and sly ways. The conniving legacy of Isambard Kirkhill.'

The badinage hurled against his employer cut no ice with Sadly. 'As long as there are wolves to prey on the flock, there'll be a need for shepherds, say I.'

'Wolftakers. Well, damn the lot of you,' spat the commodore.

'You might as well ask does the Kingdom need a future,' said Sadly. 'Do you think the sea-bishops would have got as far as they have done if the Court was still watching above Jackals, protecting the nation? Who would you rely on without us? The State Protection Board, civil servants and badly paid jobsworths like Dick Tull? Don't make me laugh. I need to report in to my superiors. You'll stay on board until we send for you.'

'I trust you will get them to see reason,' said Daunt.

'Don't you worry about that, Mister Daunt. I'm sure my nightmares are just the same as yours since I touched that cursed sceptre.'

'And Boxiron, good agent?'

'We'll take care of him in the Court's hospital. You just settle down and write me out a nice long list of all the names you saw in the prison camp's graveyard. I have a feeling there's a lot of nobles, industrialists and members of the government who are going to go missing in the next few months.'

'Don't underestimate the sea-bishops,' warned Daunt.

'Don't underestimate the Court of the Air,' retorted Sadly. 'Reduced circumstances or no, this is what we do.'

Holding the Kingdom's future in the Court's hands. Well, that was true enough. If Daunt couldn't protect the sceptre here, keep it out of the sea-bishops' clutches. There wasn't going to be a future for any of them.

When the call came to meet Sadly's superiors in the Court of the Air, Charlotte was happy to be able to leave the submersible's claustrophobic confines. It was strange to be out in the hot prickly sunshine again, her feet swaying uncertainly on the gangway across to the submarine pens. She used King Jude's sceptre as a staff, feeling like some fraudulent prophet come visiting this lost tropical island sealed away on the outskirts of the Fire Sea. Between being confined to the tight confines of u-boats and floating through the underwater alien world of the seanore, the experience of solid land and an endless sky combined to make her homesick and unsteady on her feet at the same time.

Boxiron had already passed over this gangway, borne off in a stretcher that looked more like an iron coffin; Jethro Daunt had to be restrained when the locals wouldn't let the ex-parson accompany the unfortunate steamman to his upgraded medical facilities on the island.

Nestling in the lee of the Isla Furia's great volcano and encircled by a thick red stone wall, the town of Nuyok was hidden out of sight. Some fourteen metres high, the bulwark concealed all sight of the buildings within. The wall had only been constructed, Sadly had intimated, to protect the citizens of the town from the wildlife of the jungle covering the rest of the island. This would explain its parlous state of repair – cracked and overgrown by ivy in many places, while fishermen and trappers in wide-brimmed straw hats moved slowly and deliberately in the heat across the harbour. Flat-bottomed rafts, cork-lined against the heat and sporting rainbow-coloured sails, shifted across the lake where their submersible had surfaced. At the far end of the lake Charlotte could just see a series of docks controlling access to the Fire Sea beyond, too small for submersibles, but just the right size for the small fishing skiffs.

Complaining about the wicked heat, the commodore groaned with satisfaction as he was helped into the back of a rubber-wheeled cart, the contraption pulled by a pair of man-sized running lizards. Peeling yellow-painted boards rattled as it carried the party towards a looming pair of iron gates on rollers, a partial gap opened in the portal for them to enter. Passing inside, Charlotte had never seen a city looking so ordered. The majority of buildings facing them were five storeys tall, tiered with apartment railings, each surrounded by a stretch of neatly manicured lawns formed from evenly cropped green grass. With hexagonal walls sculpted out of white porcelain glittering in the sunlight, the buildings' architecture mirrored the streets they were set in, road after road laid out in hexagonal grids. It wasn't the uniformity of the hexagonal concourses that first grabbed Charlotte's attention, however. What drew her eyes were the roads, formed out a thick clear acrylic which revealed level after level of subterranean maintenance tunnels, plumbing and pipes. *The roads are transparent.* Basement levels descended below the walled city as though the whole city was a scaled up model solely constructed to demonstrate the ebbs and flows of its sanitation.

With the flawless white glimmer from the porcelain buildings, the city had the feel of ancient times about the site, as though its inhabitants were living within a grid of oversized antiques. It put Charlotte in mind of a museum exhibition of priceless pottery from which she once liberated a few choice pieces. In contrast to their architecture, the Nuyokians reflected little of the sophistication of the buildings they inhabited. She could believe they had constructed the crumbling wall guarding the town, but the city itself? The people had the air of country bumpkins who had wandered into the place from some small village and finding it uninhabited had decided to stay. Well-tanned, Nuyokians tended the town's lawns and wandered its hexagonal roads in simple long-shirts that reached down to bare knees or drawstring trousers, others wearing sleeveless cotton tunics with blanket capes and closed-shoulder capes that provided a few garish splashes of colour. They drooped out of their balconies sucking on cuds of brown leaves or occupied themselves on roof gardens in the centre of each building. As Charlotte got closer to the volcano's slopes, she wondered at how the natives could appear so calm living in the shadow of that monstrosity vomiting out billows of white smoke into the sky. Perhaps it was from prayer? Little cupboard-sized stone temples were scattered outside the entrances of the apartments. Nuyokians busied themselves in supplication to marble statues of a female goddess, the idols kneeling with stone oil-filled lamps lit at their knees – a goddess, Sadly explained, known as the Lady of the Light. Daunt nodded in understanding, explaining that there were similar figures appearing in the mythology of other tribes of the Fire Sea islanders, gods that may have shared a common ancestry with the Nuyokians' deity.

Approaching the foot of the volcano, Charlotte discovered the hexagonal buildings swelling in size and grandeur, as though this district served as a palace quarter for the city rulers once upon a time. Rolling through large parks and gardens, the party reached a station where a series of cable car lines reached across the slopes above them. The lines passed above hundreds of farm terraces where figures could be observed tending hillside crops of wheat, rice and corn.

Leaving their cart's driver giving his running lizards a drink of water from a porcelain trough, Charlotte followed Daunt, the commodore and Dick Tull across the station concourse. Sadly led them past an ancient statue of a naked man bearing the skeletal sphere of the world upon his back, the whole thing sealed inside a larger sphere of the same transparent acrylic material that composed the streets.

The commodore indicated the open sliding door of a cable car for Charlotte. 'Beauty before age, lass. And maybe you can ask that ancient phantom knocking about your noggin to put a good word in with the fire spirits of the Isla Furia to keep us from being cooked into stone casts. What a puzzle we'd make, for some future professor of history to marvel that there were people fool enough to live in the shadow of that ugly heap of magma up there.'

'I have a feeling that the threat of the volcano has been somewhat overstated,' said Daunt, looking meaningfully at Sadly.

'It seems to be puffing away up there as happy as a sailor with a mumbleweed pipe,' said the commodore. 'I don't need to get any closer to observe it. Not after sailing past that graveyard of ships outside.'

Charlotte received nothing from Elizica, not even a feeling of unease; but the volcano's throat did seem to be simmering away on the summit, billows of white smoke folding over each other and being carried high into the clear blue sky beyond. There wasn't much about the cable car she boarded to suggest it belonged to the walled town of Nuyok, its sleek lines and glossy surface reminding her of the submersible that had carried them here. A later addition, then. The Court of the Air's handiwork. Charlotte had a good eye for such abnormalities – often all the difference between stepping on, or avoiding, a slightly out-of-place floor tile and bringing a wall of bars plunging down to trap her inside a vault.

With a low whine, the cable car lifted out of the station

and began to climb up the slopes. They passed over regularly spaced terraces and an intricate network of drip irrigation channels, plenty of farm workers in simple cotton shifts moving about the crops – plain room-sized huts for them to rest in or store equipment the only signs of construction on the incline. So where were they being taken? She looked at the Isla Furia below. As they drew higher up the rise, the party could see the landscape falling behind, smaller and smaller. The city inside its walls occupied a square stretch of territory, the hypnotizing uniformity of its hexagonal streets broken in very few places – only by parks or larger buildings – also hexagonal, which had to serve non-residential functions. Everything was constructed from the same white porcelain, reflecting bright sunlight. It stood seven miles across, Nuyok's transparent streets resembling rivers of glass this high up. Moon-shaped, the crescent of the lake surrounded the city on two sides, the volcano covering a third flank, while the distant jungle could be seen nestling against the remaining boundary. A section of their cable car network branched off and headed down the volcano, entering the distant jungle to the rear of the city. Charlotte could just discern the distant crane heads and docking pylons of an airship yard rising above the jungle, and if she stretched her ears, she imagined she could hear the distant thud of the works.

'Are you going to sacrifice us at the top, then?' asked Commodore Black. 'Is that how the Court obtains its intelligence these days – blood sacrifice?'

'The Court's agents have made plenty of sacrifices,' said Sadly. 'But they're normally paid in our blood.'

Lifting them all the way to the summit, the cable car levelled out, the pylon's chains entering a dark tunnel on the mountainside. It only took a minute to pass through, and on the other side of the darkness they emerged into the interior crater of the volcano. Rather than the bubbling lake of lava Charlotte had been expecting to find, the interior of the crater towered with buildings and massive pipe-works, a series of gantries and girders bridging the interior space. The upper edge of its rocky rim was curved with exhaust vents pumping out smoke in mimicry of a live volcano.

'There's your volcano, good captain,' said Daunt. 'The discharge from mine works. A celgas mine if I'm not mistaken.'

'The Court's greatest secret,' said Sadly. 'The only place other than Jackals where a significant vein of the gas has been found. But then we had to lift our aerial city somehow, and the Kingdom's got its own supply of airship gas sealed too tight for us to tap on a regular basis.'

'But what about the wicked molten rain, lad?' said the commodore, astonished he wasn't facing a live volcano. 'I've anchored seventy miles off this coast and watched magma coming down thick enough to leave a Jackelian ironclad more full of holes than a lump of blessed cheese?'

Sadly pointed to a crown of massive pipes encased in machinery circling the rim of the crater. 'Your rocks are real enough, but they're heated in furnaces here and then catapulted out under hyper-pressure. Our lava launchers have got a lot more accurate over the centuries since we landed here. For anyone that survives a bombardment from those, the island's coastline has concealed dirt-gas flues to choke would-be trespassers.'

'Bob my soul, but I knew there was something on the island worthy of the efforts you've made to discourage visitors,' said Daunt.

'You should consider yourself fortunate,' said Sadly. 'You may be the first people in history outside our ranks to see this place.'

Charlotte held onto the railing in the cabin as their cable

car passed through a forest of girders, elevator belts, hoists, piping, gantries, walkways and ladders suspended across the crater's heart. Something of such colossal value as celgas was always enough to pique her interest, but stealing bulky airship gas cylinders wasn't a proposition worth pursuing. That was the beauty of jewels and rare paintings, their portability and resale value. It was just unfortunate the buyers of King Jude's sceptre only wanted the piece to unleash a horde of starving demons on the world. That was one situation where having the money *wouldn't* help.

Coming across the gantries marched steammen – the human-milled variety, rather than citizens of the Steamman Free State. They were a polished copper colour, hulking things seven feet tall with a single rotating transaction-engine drum turning in the middle of each chest. On their back they had twin stacks behind each shoulder blade. Their head units resembled a cuirassier's helmet, each with three camera-like eyes giving their skulls an insectoid appearance. Some had two arms, but many had multiple limbs – four, five, six or more arms, or tools and cutting equipment serving as appendages.

Sadly noticed where Charlotte was looking. 'We've always relied on automatics on the island. Locals are happy to help out with most things, but they don't like coming inside the volcano. Old superstitions die hard.'

'All those years in your gaff,' said Dick Tull, the bitterness in his voice evident. 'Me eating that slop you served and taking whatever scraps and tip-offs you tossed my way – and all that time you had all of *this* behind you.'

Sadly didn't appear even slightly embarrassed by the subter-fuge. 'A lot more than this, once, Mister Tull. And again, soon. The Court's far subtler than the sea-bishops. A nudge here, a nudge there, and softly softly catchy monkey. We've always operated on the principle that you receive a much

301

easier ride in the great game if your opponent doesn't realize there's an opponent sitting in the chair opposite the board.'

'So it's true then?' said Daunt. 'The Court has a predictive model of society running on its transaction-engines. You really believe you can shape the world's events to a single plan?'

'You and your inquisition friends,' said Sadly, only half a sneer. 'It would be truer to say we've got a backup of the original model running now, says I. What with all that bother during the invasion. The accuracy of the new model will be up to snuff by the time the next Court of the Air is refloated.'

'You detected the infiltration of the Kingdom off the back of transaction-engine analysis?' Dick asked, not bothering to hide his surprise.

'Punch card artists are good for a lot more than working out how much has been paid in taxes and who's shelled out enough to become a duke this year,' said Sadly.

The State Protection Board officer looked grey and tired. 'I've got to get out of this bloody game, I really have. I used to think I understood how it operated, how things were done. Instead . . .' his voice trailed off.

'We're on the same side, really,' said Sadly. 'It's just the Court's in for the long haul, the long view.'

'That you are,' said the commodore. 'But this government rascal and the likes of poor old Blacky, we haven't got enough years left apiece to play along, nor the energy remaining to care for the cleverness and cunning wheezes you've got turning on your thinking machines' drums.'

'I rather think your people have lost sight of the human perspective, good agent,' said Daunt. 'For all you've tried to do here, protecting the Kingdom, our future's pivoted on the fate of young Damson Shades and the actions of myself, Boxiron, the commodore and—'

Sadly interrupted. 'But then, the Court's not the only one

with a plan, eh?' He looked at Charlotte. Still, Elizica passed no comment to Charlotte. 'And there's a thin line between assistance and meddling when it comes to the Court's calculations.'

Daunt winked at Charlotte. 'I wonder what side of the line we will be judged as occupying?'

'So do I,' sighed Sadly. 'Like I said before, we're not the organisation we used to be. Half our lot were listed as dead and missing after the Army of Shadows' invasion, with the vacancies left filled by greenhorns, agents bought out of retirement and support staff.'

They docked with a large building built into the opposite side of the crater. The commodore was the second to step out of the cable car, following Charlotte. 'The mill's been shut down, the labourers laid off, but the clerks in the counting house are still shuffling around their blessed pieces of paper, is it?'

'We're in a better state than that,' said Sadly, but something in the way he said it made Charlotte think that the old u-boat man might be closer to the mark than the agent would prefer.

Sadly led them into the building, through a nest of corridors and stairs, until the smooth rock face of the mountainous volcano replaced the metal walls of the building. Guards in close-fitting leather uniforms checked them before admitting the party any further into the complex. They carried strange-looking rifles with bulbous stocks that caught the commodore's attention. Sadly explained that they were gas-rifles, capable of firing steel darts at enormous velocities from the rotating drums above their forestock without the need to break the rifle and insert a fresh charge after each shot. They could no doubt maintain a murderously fast rate of fire. Not quite as bulky as airship gas cylinders, Charlotte had a few acquaintances back in Middlesteel's criminal underworld that would pay a small fortune to acquire such a weapon. But how to get it off the Isla Furia without getting caught?

There was a chlorine smell about the corridors they passed through. The scent sparked a memory of the public bathing rooms back in the capital – residue from the centuries of celgas mining operations, perhaps. Led into a large chamber, Charlotte saw they were left in front of a raised floor and a series of chairs, behind which curved one of the clear almost magically transparent view screens displaying the smoking vista of the Fire Sea beyond. Only one of the chairs was occupied, a balding man with two patches of wispy white hair clinging behind large ears, staring down on them over a pair of hexagonally framed spectacles. Charlotte had seen enough colleagues sent down in front of the middle court back home to know what this chamber was meant to signify. He cut a lonely figure up on the raised floor, a magistrate with most of his stenographers and court officials missing.

'This,' Sadly introduced, 'is the acting advocate-general of the Court of the Air, Lord Edwin Trabb.' He bowed towards the seat above. 'And my lord advocate, these are the group who have been frustrating the schemes of the infiltrators we now know as the sea-bishops. Jethro Daunt, ex of the church, Jared Black, ex of the royalist fleet-in-exile, Dick Tull, ex of the State Protection Board, and Charlotte Shades, ex of the flash mob and the present guardian of King Jude's sceptre.'

'The clever, the desperate, the barely competent, and the incorrigibly criminal,' said Lord Trabb. 'As strange a group as I've had presented before me in a long time.'

'You can't have many visitors out here,' said Charlotte.

'I believe you've seen the hulls of those that do,' said Lord Trabb. 'Mounds of hasty trespassers sunk on our doorstep and overgrown with fire coral.'

304

'*Acting* advocate-general,' said Daunt. 'And whom might I inquire are you acting for?'

'Ah yes, the clever one.' Lord Trabb pushed his glassed back on his nose. He seemed to enjoy lecturing them. The chamber was starting to feel less like a courtroom and more like a schoolroom. 'Well, you've given our elusive enemy a name and a face, albeit not quite the one we were expecting, so why not? I am acting for Lady Riddle, who was declared missing when the old Court of the Air was destroyed in the invasion. My department was the only one to survive unscathed, so it seemed natural for me to occupy the role. I would declare myself the real thing and dispense with the formalities, but milady Riddle has a disconcerting habit of disappearing and then reappearing when you least expect her.'

'And your department, good agent?' said Daunt.

'Section Six,' said Trabb. 'The Service and Engineering Corps.'

The commodore looked unhappy at the news. 'Ah, that's a bad turn. We've come seeking a way to keep this sceptre out of our wicked foes' clutches and instead we find grease-stained fingers guiding the tiller, not the skipper's firm grip.'

'Come now, I hardly think the desperate one is in a position to cherrypick his allies,' said Lord Trabb. 'And by your words you mark yourself out to be a fool. Who better to rebuild the Court of the Air than the very marshalling yards that maintained the old aerial city, the same academy that trained the old agents to teach the new? We have a backup model of the Kingdom's society running here, the perfect template for the perfect democracy. That is all that matters in the end.'

'It'll matter a lot less than you think, lad, when the demons chasing the sceptre turn up in their darkships, wanting to open the gates to their terrible home full of hungry ravening beasts.'

'I would council against complacency,' said Daunt. 'From what we've seen, the sea-bishops have fully infiltrated the Advocacy's leadership. When they come for the sceptre, it will no doubt be at the head of a sizeable gill-neck force.'

'I had no idea the Circlist church's remit extended to military matters?' said Lord Trabb. 'I rather had the notion you were all pacifists. To kill another is to kill myself and all that synthetic morality cant.' He waved Daunt's concerns aside. 'It is all in the model now. The sea-bishops and their schemes are fully accounted for.'

'Popinjay!' Elizica's words jabbed into Charlotte's mind. 'Am I to trust this dusty clerk, this oily-ragged boiler repairer with protecting the sceptre? Knowing of the sea-bishops' existence is not the same as having won hard experience of fighting them.'

'Tell me you can protect the sceptre,' said Charlotte. 'That you can protect the Kingdom.'

'My dear, it's what the Court's been doing for a lot longer than you've been around. The enemy are weak and far from home and dependent on secrecy and their little tricks of illusion to prosper. Now that we know what to look for, we'll root them out like a gardener clubbing moles with a spade, eh?'

Charlotte began to protest, but the acting head of the Court of the Air cut her off. 'You will have quarters made available to you in Nuyok below while our analysts follow the repercussions of your new information through our models. The course of action we need to pursue will be arrived at in good time. In the meantime, we will need to test King Jude's sceptre and see if there is a way to destroy the key-gem, to cut the sea-bishops off from further reinforcements of their race for good. I am having testing facilities prepared and we will send for it shortly.'

Their interview, it seemed, was over, and guards led the party away from the chamber.

'All my bloody working life,' Dick said to Sadly. 'I've been raised on tales of how all-seeing and omnipotent the Court of the Air is. Like ghosts in the machine, moving through the shadows and disappearing people before they ever posed a threat. All enemies, foreign and domestic, living in fear of the legendary wolftakers. And this is the bleeding reality? You're no better than the State Protection Board. Run by blue-blood idiots and leaving dross like me to get the job done right. What's that slur your people used to call the board's officers?'

'The glass men,' said Sadly. 'But this isn't the Court of the Air, Mister Tull. This is just what's left of it after the Court was destroyed. And it *will* be rebuilt and refloated again.'

Daunt frowned. 'Is that likely to happen before the sea-bishops trace the sceptre back to the Isla Furia, good agent?'

'No.'

'Then I think we better make some plans of our own,' added Charlotte. *And quickly.*

Daunt watched Charlotte lay King Jude's sceptre down on the table of the roof garden while Commodore Black quickly reached for a bottle of corn whisky Sadly had produced, as if he was worried that the sceptre's presence might contaminate his drink. 'A precious drop of the local fire water, that's what's needed to lubricate my thinking. For never was there a more dangerous puzzle than how to keep this wicked key-gem out of the clutches of its demon owners.'

It didn't seem to matter what time of the day it was, wherever you stood on the Isla Furia, you were always accompanied by the sound of the wind whistling. Sometimes it was a soft, gentle breeze. Other times a hard violent force rattling the shutters that stood ready to be lowered over the porcelain towers' windows. But gentle or hard, the whistling was a constant companion for the people of the city. Where it buffeted the slopes of the volcano, it literally whistled, seeking out the holes in the porous rock and singing through its crevices.

Dick Tull leant back in his chair. 'We could hoof it out to one of the other great powers – Cassarabia or Pericur, maybe. Someone without much love for the Kingdom or the Advocacy and able to protect the sceptre from both.'

'Who's to say their nations won't be infiltrated, or maybe the caliph and the grand-duchess will just decide to cut a side-deal with the sea-bishops like the royalists have done?' said Sadly. 'Don't trust them, says I.'

'The sceptre is as safe here as anywhere,' said Daunt. 'Which is to say, not very safe at all. And the good agent has a point; at least here we can be assured that the Court of the Air's best interests are aligned with the Kingdom's own. On foreign shores we would have no such guarantee. There would be incalculable political variables as well as the threat of the enemy's darkships arriving to seize the sceptre by force.' *Far too risky.*

'The sceptre is never going to be safe,' said Charlotte. 'Someone can always steal it. I proved that.'

'The time of the sea-bishops exercising caution is over,' said Daunt. 'They know their presence here in our world stands revealed now. I believe they will act decisively to seize back the key-gem. They need to open the gate to their home before word of their nature spreads and we locals band together to cast them out, unite to destroy them prior to their numbers swelling.'

'Just my luck. All those tales of dashing, seductive vampires in the penny-dreadfuls, and when I finally meet them, they turn out to be fish-faced monsters with a head like a bludger's wedding tackle.' Charlotte tapped the sceptre thoughtfully. 'It looks like we're going to need to split up, then. First, word of the sea-bishops' return must be spread. Second, the sea-bishops themselves must be confronted and thrown back to hell. Lastly, the sceptre needs to be protected here.'

'Is that you talking, lass, or that ancient phantom knocking round your noggin?' asked the commodore, his sweaty fingers clutching the glass of alcohol. 'Three tasks, and each of them larger than the number of brave souls we have in our band to carry them out.'

'It's the only way,' insisted Charlotte. 'I don't want to take this on any more than you do. I didn't ask for this. My easy life finished when that monster masquerading as Walsingham chose me as the sceptre's thief and a convenient corpse he could turn over to the constabulary. One thing I do know, we're not going to beat the enemy sheltering on this island, waiting for the gill-neck fleet to arrive and bottle us in here.'

Sadly nodded. 'Warning the Kingdom will be my job, says I. I'm as like to get it officially anyway, when our analysis section decides its time to move in and clean house back home.' He glanced at Dick. 'Will Algo Monoshaft believe news of the sea-bishops' invasion if we get it to him?'

'He's as mad as a bag of badgers, that one,' said Dick. 'Paranoid enough to believe his own staff were traitors. But the head might believe it, if it's me that tells him. He was halfway to getting to the truth as it was . . . he knew something was rotten in the Kingdom and it was Monoshaft who told me that the Court of the Air was back in the great game. I thought he was mad at the time.'

'As my old ma said, just because you're paranoid doesn't mean they're not out to get you.'

'Getting to him won't be easy, and that's if he's still alive,' said Dick. 'They might have already topped him by now. I don't think the sea-bishops can con us into thinking they're steammen, otherwise the head of the board'd be dead already.'

'No,' said Sadly. 'I reckon they like the shadows and pulling the strings from the backroom.' He looked at Daunt. 'There were lots of numbers twos and threes on your list from the graveyard, Mister Daunt, but not many number ones. The spotlight doesn't suit the sea-bishops.'

'As elusive as they have been,' said Daunt, 'I have a disturbing feeling that is going to change. How do you propose taking the fight to the sea-bishops, Charlotte? Or should we be asking Queen Elizica?'

Charlotte felt the queen's presence swell inside her.

'You may ask me, priest of the Circle. The only way to beat them is to enter their seed-city and steal another shield unit from their craft, use it to lock them away in a loop of time again,' said Elizica.

'Ah, you terrible phantom,' begged the commodore. 'There must be another way.'

'I can think of only one other way of stopping them,' said Elizica. 'And we should not attempt it, as it's too dangerous. Stealing one of their shield generators and trapping them in time is the best course of action. It worked before.'

'Before, my royal bloody highness, you had seven great heroes to sneak into the seed-city, and what do we have here? An ex-parson that even the church doesn't want, a thieving stage trickster, a couple of double-dealing spies, and poor old Blacky, tired and dying.'

'And with myself and Boxiron, I count seven,' said Elizica.

'The long dead and the near-dead is it?' whined the commodore. 'Is that how we will make up our numbers? Let me stay here. Let poor old Blacky stay here with a few jars of corn whisky and guard the sceptre from these demons and my wicked sister and their gill-neck puppets.'

Charlotte felt the queen make her mind up almost as soon as the old u-boat man had finished speaking. 'That is not the role I have for you. Jethro Daunt must stay on the Isla Furia to guard the sceptre. Am I right?'

'I cannot in good conscience abandon Boxiron here, as wounded as my friend is. I will stay to assist his recovery and if it falls on me to keep the key-gem and the sceptre safe, then I shall do all that I can to ensure it stays out of the sea-bishops' hands.'

'Well then,' said the commodore. 'If Daunt is to stay here and prepare for a siege, and Dick and Sadly are to warn the Kingdom of the monsters that walk among us, just who do you expect to be sneaking into the sea-bishops' evil city?'

'You and I,' said Charlotte, as the queen relinquished her voice. The plans of the spirit drifted in Charlotte's mind as if they were her own. 'An old thief and a young one. Who better?'

'Ah lass, I would come gladly with you, but it can't be done. You say the demons' seed-city is on the bottom of the great trench that cuts the world's seabed like a scar? No u-boat can go so deep, no bathysphere can withstand that pressure, not even the Court of the Air's queer submersible. You're talking about over eight tons per square inch; our hull would crumple like rice paper at six-thousand fathoms deep.'

'You are quite right,' said Charlotte. 'That's why you and I are going to need to steal the one kind of craft that can withstand that pressure, just as Elizica's raiding party did before. We need to hijack a darkship!'

Daunt and Charlotte followed the Court's white-coated functionary through a narrow corridor lined with pipes, leaking steam from ancient joins. It was warm inside. Daunt was glad they had a guide to lead them through the Court's labyrinth inside the volcano; with few clues to differentiate one area from the next, even his memory would be stretched trying to trace his steps. Opening a large metal door at the end of the passage, the guide led them into a cavernous chamber. It was small wonder the volcano still appeared active outside, venting the steam from the mine works and all of *this*. The chamber they stood in was just the first of many interconnected recesses, the neighbouring vault holding enormous transaction-engines, the thinking machines' heat driving the temperatures in the chamber close to the level of a sauna.

The first chamber they had been led to was filled with unfamiliar devices, and, of more immediate concern to Daunt, the horizontal form of Boxiron. His steamman friend lay stretched out in an open-lidded tank, half-floating in a pool of pink liquid while being tended to by engineers in white coats and leather aprons. One of the men in attendance was Lord Trabb, the lens of his hexagonal spectacles splattered with the soupy liquid covering Daunt's friend.

'You servant's recovery is progressing well,' said Lord Trabb, noting the two newcomers' arrival.

'He's not a servant,' said Daunt.

'Colleague, acquaintance, friend,' said Lord Trabb, wiping his glasses. 'The label you choose has no bearing on the process we are using.' He indicated the open casket. 'We are feeding his steamman components, which have a remarkable capacity for growth and healing, while inserting new components from our own automatics into the nutrient gel to be absorbed by his structure.'

Daunt gazed down into the tank. There was a spider's web of filaments stretched out over the gaping holes and missing limbs of Boxiron's original body, hundreds of new components laid out like a child filling in a cardboard silhouette of a figure with crystals, boards and cogs. There were more parts ready on a cart next to the tank – armoured plates and hull pieces, as if a knight in armour's plate had been assembled ready for the joust. *But he's still not conscious. Still not reanimated back into life.* If anyone could bring him back, these people could. Some of the staff moving around the chamber were under guard, their legs and arms bound by heavy sets of chains as they shuffled between the machinery. These were the more pliant prisoners the Court of the Air had snatched out of the world. Mad geniuses and master criminals and science pirates, their talents kept under check by imprisonment inside the Court's cells. Their capacity to create mischief forcibly redirected into the service of the state.

Daunt dipped a finger into the healing gel. It felt warm, like touching skin, the consistency of a conserve jam. On the other side of the tank, much to Daunt's amazement, he saw Lord Trabb fish into his pocket to emerge with a familiar old friend. 'Bunter and Benger's aniseed drops?'

'I find their consumption conducive to the efficacy of my mental quality,' said Lord Trabb.

'Indeed,' said Daunt.

'I do hope you are not a proponent of those scurrilous libels spread by their rivals in trade.'

'Not at all,' said Daunt. 'I was actually hoping to impose myself on your hospitality for the gift of one. I did have my own supply, but I'm afraid they survived the privations of the Advocacy's labour camp as little more than a swamp-water melange.'

'A tragedy,' said Lord Trabb. He eased the paper bag out of his pocket and passed it to Daunt. 'You must have these. I keep a private stock laid in from our provisioning boat to the Kingdom.'

Manners nearly made Daunt refuse, but a sweet tooth and the knowledge that the next nearest bag was lingering

313

hundreds of miles across the sea prodded the ex-parson to override the social niceties. He took the bag, extracting a sweet.

'You prove my theory, Mister Daunt, that all of the Kingdom's greatest minds find succour in Bunter and Benger's aniseed drops.' Lord Trabb obviously counted himself among that august company, but standing here with the scale of an ant surrounded by the Court's massive machinery, the purpose of half of which Daunt found it hard to fathom, who was he to gainsay the acting head of the Court of the Air?

Daunt offered a sweet to Damson Shades, but she wrinkled her nose in disgust and shifted her willowy body to one side so she wouldn't have to watch him suck on his, before pushing the remainder into his pocket. Obviously the Mistress of Mesmerism didn't seek to enter Lord Trabb's pantheon of genius through the sweets' consumption. Even with the clarity of consuming the aniseed drop, Daunt could do nothing for Boxiron but put his trust in the ministrations of Trabb's engineers and his gallery of rogues.

'Boxiron will be fine,' Charlotte reassured Daunt. 'There is still the spark of life within him. Elizica senses it.'

Daunt's fingers tightened around the edge of the tank. It was out of his hands now, there was nothing he could do for Boxiron but wait and refuse to pray.

'I see that the key-gem is still intact,' said Charlotte, pointing to where King Jude's sceptre was held tight in a vice-like affair, surrounded by massive needle-nosed instruments on wheels. The smell of cordite hung heavy in the air as if they had just finished firing cannons at it. 'As I told you it would be.'

'It is a fascinating item,' said Lord Trabb. 'We believe it somehow exists across multiple worlds, sharing its storage capacity with gems twinned in other realities. That no doubt accounts for its remarkable resistance to physical forces in our world.'

'Is there no way to destroy it?' asked Daunt.

'Not that we have at our disposal. But there is more than one way to skin a cat, eh?' Trabb's hand lifted towards the next chamber and the thousands of clacking transaction-engine drums revolving inside their vast thinking machines. 'We have successfully copied the key to open the enemy's gate onto our transaction-engines. My staff are working on decrypting the key's information, corrupting it, re-encrypting it and then returning it to the key-gem in a form that will not be rejected. We may not be able to destroy the gem, but these sea-bishop tallywackers will find it a lot less useful if it connects their gate to some random world in the universe rather than their home reality.'

'How long will that take?' asked Charlotte.

Lord Trabb pushed his spectacles up the bridge of his pinched nose. 'Months, at the very least. The encryption used is completely alien to us; it uses a form of mathematics that was hitherto unknown in this world. But have no fear,' he indicated the prisoners shuffling around in chains. 'To the world's most diabolical and depraved minds, this is a welcome distraction from their incarceration.'

Charlotte shook her head in frustration. 'Well, as long as they're entertained, then.'

Lord Trabb seemed puzzled by her lack of enthusiasm for their work. 'I can assure you, it's an astonishing achievement, being able to extract a copy of the key from the gem's substrate. It should have been impossible to accomplish, but one of our prisoners worked out a method . . .'

Daunt listened with polite weariness to a tortuous explan-ation about quantum reflections, indeterminacy and superpositions, before watching the acting head of the Court move across to a plinth where another gem was held in a metal vice. It looked to be a twin for the Eye of Fate, but Daunt knew that still hung around Charlotte's neck. This was the crystal Daunt had taken off the camp commandant's corpse before they escaped into the Court's clutches. Lord Trabb paused, lost in a world of abstract models and infinite scientific possibilities, until he remembered he was still conversing with the visitors to his island. 'By comparison with the complexities of the key-gem, this chameleon crystal is the very model of simplicity. A multifaceted device that amplifies its owner's powers to manipulate others' minds, their mesmeric ability to pass unseen as a member of another race. It also interfaces with the sea-bishop's common machinery, as well as serving as a communication, calculation and defensive tool. A veritable penknife holding a hundred blades.'

Not to mention a device for removing evidence of a sea-bishop's presence when it dies. Daunt remembered how quickly the camp commandant's corpse had combusted after he died.

'Exploring the nature of the sea-bishops' tools will not make you a better fighter against those monsters,' said Charlotte; although Daunt detected an older voice hiding among her words.

'On the contrary, my dear,' said Lord Trabb, producing a small metal device the size of a shoebox. As he brought it near the sea-bishop's chameleon crystal, a dial in the device started twitching. 'Where you detect the energies of a chameleon crystal, you detect a sea-bishop. Along with the list of names you procured from the prison camp's graveyard, Daunt, these detectors will serve as a functional method for winkling out the tallywackers hiding within our ranks in the Kingdom.'

The obituaries section of the newssheets back home was, Daunt suspected, about to lengthen by a couple of column inches if Lord Trabb had his way. Lots of shut casket funerals where a rash of accidents left the great and the good vaporized or incinerated beyond recognition.

'And with such chameleon crystals,' continued Lord Trabb, 'we have the answer to where the gill-necks developed the knowledge to cultivate their crystalline cities and other knick-knacks. Doubtless pillaged from the wreckage of the sea-bishops' last attempt to invade our homeland. I wonder what wonders of science and engineering the Court shall divine from their technology with all of our resources?'

'A way to hold off a big gill-neck armada would be favourite,' said Charlotte.

Lord Trabb didn't seem to notice Charlotte's lack of faith in the Court, wandering off deep in conversation with his technicians.

Daunt looked at Charlotte. 'It will take more than the beauty of a perfect equation to keep the key out of the sea-bishops' hands. I rather fear we don't have months. Days, perhaps, if we are lucky.'

'You're right,' Charlotte sighed. 'Elizica says she is going to call in an old marker with a friend.'

Charlotte said no more, and Daunt got the feeling that she didn't know any more herself. She walked over to the far side of the chamber, gripping the rail that overlooked the busy engines inside the next chamber.

Daunt came up beside her. 'I'm sorry myself and Boxiron couldn't protect you better, Damson Shades. I did rather promise you back in Fidelia's parish when we first met.'

He had the feeling she wasn't used to being looked after by anyone; nor the ancient spirit haunting her, for that matter.

'Just look after my sceptre,' said Charlotte. 'If I can't melt it down for gold scrap, maybe Parliament's posted a reward for its return.'

'I fear no amount of money will help us now,' said Daunt.

'That's where you're wrong,' said Charlotte, fingering the Eye of Fate thoughtfully and staring out across the rooftops of a thousand rumbling thinking machines. 'The money helps, it always helps.'

'Are you still experiencing nightmares?' asked Daunt.

Charlotte nodded. 'It's hard to separate all the memories sometimes. Which are mine, which are Elizica's, which belong to the Eye of Fate's previous owners. It's always worse at night.'

'I used to suffer something similar myself, I don't envy you. The curious thing is that since we escaped from the prison camp, my own dreams seem to have been stilled. It's as if they're in abeyance until Boxiron returns. Damson Shades,' said Daunt, glancing around to make sure they weren't being overheard. 'I need to talk with you, or more accurately, the passenger you are carrying in your mind.' He indicated the corridor back to the surface of the volcano. 'I have some questions about the prior invasion – a quiet state of meditation should prove conducive in winkling the answers out.'

'Honey, I'm usually wary about men trying to get me alone.'

'You can trust me,' smiled Daunt. 'After all, I used to be a parson.'

'Yes. You did.'

Boxiron was only dimly aware of Daunt's presence inside the large vaulted chamber, dozing in a chair next to the healing tank. The steamman's sensory levels were set to the bare minimum, as much to protect him from the burning web of pain that was his half-grown body as any results of the damage that had been inflicted on his frame by the Advocacy soldiers. None of the Court of the Air's scientists were in attendance now, in the middle of the night. None of them were there to see the strange luminescent shape coalescing into existence off to the side of the tank. In the presence of the ghostly child-like outline, Boxiron's nervous system began to reawaken, a brief hot surge of pain, before easing like balm as the ethereal silhouette reached out to touch the tank's accelerant gel. Inside Boxiron's intact skull, a private channel opened on a very special frequency. One reserved for the creator. Reserved for King Steam.

Why have you come? Boxiron signalled. *None of the people of the metal have given me succour, all have shunned me. The Loas have forsaken me, my ancestors abandoned me.*

'It is a hard law,' said King Steam, the bronzed child-like machine's image growing more distinct. 'But you know why it must be. We cannot allow our race's sentience to be copied by the fast-blooded creatures of our world. We cannot allow them to pick apart our corpses like carrion and reanimate our people as their zombie-machines. If the race of man learns how to copy our pattern, they will create a race of sentient slaves, and down that road lies perpetual warfare between the softbodies and the people of the metal. I favour the way of peace and friendship, not war.'

And I choose death, signalled Boxiron. *I have tired of stumbling through life as a pale shadow of my former self, of being an outcast among the people of the metal and a brutish curiosity among the race of man. Let me honour my vows as a steamman knight; let me pass into the great pattern.*

Boxiron sensed a wave of sadness from the steamman ruler washing over him.

'It would be the right thing to do,' said King Steam. 'Wherever our pattern has been corrupted by outsiders, self-termination is the only honourable course of action.'

Then help me, pleaded Boxiron. *Burn away this softbody*

gel that sustains my wounded corpse. Melt my soul-board and let me walk at last with the Loas.

King Steam's astral projection drifted above the tank. 'One day, Boxiron. But not today.'

Why?

'Expedience. The cruellest of masters, and one before even I must sometimes bow my knee. I have been visited by an old acquaintance, Elizica of the Jackeni, and she has helped me travel the threads that lie before us. They were not comfortable precognitions to entertain. If you die here tonight our race dies too.'

No!

'The enemies that walk hidden among the softbodies are as foul a race of monstrosities as creation is capable of producing and they have a deep loathing of our kind. They cannot drain our bodies for nourishment or rip memories from our encrypted minds, so terror of the steammen is their sole refuge. On all the worlds along the infinite string they have visited where they have found sentient people of the metal, they have burnt us out like a farmer pouring oil over a wasp's nest discovered hanging inside his barn.'

This is your law, yelled Boxiron. *Suffer not an abomination to exist. My pattern has been corrupted, end me!*

'My law to waive. And your sovereign to obey, by your rites of birth and your knightly vows.'

Please.

'I created you once,' said King Steam. 'And now I will do something I have never done in all the history of the people of the metal. I shall create you anew.'

The astral projection cascaded into the tank and the pink gel began to change colour. Without sound it began to glitter and spark, a constellation of a million burning lights.

Exhausted, Daunt slept in his chair, which was probably

just as well. Bearing witness to a resurrection was not a matter that would sit easily with a man who had once been a Circlist parson. It was always easier not to believe in gods when they didn't come calling on you.

CHAPTER THIRTEEN

Daunt stood on the edge of the Isla Furia's u-boat pens, the hull of one of the Court of the Air's strange sleek submersibles swarming with crewmen making last minute maintenance checks before she dove. Above the pens, on the slope of the volcano, part of the mountainside had been drawn aside, camouflaged doors retracted to reveal a dark sphere, an urban legend – the gas-filled globe of an aerosphere ready to lift off when Dick Tull and Sadly boarded.

'You shouldn't dally,' Sadly warned Charlotte and the commodore. 'We've detected a darkship approaching the island. They know the sceptre is here and it's only a matter of time before more of them show up to test the island's defences.'

'It'll make our job easier,' said Charlotte. 'If they're here, they won't be protecting the seed-city.'

The commodore still looked ill at ease with the plan. 'This is where we are, then. Not even waiting for the wicked demons to come and try and winkle us out of the Court's well-defended lair, an island where a man can secure a warm berth for the night and a drop of hot totty to stave off the terrors of war.

No, poor old Blacky must go out and uncover a whole nest of monsters and poke them with his sabre until they swarm out to sting him to death.'

'That's all you can ever choose,' said Sadly. 'Where you're going to die.'

'What do you care, Blacky?' said Dick. 'We're all dead men walking now, same as you. Home, here on the island, or their hole at the bottom of the sea, the odds aren't exactly in our favour are they?'

'Ah,' said the commodore. 'All the adventures and terrible scrapes I've been in over the years. My luck's dwindled away and left me beached here. Curse my mortal stars. All my luck's been used up and this is my last throw of the dice.'

Dick Tull shrugged. 'How'd you think it was going to end, you old pirate? Jared Black propped up on a swan feather pillow, surrounded by tearful grandchildren levering open the mansion's windows so he can take one last peep at the stars in the sky above? This is how men like us go. A sabre in one and hand a pistol in the other and surrounded by all the enemies we haven't outlived. At least you're going out rich. My pension's good for an evening's gratitude at an alehouse and one cold meal a day at Sadly's dung hole of an eatery.'

'Let us rather focus on that life we have left before us,' said Daunt. 'And what we might achieve with it.'

Dick Tull didn't look convinced. 'Let me know how that goes for you, amateur, when the entire gill-neck fleet's anchored off the coast. Maybe we'll meet again on the Circle's next turn. Maybe not. You used to be a churchman; you tell me where we're going.'

No heaven, no hell. The Circlist mantra echoed in Daunt's mind.

'You owe me a drink after this, Blacky, in that escape hole

323

of an alehouse you're got at the bottom of your grounds,' said Dick.

'If I'm around to serve it, you better check it for my bladder water,' whispered the commodore. 'What's the blessed world coming to when some State Protection Board man is as much a friend as an enemy?'

A sedan chair emerged from the entrance to the u-boat pens, borne with ease by two of the clanking mechanicals the Court used in its gas mines. They knelt down, lowering the chair to the ground. Silk curtains along its side were pulled back revealing Lord Trabb, the acting head of the Court swinging his legs out and dismounting uncomfortably, working the age out of his joints before approaching the group. He had two Jackelian style gentlemen's canes in his hand, but he wasn't using them to steady his gait. Instead, he tossed one to Dick Tull, the other out to Sadly. 'A departing gratuity for you both.'

'Sword cane or shotgun, sir?' asked Sadly, examining his. Made of stout rosewood, they had copper boar's heads as handles.

'Neither,' said Lord Trabb. 'We have fitted a working proto-type of our sea-bishop detection device inside each of the canes. Rotate the handle counter clockwise and push it down and the boar's eyes will glow when you are in the presence of a sea-bishop wearing one of their mesmerism crystals. The fuel source is only rated for twenty minutes of continuous operation and once the detector is activated, it cannot be turned off, so only use the cane when you absolutely need to.'

'No room for a shooter, then?' said Dick. He sounded disappointed.

'Only a suicide pill. If you pull out the detection apparatus you will find it concealed underneath. I trust you won't be requiring it, or we shall all be royally tallywacked.'

'Only when I absolutely need to,' said Dick.

Charlotte stepped in and kissed Dick Tull on the cheek, whispering a quick goodbye in his ear. The State Protection Board agent looked at her with surprise, as if he didn't quite believe his luck, then Dick and Sadly walked away towards the mountainside and the waiting aerosphere.

'You make sure your old steamer gets better,' Charlotte told Daunt. 'I'm going to need Boxiron to keep my sceptre safe. I have a feeling that the Court's engineers aren't going to be much use in a fight.'

'It's not my place to put faith in what you've got whispering away in your head,' said Daunt. 'But if I did, I would ask it to keep you safe.'

'Goodbye, Jethro Daunt, from myself and Elizica.'

'My sabre, lad,' said the commodore, exchanging a quick handshake with the ex-parson, just before he followed Charlotte along the gantry out to the Court's submersible, Maeva and the survivors from his crew mixed in with the Court's sailors across its sleek shining decks. 'That's what you can place your faith in. It's kept us alive this long, hasn't it?'

Only just.

'My Lord Trabb,' said Daunt, as the acting head of the Court was reclining back into his sedan chair. 'I trust you have been factoring our schemes into the transaction-engines running the simulation of the Kingdom's future.'

'Yes of course,' said the man.

'What do they say about our chances of success?'

Lord Trabb sighed, a look of deep melancholy settling on his features. 'Well, dear boy, let's just say if you'd recently received an inheritance, now would be an excellent time to blow the lot on fine brandies, games of chance and large tips in the most expensive hotels.' The chair lifted up into the air,

325

its poles settling on the mechanicals' shoulders, then bobbed back towards the u-boat pens.

Well, at least the gambling I'm doing doesn't cost money. Just bodies and blood, you hypocritical fool. Daunt watched his friends leave, the u-boat sinking in a gush of foam and the aerosphere drifting like a black sun into the sky, growing smaller and smaller, until it was swallowed by the smoking volcano's smoke. Daunt had a terrible premonition this was the last time he would see any of them again. *Is it because they aren't going to be around, or because I won't? My fate is my own, created through right actions.* He tried to shrug off the feeling of superstitious dread, yet still it lingered. How strange. The Court of the Air's hidden support base, with an ancient town built beyond the submerged wreckage of an even more ancient marvel. It should have felt like a lost world. Instead, it seemed to Daunt as if the world beyond was lost, and this, here, was all that was real. The horrors that lay outside would be intruding soon, though. There was no getting away from that. Daunt just had to hold on long enough for his friends to do the impossible. That wasn't so much to ask, was it?

He set off back to Nuyok's walled gate, trying to whistle away the reckoning that was blowing in from the world outside, nodding to the fishermen repairing their nets in the wall's shadow. 'There once was a Circlist priest, who found himself facing a terrible beast. He prayed not to god, but whittled a duelling rod, and instead invited the monster in to feast.'

CHAPTER FOURTEEN

'There's a mortal sight for my sore old eyes,' said the commodore, exiting the moon pool of the Court's u-boat. 'All my years and this is the first time I've seen such a thing.'

'What did you expect?' said Maeva. 'The grand congress of the seanore was attacked by the ancient enemy. How did you think our people would answer such an outrage?'

Charlotte cleared the lock of the submarine in a stream of bubbles from the pair's rebreathers. The camp they had left behind on the seabed had grown and multiplied a hundredfold, the kelp forest pierced with the clearings and banners of every clan of seanore that swam the ocean. Slanting rays of fading sunlight from the sky above dappled armoured formations of seanore shifting and switching above the underwater forest, rotor-spears glinting as they manoeuvred. Beyond the surface of the waves the sun was setting, and there were strings of burning crystals mounted on tall spears standing ready to illuminate the gathering. Was it Charlotte's imagination, or was the water warmer here now? Had the presence of so many bodies raised the temperature of the sea water, or perhaps Charlotte was flushed by the sight of so many answering the call she had sounded? Immediately below them, the crab-shelled domes of the assembly had become a series of hills – smaller domes linked by larger structures sprawling away into the distance, clusters of nomads swimming in and out through the constructions' portals like so many schools of fish. It was hard to believe this edifice was temporary.

'It is the presence of the darkships that has brought so many here, girl-child,' Elizica whispered inside her mind. 'They remember well the dangers of the demons that lurk within the trench, within the deep of the dark. The prophecy of the shadowed sea.'

A pity those within the Advocacy have forgotten, and the Kingdom of Jackals too, for that matter.

'Those who insulate themselves with the warm walls of civilization are apt to forget the lessons of the past. Lessons become words in books, and the books are quickly burnt for kindling when the world freezes. Ink runs when the seas shift and paper crinkles into dust when the world warms. But the songs of our forefathers are not so easily forgotten when they are sung well and passed down the generations. So many centuries have passed. Even my resonance fades, captured in the granite of our mountains and the flints of our fields and the stone circles of our tors.' There was a sadness in the ancient queen's voice, and a longing too, but Charlotte wasn't sure if it was for the echo's passing – that she would no longer able to watch over her people, or a yearning for the serenity of silence and a final passing after so many aeons of duty binding her to the land.

Charlotte touched the Eye of Fate, pressed tight against her skin under the diving suit. Sometimes she could feel the presence of its previous owners, all the gypsies who had held onto it over the centuries, passing the gem down their line. Madam Leeda hadn't had any children to pass it onto, nor nieces and nephews. Perhaps Charlotte had been the closest thing the old woman had to such a relative. And how had Charlotte repaid Madam Leeda? With the theft of the precious stone she used to influence the outcome of her bartering with the often hostile towns and villages she passed through. If a surrogate daughter Charlotte had been, she had proved a pretty poor one of the old gypsy – no better a daughter than the farming family had been to her. Charlotte just another crop, to be uprooted and tossed out when the rent on her field was stopped. Her real mother, Lady Mary, discarding her bastard offspring, in case Charlotte's existence embarrassed her ladyship's new husband into a divorce. Perhaps this was how history repeated itself. In the small things as well as the large. Every one of those abandonments and misfortunes rolled up into Charlotte until all she was capable of was betrayal and disappointing those that tried to show her any kindness. What use was the Eye of Fate when it could mesmerize a person in so many ways, but it couldn't make them give you the love you were owed?

'We shall find a better use for the crystal, you and I,' said Elizica, intruding into Charlotte's maudlin gloom as she followed the commodore and Maeva swimming down towards the grand assembly.

It can bring me anything except what truly matters.

'The Eye of Fate was created by the sea-bishops, never forget that,' said Elizica. 'What your heart feels is not within their understanding. All that is left of their kind is endless hunger and the desire to spread and disperse their seed across every corner of existence.'

But they used to be us – the race of man?

'Something as close to it as to make no difference,' said Elizica. 'Now I fear all they are is an abject lesson on why we should always seek to live in balance with our world and

329

never presume ourselves masters over it. The sea-bishops are the distorted reflection in a mirror we need to stare into to know what we must never become. They have become thieves of life itself. Our worst impulses given free reign and distilled over millennia into a dark, unthinking core of pure selfishness. Countless billions of sea-bishops clawing at each in cities so dense with their evil kind that bees in a hive might marvel at their fecundity. Even the walls of reality are no barrier to their dark cravings, the infinite chain of existence reduced to mere connected storehouses of fodder for them to feast on. Waiting for a doorway to open to somewhere, anywhere they might spill out for a temporary abatement of their numbers. Waiting for their scouts to signal that there is a new world fit for the feeding. Vampires in the truest sense of the world. They would suck the spark of existence out of your body and discard the marrow of your corpse as though you were a corn husk.'

Perhaps this was what Charlotte had been destined to fight after all, the magnified reflection of all the small cruelties that had been inflicted upon her.

'Your family chose to abandon you,' said Elizica. 'I did not. I have selected and saved you, Charlotte Shades, kept you in my pocket like a lucky penny for this moment. All the years you were moving through the city as its most notorious thief, you were actually training for the greatest theft in history. You're going to steal our future back from the sea-bishops, just as I once did. You will need every iota of your talent and your instincts to succeed, for the sea-bishops are the most peerless thieves of them all, and they have been stung once in the past already. I had it easy; you are going to repeat my feat when they suspect you are coming to rob them!'

Charlotte caught echoes of the ancient queen's life as she whispered through her mind. A young chieftain's daughter living a life not so different from that of the seanore – albeit one on land, in the deep endless forests of what had been the Kingdom before it had a monarch. Fighting the rule of an order of druids, one already corrupted long before the sea-bishops turned up to infiltrate its ranks. A war between the gill-necks and the tribes of the Jackeni, both sides pushed towards a conflict that could have no victor save the sea-bishops. Charlotte saw glimpses of the strange people who had helped the queen in that fight – bandits from the margins of a cursed marsh. A man who could run faster than the wind, faster than time itself. Another able to cast a lance through a mountain and see it emerge from the opposite face. A woman whose voice was able to crack steel and whose breath could blast down oak trees. Heroes that made today's people appear like pale shadows compared to such titans. What did Elizica of the Jackeni have to work with today? Not legends. Just a thieving bastard of a girl who cared merely to feather her own nest; an aging u-boat privateer on his last legs, only distinguished by being even more reluctantly involved in this madness than Charlotte.

'The passage of time breeds legends,' Elizica's reply came, 'and makes diamonds from even the crudest of coals.'

And Elizica had known tragedy too. Her father murdered by the treachery of allies who had swapped sides on the battlefield, her mother slain defending her family when the druids came to snatch the defeated chieftain's children to sacrifice on the bloody altars of their ancient oaks. Had Elizica's life played out any better than Charlotte's? She had lost a family whom she had years to love deeply, while Charlotte's had only ever been an illusion, no more real than the Eye of Fate's mesmerism. Which of them had mourned more, which of them deserved to feel more cheated by events?

'Everything that happened to me, tempered me, cast me into a woman fit to become the first queen of the Jackeni.'

And what have I done with my life?

'What you needed to do. And if you succeed in this one thing, nobody who matters will ever question your worth again.'

And what if only I live long enough to see it done?

'Then you have answered your own question, girl-child.'

There was little of the finery Charlotte had observed the first time among those assembled under the domes of the grand congress. This time, the leaders of the nomad tribes had gathered with a common purpose and their deliberations already decided. No need to impress with diamond broaches and fine seal skins and ornamental crustacean armour when there was killing to be done and a serviceable rotor-spear was all the embellishment needed to gain status over a neighbour. Word of Charlotte's arrival had spread like wildfire when the Court's sleek, strange craft had returned to their territory, and now the domes were packed with a throng of clan leaders and their war-parties' lieutenants.

They weren't waiting for Charlotte, though; rather, the echo of the ghost carried in the Eye of Fate. They didn't see Charlotte Shades standing before them, they saw Elizica of the Jackeni.

'There goes my scheme for a nice quiet bit of sneaking into the gill-necks' realm,' muttered the commodore. 'Not with this horde of rascals by our side.'

'That plan never had a chance,' said Maeva. 'I have just talked to Poerava. She says the Advocacy closed its borders to us a day after the darkships attacked. No nomad is welcome to trade in the cities of our 'civilised' neighbours now. We might as well be surface dwellers for all the welcome we will receive among them.'

'The time for subterfuge is nearly done with,' said Charlotte. 'The sea-bishops are gathering their forces for the final confrontation. Might of arms will serve us better now.'

'Is it not enough that you want to drag my poor old bones with you to steal one of the demons' wicked u-boats to carry us down into their nest of evil?' moaned the commodore. 'Now I must fight a pitched battle against the Advocacy first.'

'The seanore warriors will fight the battle,' said Charlotte.

Commodore Black did not look happy at the news. 'Tell me that the darkship you want us to steal is close by and unguarded, lass, and its helmsmen out frolicking for human blood disguised as locals.'

Charlotte shook her head. 'The sea-bishops scout force is few in numbers and concentrated around the nations' existing centres of power – the capitals of the Kingdom and the Advocacy. . . the gill-neck city of Lishtiken is where we will find our craft.' Elizica could sense the jiggers there, their presence a cancer gnawing away at the world, a cold weight pressing down on the skin of existence, slowly consuming and corrupting the world's flesh. Charlotte put her hand on the commodore's shoulder to steady the old u-boat man's nerves. 'The Advocacy's forces are being prepared to assault the island. Every gill-neck soldier we can pull away from that battle is a soldier well diverted. And while the Advocacy capital at Lishtiken is being besieged, we will have our opportunity to sneak in and seize one of the darkships the sea-bishops use to shuttle between the capital and their seed-city at the bottom of the trench.'

'It is time,' urged Elizica. 'Address the seanore, address them as their war leader!'

A shelf of stone served as a stage, netting strung up behind hung with trophies slipped through by clan leaders. Charlotte strode forward, unpinning one of the rotor-spears. As she turned around, she felt the fire of the Eye of Fate spreading across her chest. Her form was changing; or rather the onlookers' perception of it was altering. The Eye of Fate cast its spell, the ultimate piece of showmanship from the Mistress of Mesmerism. Rather than her willowy frame, they saw before them a figure of legend. A trident sharp enough to pierce armoured steel, a round shield with the moulded head of a lion and a helm with a built-in rebreather mask. This was different from any of the illusions she had cast before using the gem. They had been paltry things, accompanying sleight of hand; convincing a single person that they were at home eating a meal that didn't exist, rather than on a stage. Now Charlotte was inside the light and haze of the trickery, she could see herself as they saw her. A myth breathed into life, the phantom forms of two savage lions slowly pacing around her.

Charlotte raised her rotor-spear as Elizica raised her trident. 'Hear me, braves of the seanore. Once there was no difference between you and those that call themselves the Advocacy. Both lived in the sea of life and flowed with the current and the schooling fish. But there is a difference now. You have passed on the old songs. You have remembered the terrors of the deep of the dark, the night that clings to the scar cutting the world. The Advocacy has not. They have lost their connection to the waters of life, swaddled in glittering artificial walls and protected by the tick and tock of their machinery; they have made superstitions of the old songs and fools and witches of those that keep their faith with them. And now we have come to where we have come. Darkships cut the waters once more, and within the comforting warmth of their walls, the Advocacy has not felt the trench's chill.'

Among the assembly the nomad war leaders were jabbing their own bodies with the sharp edges of their shock-spears, working themselves up into a berserker fury, swaying and moaning to her words. There was more than one sort of mesmerism and her words held a power all of their own.

Charlotte continued. 'Within the clatter of their machinery, the Advocacy is deaf to the songs that could have warned them. Their people have paid the price for such folly. The Judge Sovereign and the Bench of Four are not their own people anymore, darkness lives within them, the stealers of shapes and eaters of souls swimming with their bodies and seeing with their eyes and lying with their tongues. The ancient enemy has begun to spread the same sickness among the surface dwellers of the Kingdom of Jackals. Soon, the surface-dwellers' airships and wheel-ships and u-boats will move completely subservient to the enemy's bidding too. Then the sea-bishops will plunge the world into war, so that there will be only bloated corpses and weeping widows to stand against them when they unlock the gates to hell and unleash their legions upon us.'

One of the war leaders leapt forward. 'My rotor-spear is thirsty for the blood of these demons; will they bleed if I cut them?'

'They bleed well enough,' said Charlotte. 'The sea-bishops rely on confusion and cunning and the cleverness of their machines. They rely on a force of numbers that would be enough to turn the sea black with their legions. But those numbers are still denied them, so now is the time to strike.'

'I will slay a hundred of them and count it a disgrace to slay so few!' yelled a seanore.

'My rotor-spear will pass through the guts of five at a time and return to my hand pleading for another throw!'

'We advance on Lishtiken!' yelled Charlotte.

The assembly dissolved into a mob as pledges of blood and carnage erupted across their ranks. Charlotte looked at the sea of eager faces, a forest of rotor-spears jabbing up towards the carapace panelled dome above. *How can I do it? Lead these people against the Advocacy? We'll be facing war machines, submersibles, trained armies – it will be a slaughter?*

'These are not simple fools that follow you,' reassured Elizica. 'They know the might of the Advocacy's military far better than you. They have rubbed up against it for centuries. Those pledges and boasts are like the war masks that cover their faces: they use it to conceal their fear. They will follow you because they know the nature of the enemy. They will follow because they understand that if they lose, it will not just be the end of their way of life, it will be the end of *all* life. Their children, their wives, their husbands, their parents, their kinsmen and their hunting partners, all of them will be hunted down without mercy and their life-force ripped from them like marrow sucked from fresh whale-bone.

'They understand perfectly that the enemy may live, or we may, but both cannot. It is a binary choice from which no sentient creature may turn its face. Do not think these people savages, do not think them fools. They have honour and they have prospered in cooperation with the balance of the sea for far longer than I have survived. To lead such warriors as these to their fate is not a tragedy; it is a privilege the like of which you will never be given again. There is no glamour being cast here and I stand revealed before them only because it is right that a warrior knows the cause they are being asked to fight and die for.'

Charlotte didn't need Elizica's council to know how few of the nomads would be returning from the gill-neck capital. A raid, the greatest raid the seanore had ever mounted – not against a rival clan this time – but against the best defended city of the most powerful underwater nation in existence. A

336

theft from the ultimate race of thieves, an attempt to steal the enemy's own magic and turn it against them.

The commodore looked out at the cheering war leaders with dismay. 'Well, lass, the fuse has been well and truly lit. Now let us see if we can survive the force of the wicked explosion.'

Daunt stood on the parapet of the keep overlooking Nuyok's walled gate. The citizens of the town were manning the walls and waiting for what was to come as patiently as the ex-parson. They kept no standing army in the city, but it seemed all citizens between a certain age – male or female – trained as a local defence force. The closest thing to a professional military company was the city's armourers who came among them, emerging from entrances in the strangely transparent streets. They came bearing crates of the Court of the Air's gas-rifles, breaking cases open and distributing guns, drums of ammunition and canisters of gas accelerant as well as sword belts among the long queues formed along the uniformly hexagonal streets. After they collected their weapons, the townspeople would pass shrines to the lady of the lamp, kneeling briefly and passing their swords over the flame, chanting prayers of the light of freedom.

The affairs of the Court of the Air and the town in the volcano's shadow had been bound together for so long that the Nuyokians spoke in a pigeon variant of Jackelian, sometimes switching into their rapid-fire flowery-sounding local tongue, other times launching into a heavily-accented take on Jackelian. It seemed to make no difference whether there was a Court agent in their presence or not: they would meander through the three modes of speaking while conversing among themselves. In Daunt's presence they would often forget he was Jackelian and drift between their pigeon language,

Jackelian and the local tongue. Then, when they caught his look of non-comprehension, they would realize what they had done and burst into laughter, their tanned faces shaking as if the fact of his foreignness was a source of endless humour.

From his vantage point on the keep's battlements, Daunt could see across the lake and the lightly wooded beach outside, rocky volcanic pebbles rather than sand, the boils of the Fire Sea simmering on the horizon. There was a permanent mist clinging to the top of the water where the thermal barrier circled the island, no sign of the approaching Advocacy forces through the seething fog. The enemy were advancing unseen, a vast fleet of war machines and submersible cruisers, but coming they were. Daunt didn't need to see the ring of markers tightening like a noose around the oval of the island modelled on the command table. He could read it in the tension of the defenders. In the way their hands clenched and unclenched around the pommels of their belted short swords. In the way they would check the sights on their gas-guns, fiddle with the seals of accelerant capsules and test the connection of their weapons' ammunition drums. Was the fear they were experiencing worse than the knot of terror tightening in Daunt's gut? He murmured a koan in an attempt to steady his nerves, but he found it almost impossible to focus on the calm of the passage. He tried instead to think of military history, all the conflicts and sieges and battlefields he had studied, but he was uncertain what lessons could be applied here. The Advocacy were a private race, they fought below the waves in their own realm to fend off trespassers and pirates and brigands. Assaulting the Isla Furia on land, their forces infiltrated by the monstrous sea-bishops, nothing like that had been recorded in history's annals.

Behind the wall, a workforce followed the armourers out from under the city, going into each of the porcelain towers and replacing the glass of the windows with metal sheets perforated with narrow firing strips. It seemed a smoothly disciplined exchange, as if the Isla Furia was laid siege to with such regularity that the city's fortification was a commonplace occurrence. The city had already been overflown by darkships, the flying submarines passing with such speed that they left little explosion of sound in their wake. The sea-bishops were no doubt confused by the thousands of signals they were receiving across the island, the radiations from King Jude's sceptre isolated, duplicated and mimicked by little devices the size of an apple that Lord Trabb's scientists had devised. Well, the best place to hide a tree was a forest. Now the enemy would have to seize the entire island and eliminate each of the false signals one by one before they arrived at where the real sceptre was concealed.

Daunt had demurred when he was presented with one of the gas rifles and a belted sword; although he had accepted the vest of chain mail offered. He had expected it to be heavy, but the slippery ceramic-like links felt as light as paper. Slipping the entire vest over his head and poking his arms out, the chain mail might as well have been one of the local's ponchos.

Coming up the steps from inside the city was Morris. For reasons best known to himself, the escaped convict had decided to stay on the island when the other Jackelians had left on the commodore's u-boat. Unlike the ex-parson, Morris had a gas-gun slung over his shoulder and heavy short sword strapped around his waist.

'Hot day for it, eh, vicar?'

'Indeed,' said Daunt.

'It'll get a might hotter when the gill-necks come calling.'

Daunt frowned. 'It sounds as though you relish the prospect of the coming battle.'

'I'm not much of a Circlist I'm afraid. Not much of one

for turning the other cheek. Those bastards had me as a slave for the best years of my life, pulling gillwort out of their pox-ridden swamps. There's not much inside me that's capable of forgiving them for that.'

'I do hope that's not why you stayed behind – the chance for revenge against your old captors?'

Morris shrugged. 'Not all of it. I like it here. They don't have money in the city here, did you know that? Although it makes sense when you think about it. Most of the trouble I ever got into was because I was trying to make some fast pennies on the wrong side of right. Funny old arseholes. Everything gets voted on by each of the towers.' He pointed to one of the soldiers on the keep wearing red chain mail. 'He's a Notifier. Red-chests get to run about telling people the results of their votes. Even now, they're all having their little ballots on how the city's going to be defended and who's going to hold what section of the wall. Personally speaking, I got my doubts on how that's going to hold up when the gill-necks are climbing over the ramparts and the air's thick with shells.'

'Yet, you're here,' said Daunt.

'Well, they know about inbreeding here, don't they? That's one of the reasons why they welcome outsiders from the Court's staff. I've got a dozen offers from different towers to stay and marry local girls. Each of the blocks has their own trade. I figure one of the towers that goes out fishing will do for me. I can sail and cast a net as well as most, and drowning worms with a rod and line was something of a pastime for me back in the Kingdom. There must be a tower of priests and shrine-keepers somewhere here. Maybe you could stay and settle down here too?'

'I don't think that's for me.' *I've spent a lifetime trying to forget about false gods without embracing this misguided people's deity.*

'Well, the trade of thief catcher doesn't exist here, see, what with no money to steal and everything being divided up among the people already. You need something you don't already have, you just borrow it from the vaults under the streets and return it when you're finished. Anyone loses their rag and murders a citizen, then they're thrown out of the city to live in the jungle as best they can until one of the beasties does for them.'

'Well then, there we have it. A Circlist priest must go where he is needed by the people as much as a consulting detective, even a lowly ex-communicated wretch such as me.'

'Won't have much need for a pacifist on these ramparts either when the blood gets flowing.'

'You might be surprised,' said Daunt.

It was the tragedy of Daunt's old calling. The science of synthetic morality had detailed volumes dedicated to the history of warfare, for if you didn't understand such a terrible force, how could you ever hope to stop it? All the factors and facets that went into causing conflicts, from political tensions to resource scarcity to familial jealousies among ruling elites. All distilled down to equations and formulae that could be manipulated and altered towards peace by the church, nudging a faction here, prodding its opposing party there. Daunt could see the branches of probabilities and possibilities narrowing to a single, inevitable conclusion. Either the race of man would survive or the sea-bishops would. This time, peace would only come with one race's complete victory over the other.

Morris left for a minute and came back holding a helmet identical to the one he was wearing, a long helm with a nosepiece made of the same light ceramic-like substance as the chain mail.

'Not for me,' said Daunt. 'I will feel too much like a soldier if I wear it.'

'You'll look like a corpse if you don't,' said Morris, indi-cating the back. There was a small rubber eyepiece and mask with a ceramic air tank on the helm's neck cover that could slide up a central rail and down in front of the face. 'There are dirt-gas vents all around the shore-line. The wind blows the wrong way and you're going to be choking on your own guts when the gill-necks arrive. And that's if the Advocacy doesn't use war gas first.'

Daunt reluctantly took the helm and fitted it over his head. At least it reflected the heat of the high sun above. *I wonder what my old parishioners would say if they could see their parson now?*

'There's the mayor of the city, Rafael Ligera,' said Morris, nodding towards a local.

Accompanied by a phalanx of the red-armoured runners, the mayor was advancing on a command platform in the centre of the keep, markers being nudged around the table by staff with wooden sweepers. The tall politician strode into their midst, broad shoulders carrying his chain mail across a ramrod straight back. But it wasn't the mayor's orders that would dictate the opening actions of the siege; those would be dispatched by the Court of the Air up in the crater of the ancient volcano. Dispatched along with the Court's u-boats now patrolling the thermal wall protecting the island, dispatched with aerospheres manoeuvring in the sky above the city. Deadly-looking weapon assemblies hung connected to the bottom of the globular airships, rocket racks and dishes of varying sizes with lethal-looking needles emerging from their parabolas. Behind the command table, citizen-soldiers wearing bulbous leather helmets with built-in speakers and voice trumpets sat at a bank of communication consoles, receiving the observations from the Court's eyes and ears in the sea and sky, relaying them to the staff adjusting the position of markers on the table. Pieces for the gill-neck fleet approaching and the disposition of the town's defenders, others for the Court's small fleet of submersibles and squadrons of darting airships. It was as though Daunt was watching a game of chess being played out. Easy to be dispassionate about the siege now, before the first exchange of fire had been traded. *Before too long this will feel all too real.*

As if the defenders had been waiting for the mayor's arrival before commencing hostilities, the volcano crater exploded in facsimile of an eruption, rocks sent spewing outwards. The roar echoing from the mount was deafening down on the city ramparts – the Circle preserve anyone inside the Court of the Air's hidden base . . . or a good pair of ear plugs. Daunt marvelled at the scale of the Court's ingenuity. He had never seen a real volcanic eruption before, but then, neither had many of the skeletons in the graveyard of vessels rusting on the bottom of the ocean on the Isla Furia's limits. None of the mariners who had sailed too close to the island had been likely to quibble about the effects as tonnes of superheated boulders began raining down around their decks.

Spouts of water fountained up beyond the thermal barrier; seemingly random patterns, but no doubt closely targeted on the advancing position of the Advocacy's underwater armada. Rocks came out faster than the eye could follow, burning specks leaving ghosts of their trajectory against Daunt's retina. Extra smoke was being vented from the Court's gas mining operation and transaction-engine chamber, and the ground around the base of the mountain trembled with the fury of the magma launchers' volleys.

For five minutes the fusillade roared out unopposed. Then, beyond the thermal barrier, the sea began to bubble and fume as Advocacy war craft surfaced. Daunt examined the surfacing fleet through the lens of a telescope borrowed from the command table. They were obviously submersibles, but unlike the Kingdom's u-boat force, the craft had none of the form necessary to preserve a little slice of surface dwelling life beneath the waves. The gill-neck craft were closer to vast ironclad warships travelling beneath the depths. Superstructures the size of citadels with cannons and turrets and decks open to the sea; mortars and bombards mounted in swivelling domes while crews of gill-neck gunners let the water sluice off their decks, carrying with it seaweed and schools of fish that had been swimming moments before across the fleet's control towers. The designs of the vessels were a curious mix of the brutally functional lines of warships combined with ornamental carvings and intricate hull sculptures. Hull plates camouflaged with the patterning of tropical fish and canon mountings wrapped with cast metal octopus tentacles. If beauties these were, it was a savage beauty.

At least a hundred of the underwater war vessels surfaced within Daunt's line of vision, and their guns didn't stay silent for long. The crash of cannons swelled into a near continuous rumble of thunder – answered with plumes of explosions from the volcano slopes and treeline, the Isla Furia's beaches shattered in a salvo of fire and shrapnel. The towering rise of the volcano shielded the Nuyokians from the worst of the invaders' barrage, warm liquid from the lake raining down as shells landed in the waters beyond the town.

The sea thrashed beyond the thermal barrier, water frothing and bubbling as the gill-necks expended underwater projectiles and torpedoes by the tonne trying to destroy the devices creating the heat field. Daunt was no engineer, but even he knew they weren't going to break it that easily.

Given targets unshielded by the sea, the volcano's spitting fury had swelled to a crescendo, rocks spinning out towards the surfaced fleet, passages traced with fiery spirals, contrails of dark volcanic dust marking their wake. The projectiles disappeared, tiny motes in the sky, followed by explosions flowering across the fleet. The volcano's hidden launchers were firing with a rapidity that no natural eruption could match. The Court had abandoned their base's camouflage as a natural phenomenon, launching projectiles so fast that their launch pipes were echoing with hollow reverberations, a stuttering expulsion of rocky mass. To the sailors and marines on the Advocacy fleet, the missiles must resemble gull motes swelling to the size of houses, a brief prayer to the mother of the ocean that they would land somewhere else, then their fierce impact, tossing the massive war machines in the sea. The impact on the gill-neck armada was apparent now, the rain of high velocity rocks striking the enemy hulls, flying vessel fragments and explosions of debris audible from within the town's walls. A tinny booming as if the invaders were beating drums on their approach.

From back inside the city came a jarring screech. Daunt turned to see a pair of gigantic cannons being pulled down the translucent streets, a caterwauling rising from their steel wheels, eight on either side of their recoil carriages. Articulated barrels stretched over ninety feet, with each of the red-tipped shells following in a long ammunition train standing taller than Daunt. These two giant artillery pieces were clearly of the city rather than the Court, the barrels raised on hydraulic struts with carriages constructed to be anchored on steel turntables waiting either side of the gates. Shrine keepers walked backwards in front of the rumbling monstrosities, swinging globes of scented oil and tossing holy liquid and blessings over the advancing gunnery. The antique artillery pieces were every bit a match for the ornamentation crafted into the Advocacy war cruisers halted outside the thermal barrier. Both barrels gleamed evilly as dragonhead jaws,

345

angelic-winged women coiled around each piece, while their wheels turned as gargoyles with grinning, leering metal teeth as spokes.

Morris cursed and one of the Nuyokian soldiers on the line clapped Morris's back between the shoulder blades. 'Is Santo Ruidoso and Santa Bocainfierno, yes? They speak for the city today.'

'It's not those two howitzers that worry me, it's the automatics you got manning them.' He pointed to the chains being used to haul the pair, each the weight of anchor chains and borne by thirty to forty metal forms lugging the tonnage forward. It was more of the same automatics the Court set to work in their volcano's gas mine, the hulking machine-men – as large as they were – clearly straining against the mass of the town's artillery.

'Who better to pull those two brutes?' said Daunt.

'The cardinal rule of soldiering,' said Morris. 'You never bring automatics within a mile of real battle. They haven't got the brains for it, see.'

Daunt frowned. 'I believe you'll find the steamman knights would beg to differ on that point.'

'I'm not talking about King Steam's lads,' said Morris. 'I'm talking about the kind of automatic that clank fresh out of a Kingdom mill with the badge of one of our industrial lords stamped across its shiny bum-cheeks. You can train their kind to simple tasks with enough repetition, but stick them in a fighting regiment and as strong and as armoured as they be, you'll end up with as many casualties on your own side as the enemy's.' He pointed to the creations setting up the cannon. 'Rely on them as loaders and they'll be fine for a few shots, until one of 'em has a funny turn. Before you know it, a shell will be slotted in nose facing down-ways rather than up-ways, followed by an explosion that'll tear the gates off the town walls. Every few years you get some green-arsed colonel that sets up a battalion of automatics, promising a revolution in warfare. They're usually cashiered out after the steamers have bayoneted a few too many of our own side's redcoats, that's if the officer's pretty head hasn't been sabred off by one of his automatics.'

The Nuyokians had obviously reached the same conclusion as Morris. As soon as the two cannons were nestling behind the walls, their barrels raised over the battlement like metal giraffe necks, the automatics lined up and marched back down the streets towards the volcano. Human artillery crews swarmed over to crew the weapons. Daunt looked up at the volcanic slopes of the Isla Furia. Somewhere up there, Boxiron was recovering in the Court's healing tank. Still oblivious to the world and the turn of events that had brought the forces of an entire nation hammering on the walls the steamman and Daunt had taken refuge behind.

It didn't take long for the city's two cannons to add their fury to the fusillade from the Court's volcano launchers, the length of the barrels recoiling back along their pneumatic segments, shortening as the great guns rocked on their carriages. They sucked in the air after each ear-splitting shot, dozens of the gunnery crew mounting the ramparts' steps with hand pumped water hoses and spraying down water that sizzled and turned to steam along the length of the pieces. Nuyok's long-guns sounded more like instruments of war than the mock eruption from the volcano, but the flowers of destruction that blossomed among the distant fleet was distinctly less impressive than the savage impact of the Court's hidden launchers. Still, the artillery crews cheered wildly, while all along the ramparts the armed citizenry joined in, hollering and waving their rifles in the air.

Hovering above the volcano's slopes, the squadron of

aerospheres turned as if tracking something. The reverberation of a darkship clapped above their ears in the sky while the weapon assemblies beneath the Court's airships traded electrical lightning between their dishes, a web of burning energy traced in the air above the city. The darkship passed through the lattice, a second later shattering into an explosion of waxy fronds, leaving the air above the lake filled with smoking, drifting strips of an oily dark substance. Boxiron created a similar effect when he held his monthly bonfire of all the newssheets and periodicals which Daunt subscribed to.

There was a second clap, another darkship operating in the air, this one flying underneath the web of deadly energies cast by the Court's globular airships. At first Daunt thought the darkship had been affected by its proximity to the energy web, its mantaray shape diving into the lake's waters. But it regained a semblance of control and skimmed out towards the distant harbour gate, bouncing like a tossed stone and clearing the inlet before ricocheting off the sea and back into the sky. In its wake, Daunt saw the evidence of the curious cargo it had deposited before fleeing. A slick of pollution bubbling to the lake's surface, followed by a bobbing school of egg-shaped objects, each constructed of the same inky substance as the darkship.

'That thing's laid some spawn,' said Morris.

'Bob my soul, but I believe you are right,' noted Daunt.

The slick crawled up towards the shore of the basin, forming an unctuous crescent in the corner of the lake. The eggs appeared to be rolling towards land. As they touched down on solid ground, they each sprouted six pincering legs and the rise of the volcano turned dark at the foot of the shore. The Isla Furia's queer invaders were moving up through the beard of tropical woodland and into the crevices of the mountain. Swooping downwards, the Court's squadron of aerospheres came in to investigate, their weapon assemblies rotating as they dived, preparing to lash this peculiar black army of fist-sized marching spheres with the energies stored in the airships' capacitors. A hideous screeching sounded from the little eggs as the airships plunged to fifty feet above the shoreline.

Where have I heard that infernal sound before? Then it came to Daunt. Inside the crystal machine of the sea-bishops when they were attempting to plunder his memories. It was a hideous murdered baby noise, far worse than fox baying. With a sudden flurry of explosions, the eggs that were still bobbing in the inky pool on the lake rocketed upward, breaching the fuselage of the Court's squadron of aerial vessels. The aerospheres began to twist and judder, a flight of birds that had ingested a swarm of wasps and were now dancing with the pain of stings in their gullet. Then the spherical hulls of the Court's airships started to buckle and warp, the weapon dishes underneath discharging at random before each of the craft detonated. Showers of burning metals and hull plates glanced off the lake, hissing and burning, floating briefly before sinking.

'There goes the bloody RAN,' said Morris in mocking reference to the Kingdom's force of airships.

Moans and wails mixed with angry curses along the wall. Daunt could sense the change in the population's temperament. It wasn't surprising. The Court of the Air had arrived from far beyond the unbreachable Fire Sea, benefactors who had helped end the Nuyokians' isolation, their periodic famines and dependence on erratic rainy seasons for their crops. The Court had squatted in the volcano's remains for centuries like fire gods, protecting the islanders in return for their humble labours. And here their benefactors were, being lain low by the invaders. Daunt looked up from the flaming devastation spread across

349

the lake's surface. He had been distracted long enough for the scuttling eggs to have formed into narrow black fingers crawling up the slopes, advancing towards the throat of the volcano. Oblivious to the creeping threat below, the volcano's guns were still raining a furious toll of destruction down on the armada halted beyond the thermal barrier.

The Court continued its shaking volley in mimicry of an eruption, right up until the top of the volcano was seething black with the fist-sized invaders, then the spider-legged eggs started leaping over the edge, the rolling barrage of super-heated rocks violently halted by clouds of exploding trespassers. Daunt could imagine the eggs rolling down the vent of the crater, twisting the launchers into ragged lines of punctured metal with their explosive fury. Others leaping into the nest of gantries and stations and blowing apart walkways and murdering the Court's personnel by the dozen with each detonation. Surely Boxiron would still be safe, deep inside the rocky chamber alongside the fruits of the Court's super science and their great transaction-engines? The sea-bishops wouldn't want to waste the time digging their precious sceptre out of a mountain's worth of rock fall, would they? Daunt could hear the rolling firecracker detonations echoing inside the vent, the louder explosions of the Court's launchers silenced, overwhelmed by this ugly black tide flowing up the slopes, filling the crater's space with fury. As the last of the swarm disappeared over the edge a sudden silence settled over the island. No barrage from the fleet, no shelling from the Court's launchers, no small-arms fire from the wall. The distant cheeping and whistling from the jungle beyond Nuyok's walls, monkeys and birds, filled the quiet. The chirruping was added to by shouts along the wall, defenders pointing to the boiling ocean beyond their shoreline. Daunt raised his telescope for a better look.

Outside the thermal barrier the same class of metal war machines the gill-necks used to entangle the Jackelian convoy's flagship had surfaced. Starfish! They were spinning around, launching ordinance up and over the thermal barrier. Daunt wasn't sure what they were throwing across the barrier protecting the island from the ocean, but he was certain it meant no good for their chances of keeping the city in human hands. Daunt passed the telescope across to Morris and the old Jackelian adventurer swore under his breath.

'Do you recognize what they are tossing over the barrier?

'Our fleet sea arm call them rolling-pins, on account of what the buggers look like,' said Morris. 'Landing boats, good for crossing the seabed and advancing up a shore. A big steel tube with caterpillar tracks on either end, spiked with guns and lances. I wouldn't want to be one of the Court's soldiers dug in on the beach – they'll do a roll and crush job on their positions down there.'

'I trust the city's walls will hold the machines at bay?'

Morris shrugged. 'They're not much good as a ram against walls this thick and high, but they won't need to be. Each rolling pin will be carrying thirty to fifty gill-necks, depending how tight they've packed their marines in. There'll be sappers with explosive charges, snipers, grenadiers, and portable artillery pieces and assault troops pounding on our walls within the hour.'

'Oh dear.'

'We've lost our big guns up there as well as our Jack Cloudies. There'll be too many rolling-pins coming in for the few u-boats the island's got patrolling inside the barrier to pick even a fraction of the armour off.'

'What would you say a realistic estimation of our chances are?'

Morris patted his gas-rifle. 'With these fancy shooting irons,

351

we've got seven or eight times the gill-necks' rate of fire, but—' he indicated the citizenry lined up along the battlements, '—you're talking about one of the world's great powers lining up against us out there. The Nuyokians are a game bunch, but they're not professional soldiers, they're farmers and shopkeepers with guns and a couple of weeks' militia training every year. Even with the Court's soldiers as our backbone, we're outnumbered a thousand to one. So what are our chances, vicar? I would say our bun's been well and truly baked. It's not if we fall, it's when.'

Daunt felt his soul shrivel at the ex-soldier's estimation of their odds. *We have to buy Charlotte and the commodore the time to reach the seed-city.*

Morris pulled back the safety bolt of his rifle. 'On the plus side, I'm going to get my choice of Advocacy heads to put bullets into. One for every day the arseholes had me as their slave, see. You might want to be getting off the wall sharpish.'

'A priest's training includes physical healing, as well as tending to our parishioners' souls and mental wellbeing.'

Morris pointed down to the aid station tents set up close to the wall, rows of stretchers and tables bearing bone saws and tubs of boiling tar to quickly seal wounds, all lined up incongruously across the neat lawns of the nearest row of hexagonal buildings. 'There'll be work for you soon enough, then.'

His words were cut short by the wailing of sirens coming from inside the town, no obvious sign of the source, but the noise seemed to shake through the transparent streets from every point.

One of the nearby locals tapped his nose and indicated his gas mask. 'Air, for face.'

Morris pulled down the gas mask on the back of his helmet and Daunt followed suit.

'There she goes.' Morris's voice sounded muffled beneath the ceramic air drum and rubber visor, great clouds of yellow-tinged gas seeping down from midway up the volcano's slopes, rolling across the shore and making a fog across the sea. Whatever damage had been inflicted inside the crater, the Court's facilities were intact enough to release their final defensive barrier. As a cornered squid releases a mist of ink, so the volcano was putting out the shroud of poisonous death that accompanied a genuine eruption. Flags lifted up along the wall to monitor the direction the wind was blowing. Luckily for the city, the breeze seemed to be carrying the poison gas along the shoreline and out to sea. Unfortunately for the islanders, Daunt mused, the Advocacy fleet wasn't a convoy of merchantmen chancing their luck against the Isla Furia's ferocious reputation. The landing force would no doubt be wearing water breathers, and the poison gas would be of nuisance value only. It did have the effect of concealing the Court's defences along the shoreline, though. When the initial sounds of battle began to drift across the lake, the sights of the fighting were completely enveloped by high waves of rolling poison. Along the beach, different strands of coloured smoke began to mix with the yellow war gas, trenches laying down smoke cover, other forces signalling with smoke canisters. The two massive cannons behind the city walls responded to the coded signals, pounding out volley after volley, the results of their work hidden from view, but audible from the distant whoop of detonations. It was a surreal sight, the mist and clouds veined as though a rainbow, all sounds of conflict distorted by it. The distant fighting continued for over an hour and there seemed no let up in the gas – as if the volcano – having its fire silenced, was pouring all its fury into this boundless toxic veil.

Signalling the collapse of the shore's defensive line, the

lake's ocean lock burst open in a massive explosion, pieces of concrete blown across the lake, a deadly shower of wreckage sweeping across the battlements. A second after the detonation, the screams of pain and terror from the defenders who had taken the shockwave reached Daunt. Some townspeople had been flung off the wall, others maimed and ripped apart. Behind the city's wall, one of the clean gleaming white porcelain towers stood with its top two storeys shaved off by the scythe of rubble.

'This is how it begins,' whispered Daunt. Then he shook himself. It was almost as if he had been possessed by the old gods again when he had spoken.

'Reckon you're not wrong,' said Morris, resting his rifle on the battlements. There were two little metal legs underneath the barrel, and he had opened them up to rest the gun against the stone, swivelling the stock experimentally. 'You been through anything like this before?'

'Jago,' said the ex-parson. 'I was on Jago when it was invaded.'

'Then you know what to expect.'

'I presume you've tasted similar when you were in the regiments?'

'Once.'

'So you showed the good wit to get out,' said Daunt. 'Sickened by the senselessness of it all?'

'That wasn't why I deserted,' said Morris. The convict's body language closed up. 'Eyes front. They're coming. Can you smell them? Can you taste them? Bloody gill-necks.'

Out towards the sea the wind had changed direction, war gas drifting across the lake, providing the advancing Advocacy forces with a haze screen of cover. The Court's own deadly cloud was working against them now. Daunt saw a couple of runners outside the battlements, sprinting down the ground between the wall and near shore of the lake, pegging small triangular pennants into the dirt. *The effective killing range of our rifles, so our defenders don't expend ammunition needlessly.* There wasn't much cover in the stretch of land between the lake and the city – wooden jetties for fishing boats, a few shacks for storing nets, eeling skiffs lying beached in the reeds. Apart from the runners desperately marking out the ground, the rest of Nuyok were sheltering behind their town's thick, tall walls.

Daunt quickly tipped up his gas mask and wiped the salty sweat off his forehead before it could sting his eyes again. Even the wind on the island was hot, playing against his skin as if it had been blown off the coals of a Jackelian tavern's fireplace. Matters were about to get devilishly hotter. Out on the border of the lake, a rhythmic clanking filled the air as hundreds of rolling-pin tanks began to rise up out of the lime-coloured waters, tracks at either end of the metal vehicles dragging them off the lake bed and up onto the surface. Almost before the landing craft had cleared the surface, the guns studding their armour spewed out a hail of fire. They were moving up in a coordinated assault formation – some halting for hatches at their rear to fall down and disgorge marines, others coming to a standstill in the shadows of the battlements, dozens of weapons bristling up on their maximum elevation and peppering the battlements with shot and shell. These soldiers had come for the long haul, bulbous crystal helmets filled with water connected by hoses to their version of rebreather packs, bodies weighted down with pouches and entrenchment equipment. Protected by the initial landing force, more rolling-pin armour emerged out of the lake waters. Some were dragging spherical cargo containers, others mounted with trench digging prows and siege machinery. The appearance of this assault was met by

355

a hail of fire from the Nuyokians, the roar of their rifles firing a thousand baby rattles shaking in anger. It resounded across the lake like no gunfire Daunt had ever heard before. Not the wood-like splinter of explosive charges being ignited and discarded manually, but a hollow thwacking as the firing bolts in the side of rifles jolted back and forth with the discharge of super-compressed gas. The defenders' furious response was accompanied by a clockwork clack of ammunition drums rotating on top of the rifles as the city's militiamen emptied their magazines down onto the ground in front of their home. A fierce drumming echoed from the rolling-pin tanks as rifle balls glanced off their armour. Where the gill-neck marines were out in the open, unloading their siege and entrenching tools from the landing craft, soldiers' corpses spilled into the dirt and crumpled back into the lake's reeds.

Behind Daunt, the two long guns of the city were still discharging every few minutes, tossing shells at the stalled battle fleet of the Advocacy as fast as the city gunners could reload shells into the breeches. Daunt ducked as a spray of shots whistled past his head. Morris was keeping down, swivelling his gas gun on its leg mounts and aiming careful bursts at the invaders below, laughing as if the vista of carnage below was a theatre production laid on purely for his amusement. At the receiving end of each spray of bullets, Advocacy soldiers collapsed to the ground with shattered breathing helmets, their crab-shell armour torn and holed. Elements of the landing force were trying to storm the slopes of the volcano, no doubt trying to find elevated positions from where they could shell and snipe at the city below. Fortunately for the Nuyokians, the close-defence mechanisms of the Court of the Air were coming into play. Fake rock fronts were drawing back all across the mountain side, cannons, mortars and banks of rapid-fire rifles emerging into the light of day from camou-flaged bunkers, cutting down each wave of Advocacy marines as they attempted to scale the rise.

Stretcher-bearers ran crouched along the length of the battle-ments, rolling collapsed bodies onto stretchers and manhandling them down the steps towards the surgeons' tents on the lawns of the nearest towers.

All around Daunt the defenders were intent on murder, focused on killing enough gill-necks for the Advocacy to abandon its beachhead. *This is your war, Jethro Daunt, and welcome to it*. He bent down and went off to see how many of the wounded he could save.

CHAPTER FIFTEEN

Dick and Sadly stood in the shadows of an alleyway, occupying one of the narrow passages between the imposing marble facades of the capital's moneyed districts, a wide boulevard disgustingly well-lit by gas lamps even in the middle of the night. As head of the State Protection Board, Algo Monoshaft was entitled to a grace and favour residence supplied by the state. In this case, a series of rooms atop Victory Arch.

Dick had always considered it fitting that the civil servant charged with the protection of the realm from its enemies should be ensconced inside a monument built to celebrate Parliament's victory in the civil war. *If me and Sadly get in there alive, who knows, maybe the old arsehole'll continue doing the job.* That didn't mean Dick failed to begrudge Algo Monoshaft his polished walnut floors and his servants and his expensive antiques and every penny of the luxuries he enjoyed while Dick had shivered in the cold comfort of Damson Pegler's cheap boarding rooms. Perched in gilded opulence atop the ceremonial gateway's four arches. Well, at least Dick knew where to find the senile sod, even if it was in the lap of state-patronized luxury. They might have had an easier job of it, if the head had lived in Steamtown with the majority of the capital's other steammen. But Algo Monoshaft was living high on his perks, so here the head was, and across there Dick and Sadly would have to go.

Sadly checked outside the alley. 'Nobody watching that I can see, but that doesn't mean they're not out there to get us.'

'Oh, they're watching all right,' said Dick. 'Walsingham isn't going to let anyone he doesn't trust within a country mile of the old steamer.'

'They can't all be sea-bishops across there,' said Sadly. 'They don't have the bleeding numbers to impersonate everyone, says I.'

Dick cradled the heft of the Court's heavy gas rifle. It was a queer-looking weapon, but it'd plough a furrow through anyone standing between him and the master of the board. 'Doesn't matter. There's an execution warrant out on the both of us. If there's dustmen inside the arch, they'll cut our throats first and ask questions later. Won't have time to separate intentions inside there.'

'Well then, Mister Tull, some good men are likely to die for a misguided cause.'

Sadly's rodent-like features were darting about and he looked like he was ready to sprint out to the cover of the nearest building, but Dick laid a hand on the Court agent's shoulder. 'We're not going to run up to the front and shake scullery windows looking for a way in. If it's an assault you're after, we could've landed that aerostat of yours on the roof and kicked in a skylight.'

'How then?'

'I don't know what trade-craft they taught you in the Court, but me, I was taught by good old Sergeant Childers back in the day. I'd say he was a grim old bugger, except I think I've turned into him.' Dick led Sadly down the narrow passage and into a small square off the side. There was an oblong of grass bounded by seats on four sides, the kind of place clerks and clackers would come during their lunch to sit and stare at the prestigious volume of pigeon droppings painting the marble statues lining the path. 'Always good for a lesson, was Childers, and a kicking if his education didn't stick in the head of the young fools palmed off onto him to train.' Dick approached a life-sized statue of a man clutching the pommel of a great sword with two mailed hands. He eased himself behind it enough to slip his fingers towards a shadow on the statue's back, twisting his hand around an awkward angle to reach inside the hidden shelf – feeling for the cobweb-ridden rusting lever he had once been shown. 'Lessons like never enter somewhere you haven't located the back door.' As Dick twisted the lever, the statue ground forward on its plinth, revealing a square well with a metal ladder riveted into the shaft. 'And a back door can be a front door too, when you don't want to be seen going in.' *Maybe I would have shown it to that young oaf William before I'd retired. Not that Billy-boy would've listened.* He hadn't thought there was much that Dick knew worth the passing on.

Climbing down into it, the shaft led to a narrow tunnel, a ceiling low enough they both had to stoop. Dim shafts of light emerged from vents intended for ventilation and there was a layer of dust thick enough to indicate the tunnel hadn't been used in quite a time. Sergeant Childers had been right about this, but then the sod had been old school. It was a depressing thought to Dick, but now, so was he. As long as you didn't count getting ahead in the board, there were quite a few tricks and skills he would be taking with him unpassed when he left. Plenty about doing the job right. Not that effectiveness counted for much among the quality that ran the civil service. Being in the appropriate place to take credit with the right accent was more important to preferment than anything so grubby as consistently getting results. That was what the proletariat was for. But if Dick lived through this, if he got *this* job right . . . *they won't be able to steal the credit for this result. Rooting out conspiracy within the board; nobs like Walsingham not just exposed as enemy agents, but revealed as abhuman.* The state had awarded large discretionary pensions to fools for far less than Dick was attempting to do.

There was another vertical shaft at the end of the narrow corridor, a claustrophobic climb up into the bowels of Victory Arch, then a series of horizontal passages branching out which the two of them had to traverse crawling on all fours. Built into the floor at irregular intervals were little wooden flaps that could be lifted up, revealing small eyeholes giving onto the rooms below. When it came to tradecraft, you had to forget what you read in penny-dreadfuls and saw on the stage. No self-respecting spy would order a builder to construct a surveillance hole in a wall, much less behind the eyes of a strategically placed oil painting. Marks waiting in a room would get bored, would look around – and wandering eyes were quick to spot little flickers of movement on supposedly static surfaces. But a ceiling? Nobody looked up at ceilings; crane a neck for too long and all you were going to get for your trouble was a neck ache. And sounds, they carried up quite naturally – just ask anyone in the slum tenements of the rookeries about how noisy their neighbours were. Of course, sound carried down too, which is why the dusty passage Dick was squeezing through was lined with a stretch of cork across its floor and walls.

Dick was in the lead and he laid down his gentleman's cane

and indicated to Sadly that they should halt, taking the time to lift the wooden flap off a surveillance hole. It proved to be a good spot, right above a chandelier, the top of which had a hidden ring of mirrors around the crystals, giving angled views of the entire chamber below. There were glass cases containing old swords, armour and a variety of personal items that had belonged to prominent parliamentarians centuries ago. They were still above the public part of the arch, where the idle and curious could pay a penny or two to gawk at the faded glories of the monarchist's defeat. He closed the flap. They continued on their way, ignoring the hatches in the passage's roof that would lead up into concealed entrances inside the apartments. Dick had been here twice before, inside the arch, not its hidden passages. Both times when he was starting out in his career with the board, bearing official document pouches for the head to peruse and sign. From what Dick could see of the rooms through the surveillance holes, they hadn't changed much in all those years. Burnt larch panelling, antiques on display, the occasional night watchman patrolling with a gas-fed lantern and a belted cutlass. The private apartments above were much the same, except the watchmen were board officers. Far too many of them for a normal night's duty in this place; far too alert and well armed.

Dick lowered the wooden flap on the surveillance hole. 'They really don't want any bugger getting in to see the head.'

'Then they're due a disappointment, says I.'

'Sergeant Childers told me the head's private rooms have an escape hole. He's up top, we have to climb another two storeys.'

'Let's be about it, then, eh, Mister Tull.'

It was slow, careful work. Dick hoped that Monoshaft would be able to squeeze though these passages on the way down. They had been built in an age before the old steamer had taken charge of the board's resources. They reached the staff quarters below the head's private apartments, and surveying the corridors, Dick spotted Corporal Cloake sitting at a table in the main corridor, a number of burly-looking men lounging about, some playing cards next to a pile of coins. Dick lifted his cane up and made to activate the sea-bishop detection mechanism, but Sadly tugged on the cane to stop him.

'Don't be wasting its charge,' whispered Sadly. 'That one's got to be one of them. He was at Tock House when they came for us.'

'You're right, some of the guards too, probably.' *But not all of them, or I doubt if they'd be playing cribbage on the table.*

Sadly pulled the gas gun slung across Dick's back. 'This'll sort 'em out, either way. Come on.'

Dick was about to shut the surveillance flap when a figure walked down the corridor and the sergeant had to stifle his reaction. *Jethro Daunt.* It was one thing to know at the back of your mind that people like Cloake and Walsingham had been murdered and replaced by doppelgangers – Walsingham had never seemed particularly human to him in the first place. But to actually see one of the sea-bishops mimicking a man Dick knew was presently hundreds of miles away on the Isla Furia sent a waterfall of chills crawling down his spine.

'What is it, Mister Tull?'

'It doesn't matter. Let's go.'

Reaching their destination, Dick used the butt of the rifle to hammer aside the rusty bolts securing the hatch above his head, a shower of oxidised metal flakes falling onto his sweating face. There was a clockwork box meant to trigger the escape route from outside but it had stopped functioning

– possibly centuries ago. The hatch opened above the crawl space. When Dick pulled himself out he found himself in a large wardrobe littered with mothballs but no clothes – attire superfluous to a steamman's needs. There was an oblong of angled slats in the wood giving a view out onto the room beyond.

'Any guards?' asked Sadly, coming up behind Dick.

Dick shook his head. 'Monoshaft's said to only allow a single house servant inside to clean. Doesn't trust anyone not to nose around his papers and notes.'

'Just because you're paranoid doesn't mean they're not out to get you.'

Clicking open the wardrobe door, Dick was at a loss to know what cleaning the unlucky servant was actually allowed to do. All around the room, every surface was scattered with pieces of paper covered over with half-mad scrawls, annotated cutting from newssheets and pieces of string and chord connecting the scraps like veins on a drunk's face. It was as bad as the mess back in the board's offices. Sadly picked up a faded cartoon cut out of the front of the *Middlesteel Illustrated News*, a drawing of two senior members of the government pinching each other's noses. The speech bubble had been scrawled over, frantic handwriting demanding, *Why is this here? Why, why?*

'He's not playing with a full deck of cards anymore, is he?' said Sadly.

'Give him his due. He'd worked out the Court was back in the great game when I thought he just blowing steam from his stacks,' said Dick, 'He connected the gill-necks and the royalists working together before anyone else.'

There was a noise from the connected room and Sadly unshouldered his rifle while Dick padded silently up to the door. The Court's agent was holding his rifle ready, lowered

and angled towards the floor, and Dick rested his cane against
the wall, then tipped the door open before springing into the
room with his gun gripped in both hands.

'You!' Algo Monoshaft was scrabbling around the floor,
laying lengths of string around the spirals of paper littering
his expansive carpet. He had a dozen pots of dye of different
colours scattered around him, and appeared to be painting
the strings according to the strictures of some mad colour
code. Monoshaft didn't sleep much, but at least they had
caught the board's head unawares.

'You murdered William Beresford. I knew it would be you
who came for me, sergeant.'

'Stay where you are, sir,' said Dick. 'I don't know how
many hidden buttons you've got to call for help, but I reckon
a cautious old steamer like yourself will have a few.'

'I though you were too trivial to be turned by them,' said
the steamman. 'But here you are to kill me, just like you slew
poor young Beresford softbody.'

'The opposite of that, sir,' said Dick.

'Sweet lies. Always lies, when the treasonists are everywhere.'

'Just who do you think sent us?' asked Sadly.

'The vampires, of course,' said Algo. 'They have been
turning all of my officers, corrupting them into the half-living,
feeding on the people's blood and spreading their sickness.'

'Not quite, sir,' said Dick. 'But you were right about the
Court of the Air, and you were right about the gill-necks
working with the royalists. You were bang on about that.'

'That's it sergeant, flavour a lie with the truth. You can
transmute your form into bats and vermin, that's how you
slipped past my soldiers outside. But you can't drain my
blood; I have only oil and vapour for you. That's why I
have to die. Then you'll have one of the section heads

replace me, they're all your vampiric allies now. I can't trust any of you.'

Dick lifted his rifle out and as a sign of good faith placed it on a tabletop to his side. 'I'm not here to kill you, sir. I'm here to ask for your help. We have been infiltrated all right, but not by what you think. I've just come back from what passes for the Court of the Air these days and I need your help to rescue them from the gill-necks. I need the RAN and the fleet sea arm to go to sea in defence of the nation and our interests or there'll be nothing left of the Kingdom by the end of the year.'

'Lying,' spat Algo with enough venom that his voicebox shook. 'It's a war you want.'

'Only against the real enemy.'

'I couldn't agree more,' said Sadly, raising his rifle to the ceiling and loosing a chattering burst into the plasterwork before dropping the barrel towards Dick and the steamman.

'What are you doing?' Dick shouted as the sound of panic and guards clattering outside the private apartments began to filter through to where they were standing.

'It's not a war, says I. No more than when a farmer brings his swine in from the field and takes a razor to their throats. What do you call that? A harvest?'

'You bastard, Sadly, you've sold us out.'

'I told you,' warbled Algo. 'I warned you to trust no one. There are treasonists all around us.'

Sadly activated the sea-bishop detection mechanism on his cane and tossed it towards Dick. The eyes in the copper-boar's head handle were filled with orange light and burning with a fierce urgency. 'Well, someone in the room is not of this world, and you must be fairly sure *you're* still a human.'

'You can't be one of *them*,' said Dick, reeling in shock. 'Daunt can sniff their kind out. The amateur pegged Vice-admiral Cockburn for a sea-bishop straight away, like a walking blank he said.'

Sadly leered. 'I find your nickname for our race almost as disgusting as having to bear your fetid appearance, cattle. We know our kind as the Mass. Our numbers are as infinite as our dominion is eternal. While you are as dull as you are repellent, so let me explain for you, we discovered Daunt's ability back on the island. That was where Barnabas Sadly was taken – that was when I replaced him. To fool Jethro Daunt, all I needed to do was intensify my mesmeric field and convince the creature he was now seeing all the physical cues he expected to observe from his fellow cattle.' The creature laughed without warmth. 'Your crippled friend really shouldn't have brought a cane filled with a tracking isotope into the prison camp, even an inert compound. You animals make it too easy. I let you escape and lead me straight back to the location of the key-gem, *Mister Tull*. Days spent on the Isla Furia, listening to your pathetic plans to defy the Mass, time well spent making sure the memories of the defences I ripped from the Court's agent were reliable and up-to-date.' The Sadly creature's rifle barrel twitched as he saw Dick glancing towards the rifle he'd laid aside. 'I wouldn't reach for that gun, animal. It would be a shame if you were to die immediately. You have assisted the Mass so well. You deserve to see our people's final victory, even if you don't live quite long enough to fully regret it.'

There were the sounds of a door breaking, the crack of approaching boots on the floor. 'I wanted to see how much the head of the State Protection Board had uncovered of the Mass's activities on his own. But here he is – half-senile and blinded by the superstitious myths of your primitive land – foolish machine creature. Your kind must have built his, once, animal. He's exceeded his creators only in longevity, not in intellect.'

'You can't turn me into one of you,' said Algo. 'I have no veins to spread your vampiric sickness.'

Sadly laughed and his shape began to shimmer, reforming as a facsimile of the old steamman. 'I don't need to bite you to become you, senile contraption. It's your memories I am unable to steal. Too well encrypted by that rusted calculating device you call a monarch back in the Steamman Free State. But it matters not. Your kind is as few in number as mine is legion. Perhaps we shall keep some of you functioning as slaves – that was your original function, was it not? There is certainly no sustenance on you to feed the Mass.' The sea-bishop jabbed his gun towards Dick. 'You shouldn't feel too bad, animal. You are livestock and we are wolves and that which preys on a creature is always quicker and faster and more intelligent than it. The best plan you could come up with is attempting to repeat the same trick your bitch-queen played on the Mass centuries ago, sealing us in a trap of time. Even if your friends weren't going to be walking into an ambush, your witless scheme would never have borne fruit a second time. The shield technology she modified to trap us is under constant guard. What is it you animals say? Fool me once, shame on you; fool me twice, shame on me.'

The creature kept Algo's appearance as behind him, the room was filled with armed men, Corporal Cloake and the fake Jethro Daunt among them.

'Bob my soul,' said the Daunt creature, its eyes lighting up with a passion that the original rarely showed. 'It seems we have bagged a couple of intruders.'

'This assassin broke into my apartments,' said the sea-bishop masquerading as the head of the board. 'One of our own officers gone rogue. Yes, there's an execution warrant outstanding on Sergeant Tull here, and the mechanical is a poorly designed automatic engineered to impersonate me.

Take them away, Jethro softbody. Consider your commission with the board fulfilled. Lock them away deep where we keep our most dangerous prisoners.'

Dick moaned. He had failed. The sea-bishops held the Kingdom and the Advocacy in their thrall, they had the measure of the Isla Furia's defences and that old sea-goat and Charlotte Shades were walking straight into a trap. Dick's retirement was finally upon him, and he wouldn't end up struggling on his scanty pension. Not in the slightest.

Many cities were said to glitter metaphorically – to gleam with gas lamps and hotels and expensive restaurants and the moneyed classes chasing their dreams by opening their wallets. The capital of the Advocacy, however, didn't need metaphors to sparkle. Lishtiken lay there on the underwater plain with its diamond towers and its ruby-shaped domes running along the seabed, silhouetted against the underwater mountains and shining like a thief's dream. The Advocacy had grown a coral-like city out of crystals, the splendour of its gem buildings overlaid with knots of pearl-coloured spheres clustered together, fish spawn clinging to reeds. There was movement all across the vista – gill-necks swimming freely in every dimension between thousands of openings, larger chariot craft bearing citizens between buildings. Connecting everything as though a fine mesh, transparent tubes hung as a capsule-less version of the Kingdom's atmospheric network – artificial currents sucking swimmers effortlessly on their way across the capital.

But for all its obvious wealth, Charlotte wasn't here to loot Lishtiken, and nor were the thousands of seanore warriors picking their way carefully through the sea farms on the capital's eastern flank.

The commodore's voice sounded in Charlotte's diving

helmet. 'They're lax today, lass. All this way up to their mortal doorstep and hardly a patrol boat to make us duck on the whole journey.'

'Their fleet will be busy and bloodied at the Isla Furia by now,' said Charlotte. 'With word of the sea-bishops' presence being spread among the nomads, the monsters must be growing desperate to get their hands on the key-gem.' *Of course, the sea-bishops' infiltrators inside the Advocacy will be quick to write such stories off as the ramblings and propaganda of superstitious savages, and that will hold up, at least for a while.*

'Ah,' the old u-boat man grumbled, 'in my experience, when something is too good to be true, it usually is.'

Vane came up behind them, the nomad chieftain so weighted down with rotor-spears, armour and weaponry it was a wonder he could cut through the water with the ease he did. 'There are darkships secreted in the city?'

'At least two of them,' said Charlotte. She could feel the press of their presence like a cancer, an illness upon the world. 'And their masters too.' Ensuring their grip on the Advocacy's leadership did not weaken at this pivotal point in the invaders' fortunes.

'We will give you half an hour to get inside before we begin our attack – you will find that adequate.' He waved his arm and Maeva came forward, travelling lightly armed compared to her fellow nomads. 'Maeva has been inside Lishtiken many times, leading our trading parties. She knows its ways best and shall guide you.'

The commodore didn't look pleased by the prospect. 'You don't have to be doing this now, Maeva.'

'You would get lost two feet behind your own sleeping bubble,' said Maeva. 'It's best someone who knows which way the tide flows is on hand to guide you though the city-dwellers' defences.'

'You should stay here,' he insisted. 'I had a mortal strange dream last night. I don't think things will end well, and I don't want you along to share my fate.'

'I've as many grey hairs as you, Jared Black. I'm not planning on living forever. It is done. I will be your scout. This is my decision to make, not yours. You don't get to do that again to me.'

'You will lose many fighters in the assault,' Charlotte warned Vane.

Vane shrugged. 'I was not planning on living forever, either.'

'Remember, we only require a diversion,' said Charlotte. 'Nobody among the grand congress is expecting you to lay siege to Lishtiken and successfully seize the capital.'

Vane shivered with the thought of it. 'Enclosed by walls and corridors, unable to feel currents running across my skin. Hiding my face from the tides like a frightened hermit crab drawn down into its shell. What would I do with a city? Such a life would be as living entombed.'

'Remind them of the old ways then, lad,' said the commodore.

'I am glad you are going, silver-beard,' said Vane. 'If you stayed too long with the clan I would probably have ended up killing you.'

'Better an enemy should kill me than a friend,' said the commodore. 'Let's give those dark-hearted demons down there first crack at my old bones.'

'Half an hour!' the war leader called after them as they left. 'Move fast and true.'

Urged by Maeva, the three of them connected voice lines between their suits and they travelled forward joined together as though by a long umbilical chord. 'No open communications from here on in,' ordered Maeva. 'The edge of the city is patrolled by dolphins and they can detect voiceboxes at a distance far beyond any clansman's hearing.'

'It's an exposed approach,' said Charlotte.

'Not through there.' Maeva's gloved hand indicated the vast nets of fish pens floating tethered along the sea farms. 'We cut a small hole through the mesh and move with the schooling fish. Too much activity inside for three uninvited guests to be spotted.' She smiled beneath the visor of her helmet. 'We just have to hope that no farmer tries to spear us for poachers.'

They made the journey unimpeded, observed only by silvery clouds of darting garfish. All the farmers they spotted outside the nets were busying themselves by their feeding pipes, testing water inside the pens, dipping nets inside to check catches for diseases that could kill their livestock. Before they broke cover, Maeva sketched a rough outline of the city and asked Charlotte where she sensed the darkships' presence. Charlotte tapped a section more or less in the centre of the underwater metropolis.

'That is the heart of the Judge Sovereign's rule,' said Maeva. 'The Temple of Judgements, or somewhere very close to it.'

The commodore groaned. 'Poor old Blacky and his unlucky stars. Why could these demons not be hiding their wicked darkships in a cavern on the outskirts of Lishtiken? They have to be in the best-defended spot in the whole nest of gill-necks.'

Charlotte shrugged inside her diving suit. 'Honey, the sea-bishops feed on power as much as blood. I wouldn't expect them to be anywhere else.' She tapped the crystal hanging around her neck, a small bulge beneath her suit's fabric. 'If it comes to it, I can use the Eye of Fate to convince any Advocacy soldiers we meet that I'm the Judge Sovereign himself.'

'What about the sea-bishops, lass, will that little geejaw of yours work on them?'

'Queen Elizica once used it to convince the enemy that she

was a sea-bishop wearing a human form,' said Charlotte. 'I hope I can do the same. Their minds are a lot stronger than ours are – bred to be resistant to their own trickery.' *But I've been using the crystal for far longer than Elizica when she crept into the seed-city. Surely that must count for something?*

'Hope? On such a small hope swing the lives of us all. The blessed Eye of Fate is well named, so it is.'

Maeva pointed to a stretch of Lishtiken's waters that seemed darker than the rest of the sea. 'That is where we must go. There is a way to bypass the city's defences and patrols over there.'

'That's a cloud of plankton, Maeva,' noted the commodore. 'Is it doing what I think it's doing?'

'Maybe. Do you believe it's feeding on the city-dwellers' waste?'

The commodore's face frowned inside his rebreather. 'Crawling along pipes full of turds. Is that what you want to inflict upon me? Is this your revenge on poor luckless Blacky for taking off all those years ago?'

'It's a start, Jared. A start only.'

CHAPTER SIXTEEN

Shortly after the gill-necks' rolling-pin tanks had dragged up large black spheres studded with spikes, the lines of ugly globes began launching out fizzing rockets which landed harmlessly enough, leaving each rocket pouring out smoke cover to mask the invaders' exposed position in front of Nuyok. Unable to effectively sight on the invaders, the militia along the wall had been reduced to firing blind into the fog, emptying magazines into the billowing clouds. The battlements themselves were now shrouded inside the choking veil, and Daunt's war had been reduced to a couple of feet's visibility either side of him, stumbling through a hell he had been trained to deny.

Out beyond the wall the Advocacy forces had assembled gallopers – small mobile cannons that could be broken into pieces, transported by the landing boats, and then put back together to hurl small but deadly projectiles towards the city. Daunt couldn't see them, but the effects were being felt around the city, shells tearing into the walls, others passing overhead and wrecking devastation amid the towers' clean white porcelain spires. Particularly devastating was the enemy's chain shot, twin cannon balls linked by thick rusty chains that rotated as they flew, deadly bolas decapitating defenders where they stood.

Nuyokians were heaving out poles designed to push back scaling ladders being lifted up against the walls, others lugging drums of acid-like oil to pour through siege drains, spraying their deadly contents out onto the assault. From the anguished screams and yells that greeted the dispersal of each drum of corrosive liquid, the gill-neck sappers and engineers were hard at work on the ground below. It was only a matter of time before the attackers managed to successfully set enough explosives to blow open a breach in Nuyok's walls.

Daunt was moving along the battlements, thick with smoke carrying the distorted cries of the attackers and the defenders' curses and rifle fire. Militiamen bent over the ramparts and emptied their magazines in a desperate attempt to halt the surge of numbers coming at them, heaving out at siege ladders with their y-shaped poles, others hacking at grapple cables sunk into the stone walls. Each of the gas guns contained a bayonet, spring-mounted to extend like a penknife's blade. Many of the militia had triggered theirs, adding a foot of serrated steel to the length of their rifles, hacking out at the crystal-helmed gill-neck faces trying to struggle over the wall.

Weighed down by a medical satchel given to Daunt by a surgeon at the aid station below – one of the Court's personnel, not a local – he crab-crawled his way toward the next cluster of men shouting for assistance, bullets whining like hornets past his helmet.

This was far removed from the Circlist church's medical training. The priests back at Daunt's seminary would have been horrified at the scale and severity of the injuries. A world apart from the delicate balance of pastoral care, diet, exercise, meditation exercises and identification of physical ailments that could throw out of kilter the miraculously sophisticated organism that was the race of man. Soldiers blinded by shards of stone from cannon impacts, missing arms and legs from the bombardment, punched down by rifle balls, felled by grenades and blade cuts, bones broken and spines shattered slipping from the battlements. Already the orders had gone out from the mayor's command post that wherever they could, the injured should make their own way down the wall's stairs to the aid posts. So hard-pressed on the battlement that no fighters could be spared to supplement the stretcher-bearers by carrying down their wounded comrades to the Spartan medical facilities. Daunt reached the militiamen yelling for a medic, half of the company jabbing out with bayonets, the remainder standing back and aiming shots over their comrades' shoulders. At their boots was a militiaman doubled up on the rampart, surrounded by nets filled with the ammunition drums and gas propellant canisters he had been distributing among the defenders.

Daunt rolled the body over; only noticing the fourteen-year old's agony-contorted face after he had pulled his hand away from the bubbling ruin of his chest. Try as he might to suppress it, Daunt felt the wave of anger rise within him like an overwhelming tide. 'What's he doing here? He's too young to be fighting.'

'His city too, Court-man,' snarled one of the fighters, not looking away from sighting his rifle. 'Take him to medicos.'

'I can't bandage him up; I can't move him by myself. Damn your eyes.'

The soldier pulled off his empty ammunition drum and threw it over the parapet as if it was a discus. 'Damn theirs instead.'

'I can't die,' moaned the boy, as if the fact of his mortality was more of a shock to him than his wound. 'I can't.'

What had this been to the child, a game? A chance to show off to his friends, to impress his elders in the city? The chance to get a piece of cannon shrapnel lodged in his gut, the random hand of fate selecting who survived and who didn't. Daunt felt like screaming out at them to stop, begging both sides to end this butchery. But this slaughter was necessary to hold onto the Isla Furia, to keep the sea-bishops' prize out of the invaders' clutches for as long as possible. *This is my doing, my design, and all I can do to assuage my guilt is wrap bandages around the limbless cripples I am creating here today. Maybe I should have tried to run with the sceptre? Led the sea-bishops on a merry chase across half the world. Bought time with my shoe leather, not the blood of these poor islanders.*

With the militiamen fully engaged by the gill-necks crawling up the siege ladders, Daunt yelled out to Morris to help him shift the wounded boy, the Jackelian setting the timer on a stick grenade before tossing it over the parapet.

'This is work,' Morris panted with a savage jollity, slinging his rifle over his shoulder as he came running over. 'They'll know they've been in a fight before the night falls right enough.'

Now Daunt reconciled Morris's desertion from the army with the cues from his body earlier – his ambivalence and disgust and shame. A sudden epiphany. Morris hadn't left the army because he had been disgusted by the carnage of war; he had left revolted by how much he had *enjoyed* it.

'Lift his boots; I'll bear his weight behind the arms. As gently as you can down to the aid station.'

'Don't worry, boy,' Morris encouraged the young soldier. 'It takes a man's weight in lead to kill him. Bit of shrapnel like this, it's only good for a souvenir to hang above your fireplace.'

'Why me?' The young soldier didn't appear to be addressing anyone in particular, his head lolling from side to side as he was borne down the steps.

'Because you're here, boy, because you're here.'

'Don't talk,' Daunt advised him.

'Those ammunition bags you were lugging, fine bullets they are,' said Morris. 'Been sending those arseholes out there back to the ocean all day with them. Lake's running red with their blood when you can glimpse the waters through the bloody gas.'

The ground they were carrying the soldier along shook with the cannonade of the city's two giant artillery pieces. Across the lawn of the aid station, bodies lay strewn outside the tents, a cacophony of moans and pleas and screams from militia fighters lying on their stretchers. If war was a mill, this was what it produced. The dead and the dying and the barely saveable; begging for water and the attentions of someone, anyone, who could take away the pain, grow them another limb, close the sight of organs that were never meant to be exposed to light.

'Attend here!' Daunt yelled out, lowering the boy down to an already bloody blanket, its previous occupant shrouded and piled on one of the yellow carts waiting behind the tents. 'Surgeon, attend here!'

'It's no good,' said Morris. 'The lad's gone.'

Daunt looked down, stunned. 'He can't have done. The boy was moaning, he was calling out in pain just seconds ago.'

'That was minutes ago. You can see it in their eyes, the ones who don't want to go on. The look always tells you more than their wounds do.'

I know that look. I used to see it in the mirror most mornings. Daunt touched the boy's neck, feeling for a pulse. The young soldier was stone cold. It was as if he had been dead for days. 'He didn't want to die. This, this was my doing.'

Morris checked his rifle. 'Some people just can't take it. It's a crucible up there. Some melt. Some temper. And I promise you, vicar, this ain't your doing. It's them arseholes over the other side of the wall, see. Fairly definite about that.'

'He didn't want to die.'

'Take a rifle, vicar. Take some revenge. You'll feel better.'

Daunt suppressed something deep and primeval that called out for him to do just that. 'It's not what I'm for.'

Morris shrugged. Behind him there was a bubbling vat of cauterisation gel, a soldier with a stump of an arm yelling as two orderlies either side of the man shoved the bleeding remains of his shoulder into the liquid.

'Come on, climb back up to the wall with me. It's not really healing you're doing here, is it? You're only pushing the dents out of the armour, grinding the chips out of the blades before tossing 'em back into the fray.'

'Just hold the line, Mister Morris.'

The stocky Jackelian gave an ironic salute and loped back towards the fierce combat along the top of the battlements. Daunt had seen death before . . . on Jago, in his parish back home, in his trade as a consulting detective. But this destruction was on a different scale. He might as well have been the city's commander, dispatching thousands to their end with a causal wave of a marshal's baton. He took the boy's cold hand in his, rubbing the fingers. 'You have to be careful with murder like this, murder on an industrial scale. It can do things to you. Send you mad enough to start listening to the old gods, and that can land you in all sorts of trouble.'

I can't die.

'No energy is ever lost, young man,' replied Daunt. 'Only transformed. That's how the world works.'

All along the battlements: screaming, yelling soldiers, and the thud of their rifles, the war cries from gill-necks, bayonets being thrust into gas masks and rebreathers as the battle desperately surged back and forth for control of the wall, just energy, trickling from one state to another. That was all it was. Trickle and flow, trickle and flow.

A passing surgical orderly kicked Daunt in the small of the back. 'Get to the wall, Court man. There are more wounded who need carrying down.'

Daunt reached into his pocket and pulled out his bag of aniseed balls. 'How about you, would you care for a Bunter and Benger's?'

'This is a war, Court man, a *war*. Get off your arse and help us.'

'Yes. I am rather afraid this war belongs to me.' He stood wearily up.

The orderly shoved a red crayon-like stick in Daunt's direction. 'Move down the line of wounded. Anyone you think can be saved, mark their forehead with a cross.'

'Mark them all with a cross,' said Daunt. 'We're pulling back. Prepare to move the aid station.'

'Back, where?'

Daunt pointed to the volcano. 'Inside there.'

He picked his way through the wounded littering the lawn, treading through the human debris of war, oblivious to the calls of the surgeons and their medical staff. Up on the gate's keep, the command table holding the plans for the siege was nearly depleted of counters, only a few of the mayor's staff left at the table and communication desk to push around the surviving units. The rest were at the battlements, firing desperately out into the wall of smoke. The mayor himself was unchanged, striding between the table and the defenders, a gas rifle cradled under his right arm.

380

'Fall back,' Daunt ordered the mayor, who was looking down at this strange foreigner with a mixture of curiosity and hostility. 'Fall back to the volcano. There are chambers underground large enough to shelter the town's population.'

'This is our city, Court man,' boomed the politician. 'Our forefathers—'

'I know, I know. Lie under the ground, died defending it, you'll bring everlasting shame on our Lady of the Light. But here's the thing. The battle of Clawfoot Moor. Same situation. Last great siege of the civil war, and the royalists lost, because just like Nuyok, your perimeter is too wide to mount an effective defence. The Advocacy has enough numbers to swarm over your city and your towers can't be fortified adequately to hold them off. The volcano complex on the other hand had got limited access points and you can funnel your attackers down to narrow enough streams to make your rifles count. If you stay here and fight from your towers, they'll become nothing more than coffins for your people. The Catosian city-state of Sathens achieved the same thing I'm proposing against a polar barbarian horde using the Valley of Egon's slopes. Fall back now, while you can still control the wall well enough that the gill-necks can't harry your retreat. Pull back your two great guns for protective fire to cover your withdrawal.'

'Are you a general of your people, Court man?'

'I understand war, good mayor. Well enough to know this is the only way the people of your city will survive the invasion.'

One of the communications signallers turned around. 'Sappers have breached the wall on the forest side, a fifty-foot section collapsed. Gill-necks are emerging from the trees and trying to storm the rubble. We are being over-run and the city reserves have all been dispatched.'

'The Court has always protected us.' The mayor sounded as though he was trying to convince himself.

'We will, I vow to you we will.'

It was on Daunt's hands now. Failure or success. A pacifist general was leading the army to victory or defeat.

The barrel of a gun pushed Dick inside a large windowless cell, the space matted with dirty straw and scattered with a dozen unkempt prisoners in a variety of clothes. Algo Monoshaft was rudely shoved in after the officer.

'I've seen better looking cells,' said Dick.

'It's not so much a cell,' said the guard. 'More of a larder.'

'The Mass must feed,' agreed the second guard. 'But we're not fussy about our prey being alive, as long as your flesh hasn't turned rancid.'

Dick looked at the thick metal door, sturdy enough despite turning rusty from the damp. 'How many of you things are there?'

'Not so many here. Where we come from, you have no idea.' The guard tossed Dick his cane. 'You're solely among fodder in there, though. You can use your little toy to confirm the truth of my words. You won't need the cane when it's your turn to be taken. You'll be able to tell who among you is the Mass quite easily, because we'll be the ones dining on you.'

The creature masquerading as Sadly appeared, wearing the Court agent's form again rather than Algo's. 'You'll be pleased to know, I checked your cane and left you your Court-issue suicide pill underneath the detection mechanism. I have a wager with my brothers here. They think you'll take it after you've seen us feed. I say you won't.'

'What's the prize?'

'The little sustenance that's hanging on your scrawny bones

is enough of a wager. I prefer younger meat myself, but waste, not want not, as Sadly's old ma used to say.'

'Choke on it, you jigger.'

Their laughter echoed outside as the cell door clanged shut.

'Not to trust anyone,' moaned the steamman. 'I told you. I warned you.'

'That's been my bloody life, sir.' *My death now too, from the look of it.*

The other prisoners in the chamber seemed cowed and cowering. It took a second glance from Dick to realize he recognized one of the figures. Vice-admiral Cockburn bore little relation to the commanding figure Dick has seen on the convoy's flagship. An atrophied figure now, sitting rocking in his own filth. There were a number of plates shoved through the feeding flap at the bottom of the armoured door – the plates piled with cubed vegetables – turnips, parsnips and other root vegetables. Dick scooped up the plate to take to the gaunt officer of the fleet sea arm. 'Eat, man. You're wasting away here.'

'Eat,' giggled the vice-admiral through a scraggly grey beard. 'You fool. They always take the fattest first. Don't eat. Never eat the food.' He spilled the plate angrily in front of Dick. 'You'll see, when they come to choose. They feed outside the door. You can hear them. You'll be the first. Look at you, like a pie seller with that gut. You first.' He broke down into a fit of snorting coughs and Dick reeled back. He was disgusted by how far the navy officer had fallen. Even the prisoners back in the gill-neck's slave camp had held onto more dignity than this. How long had the officer been held inside here?

Algo's metal skull swivelled around the room, taking in the dozen or so prisoners, 'You have a device to detect the presence of vampires, sergeant? Inside your cane? Use it now, there are treasonists among us, my olfactory sensors can detect the stench of the enemy, and the fact that monster told us there are none in here merely confirms it to my mind.'

'The enemy aren't vampires,' said Dick, checking his cane. 'We've been calling them sea-bishops, an underwater race from a bloody long distance away from the Kingdom.'

'Names, names, I heard you, sergeant, just as I heard the vampire. Sea-bishops, the Mass. They feast on human flesh, they can alter their form, and they walk unseen among us. What else would you have me call them but vampires?'

'Fair dos,' said Dick. 'But this cane isn't going to find them.' He pulled out the detection device, locating the tiny white pill sunk on a small velvet-lined niche underneath.

'What do you mean? That is a device of the Court of the Air, is it not?'

'One of the civilians I've been working with, Damson Shades, otherwise known as the Mistress of Mesmerism. Before I left for the capital she whispered something in my ear as I was saying my goodbyes. *Your detector doesn't work. Tell no one, until it's too late.*'

'By the beard of Zaka of the Cylinders, sergeant, why would the Court send you here with a defunct vampire detection mechanism?'

'Bugger me if I know. But a force that's been around the maypole a few more times that you or me has possessed the girl. Let's see what this cane does do, then.' He re-inserted the tube of coiled machinery and twisted the handle as Lord Trabb had instructed him back on the Isla Furia. The eyes on the copper boar's head started glimmering orange just as Sadly's cane had done within Victory Arch. But unlike the fierce orange glow, the illumination of Dick's cane's ornamental handle spluttered and flickered weakly. *That's it then? Just broken like the girl said it was?*

Algo Monoshaft seized the cane from Dick's hands, and

for a moment, Dick thought the batty old steamer was going to use the confirmation of the light to accuse him of being a sea-bishop, but the head of board seemed intent on the handle's eyes.

'What is it, sir?'

'A coded message,' said Algo. 'From someone who knows a very ancient secret . . . that steammen can pulse their vision plates to communicate privately between each other, and an individual who also has access to King Steam's royal cipher. Ah, here's the writer's signature. Did you meet a Lord Trabb inside the Court of the Air?'

'That I did. Your opposite number in the Court.'

The flashing in the handle finished and the steamman unscrewed the knob, pulling away the detection apparatus. Algo tapped out the suicide pill, holding it up gently between his iron digits. 'It is time for your vampire friend to lose his wager, sergeant. You are going to have to ingest this pill.'

Dick looked at the senile old sod as if he had gone mad.

'It's only fair, sergeant, as I fear I am going to have to commit suicide too.'

Whether through good timing or having to slowly navigate their way against the current of nightsoil and effluence, by the time Charlotte, the commodore and Maeva dislodged the sewer port into the gill-neck's capital, the city's defence – and their diversion – was already well under way. Charlotte's suit carried the distant sounds of the underwater battle, amplified and tinny to her ears. She hardly noticed the clash, last out of the claustrophobic tunnel, the commodore and Maeva helping her out into a tight space between two buildings.

Lishtiken, remote and hidden from all surface dwellers' sight, was even more imposing close up. It seized the light of its own lamps and hurled the illumination across the cityscape, dancing and reflecting from a thousand crystal surfaces, mirrored and distorted by the planes and waters. Only the constant movement of swimmers and their submersible vehicles anchored the vista as real, rather than a hall of mirrors glimpsed through the prism of a glass of water. The scale of the city and the way its illumination twisted and shimmered around Charlotte was enough to make her feel dizzy. Many of the crystal surfaces were transparent, exposing chambers inside – a few filled with liquid, others airtight, betraying the gill-necks' origins as an amphibious offshoot of the race of man. At close quarters she could observe the organic nature of the vast steepling constructions running together like a cliff line, crystalline buildings branching out to search for the surface's scant light. On the outskirts of the city low flashes of light bounced around Lishtiken's margins, rotor-spears exploding and the distant magnesium flashes of shock-spears discharging bolts of wild energy. How many nomads were losing their lives out there, buying them the time to carry out her plan? When Charlotte looked closer, the flow of traffic between the buildings was bustling with a single purpose now – getting to cover. She touched the reassuring heft of the shock-spear holstered like a splint against her calf. They had decided not to enter the city with the man-high rotor-spears . . . waving one of the ranged weapons would have been akin to unfurling a nomad standard in the centre of Lishtiken.

'The Advocacy is not used to this,' said the commodore in a coughing chortle of mischief. 'They've had mastery of the mortal deeps for so long they've forgotten what it's like to have their noses tweaked. I have the feeling they don't much care for it.'

'Lishtiken has never been attacked,' said Maeva. 'Not in my memory. The Temple of Judgements is over there. If we meet anyone who questions our presence, tell them we're with your sister's people. You can still pretend to be a royalist can't you, Jared?'

'I've spent most my life pretending not to be one; the reverse won't be any harder.'

Charlotte slipped into her old familiar routine. Just another theft from the rich and powerful. Something she needed to do. Not to alleviate her poverty this time; an extra layer to the blanket of wealth she used to keep the desolation at bay, all her fears of being abandoned with no one willing to help her. Her commission was stealing one of the enemy's dark-ships. A way to transport her into the monsters' lair. She could hardly enjoy her life if every iota of her blood was sucked out to satisfy some horde of fish-scaled monsters, could she? The sea-bishops had immense power. They were greedy beyond avarice, and like so many back home, they had tried to use Charlotte, then discard her. Arrogant. Selfish. Calculating. They were overdue for a fall and who better to humble them than Charlotte Shades, Mistress of Mesmerism?

The raiding party kept to the lower levels of the city, as Maeva led them through the shadows of the gem-like towers, a maze of pipes and gantries, exotically coloured seaweed clinging to any stretch of seabed not built over. At one point, the nomad woman led them on a diversion to skirt an access station for the transport tubes sending gill-necks to far-off sectors of the city. The way ahead was thronged with locals trying to get into the heavily overcrowded transport system; to travel home and check their families were safe from the raiders. Squadrons of armed and armoured gill-necks manoeu-vred past, soldiers riding something Charlotte hadn't seen before. Massive squid-like creatures, rubbery flesh saddled with a single rider above stabilising fins; flashes of sinuous skin and quivering tentacles as the squadron propelled past.

'Monitors, lass,' said the commodore, keeping low on the

seabed next to Charlotte as he watched them flash down the gap between the towers. 'Same as our Kingdom constabulary.'

'They are stabled at the Temple of Judgements,' said Maeva, sounding pleased. 'Fewer of them for us to bluff our way past.'

Shaped like a crown rising majestically out of the surrounding buildings, the Temple of Judgements reached up as grand as any palace. Charlotte ran her eyes over the fortress-sized structure as she squeezed out of a narrow passage. Dozen of crystalline towers climbed out of a central wheel structure, points on its coronet circled by spirals of pearl-white bubble-buildings, each wreath set among a helix of winding arches.

'Can you still feel the darkships inside there?' asked the commodore. There was a tone to the old u-boat man's voice that made Charlotte suspect he would have been relieved if she said no.

Charlotte pointed to the side of the Temple of Judgements, near the seabed where the red crystal wall sloped dotted with tunnel entrances. 'They are inside those passages.'

'U-boat pens,' said Maeva. 'They'll be mostly empty by now. Anything with torpedo tubes will be out chasing our warriors.'

'They won't have sent the darkships, not yet,' said Charlotte. That wasn't the sea-bishop way. They might send their forces to tip the balance, but why risk their precious lives when they commanded so many expendable cattle to exhaust first? 'I can sense at least two vessels inside.'

Elizica was worryingly silent on the matter. *Yes, because I'm doing such a good job by myself.*

Charlotte gazed up at the waters above the city. Was it her imagination, or were the flashes of fighting at the margins of the capital growing less frequent now? Savages against the well-defended heart of the Advocacy's hegemony, how long had she expected the nomads' war party to be able to mount a diversion? Charlotte singled out an entrance down which she sensed the darkships lurking and they quickly crossed the open plaza to the temple.

Inside the tunnel entrance, the water was dark and still. They only took a minute to swim along the smooth crystal surfaces. As the light inside the submersible pen began to brighten the water, Charlotte realized the sloping tunnel floor was clear of liquid before them. 'There's air ahead of us.'

'Always better to do repairs on your blessed boat out of the sea when you can,' said the commodore. 'Welding is welding.'

'The oxygen will be enough to keep the casually inclined away from their pens,' said Maeva. 'Our ride is topside?'

'Let's see.'

Breaking the surface of the tunnel alongside her two companions, Charlotte found herself in an oblong chamber, a crystalline ramp with multiple launch rails running across its floor. A couple of open-to-water gill-neck craft hung from gantries above, and at the back of the pen, a pair of black oily-hulled darkships skulked. Two massive malevolent stingrays – they appeared to be steaming in the air, as if their presence was enough to make the very substance of the world crawl. Arches at the rear of the chamber led deeper into the Temple of Judgement, sealed with glass doors – but of crew, engineers and temple staff there was no sign. The three of them walked cautiously up the incline, pushing the visors of their diving helmets up into their helms. Disconnecting the voice line that tethered the three of them together, they pulled out shock spears and crept up alongside the launch rails, dripping water down onto the hangar floor.

'Why do I feel like a mouse, lass?' whispered the commodore.

'Creeping up on a piece of cheese dangling from a bait clasp?'

Charlotte craned her neck, looking for any signs of movement in the dock. 'That's the point of the assault. Any sea-bishops masquerading as Advocacy commanders inside the temple will be overwhelmed by officials pestering them for orders on how to defend the city.'

Charlotte approached the alien black mass of the ships. It was as if the substance that formed them was alive, throbbing with dark intent.

'How many can one of these evil boats carry?' asked the commodore.

'Two pilots. Up to ten passengers,' said Charlotte. *At least, that's how Elizica remembers it.* 'Enough to hold the three of us.'

The commodore appeared as though he'd been hoping for a smaller capacity – perhaps one less than his number. 'Two craft to choose from, but we need to name them for luck. The one on the left we'll call the *Revenue Man's Soul* – for it's a fact well known that they have none – and the one on the right should be the *Witch of Jackals*, for it's her dark magic we must rely on to survive diving to thirty-six thousand feet. Which one of the terrible pair are we to seize?'

'I'll take a witch over the office of tax,' said Charlotte. She approached the craft on the right and touched the crystal under her diving suit. A circular port irised open in the darkship's hull and a ramp extruded like a lolling tongue. One foot on the ramp and Charlotte was punched backward by a weight wrapping her with a murderous constriction, then she was falling down to the dock. She managed a single surprised croak before a blaze of agony burned across every nerve she possessed. As Charlotte tumbled, she saw Maeva weaving around, her shock-spear blazing erratic bolts of energy towards the craft behind them, loosing bolts even as her body jerked and lurched, spouting blood off her diving suit in a hail of rifle balls; falling, shooting, falling, shooting. Charlotte hit the chamber's floor as a dead weight, exhaling and gagging, the strangling netting repaying her every movement with sparking pain. Laid out across the hanger, Charlotte's eyes twisted up, the one thing she could still move without being lashed by the cruel embrace of the capture net. A lock had opened in the craft behind them, spilling sailors with guns – Jackelians by the look of them, the ancient royalist arms of the Kingdom sitting on their Jack Tar hats.

Commodore Black stumbled towards Maeva, clutching a red weal of blood on his shoulder. Shot-drunk and trembling, he landed on his hands and knees by the nomad woman's side. 'Don't move, lass.'

'I've found a way to punish you after all, Jared,' she grimaced.

'Save your strength now,' the commodore pleaded. 'We'll patch you up. Just be quiet and let me look at you again.'

'And how do I look?' Maeva coughed.

'Fine, lass. Just like when we first met.'

'You always were a honeyed-tongued pirate.'

'Privateer, Maeva. Never a pirate.'

A grey-haired woman emerged from the darkship portal Charlotte had opened, more sailors at her side. Alighting on the dock, the woman smoothly kicked the commodore off all fours and onto his back. 'There you are brother, lying on your fat arse. That's the way you like to spend your wars. Before you run away, at least, leaving the rest of us to die.'

'Mercy,' coughed the commodore, raising an arm. 'Parlay.'

'One privateer to another? I think we're a little beyond that, don't you?' Gemma bent down and reached through the netting binding Charlotte, a blade in her hand. Slicing open Charlotte's diving suit, the woman reached through and ripped

391

the amulet painfully from Charlotte's neck. 'No more stage tricks from you, Mistress Shades. Our mutual friend Mister Walsingham is looking forward to renewing your acquaintance. It seems you owe him a sceptre and he's not very pleased with all the hoops you're making him jump through to retrieve it.'

Charlotte tried to speak, but the burning agony was as bad as plunging her fist into a stoked fireplace.

'The capacitors on the net are very sensitive,' smiled Gemma Dark. 'I'd keep your witticisms to yourself, thief girl, until you're safely locked up in the feeding pens. You did want to visit my allies' seed-city, no? It's a long dive down. I'm here to save you the trouble of stealing a darkship. Always happy to give any friend of my brother the scenic journey.'

Maeva groaned on the floor, her fingers reaching weakly for her fallen shock-spear, but Gemma Dark's foot swept the nomad's weapon a couple of inches beyond her dying grasp. 'No, I don't think *you're* coming along for the ride. You'd bleed all over my darkship's cabin, and while our allies do so appreciate human blood, I'd rather not have to mop it up for them.' Gemma Dark knelt down alongside Maeva. 'Your filthy nomad vermin outside Lishtiken didn't last very long, I'm afraid. The city wasn't as unprepared for your arrival as it appeared. Time for you to join your friends.' The commodore's sister produced a pistol and shot Maeva through the heart, her body shuddering on the floor. Charlotte jounced in shock at the cold-blooded slaughter, the commodore's moan coming out as half a sob.

'That's as much mercy as I have for your kind, sea-wanderer. Same as your seanore friends showed any royalist unlucky enough to be captured crossing your hunting grounds.' She pushed the commodore away from the nomad's corpse with her boot, clicking her fingers for the mob of sailors to come and secure him with manacles. 'Don't worry, you're not getting off so easily, brother. We'll have a proper family reunion, you and I, appropriately unhurried. The sea-bishops have a machine that allows them to drain a mind as if it's a swamp, but where's the sport in that? I'll handle your interrogation the way all traitors to the cause should be treated . . . your fat arse, an iron bar, and your dear little sister for company.'

'You didn't have to kill Maeva,' whispered the commodore. 'You didn't have to.'

'Oh, I think we should start as we mean to go on, don't you?'

Charlotte lay on the deck, the sailors deactivating the shock net only to manacle her arms and bundle her up inside the darkship. At least she was free of the vicious shocks pursuing her every roll and twitch. 'You can't trust the sea-bishops! Those monsters don't have allies, they have herds. You're not their partners. To them, you're only their supper – delayed.'

'Trust has always been a pliable notion, thief girl,' said Gemma, boarding the craft and stuffing Charlotte's amulet inside her jacket pocket. 'And when it comes to the hunt, better a flea on the hound, than a flea on the hare, hmm?'

After the shock of the net, Charlotte could hardly stand, and the sailors rolled her into the back of the darkship's cabin, a featureless dark tunnel leading up to the cockpit. The surface was slightly sticky and wet, as if they were being held in the belly of a beast. She turned over as she slid across the floor, landing next to Commodore Black. With her hands and the old u-boat man's securely bound, Charlotte noticed the sailors were passing their rifles to one of their number, a young pock-faced man who then exited the darkship with a pile of rifles in his arms.

'Is that the limit of the alliance you have struck, honey?' Charlotte called to Gemma. 'The sea-bishops won't even let you in their city with ranged weapons?'

Gemma patted the sabre resting by her side. 'Hold your filthy mouth, thief girl, lest you lose it. I still have this, and its edge is sharp enough for your wagging tongue. My allies don't need your prattle during interrogation. They can rip your thoughts out with their queer machines.' She turned back to the cockpit and then ignored her prisoners.

Jared Black shook his head sadly. 'Sorry lass. This is it for our schemes. Why did Maeva choose to follow me? She always knew what follows at my heels. I'm an old fool whose life has drained away into the sea, but a young doe like you deserves better.'

Charlotte watched the controls at the front of the darkship twisting around the pilot, carnivorous black ivy wrapping itself around a victim. 'We all deserve better, Jared.'

'Aye, but this is all the wicked world has for us.'

CHAPTER SEVENTEEN

Corporal Cloake pulled back the viewing slit on the feeding pen's heavy iron door. The sea-bishop glanced inside, noting the figure stretched out across the floor. The rest of the cattle were herding fearfully to the rear of the chamber, while the nanomechnical creature that had until recently been head of the State Protection Board was shaking near the corpse as if a disease was inflicting it.

'I have lost my bet,' said the sea-bishop wearing Sadly's body. He was standing behind Corporal Cloake along with the pair of guards standing sentry on the feeding pens. 'It seems as if the Tull animal chose to suicide.'

Cloake nodded towards the guards. 'You two, drag it to the rubbish pile.' He opened the feeding pen door, the stench of cattle defecation flooding out, added to by the foul reek of Dick Tull's corpse.

'By the dark between the worlds, what a malodour,' grunted one of the guards, hesitating before stepping through the door.

Corporal Cloake entered the pen. As he set foot inside, he stepped into a pile of decaying feed used to fatten the cattle. Cursing, Cloake brushed his foot off against the pen's sides.

What was the point of feeding these dumb things if they wouldn't eat? Well, they still needed to consume plenty of water. He would have to remember to order the herd master to add a hunger stimulant to their liquids. Then the cattle would be as fast at the feed as the filthy rodents scattering across the floor before him.

Cloake bent down, checking the corpse's cold, pasty skinned neck for a pulse, before feeling for a heartbeat. Nothing. The animal had been sweating before it died, its jacket drenched in its own disgusting sweat. By Tull's side was the cane to detect the brethren of the Mass, the pommel carving's eyes dead, power source drained and partially disassembled to reach the suicide pill. 'Powdered root in the suicide pill, similar to those issued by the State Protection Board. The fever stopped its heart. It's the poison you can smell on its skin.'

'Its blood is rancid,' said the guard, grabbing hold of a stiff leg. 'The Mass must feed.'

'Indeed we will, but not on this debased flesh,' hissed Cloake. 'How many do you need? Animals overrun this filthy city. Breeding in their slums, lying hop-addled in the gutters outside their taverns. You can't cross the street without tripping over sustenance.'

Sadly helped the guards drag the corpse away, while in front of Corporal Cloake, the deposed head of the State Protection Board was vibrating and shuddering, adding its mad ramblings to the insane sing-song whine from the dirty cattle clustering at the rear of the pen.

'Treasonists, treasonists, everywhere. Vampires, vampires, on the stairs.'

'So, your mind's finally become as broken as your body, you primitive bucket of bolts?' Cloake drew out his pistol. He was eager to pay back this half-witted calculating device for the ignominy of far too many years having to pretend to take orders from a mere nanomechanical, of having to subjugate the superior intellect of the Mass to this ridiculous half-sentient machine-born monstrosity. 'Don't you have any orders for me? Speak, tell me how you are the head of the board and I must rush to do your bidding . . . order me to let you live!'

Dragging Dick Tull's corpse out of the cell, the sea-bishop wearing Barnabas Sadly's form turned and took in the vista of the Algo Monoshaft's violently shuddering body, Corporal Cloake standing in front of it and about to pump a bullet though its useless, shaking skull.

'Don't!' shouted Sadly. 'That's—'

Cloake ignored his brethren. 'We can't take an imprint of this thing's memories. I want to see what it looks like in pieces.'

'—how their race use their body as a—'

With stacks sealed for hours, its boiler-heart circulating and building pressure, the pressure inside Algo Monoshaft's frame became too much for its ageing hull-plates to hold.

'—suicide bomb!' The steamman transformed into a grenade, shrapnel and fire scything out, instantly killing all the cattle and cutting Corporal Cloake in two, both halves of his body collapsing across the filthy pen floor. Cloake's mesmeric field collapsed along with the shredding of his crystal. The sea-bishop's distended head had enough life left to watch the other guard caught in the blast. Writhing across the floor, the sea-bishop's field flickered on and off as he lost control – switching between his human and natural form – then, judging its host life lost, the evidence removal function of the crystal activated and the guard flared into ashes. Cloake reached for his own crystal, but it had been blown to pieces, his fingers only coming away with splinters. He wasn't going to experience the sudden clean death of the crystal's mercy.

Sadly and the remaining guard were peering around the doorway at the silent shrapnel-embedded walls of the pen, peering horrified through the smoke at the ruins of their brethren's body.

Corporal Cloake moaned. The last thought that flickered across his dying mind was how damned hungry he was.

Crowds snaked up on the slopes of the volcano, the hangar doors of the island's destroyed airship squadron held open while thousands of Nuyokians abandoned their city, ordinary citizens deserting their porcelain towers and hexagonal streets for the safety of the Court of the Air's underground chambers. Daunt considered it something of an irony they would be packing in around the house-sized transaction-engines of the Court, the steam-driven thinking machines maintaining the model of Jackelian society and the supposedly safe course the Court was charting for it. There was nothing *safe* on the Isla Furia anymore. The city wall overlooking the lake was holding, but only just. Mainly thanks to the fact that the parapet on the city's jungle side had been breached in so many places that it now made sense for the gill-neck invasion force to concentrate their forces on the breaks to the north-east. Leaking invaders into Nuyok, storming the rubble of fallen battlements. It wouldn't take long before the Advocacy commanders realized that only token militia volunteers manned the city towers in front of them. Daunt was introducing a new thing to the city today – a terrible lesson for any pacifist to pass on. Guerrilla warfare. Hit and run. It was the only way to slow down such a vastly superior force. Give the Advocacy the impression that every hexagonal tower they faced was a fortress needing to be reduced to rubble, every savage inch bled for, while small mobile companies charged across the streets, harrying the gill-neck invaders. Hope what was left of their defences held until the populace was evacuated.

It was a risky plan, but the only one Daunt had. Every minute he slowed their advance was another minute for citizens to seek out the safety of the Court's deep vaults. Poor devils. The Nuyokians were like refugees everywhere, all the worse for being dispossessed inside their own city, the city monitors shouting at the crowds to toss aside any possessions slowing the lines down. Wrestling carts of goods away from some and pushing them off to the side of the lawns. They took it in better humour than a similar mob of Jackelians would have – no doubt a side effect of their communal society and particular ideas about ownership.

Morris counted explosions flowering around the collapsing defences on the far side of Nuyok, then looked at the mob herding up the slopes. 'I don't like it. That place up there might be laid out like a fortress, but the Court was never built to house so many civilians. The gill-necks will be able to wait us out for as long as it takes for us to starve. Once the hares are inside the warren, there's no way out that won't be weasels all the way.'

'I'll settle for as long as it takes,' said Daunt. 'Time is what we need.'

'Time for what?' asked Morris, wiping the sweat off his brow. He had pushed his gas mask back up his helm. 'You don't really think Dick Tull and Sadly are returning to the island with a flight of Royal Aerostatical Navy squadrons in tow, do you? And I don't particularly rate your girl and u-boat skipper's chance of rousing the nomads of the sea up against the gill-necks, either.'

'I fear we must have faith, Mister Morris.'

'When a Circlist parson starts talking of having that, I know we're in bloody trouble.' He spat onto the ground.

'Well, at least the poor gits will be better shielded in the gas mine's tunnels than inside the city. Porcelain walls might keep you cool from the heat, but they're bloody shrapnel coffins in a fight, see.' His last few words were mangled by the detonations of the two giant cannons, their artillery relocated in front of the cable car station and landing shells within the city boundary. It was a hard thing to do, to order gunners to land shells on their own people. But the forces along the jungle-flanked wall had become so intermingled that the impact of the barrage was killing as many Advocacy soldiers as locals. Out beyond the thermal barrier surrounding the island, the invasion fleet was now bridging the killing zone unopposed. More soldiers to pour across the island, more predators to prowl the set Daunt was trapping the citizens inside.

Eventually the sea-bishops hidden among the invaders would track down and eliminate the faked signals emulating King Jude's sceptre and then there would be only one hiding place left. The volcano. They would throw the entire gill-neck military machine against the slopes, with not a care for the natives sheltering inside. It all came down to time, if only he could buy enough time. Buy it with bodies. *What a bitter currency to fund my strategy.* A line of detonations stitched their way across the cable car concourse, the distant whoop of gill-neck mortars falling across their position.

Daunt ducked reflexively along with Morris behind the makeshift command post in the volcano's shadow. A hailstorm of tiny stones and dirt jounced off the sandbags and ricocheted off the cable car station behind them. As the dust of the explosions cleared, Daunt saw that the columns of fleeing Nuyokians had been broken, limbless bodies scattered as though seeds from a dandelion head, wails of moaning rising around smoking craters. The rain of mortar shells on their position had left Daunt with a dusty, gritty taste on his tongue, his clothes covered with a layer of dull volcanic dust. A sudden wave of fatigue washed over him. How long since he had last eaten or slept? Everything was war; it was as if there had never been a time when he had known peace. Daunt couldn't faint now. This was his slaughter. He would look the refugees in the eyes as they passed. He would feel their fear and taste their pain. The Circle save him, but the ex-parson's ear was attuned to this carnage now. Daunt could tell the difference between heavy bombards and light gallopers, between the short-barrelled cannons on the rolling-pin tanks, tracks pulling them over the rubble of the walls, and the heavy howitzers that the gill-necks had assembled on the island's shores. The pacifist had a day of practical lessons to add to his years of book learning. A day stretched into a year, subverting the lessons of the church. From how every battle could be avoided, corrupted into by what means their lost cause might be turned around.

Running across the ground of the mud-trampled parkland opposite, one of the city engineers came skidding past the sandbags. 'The blasting barrels you requested have been assembled, Court man.'

Daunt turned to the crumpled map of the city he had procured, laid out across a porcelain bench. 'We don't have much time. Bring down the towers along this line—' he tapped the map, '—and then this one.'

The engineer looked indignant. 'You are asking me to destroy our city?'

'Walls and halls are not your city,' snarled Daunt. He pointed to the struggling lines of citizenry pouring past their position. '*They* are Nuyok. Bring these two districts down, collapse their under-streets into canyons and we will force the gill-necks to funnel through this central area. A mountain pass for us to defend, such as the steamman knights held in the Battle of the Gauge Heights.' The engineer looked as if he was going to argue further, but Daunt silenced him with a jab towards the low buildings on the far side of the parkland. 'These palaces need to come down too. The Holy Kikkosico Empire's defence of Los Tarral showed that it's many degrees harder to assault through rubble than through standing structures.'

'Those are not palaces,' the engineer sounded disgusted. 'That is the great Library Publico of Nuyok.'

'Good engineer,' Daunt seized the man by his ceramic chainmail. 'I have killed thousands of men, women and children today. Let's burn a few of your books on their shelves too.'

The engineer stumbled back, looking at Daunt as if he was mad. 'We will clear the shelves, where we can, where we have time.'

'Who will read them?' Daunt shouted as the engineer exited the command post. 'Can corpses read your precious shelves of books?'

Morris pulled his rifle in tight on his shoulder, flashing a look of concern at the ex-parson. 'You need to rest. I slept an hour at the back of the station on one of the spare stretchers.'

'I can sleep when I'm dead,' said Daunt. He pushed Morris away. 'Monsters win battles, Mister Morris. That is the real lesson of history. Cold, heartless madmen who march innocents into the mincing machine of war. We face monsters, but what are we? What must we become? Monsters killing monsters.'

'You won't get the taste for it, vicar. Not you. For some this is beer and mumbleweed and sex. But you're better than us.'

'Better!' Daunt thumped the map. 'Everyone in the Northeast of the city will be cut off in a few minutes. My last order to them was to fight to the end. No quarter. No retreat. I *am* better. You thought we'd have folded by now, surrendered. You gave me odds on it. But the city is still fighting. How many generals could have done that? How many colonels and field marshals could have prolonged the killing here for so long?'

'You'll know when it's time to stop,' said Morris, sitting down. 'And that's better than most.'

One of the Court's guards came into the post, pushing back a strange black mask that covered his face, an evil grasshopper head made of rubber and leather and twin respirators, one hanging on either side of his visor. He passed a wax-sealed tube across to Daunt. 'Lord Trabb's complements sir.'

'What is it?' asked Morris as Daunt scanned the message pulled from the container.

'Bob my soul, but just once I would like to receive some good news today. The Court's spotters on the rise are reporting the fall of the wall on the south side. Lord Trabb's worried that the advance of the gill-necks towards us will trigger the Court's defences. Their automated gun ports on the slopes won't differentiate between refugees and Advocacy marines right now. It'll be a hard pounding for everyone.'

'Then turn the damn things off,' said Morris.

Daunt handed the tube back to the Court's messenger, addressing him directly. 'No. Keep the artillery running. Any stragglers will have to come in under fire.'

Morris looked horrified, his eyes flicking towards the frightened women and children filing past them. Another round of mortar shells scattered across the concourse, militia yelling and screaming over the impacts, trying to shepherd the mob into the safety of the mountain refuge.

'I won't pick up a gun myself,' Daunt told Morris. 'Because I'm a good Circlist and a better hypocrite. I won't pick up a weapon because I've got you and everyone else to do that for me.' He picked up the map and left the post, glancing back at Morris. 'On your feet, sir. It's not time to stop yet.'

Down the darkship sank, spinning slowly, the only signs of the trench's fierce depth the occasional animal-like tremor along the craft's oily floor, something to accompany the creaking from its hull. Unlike a Jackelian u-boat, there were no gas lanterns to light the drop into the abyss, but the craft seemed to emit a hellish red glow which the pilot's viewing port could translate into a form of vision. The occasional snake-like trench dweller passed the darkship in front of the jagged, falling walls of the trench, moving through a sea of blood.

Gemma Dark came strutting down the narrow cabin, cock-of-the-walk since she had captured Charlotte and Commodore Black. In a rare flash of generosity she had ordered Jared's shoulder bandaged, although Charlotte suspected that had more to do with a desire to prolong his time under interrogation, rather than any softening of heart towards her brother. 'You want to know an irony, brother? It was the airships of the Royal Aerostatical Navy that first chased me down here, their depth charges that set off a rock slide, breaking the ancient machines holding my allies locked in a snare of suspended time. Parliament freed them, but my wrecked u-boat was the first thing their scouts came across.'

'A pity they didn't gorge their chops on your bitter old bones,' growled the commodore.

'Oh, they killed a few of us,' said Gemma. 'Stripped our minds and fed on our blood. That was when they realized the similarities between our two peoples. Both of us hunted and harried to the ends of existence, persecuted for who we are. They needed allies to take their first tentative footsteps outside, re-entering our brave new era, and the cause had run out of friends a long time ago.'

'Only because you'd seen most of them killed, sister,' muttered the commodore.

'Not quite as many as I should have done.'

'You've made a bad bargain,' spat Charlotte.

'Tell me that when I am sitting on the throne of Jackals as the Kingdom's first true queen for over seven hundred years.'

'You won't be queen,' laughed Charlotte. 'You'll just be in charge of the abattoir for a short while.'

'We shall see.' Gemma pulled out Charlotte's amulet and swung it tauntingly inches from her face. 'What are you without this trinket? Only a petty housebreaker, and probably not a very competent one without my allies' tricks to bend weak-willed minds to your thievery. Walsingham tells me that you're the illegitimate daughter of an industrial lord, that filthy parliament of shopkeepers, tradesmen with their dirty stolen titles. What a *fancy* pair of doves flapping in my snare. A shopkeeper's bastard, working with a traitor to the cause . . . a lapdog and informer for the State Protection Board.'

Behind Gemma, the cliff-face through the darkship's port had stopped rising past, her darkship turning to reveal the trench floor. Further than any human should have been able to reach, the deep of the dark. It was still, currentless and cold, but not entirely without movement. Charlotte could see the sea-bishops' seed-city ahead, a vast ebony disk blocking the floor of the trench. Above it, moving sedately with the vast pressure, were darkships, as well as figures wearing diving suits that looked like collections of joined spheres. They were putting the finishing touches on a massive curved arch, jagged, crystalline, an architecture of pure evil. Large enough to pass the seed-city squatting before it through the vault, and with good reason. When the gate was activated, Charlotte's world would be joined to its dangerous mirror image across the well of infinite possibilities. How many seed-cities would pass through that gate then, how many countless sea-bishops, arriving to feast until every living creature in her world was extinct?

'Nothing should be able to prosper this deep down,' said the commodore.

'Walsingham's people like to toil far away from the gaze of their enemies,' said Gemma. 'And as I have had it explained to me, my allies need the incredible forces of the pressure down here to anchor the energies released when unlocking the portal to their home.'

'How can you talk like that about helping them?' asked Charlotte, stunned by the royalist's disregard for the implications of her words.

'Why don't you ask my brother?' laughed Gemma. 'We were both born with a price on our head, weren't we, Jared? The children of rebels with long-lost titles and nothing else except a world full of enemies and assassins and turncoats ranged against us. You want to know why I'll choose those treacherous reflections of humanity as allies over my own race? Just the chance of getting my hands on my brother would be worth all that I have done in their name and all that I yet will. I would crawl across every cold inch of hell merely for the chance to tweak this jigger's beard.'

Charlotte found it hard to believe anyone could hate the way this woman could. Beyond reason, Gemma was clinging to it like a life raft. She was hollowed out with hate. 'Once you open that gate, there will be no closing it. The sea-bishops will come here in numbers beyond legion to feed on us.'

'Quite so,' said Gemma. 'Fortunately there are so many nations around who are entirely superfluous to my coming reign. Those shiftie bastards, those king-murdering regicides on the First Committee in Quatérshift, for instance. I think a world without them would be for the better, don't you? And the Steamman Free State? Where were they when Jackelian shopkeepers were hunting my ancestors, foxes to the hounds, across the moors? An internal matter, can't intervene. Let's see how the steammen like a taste of neutrality from their neighbours for a change. The caliph down in Cassarabia, drip-feeding the cause crumbs of support from his table only when it suited his glorious highness? Well, he likes crafting monsters out of slave flesh, he can meet my monsters and we shall see who comes out best from the arrangement. The Mass must feed, that's what my little darlings are always saying. Let them!'

Charlotte stared up in shock at the commodore's sister. 'You've lost your mind.'

'Just running to the bitter, that is all. Ashes are what the world has given me. I'm only riding my luck and making the best of it.'

'You can't trust them!'

'Am I an idiot, thief girl?' snarled Gemma. 'I trust them as much as I trust my dear brother here. But I have worked with the Mass for long enough to understand them far better than you ever will. They are cowards. They are a hundred times as far ahead of us in engineering and technology as we are above the most primitive tribe of polar barbarians, and yet the Mass will never fight until they have overwhelming numbers on their side. Even then, they prefer to sidle up behind you masquerading as your grandmother to slip one of their blood-draining daggers in your spine. They live in fear. Fear that one day they will connect to a reflection of their world carrying a race as far beyond them as they are beyond us. A race that will follow them back to their barren piss-ridden world and burn them out for the plague they have become.' She bent in close to Charlotte and winked. 'Every day I've lived I've faced and fought against impossible odds. The sea-bishops don't know it yet, but they've found the world they've been dreading all these millennia. It is ours, and I shall be its sole ruler.'

'They're not quite the cravens you take them for,' said Charlotte. 'You know what happens when sea-bishops reach a world with a species judged too hostile to be conquered? They detonate their seed-city and all on board die rather than risk capture and having their home traced. Self-sacrifice, all for the Mass. They are experts at judging the odds.' She pointed to the seed-city, its black expanse approaching closer to the darkship with every second. 'Does that look like a race of creatures uncertain about their chances of victory against us?'

'Suicide is usually the way cowards leave the world,' said Gemma. She turned to her royalist sailors inside the darkship. 'Never give up the cause. Never surrender. To live is to fight and to fight is to live!'

The u-boat crew raised their fists and punched the air, shouting back her words like a war cry, making a holy mantra of the cry. Gemma turned around and slammed her boot into the commodore, doubling him up in agony. 'Look at you, brother. Always fighting when you should be running and running when you should be fighting.'

The commodore groaned and raised a hand weakly towards the approaching seed-city. 'We're like those demons lurking out there in the night, Gemma, the fleet-in-exile, the royalist cause. We should have died out an age ago, surrendered to history and the blessed march of progress.'

'If that's the limit of your defeatist cant, maybe you could have had the courtesy to move along the Circle before you went and got my only son bloody killed,' snarled Gemma.

'Bull died like a man,' said the commodore, 'facing down true enemies of the Kingdom.'

'Another lie. You paroled him out of prison just to get him murdered on one of your dupe's adventures, your pockets lined with an industrial lord's gold to do it. Well, brother, you and your fancy piece here can share Bull's *glory*. But not before you've seen my allies have their fun.'

'I'm sorry about Bull; that much is true.'

'Sorry! You've never had a child die. You don't have the right to be sorry.'

'You're wrong about that too, Gemma.'

'Been sowing your wild oats out there have you?' sneered the commodore's sister. 'Yes, your noble bastards are probably scattered in every port from Spumehead to Thar. But don't expect me to mourn one less of your seed, brother. Your half of the family tree is about to come to an abrupt end, while mine is only just beginning.'

'Ah, sister,' wheezed the commodore, 'you're sixty now if you're a year. There are no more children for your old body.'

'That's where you're wrong. The Mass are going to alter my flesh to make me like them. I will live forever, my youth restored, my womb fertile again. By the time I am finished, this world will be filled with *nothing* but my descendants. You and everyone else in the world are nothing but my meal ticket to power, quite literally. So let me tell you how things sit. Your pathetically desperate plan to alert the State Protection Board to the sea-bishops' presence has failed. The siege at the Isla Furia is about to end the only way it could, and you two fools are going to live just as long as it takes for that gate out there to be opened.' She smiled coldly at them before she turned to watch the seed-city swallowing their craft. 'After all, it is true. The Mass must feed.'

When the door on the seed-city's dimly illuminated cell opened it was more like a mouth widening. The manacles were unlocked on Charlotte and the commodore before royalist sailors shoved the two of them inside. The surface of the cell was wet and slippery and a silhouette rose up out of the shadowy prisoners huddling on the floor towards the cell's rear. As he drew closer, Charlotte recognized the man. 'Sadly!'

Barnabas Sadly rubbed at raw red eyes, as if he didn't quite believe what he was seeing. 'They've caught you too?'

'That they have, lad,' said the commodore. 'My sister and the sea-bishops both.'

'Sea-bishops?' said Sadly. 'Is that what you're calling those things?' He saw the look of confusion on the commodore's face and continued. 'Those monsters have the spit of me walking around. My face, a parcel of memories they ripped out of my mind inside the gill-neck prison camp. But I, it certainly ain't. It's one of the wobble-headed beasts. I've been here ever since they stole my shape and shipped me out of the prison camp, trying to avoid looking chuffing fat enough to make a good mouthful for these monsters.'

'That's how my sister knew we were coming,' groaned the commodore. 'Sadly a cuckoo in the nest. You're well out if it, Barnabas. The Court of the Air is about to fall to the enemy on your people's island. Me and the girl here were the Kingdom's last hope to survive.'

'That's a poor turn,' sighed Sadly. 'So my cover's blown and the Kingdom's odds are as low as the rest of ours?' He indicated the prisoners huddling sullenly at the rear of the cell. 'Meet the survivors of the convoy that weren't sent to die on the Island of Ko'marn. The beasts dispatched me here along with the choice cuts, so you lot wouldn't spy the fact there were two Sadlys limping about the prison camp.'

Charlotte looked at the whimpering mass of broken prisoners hugging the cell wall behind the Court's agent. This was a terrible sight to see. The sailors in the feeding pen were utterly broken. Men of action and violence and discipline, used to facing death. Withdrawn into sullen madness, shaking and trembling and mercifully unable to engage with the daily routine of being available for consumption. But not Barnabas Sadly. He was still here, dirty and unkempt and soiled, still standing and thinking and ready to fight back with whatever his hands could fashion and his mind devise. 'You've lasted all this time down here?'

Sadly thumped his mangled leg. 'I think the first few weeks they kept me in case they needed to pick through my mind again. Now, I'm limping along on the fact I'm hardly choice meat. But I don't know what's worse. Being selected, or being left for another meal day after day. It's as good as running mock executions for breaking prisoners' souls. Look at these poor devils. They were our fighting men, once, the bravest of the brave.'

'You seem to have outlasted them, lad,' said the commodore.

'Well, as you seem to have rumbled during my absence, I'm with the Court of the Air. They take out our souls shortly after we join.'

'What you believe of your essence is irrelevant. We only select cattle based on your vitality,' said a familiar voice behind them.

Charlotte swung around. Walsingham was standing at the entrance, two hideously wizened sea-bishop guards either side of him, clutching long dark rifle-shaped crystalline weapons, their elongated heads black bishops' mitres, swaying as they stood ready to open fire. 'Not too much fat. Plenty of tender young flesh. We can't abide the oily taste overweight over-aged

411

animals like you—' he pointed at the commodore, '—leave on the palate. But that's fine, your sister wishes to toy with you a little, so for the sake of diplomacy I shall humour her.'

'Why don't you show us your real form, *Captain Twist*,' said Charlotte.

'Oh, I am sure the members of the Mass all look alike to mere animals,' said Walsingham.

'You can eat my cursed sister, then,' said the commodore, 'and let us three go.'

'That would be a poor decision,' smiled Walsingham. 'A farmer must use dogs to hunt down wolves, even if he has to eat a little hound during the depths of winter when the larder runs low.' Walsingham raised the amulet Gemma Dark had ripped from Charlotte's neck. 'Not quite the gem I hired you to retrieve for me, but judging by my reports from the siege at the Isla Furia, I should hold that by the end of the day too. As for my animal semblance, it serves as a good example.' He called out to the corridor and a miniature sea-bishop walked tentatively inside the cell, passing a pair of royalist sentries outside, the creature standing no higher than Walsingham's waist. Like the two sea-bishop guards, it wore a rubbery skin-suit with a crystal held in the centre of its chest as though it was a beating heart. The royalist sentries outside were trying hard not to look in the prisoners' direction. They knew what was coming next.

Walsingham placed a hand on the little monster's shoulder. 'This is my son, Child 722 from my twelfth brood-wife. Select your animal. Speak only in Jackelian.'

The alien child walked forward, lights in the ceiling growing painfully bright in response to an unseen command from the child's crystal. It pointed to one of the men at the back: tall, strong, a tattered sailor's uniform reduced to filthy rags by his incarceration. 'That one, father.'

'An excellent choice. Now, switch to amplification mode and focus.'

As the gem glowed in the centre of the young creature's chest, the sailor stumbled away from the rear wall, mumbling the same name over and over again – Sally, Sally – one of his own children, perhaps. Charlotte looked on, frozen in horror. Behind the selected sailor the other prisoners were shaking and keening, an animal noise she didn't think it was possible could rise out of any human throat.

'Maintain your hold,' ordered Walsingham. 'Bring the animal in closer, closer.'

The sailor was a foot away from the miniature sea-bishop, when the child monster produced the same style of crystalline tuning fork-shaped blade that Corporal Cloake had once tried to use on Charlotte. It seemed to seal into the child's tiny hand, growing and moulding into the veins around its black, withered wrist, then the thing stabbed upwards with the blade while the sailor was bending down, reaching out with his arms to hug whatever projection of familial love was in his mind's eye.

'Inject, reduce, ingest,' called Walsingham.

Charlotte couldn't tear her eyes away from the sickening sight, the man's frame diminishing, blood and liquefied meat flowing up the crystalline prongs, the young creature's stomach swelling as if it were pregnant. Flicking out talon-like, the prongs of the feeding blade withdrew and a crumpled husk, little more than sack of mummified skin, flopped to the oily surface of the cell. *This is what happened to Damson Robinson back in her pie shop, the Circle preserve her soul. They did that to my friend! I never had so many I could afford to lose them.*

'Very good, child. A perfectly clean cull,' said Walsingham, patting the hideous thing's distended head. 'Tomorrow we will practice feeding and see if you can push your cattle semblance into the minds of *all* the animals here, not just your prey's.' He turned to Charlotte. 'It is relatively painless. The blade sedates as it drains, just as our mesmeric trance convinces the animal it is in the presence of its own herd.' He pushed the sailor's desiccated remains away with his foot. 'Very little sustenance is wasted, which is of paramount importance.'

Charlotte bent over, clutching her heaving stomach. Charlotte had seen this in the memories Elizica had dredged up in the sceptre's recordings, but watching it in person, the visceral sight and the stench, was almost more than she could stand.

Walsingham appeared amused by her reaction. 'I remember the night we first met. Before you took to the stage in front of the guests, one of his lordship's servants fetched you a plate from the kitchens and you ate. Did you weep tears for the cuts of roast pork you piled into your primitive digestive system? Did you mourn how long the animal had hung in a dirty shed, its neck inexpertly slit and its blood pouring away? Do you know how much genetic similarity you share with that swine? I could rip out its heart and have it sown into your body with as little inconvenience as changing the power cell in my guard's rifle. But does that stop your saliva running when you smell roast crackling? It does not. This is the way of nature. Predators and prey, always.'

Charlotte glared hatred at the creature. 'Don't expect your prey not to go down scratching and biting.'

'Oh, you've inconvenienced me quite enough thus far. You should view you and your rabble through our perspective, understand how pathetically short-lived you are. The Mass have purified our genes – we can live for thousands of years, near immortal. To us, you animals pass like mayflies in the burning of a single afternoon. You should be honoured that your flesh serves the Mass. Well, we're preparing a recorder to rip a memory imprint from you. We will discover just what tricks you have played on us. After that . . .?' He smiled at her, licking his lips. 'My progeny shall see how the bacon sizzles.'

As the sea-bishops departed, the wall sealed up, leaving not a trace of a join behind them.

Commodore Black stumbled after the creatures, slamming his fist into the cell's damp featureless surface. 'Look at this foul black stuff, dripping with evil and cunning. How can I pick the lock on this? A swallowed man tickling open the guts of a whale? How am I meant to bring my mortal genius to bear on such a foul prison?'

'Don't worry, Jared,' said Charlotte, laying a hand on the old u-boat man's shoulder.

'Why, because our worries will be short, lass? I always knew in my bones that it would be Elizica's games that did for me in the end. All my life, running. You can escape from almost anything, but you can never escape the who or how of your birth, not who you are.' Big wet tears tolled down his cheeks and he rubbed them away with half a sob and half a snort of laughter. 'These tears aren't for me, lass. Not old Blacky. Sick and dying and hardly missed when he's gone. They're for you and all my friends back home. I've saved us all Charlotte, that I have. I've saved us all a dozen times over. I've faced mad revolutionaries and madder gods, fought our enemies from Cassarabia to Quatérshift, battled villains from the deserts of Kaliban to the black halls of Jago, but here's my end. A cell with no lock is an escape even old Blacky can't manage.'

Charlotte shrugged. 'Housebreaker, animal, cattle, prey, bastard, thief girl – that's all that Walsingham and your sister see when they look at me. But while I dabble as a thief, I'm also Charlotte Shades, Mistress of Mesmerism. I didn't fall onto the stage by luck. I didn't become the quality's act of choice just because they wanted to gawk at the bastard daughter of one of their own, fallen, capering about for their amusement. I learnt the craft the hard way: memory tricks, cold reading, sleight of hand, pickpocketing and hypnotism. I studied under the best in Jackals and stole to pay for it. And you know what, we're the best in the *world*. I can read any mark for their weakness and I know what the sea-bishops' real flaw is – it's their bloody sense of superiority.'

'Push a sabre in these poor old fingers and I'll take on any horde of demons, but I can't beat a pack of monsters with their own arrogance.'

'I think you can,' said Charlotte as she leant in. And began to tell the commodore the truth.

CHAPTER EIGHTEEN

'All I wanted when I was younger,' said Morris, the gas rifle shaking against his shoulder as he fired behind the sandbags, 'was to be rich. And now I'm older, all I can think about is getting a little peace.'

'I would settle for a little peace myself,' muttered Daunt.

There was scant cover in front of them now, the parkland cleared and barren. Trees felled by the Nuyokians to give a clean field of fire and ornamental gardens churned to pieces by the Advocacy's artillery. Zigzagging gill-neck skirmishers fell as they advanced. The town's militia had held onto the ruins of the library for as long as anyone could have expected them to, only falling to the massed ranks of gill-neck columns advancing up the transparent streets, countless thousands of the invaders in the city now. Their enemy had numbers enough that they could afford to ignore the surviving groups of militia guerrillas still holed up in the porcelain towers, other citizens using the maintenance levels under the city to pop up behind gill-neck positions, loose a few bursts, then disappear into the subterranean warrens under Nuyok. There were telltale columns of yellow smoke rising up. The gill-necks pumping

417

dirt-gas into the undercity, trusting the respirators on the militia's masks would expire before the invaders' supplies of war gas. How many of Daunt's decoy signals were broadcasting now, in imitation of King Jude's sceptre? Probably only the real one locked in the Court's hidden depths. On the foot of the slopes, Daunt could gaze out across Nuyok's length. Its white porcelain symmetry, the hexagonal perfection of her spires shining in the light of the tropical sun. The hypnotizing symmetry of avenues broken where towers had fallen, lying in piles of rubble. Fires burned uncontrolled through the landscape, palls of smoke blending in ugly rainbows with poison gas and the smoke of the gill-necks' guns.

The Advocacy forces were massing on the other side of the ruined library, using the burning rubble to shield themselves from the militia's sniping. They had cleared enough of a passage to bring up rolling-pin tanks, clambering uncertainly onto the rubble, clacking tracks halting, leaving the armour a clear field of fire onto the militia survivors ranged against them. The rate of fire of their respective weaponry was dictating both sides' tactics, exactly as Daunt had counted on. With single shot rifles, each old charge needing to be cleared and a new one breech-loaded, the gill-necks were coming at the Nuyokians in columns and massed squares, the traditional marching lines the Kingdom's regiments used. The gas rifles supplied by the Court lacked their enemy's range, but put out a ferocious rate of fire in comparison. Each soldier able to pour a company's fusillade against the gill-necks. Daunt had his forces scattered and dispersed, small units operating in support of each other, but the time for hit and run was disappearing with every foot of territory lost.

This was the future of warfare Daunt was inventing here. Of all the prizes to claim, this was a terrible accolade Daunt had never imagined possessing. If the ex-parson had any consolation, it was only that nobody would survive on the island to enter his name in the history books for originating this slaughter. Not the Nuyokians, not the gill-necks. The invaders didn't want to be here, fighting in this alien realm. Whatever lies the sea-bishops among the Advocacy's leadership had concocted to set their invasion force against the Isla Furia, the invaders had no passion for it – fighting the surface-dwellers outside the womb of the sea, dying in the beating heat across such strange, unfamiliar streets. No desire to die here. Only a grim murderous determination now to repay the casualties inflicted upon them. A butcher's bill unlike any battle in history. Slaughter on an industrial scale. The Jackelians had mills for everything, now one of their numbers had established a manufactory for murder. All hail the pacifist commander – inventor of the scientific method, warfare as science.

'Gaze upon the future, Mister Morris. I am the master of it,' said Daunt. *How am I better than the sea-bishops? They have their dupes lined up for the slaughter and I have mine. And here in this peculiar city of the past and city of the future, our proxies are dismembering each other to decide which race will endure.*

'Nothing modern about this vicar. We've been at it long before you lifted the marshal's baton.' Morris glanced back up at the volcano's slope, noticing the guns had fallen silent in their camouflaged bunkers. 'We're not going to fall back under barrage?'

Daunt pointed to the massing forces in the ruins of the once palatial library opposite. 'There's more of the enemy now than Lord Trabb has shells left in the stronghold's magazine.'

'So we're only to fire when we see the whites of their eyes. Not that you can see their peepers with those fish tanks they've got on their heads.' Morris spotted something out of place on the farm terraces above them. Figures moving among the spouts of fire being thrown up by the Advocacy artillery. 'What's that? Tell me some arseholes aren't still ploughing and watering the paddy fields up there?'

'I've made arrangements with Lord Trabb,' said Daunt. 'Something more gainful for his labour force of mechanicals to be doing than tunnelling fresh mining shafts.'

Morris shielded his face against the high sun with a hand. 'They're digging a network of fire steps up there!'

'Trenches,' said Daunt. 'Trenches are what they're digging.'

Yes, Daunt had formulated an equation for his new style of warfare. And the Advocacy was about to discover that as hideous as their losses had been to date, they could get a lot worse.

Dick Tull shivered as he woke up, his teeth chattering and his fingers trembling against the frost-covered pile of rotting vegetation. Circle's teeth, it was night cold outside. At least the hill of decaying turnips, corn heads and blackened potatoes serving as his bed were frozen solid enough for his body to be laid across the top of the mound, rather than drowned underneath a rotting slush.

There were dozens of other bodies thrown across the mound, the mummified sacks left by the sea-bishops' feeding, and Dick had to work hard not to retch at the sight as he pulled himself up. He recognized the tall buildings surrounding him, the grand crystal canopies glinting in the moonlight. This was the State Protection Board wing of the civil service complex at Greenhall. So, they had dragged his corpse out of the cells without feeding on his poisoned flesh. *And all I had to do was stop my heart for an hour to get here.* Dick smelt the tang of his jacket, rank even to him. Garlic powder the contents of his cane's suicide pill, along with the Court of the Air's cardiac drug. *Garlic*. He tried not to chuckle through the cold burning agony of his throat. It was strange how many myths had their basis in reality.

There was a clanking from inside the bottom storey of the building, the light of a furnace burning inside. Best to be out of here before the sea-bishops on the janitorial staff showed up and tried to feed him into a fire.

Dick patted his jacket pocket. *Still there*. It wouldn't do for Algo Monoshaft's sacrifice to be for nothing.

Gemma Dark's men opened the cell door and pushed her coughing brother, manacled anew, out into the corridor. Gemma glanced behind her. The dregs of Parliament's cowardly Fleet Sea Arm were cowering along the back of the soiled chamber, along with Jared's fancy piece, still standing tall, defiant to the end.

'You won't be so cocky, thief girl, not after Walsingham has run you through his mind ripper. You'll only be provisions for his people's larder after that.'

The dirty little whore flashed Gemma her fingers in an inverted 'V'. That obscene gesture of defiance, the lion's teeth, never went out of fashion back in the Kingdom. Gemma snorted in amusement and sealed the cell door.

Commodore Black tried to say something but broke into a fit of coughing, unable to cover his mouth with the weight of his chained hands.

'Don't worry brother. She's got an hour or two before my allies come for her. Your troubles, however, are a lot more immediate.'

'Come on now, Gemma, you won't do any harm to me. We're family, aren't we?'

'Blood's thicker than water? Let's spill some of it and see.'

421

'At least let the blessed girl go free, then. What harm has that poor lass done to you?'

'The Mistress of Mesmerism means something to you, brother, and that means something to me.' Gemma turned to her escort. 'Stay here. After Walsingham has ripped what he needs from the thief girl's mind, make sure she's pushed to the front for the first hungry pack that turns up with an appetite.'

The commodore groaned and Gemma laughed, shoving him down the corridor. She had a more old fashioned arrangement lined up for her brother's interrogation. 'I think that counts as a kindness, don't you? She'll probably be sucked dry by the time you get back to the feeding pen. You won't have to watch my allies exercise their shockingly crude table manners on the silly little thief girl. Just a sack of skin and bone discarded in the corner for you to remember all the good times you had together.'

Her brother was sobbing, but Gemma felt no pity for the traitorous dog. His crocodile tears were oil to the flames of her rage. How dare he care for *her*, a Middlesteel guttersnipe, when he had cared so little for the thousands of his people he'd abandoned to their deaths at Parliament's hands? Fleeing when the fleet-in-exile had been burnt in its u-boat pens, betrayed by renegades among their own ranks. Getting her darling Bull killed after he'd been captured, selling out to the enemy's secret police when push came to shove, just to preserve his own cowardly hide. All that Gemma had done, all that she had seen – it all should have been her brother's fate. Instead he had tossed it over to her. A final bitter legacy as cruel as the one her parents had heaped onto their offspring. The children of exiles, hunted and pursued to the ends of the globe. Rebels by birth and blood. Well, the world had made her a privateer, every new breath a victory, and now they would drink from the bitter chalice they had mixed. Let the world choke on it. She would rule over its survivors. Gemma would be their saviour, wringing gratitude out of the people like blood from a soiled rag discarded from a surgeon's table. But there was still her brother to deal with. Too weak to rule, too headstrong to be ruled.

'Don't torture me, Gemma. For old time's sake, just put a bullet in my head. Don't let me linger in this wicked nest of demons.'

Gemma didn't deign to reply. They headed through the dark, unpopulated lower levels of the seed-city. Water dripping from its black, bony organic hull. This was where her allies made their royalist puppets live and work. Indicative of how they viewed their relationship. Tossing Gemma meagre scraps from their table. She got to the room she had readied, pushing the commodore inside. At her command, the floor of the middle of the chamber rose, forming the shape of a chair. She pushed the commodore savagely down into it, and at her direction, it wrapped tentacles of black coils around her brother's chest and arms, sealing him in its grasp as securely as if she had whittled both chair and sibling out of obsidian. A curving table shaped into existence just in front of them, rising out of the floor's oily substance.

'In an hour the Star Chamber will arrive here to try you. There are a few old faces you'll recognize, Jared. Crew that served with the fleet-in-exile. They're not up to much, to be honest. All the good ones stayed and fought and died at Porto Principe.' She walked to the edge of the chamber and returned with a long length of black metal. 'You recall what used to be done to traitors to the cause, brother? We saw it done ourselves often enough in front of whichever captains were in harbour at the time.'

423

'Why do you think I left, lass? We'd become no better than murdering pirates.'

Gemma leant forward with the pipe and casually winded him in the pit of his gut with the end of it. 'Pirates steal what is not theirs. Any shipping that fell to the fleet-in-exile's u-boats was already ours!' Gemma didn't give him time to reply, but lashed down against his kneecap, hearing the crack of it shattering with as much satisfaction as she was capable of. 'Stealing from thieves who had stripped us of everything we possessed, executing all the prisoners we took. That wasn't piracy. That was pure justice.'

The commodore moaned something and she shut the filthy turncoat up with a quick slap of the bar across his mouth, blood and teeth flying over her boots. 'How did my boy look when he died? Something like you, or do I need the rest of our hour together to work towards that?'

'Shoot me,' mumbled the commodore, the words lisping and mangled through what was left of the lower part of his face. 'I'll tell you anything.'

'Of course you will,' said Gemma. 'But that's not really the point of this, is it? You've never known anything worth knowing. Only how to run and lie and betray.' She jerked up his scalp and looked him straight in his pathetic, puffy face. 'And that's not enough, this time. You'll get your bullet after your trial, after my coronation. Unless I decide to bring back disembowelling for treason as my first act as sovereign.'

The door opened behind her and Walsingham entered. She slapped the bar across her brother's ribs, laughing as they shifted and snapped, then turned to face the creature.

'What are you doing?' Walsingham demanded.

'Exactly what we agreed,' said Gemma, raising her bloody length of metal. 'I don't need his mind ripped to administer royal law.'

'You are beating an empty chair,' said Walsingham.

Gemma looked confused towards her brother's beaten body lolling in the clutches of the seat. 'What are you talking about? I'm working to keep my brother breathing; just alive enough for his trial, just alive enough for him to see my victory.'

Walsingham strode forward in fury and slapped Gemma, knocking her to the floor. 'You foolish animal, what have you done here?' He pulled out the pendant hanging around his neck and shouted at it. 'Send a fully armed cohort to secure the feeding pens. Send another to the engine rooms. Order all guards on duty to admit no one. There are escaped animals on board who have possession of one of our chameleon crystals. No shield generation equipment is to be removed under pain of execution!'

'My brother,' moaned Gemma pointing at the bleeding figure slumped in the seat.

'Is not there! You have been mesmerized, animal.' He kicked Gemma in rage. 'You are talking to thin air and attacking an empty chair.' He knelt, his human form vanishing to be replaced by the dark leathery-faced features of a sea-bishop, fangs glistening at Gemma. 'If the savages on this world succeed in locking us away in eternity's cold grasp again, I can promise you and your royalist herd, it will feel so much longer than forever for *you*!'

CHAPTER NINETEEN

Dick Tull had acquired a heavy blanket from the doorman of the Embassy of the Steamman Free State, though the Circle knows where from. It was not as if the sentient metal creature had much use for it.

He felt like a beggar as he was ushered shivering in front of the ambassador. The transparent dome-skull of his Excellency Grinder Longbody sparked with unrestrained curiosity as Dick was ushered into the ambassador's office.

'Your possession of the embassy's pass code would have gained you an audience by itself,' announced the steamman official, 'without the ridiculous notion of a Jackelian citizen wanting to claim political asylum with us.'

Dick coughed, still trembling. 'Belt and braces, your Excellency.' He reached inside his pocket and removed a slim oblong of semiconductor substrate inlaid with a fine filigree of glowing lines.

'And by the beard of Zaka of the Cylinders, what would that be?'

'A soul board,' said Dick.

'I know that, you impertinent softbody,' snapped the ambassador. 'Are you a common gravedigger, violating our corpses in the hope of a reward? Which of our people's cadavers did you violate to steal that soul board?'

'It was freely given while its owner was alive,' said Dick. 'And it contains more than the soul of Algo Monoshaft. It contains a suggested modification for your brains, courtesy of the Court of the Air.'

'Algo Monoshaft, the head of the State Protection Board?' crackled the ambassador's voicebox. 'If he gave you this, then he is dead! He could not live for longer than an hour without it.'

'Indeed he didn't. He blew himself up, turned himself into a suicide bomb.'

'But such an extreme end can only be granted with the permission of our maker, King Steam – it is almost unheard of?'

'Your king's spirit visited Algo Monoshaft in the cell of our enemies. Royal sanction was secured. Algo's sacrifice was necessary to guarantee the survival of both your people and mine.'

'How am I to believe these outrageous claims, softbody?'

'Algo said you could verify my words by lifting the seal on this thing's circuits and reading his final memories.'

'What possible modification to our hallowed architecture would be important enough for Monoshaft to pass into the Hall of Ancestors for?'

'Let's just say you'll be able to see more clearly,' coughed Dick. *Clearly enough to see the monsters walking among us.* 'And after you do, the head of the State Protection Board has petitioned King Steam for every steamman living inside the Kingdom to go out into the streets on a bit of a hunt. You see,' said Dick, leaning in close, 'and this is the nub of the thing. There are treasonists *everywhere.*'

Charlotte, Sadly and the commodore moved down the dark-ship's corridor as fast as they dared. To anyone who caught sight of the three of them, hopefully all they would notice was a sea-bishop, the commodore in a purloined royalist sailor's uniform and their prisoner – Sadly – being taken to an interrogation room to have his mind probed. Hopefully, that is, as long as Charlotte's control over the Eye of Fate stayed strong.

It didn't come easy to Charlotte. She was using the amulet constantly now, as a sea-bishop would. It was intensely painful keeping up the appearance of a sea-bishop, pushing the mesmeric field out. Her head was aching from it, throbbing with the mother of all headaches. Charlotte's usual acts of mesmerism were restricted to ten-minute turns of a stage, and more often than not, one-to-one acts of suggestion. She had a new-found respect for the sea-bishops' abilities. To be able to walk undetected among the race of man's teeming masses unnoticed for months at a time without letting the illusion slip. No wonder they needed skull cases as tall as a stovepipe hat to hold such powerful brains.

'Don't worry, girl-child,' said Elizica, her smooth voice slipping through Charlotte's mind as though a memory. 'This is what the Eye of Fate was meant for. Not relieving noble-born dupes of their wallets, not tricking local dignitaries into stabling gypsy caravans on their land.'

Charlotte rubbed the smarting skin under her breasts, scratching the remains of the artificial skin she'd torn to reveal the real Eye of Fate's hiding place. The Court of the Air was expert at creating such nooks for their agents.

I would like to see Gemma Dark's face when she realizes that the crystal she ripped from my neck belongs to a dead prison camp commandant.

'I would not,' whispered Elizica. 'This cursed vessel's halls are filled with enemies. Once Gemma Dark understands you mesmerized her and compelled her sentries to open the door and surrender their weapons and uniforms, your ability to mimic a sea-bishop's form will count for little.

The commodore shuffled along, a hand on the pommel of his purloined sabre to stop its length tripping his legs. 'Don't think I'm not grateful for saving my old bones from what my sister had in store for me, but . . . answers, lass. You promised you would tell me the truth back in the cell, a promise cut short by Gemma's arrival. How did you know to be wearing another crystal and have the Eye of Fate hidden away under the Court's cunning prosthetics?'

'You have the canny eye of Jethro Daunt to thank for that,' said Charlotte. 'He spotted that Sadly had been replaced by a sea-bishop when he was escaping from the Advocacy prison camp.'

Sadly looked confused. 'But the sea-bishops realized Daunt could smell their kind out, they taunted me for days with how cleverly they had replaced me. They thought their infiltrator could supply Daunt with all the missing signs that gave them away?'

'Oh, but they did,' said Charlotte. 'He was quite impressed how fast the sea-bishops learned to fool a priest's senses. Your doppelganger planted Daunt's mind with every cue and tell a churchman needs to read a person like a book. It was a perfect impersonation.'

'Then how did . . .?'

Charlotte brushed Sadly's bad leg with her fingers as he limped forward. 'Your doppelganger's footprints on the beach as he was limping out towards the Court's rescue submarine. A pair of boots walking normally left them, without the irregularity of the limp Daunt was observing.'

Sadly grunted in understanding.

'All those legends about vampires and mirrors, there's some substance to the myths,' said Charlotte. She brushed the Eye

429

of Fate. 'This can work a lot of mischief inside a mark's mind, but you constantly have to be a master of the small details, like remembering to project your false body in the reflections you leave on surfaces. Easy to forget.'

'Ah, that sly churchman,' wheezed the commodore. 'But Jethro Daunt didn't think to tell poor old Blacky about his wicked little discovery.'

'Only myself and the head of the Court, Lord Trabb,' said Charlotte. 'We had to let the sea-bishops think they had infiltrated us, so the fake Sadly could return and betray what he believed were our plans. It was the only way to get us inside the seed-city. Daunt realized from the outset that simply trying to repeat Elizica's original feat centuries ago would fail. The sea-bishops would never permit us to steal a darkship again and reach their home. Misdirection was the key. And what better way to infiltrate a stronghold than to have your enemy carry you inside their walls?'

'Then you knowingly sent that wretch Dick Tull walking into the enemy's hands with a devil by his side. Maeva, all her seanore warriors, you let them all sacrifice themselves for *this*, lass.'

'And all of the Court's staff and thousands of Nuyokians back on the Isla Furia. There's enough blood our hands for everybody. I'm sorry about what happened to Maeva, Jared, truly, but we're all dead anyway if we don't stop the sea-bishops. Better we have a fighting chance . . .'

'That's the Court's way,' said Sadly, almost approvingly. 'Whatever it takes, whatever the cost.'

The commodore rubbed his bandaged shoulder. 'That, it may be. But it's poor old Blacky and his friends that must do the bleeding for your dirty schemes. This is a fool's chance. You heard what Gemma said when she had us on the dark-ship sinking down to this black pit of hell. The shield device you would have us steal to freeze these demons in a trap of time is under heavy guard. Will the trickery of your clever gem pass a sentry's close inspection by an army of sea-bishops? Will you pretend to be Walsingham and have him order the demons to pass out what they have no doubt been ordered to secure with their very lives?'

'Oh, I don't know. It might work. Misdirection is the key, remember.'

Sadly pointed down the corridor to a side passage. 'That's the way to the airlock where the darkships are docked.'

'How can you be telling that, Sadly?' moaned the commodore. 'All these dark, dripping corridors – all alike, we might as well be passing through a leviathan's veins.'

'I have a very good memory, Mister Black,' said Sadly. 'That's my training and I was working *very* hard to memorize the way to get out of here when they hauled me down to the feeding pens.'

'The city hasn't changed much since Elizica was last here,' said Charlotte. 'But we're not leaving. Our path lies that way.'

'Ah, why not,' whined the commodore. 'I'm a dead man walking anyway. At least I'll be going down with a sabre in my blessed hand.'

'Withdraw!' Daunt's shouts sounded hollow through his gas mask. Never was a weapon so pointlessly deployed as this war gas, yellow blankets of blistering poison drifting over the volcano's slopes with both sides protected by their helmets. Both factions only inconvenienced by the foul fog. How Daunt longed to rip the cloying device off, to take a breath of real air. 'Why are they not withdrawing?'

The Notifier standing next to Daunt stared down at the ring of trenches below, the thud of gas rifles growing frantic as the gill-necks' massed ranks marched forward, advancing under the hazardous cover of a rolling barrage from their own artillery. The red chainmail across the woman's chest made her appear as if she had been wading through blood all day. Perhaps she had. 'The first trench has not had their votes tallied yet. To retreat is a serious matter, Court man.'

Morris snorted in rude amusement on the firing step of the trench. Daunt bit his tongue. Above them was the next trench ring, higher, its tighter circumference designed to accommodate the diminished number of fighters that would be falling back from Daunt's present position. Higher still, another trench circuit still being dug by the Court's mining force, working as they laboured under the fierce fire. The occasional miner malfunctioning from enemy shelling would come lurching down the incline, oblivious to the battle and ploughing into the advancing gill-neck formations where it would be battered into deactivation. The survivors could only fall back, regroup and concentrate their fire, however, if they actually *followed* Daunt's orders rather than constantly putting them to the ballot.

'Bob my soul, but dying down there is a serious matter,' said Daunt. 'Falling back to a prepared position is a serious matter, keeping the townspeople alive is a serious matter.'

'Freedom's light burns within each of us. It can never be diminished,' said the Notifier.

Damn her foolish religious cant. Did her faith offer any succour to those dying and maimed, as their light flickered from the world? *Superstition is the enemy*, that's what the seminaries taught back home. Well, the Circlist church's teachers had never had to crouch in the dirt and be pounded by gill-neck artillery all day long. There was a sudden surge of movement as militia fighters below flooded into the narrow communication trenches, surging up towards Daunt and the next defensive ring.

'Prepare the charges!' Daunt yelled. Along the firebay one of the engineers began fiddling with the ignition wires, readying to detonate the barrels of liquid explosives in the communication passages, sealing their defences against infiltration counterattacks from below.

'They have come out in support of your plan,' said the Notifier, somewhat superfluously.

'See if they can convince those gill-necked bastards down there to vote on going home,' said Morris.

The town's fighters poured into the trench, taking posts in the firebays and fixing their sights on the slopes below. Their chainmail armour was covered in mud, those portions of their faces that were visible under their gasmasks streaked with soot and tears and sweat. Manoeuvring through the narrow gap of the trench, the militia's young powder monkeys sprinted, sacks of ammunition drums and propellant jangling as they squeezed through the confined space, voices calling out for patronage in a cruel imitation of a street hawker's cries. The day was edging towards twilight. When night fell, the gill-necks would have the advantage, their eyes born to the half-light under the waves.

Daunt indicated the powder monkeys. 'Their sacks are half empty.'

'That's the problem with putting out bullets like a hailstorm,' said Morris. 'We're running low of ammunition.' He patted his gas rifle. 'Anyway, that's what the cutlery on the end of this if for. Never thought I'd be pig-sticking on a battlefield again.'

Daunt nodded grimly. He gazed down at the massed gill-neck ranks climbing relentlessly towards them. The heavy bunker guns along the slopes had fallen silent half an hour ago, preserving their shells for the moments when the rolling-pin tanks rumbled forward. Where previous advances had been halted, burning formations of gill-neck vehicles of war littered the blackened parkland in front of the volcano.

'Fire in the hole!' yelled the engineer as he plunged the stick down on his detonator.

A wall of rubble and fire erupted into the sky, showering the gill-necks' forward ranks with shrapnel and rock shards. The defenders' abandoned trench circuit had collapsed in on itself, any dead fighters left inside incinerated along with the front of the invaders' line. Hundred of bodies lay piled on the lower slopes, a few wounded gill-necks trying to struggle out of mounds of shattered flesh even as the next wave of Advocacy marines beat their way over their own dead and dying. Rifles discharged along the Advocacy ranks, a rippling line of smoke from their guns as bullets bounced off the lava slopes and caught some of the defenders in the head. The line that had just fired halted, clearing their rifles and pulling out a fresh charge, allowing the soldiers behind to step forward and bring their guns up towards the trench.

One of the militiamen to Daunt's right slumped against the revetment, his dying body shuddering as a companion pulled him off the firing step, clearing the way for another fighter to take his place on the trench board. He wasn't a man anymore, a living being with dreams and hopes and interests and family. He had become a dead weight clogging the workings of Daunt's killing machine.

'Wait for, wait for it. *Range!*'

A bass roar sounded the length of the trench, rifles jolting with the thud-thud-thud of their volleys. Each defender had the legs extended on the end of their gun barrel, sweeping the rifle left and right, invaders collapsing at the receiving end of their deadly arc of fire. Overhead, the whine of their foes' falling shells droned louder and louder, a fountain of explosions shaking the slopes above Daunt. Rock fragments scythed the trench from the rear, Daunt feeling the impact across the back of his helmet and chain-mailed spine as if someone was trying to drive nails through his back. Further down the line, larger shards had decimated the defenders, militia crawling wounded over the trench's dead. There were gaps in their firing line. Gaps Daunt had no one left in a healthy enough state to plug. Daunt turned to the rear revetment, the smoke of the artillery barrage landing obscuring his view. The next trench ring was still being carved out of the rock by Lord Trabb's automatics. They had nowhere left to retreat to. The locals no longer had the numbers to hold the line long enough for the mining machines to finish the job.

Morris extended his telescope to peer down at the ruins of the town's once palatial library. 'Bugger. They've brought their howitzers up. They must have been counting our counter-battery fire. They've guessed our magazine is as good as empty. Nothing to throw back at them but spit and words. We're in trouble.'

'If we're not, Mister Morris, it'll do until the real thing comes along.' Daunt took the telescope and peered through it. Beyond the cannons lined up behind the library's rubble, a long column of armour advanced trundling up one of the streets, the guns spined along the length of the tanks raised as if in salute . . . or elevated for an attempt at storming the slopes of the Isla Furia.

Along the rubble, the Advocacy's gunners had finished reloading their big guns and the carriages began to slam back as they expelled thunder. More accurately ranged this time, explosions flowered fore and rear of the circuit of trenches. Daunt fell back as a shockwave snarled itself around his body and hurled him off the firing step. He grasped the bare skin of his face. His gasmask had been blown off his helmet, the smell of cordite overwhelming now. As Daunt struggled up

435

through the dust, a rockslide from the trench walls nearly toppled him onto his back again. In front of Daunt, Morris lay stretched out, his body covered in dirt . . . but only some of his body. Morris's legs were visible protruding from the landslide, too far away from his torso to still be connected to the Jackelian.

Morris reached his hand out towards Daunt, his gas rifle clutched in bloody fingers, an offering of war. 'Take it.'

'I can't.' Daunt's voice came out like a husk, a rasp of dust and blood clearing his throat.

Morris weakly pushed his rifle out again towards Daunt. 'I bloody love this, vicar. And I'm getting out in good order. You can revel in the fury. But the end's always terrible. When it stops. Your rage fades. Just thousands of corpses. The cries of the lost and dying.'

Daunt crawled forward, the smoke clearing in the trench. So few standing, so few bursts of fire replying to each new shelling. The ground shaking and vibrating. If the crack widened under them, would they plunge down into hell?

'Do you have a hell?' Daunt yelled down the trench, his cry lost on the surviving fighters. Some crouching, others dying, survivors releasing the blades folded under their rifle barrels. Preparing for their last stand. *Or is this it?*

'I can feel it,' moaned Morris, his words bringing Daunt out of his shock. 'My soul leaking away back into the world, mingling with it all. Tell me I'm going to come back as better people, vicar.'

We'll learn the lessons of this life. Return to the one sea of consciousness, diluting into the infinite until our essence is cupped back out again into the world. Daunt took the Jackelian's ice-cold hand. 'We all will.'

'I already have!' Out of the smoke and fire along the slope he stepped. Iron feet crunching the ground. A scarlet pulse running down his vision plate as strong and steady as a heart-beat. His chest shining and bright. Boxiron. *But not Boxiron.* The creature of the metal combined with one of the Court's human-milled marvels, sealed and connected by a power far beyond that of the race of man. As the smoke drifted sideways, Daunt saw hundreds of the Court's miners stood lined up behind the steamman. Bunker doors were springing open across the slopes, no cannons emerging – only the massed ranks of the Court of the Air's mining force. They emerged unconcerned into the blast waves of the Advocacy strafing, stone shards rattling off their hull plates as they formed into long columns. Then the legion charged down the Isla Furia.

'Boxiron?'

The steamman's head slanted down, taking in his shining polished brutal new body, as if he was seeing it for the first time. 'Yes—' he raised his fist and behind him a legion of miners raised theirs in a mirror reflection of the steamman, '—I think I am upgraded. By the will of King Steam.'

Daunt gawked. *A slipthinker.* Boxiron was now a slip-thinker, able to inhabit multiple drone bodies and make their will his. The highest caste of steamman society. Unlike the empty shells back in Tock House, so many suits of armour without their controlling presence in residence. But Boxiron didn't have an army of inactive drones. He had an army of hulking mining mechanicals, their fists spinning as drill-bits and shovels and pickaxes. Able to carve caverns out of solid rock, or chunks out of an invading army.

'Mechanicals,' groaned Morris. The dying adventurer's words came out through gritted teeth. 'Mechanicals can't fight.'

Boxiron stepped down into the trench, the metal legion to his rear following a second later. He scooped up the gas-rifle in front of Morris. It looked like a stick in the hulking brute's hand. 'Perhaps, but a steamman knight knows little else. They are not your mechanicals anymore. They are mine.' Boxiron's proud head swept the sight of the trench, the surviving militia scrambling out of the way of the metal titans landing among them, then Boxiron took in the ruins of the city below. 'A defensive funnel to concentrate the enemy's formations. A variation of the Battle of the Gauge Heights.' He looked at Daunt, the light of his vision plate skipping slightly in surprise. 'You are in command here?'

'I believe I was.'

Boxiron pulled back the firing bolt on the gas rifle. 'Interesting. You would have done better to build a series of redoubts rather than a continuous trench, that would have concentrated your enfilading fire. But this is no longer a defensive action.' The words from his voicebox were nearly overwhelmed by a fierce roar from hundreds of drill-bits spinning into action, tool arms testing the air in unison. 'Do you mind, Jethro softbody?'

Daunt lifted his hand weakly over the top of the trench. 'That was never what I was for.' He tried to sit up and watch the charging waves of mining mechanicals, but it was so much easier just to prop his back up against the trench walls, holding Morris's still, cold hand. Daunt's head nodded, little waves of dreamless sleep, sheer exhaustion overtaking him. Sounds and screams and explosions from below punctuated each wave of blackness. Loud at first, then increasingly distant as Boxiron's forces pushed back to the distant margins of the city. It was dark now, twilight passed into night. He was so tired, beyond what he should be.

Shaken awake by a Notifier, Daunt blinked sleep out of his eyes.

'How do you vote?' demanded the man. 'Do you vote to advance towards the shore?'

438

Daunt lifted his hand, still holding Morris's cold finger into the air. 'We vote to sleep.'

'He cannot vote. He is dead.'

'No, I don't think he is.'

'Are you voting to stay here in a defensive posture?' asked the Notifier, indicating the distant clash of fighting.

'I know when it's time to stop.' Daunt shut his eyes. For the first time in ages he allowed the dreams in.

CHAPTER TWENTY

Charlotte nearly slipped on the underwater city's oily floor as a familiar figure emerged out of a side turning ahead of them. Gemma Dark. She had her sabre in her hand, and her appearance was answered by a hiss of steel as the commodore drew his blade.

'I knew it,' called the commodore's sister. 'They're all at the other end of the city, sweeping the engine levels for intruders, and here you are, heading in the opposite direction. Whenever my brother is up to mischief, just head for where you're not expecting him, and there he'll be.'

Charlotte let go of the image of the sea-bishop with relief; the strains of keeping up the illusion dropping away like a lead weight. 'The sea-bishops have a very low opinion of their cattle's intelligence. I suppose it helps to loathe what you must consume.'

'The lifeboats are back that way,' said Gemma.

'Oh, I don't need a darkship,' said Charlotte. 'Not after you were so kind as to pilot me to where I needed to go. I don't suppose your stock is very high with Walsingham now, or he'd be standing here beside you.'

'We don't have time to dally,' hissed Elizica inside her mind.

440

'When the enemy realize we're not hiding from them in the engine levels, they'll reach the same conclusion as this filthy collaborator.'

'Can you keep this witch engaged for a while?' Charlotte asked the commodore, sotto voce.

'We shared the same fencing masters growing up,' said the commodore. 'But I've had a few hard lessons since. Let's see what a dying man's old bones are good for.'

Charlotte squeezed his shoulder. 'End of this passage, second corridor on the left. Be lucky.' She didn't add the unspoken: *If you live long enough.*

'There's a first time for everything, lass.' The commodore slashed his blade left and right, testing the air, even as Gemma Dark sprinted forward, roaring in rage.

Charlotte and Sadly slipped past against the wall as the brother and sister's razor-edged steel sprung off each other, sparking in the gloom.

'I think she hates him a lot more than she wants to be queen of the realm, says I,' observed Sadly as they moved rapidly down the passage.

Charlotte glanced back at the furious duel behind them. *Almost as unwholesome as my feelings towards my mother.*

'You're not doing what the enemy expect you to, are you?' noted Sadly, his tone complimentary.

'Actually, I'm going to do the sea-bishops something of a favour,' said Charlotte. 'I'm going to give the bloody monsters exactly what they want.'

Commodore Black deflected his sister's thrust with an angry scraping of rasping metal. 'Our age has passed. The trail of our comet has faded into the night, lass. We're the last of them. All that is brilliant has waned and it's time for us to go too.'

'Never!' yelled Gemma, drawing back, panting. 'It is my right to rule and I shall!' She feinted left, then thrust to the right, the commodore only just parrying her blow in time. Jared was getting tired, his arm as heavy as if his flesh was formed from concrete. She was younger than him, and her muscles not addled with a wicked black rot eating her body away from within.

'You wouldn't be ruling, Gemma. You'd just be warming a hard lifeless slab of stone cut to resemble a throne. We only ever ruled with the people, not over them. When our ancestors forgot that, we lost all the rights we ever had.'

'You lying, cowardly, useless jigger,' Gemma sneered, the sabre raised over her head and turning in her hand. Jared would take his eyes off that hypnotic windmill of hers at his peril. 'How dare you stand there and spout base parliamentary propaganda at me. You betrayed our family, our line, the bloody *cause*. You left me to shoulder the legacy that should have been yours. All the times you ran away and here you are, choosing to stand for *this*? After all these years, have you found something you'd die for at last?'

'I'm already dead, lass.'

Her sabre lashed out, nearly skewering his forehead as he stepped aside. 'On that much, we agree.'

'I promised our father that I would look after you, Gemma.'

'A promise broken along with the fleet-in-exile,' spat his sister.

He stumbled back as Gemma Dark showed him how fit she still was, her blade dancing from side to side, shifting with a fierce energy. Hate could do that, so it could. All their years together. Did she still remember the first lesson their mortal fencing master had taught them? A brief one, words only, rather than the long tiring drills that followed, *high outside, low inside, thrust, parry*, administered in the cramped

confines of their u-boat and the royalists' clandestine underwater harbour?

The art of combat is the art of the unexpected.

She thrust out towards his heart even as he dropped his
guard, stepping sharply forward and to the side, taking the
steel in the centre of his bandaged wounds. There was a brief
glimmer of shock in her eyes as the realization dawned that
she had trapped her blade in her brother's body, skewering
him. Then the terrible widening of her eyes as she felt her
brother's blade sinking through her body and emerging
through her spine. She tried to speak, to curse and swear, but
a throttled line of blood was all that emerged as she stumbled
down towards the floor of the demon city, her brother
clutching her tight.

'My vow is true. I've saved you, Gemma. Our family was
never meant to rule over these bitter ashes.'

Gemma tried to splutter her rage at him as they fell back
on the oily deck. He whispered in her ear. 'I'm a dead man
walking, lass. Dying slowly, painfully, as my blasted body eats
itself from the inside courtesy of the dark rot. I'll be seeing
you soon.'

She gurgled something, a last half-satisfied exhaling of
breath.

Bellowing in pain, the commodore pulled himself off her
sabre and pushed himself shaking to his feet. 'That's my luck,
Gemma. Still alive for a little bit longer.'

The words came out as strangled sobs. He withdrew his
blade from his sister's body, wiping the steel on his trousers,
then stumbled down the corridor following Charlotte Shade's
parting directions.

At the end of the passage a door had been opened into a
long oblong-shaped chamber, Charlotte Shades and Sadly
standing over an evil-looking control panel set beneath a wide

screen staring out onto the deeps of the dark. The waters at the bottom of the trench were pitch black, but there was an arc of light so bright he could hardly stand to look at it. The illumination was coming from the vast crystal portal, the gate that could connect their world to the sea-bishop's terrible homeland.

'What are you doing?' moaned the commodore as he lurched into the chamber. 'Is that not the gateway to these demons' spoiled world, thick with their hateful legions?'

Charlotte tapped the Eye of Fate, glowing now around her neck, filling the dim chamber with a light as terrible as the one outside the city. 'The Court of the Air took a copy of the key from the sceptre. Originally they were hoping to corrupt the key and reintroduce it to the sceptre. Instead, we copied its imprint onto the Eye of Fate.'

The commodore pointed to the glowing portal outside. 'You've activated their dark portal, lass. Are you mad?'

Sadly winked at him. 'Not just activated it, but signalled the beasts that here is a world safe for them to feed on. They're on their way to the feast.'

Commodore Black raised his sabre at them. 'You're bloody mesmerized! The demons've nobbled the pair of you.' As he spoke the seed-city shifted and quaked beneath his boots, the weak u-boat man's stance on the deck nearly unbalanced.

'There's an armada of seed-cities hurtling towards us down their tunnel,' said Charlotte. 'It seems only fair to send them one back.'

Sadly grinned as he worked the controls. 'You know what happens when an immovable object meets an irresistible force, you old rascal? A ruddy big explosion, the kind you can't even measure on the chuffing scale!'

'I need to stay here with the Eye of Fate,' said Charlotte. 'To pilot the city in and seal the portal at our end just before the impact. Otherwise our world will share the force of the explosion along with the sea-bishop's home. You two get back to the docking bay and bail out on a darkship.'

'I'm not leaving you alone here alone, lass.'

'Do it!' ordered Charlotte. 'The Isla Furia will probably have fallen by now, the Court exterminated along with Jethro. Dick Tull is likely dead too. Someone needs to make sure these bloody vampires' last survivors don't rule the Kingdom and the Advocacy for the new few centuries. Expose them, root them out.'

The commodore put a hand on Charlotte's shoulder. 'You're as plucky as my daughter ever was, lass. Goodbye to you, and as fair a wind in your sails as I never had.'

'Go! You too, Sadly. I'm going to use the Eye to seal this chamber off for good.'

Commodore Black smashed the back of the girl's head with the buckler of his sabre, catching her as she tumbled back, pulling off the Eye of Fate and slipping its chain over his head.

'I wondered if it was going to be you or I to do that,' said Sadly.

'Ah, Barnabas, the Court trained you for the job,' said the commodore. 'But I was born for it. And now I'm dying for it, too, curse my unlucky stars.'

Sadly picked up Charlotte's unconscious form and slung her over his shoulder, holding his hand out for the commodore's sword.

'Get your own steel, lad. You'll find one by my sister just down the way.'

Sadly nodded. 'You would have made a good agent for the Court.'

'I'm a heartless jigger, lad, but I was never that evil a brute. Keep her alive or I'll come back and bloody haunt you.'

He listened to the agent's sprinting footsteps fading down the corridor and touched the glassy surface of the Eye of Fate. *I always knew you would be the one to get me killed.*

'How else is a royalist to die?' Elizica's voice echoed in the commodore's mind. 'But in the service of a queen?' The chamber door sealed as if it had never existed while the meaning of the controls flashed through his mind. 'Don't wait too long, Jared Black. I can sense alarms activating throughout the city. They know someone is inside their pilot's chamber and that their portal has opened.'

I think it would be good if someone lived to tell of this, my bloody royal sovereigness.

'The world must live, Jared Black. Our two friends understand this too.'

Jared worked the controls, the seed-city shifting from side to side as it dragged away from the bottom of the trench, a mist of dark silt spewing up around them. The commodore counted the time down in his mind, ignoring the blood leaking from his shoulder, ignoring the angry burning in his lungs. His body afire with the pain of his illness and the strange connection to the Eye of Fate. Had Sadly made it? The agent'd used up his time and so, curse his stars, had poor old Blacky.

There was a terrible shaking as the seed-city passed through the crystalline arch, the pit of Jared's gut falling away as they smoothly entered a realm of fractional unreality, mere probabilities between the infinite chain of worlds. Through the Eye of Fate he felt the throb of the shield generators activating, protecting them from non-existence in this queer realm beyond matter and reality. Sealing them in a bubble of time impervious to the raging non-existence outside. Jared Black felt something else too. The presence of Walsingham beyond the door, raging at the other sea-bishops outside to bring up equipment capable of cutting their way through the seed-city's self-repairing structure. The sea-bishop's face appeared floating above a projection panel on the commodore's console, its hideous real face, not the stolen human features of a long dead State Protection Board officer.

'Do not do this thing – pilot us back to your plane of existence. I will offer you the same deal I had with your sister. You shall be sovereign of your people, the new king of Jackals, ruling supreme and absolute. Your nation will be favoured among the entire world, master of all the others. Your enemies will bow down before you.'

'Lead bull on the farm, eh? Siring lots of fat juicy cows for the plate.' The pain in his shoulder was vanishing, burnt out by his unearthly connection with the Eye of Fate.

'You shall be king!' roared the creature.

'I had a strange dream the last night I spent with the nomads of the sea,' said the commodore. 'I was on a station platform in the centre of town, waiting for a capsule with all the clackers and clerks to take me home, when I saw my father. He's been dead for years, of course. Which is why I was so pleased to see him. We talked for hours about all the things we'd been doing, catching up, his life and mine. Ah, it was good to see him again, after all this time.'

'What are you prattling about, animal?' bellowed the sea-bishop. 'Turn us around. Take us back through the portal!'

'What am I talking about, you wobble-headed, blood-drinking, black-hearted bastard? It's time for me to move along the Circle. But here's the thing . . . you pack of jiggers are going first!'

Slamming his hand on the controls, the commodore sealed the portal behind him and killed the engines, their seed-city hurtling towards a hundred thousand identical cities closing in on them down a narrow thread of probability that shouldn't exist. And then, in a searing noiseless explosion beyond even the power of the sun's last gasp, it didn't.

EPILOGUE

Lord Donaldson warmed his hands in the pockets of his overcoat as he waited for the door of the luxurious shop-front to be opened. His coat contained little rubber capillaries that circulated hot water from a heating stone secreted in its false lining, a fact for which he was grateful as the winter wind bit against his young six-foot frame.

'Is this really necessary?' he asked his manservant, Fisher.

'Do you mean the procurement of a gem for your engage-ment ring, sir?' said Fisher. 'I rather think Lady Amanda will be expecting one.'

'I mean all this,' said his lordship, pointing to the transaction-engine drum turning in its armoured lock, processing their calling card with a rumble of suspicious clicks and clacks. No doubt cross-referencing their bona fides with the shop's appoint-ment book. 'All this blasted security? Isn't it more normal to go direct to a jeweller and leave the sourcing of one's gem to the tradesman?'

'Indeed, sir, indeed. Unfortunately, Lady Amanda has been very specific with her requirements. And this boutique doesn't deal directly with jewellers. Those of quality who wish to buy must present themselves in person. It is something of an *exclusive* establishment.'

Their calling card accepted, the armoured portal began to vibrate as very large bolts began to slide back automatically.

'I'm afraid the nature of the prices will serve to underline the nature of this exclusivity,' explained the manservant. 'And I should warn you, the proprietor is somewhat prickly. She threw out the Baroness Peery last week over some misunderstanding. A very slight matter indeed. I heard it from her chauffeur.'

'How droll. I can see why Lady Amanda is attracted to such a place.' Lord Donaldson sounded bored. But then, wasn't this what having obscene amounts of family money was meant for? Smoothing out all such tiresome obstructions to his whims and humours?

Passing through the vaulted corridor, grilles and doors retracted, the pair entered a large airy sales room of polished black marble floors and solid oak display cases arranged so the glass tops caught the light from high above. Fisher nodded to staff dressed as footmen, standing sentry-still by a rectangle of Doric columns towards the room's centre. Guards, obviously, but not dressed as such, lest the fairer sex be put into a faint by their intimidating presence. The contents of the row of cases did not shame the opulence of their surroundings – colours and shapes and cuts quite unlike anything to be glimpsed in the dozens of jewellers lining the fashionable street beyond.

'This,' Fisher announced, 'is my Lord Donaldson.'

Lord Donaldson noticed a cloaked female figure emerging from behind one of the columns. 'A rare collection, damson. We should start with your most precious gem first, so her ladyship may feel this afternoon's work not better done with her presence, which would, I believe, be unlucky.'

'If you place stock in such things,' said the proprietor. 'I am afraid my most precious gem was lost some time ago. But I am sure I have many here that will suit.'

Lord Donaldson peered in closer at the case. Some of the gems actually seemed to have been whittled as though they were ivory in a bored sailor's hands. Tiny crabs the size of fingernails, formed as effortlessly as they had been poured from liquid diamond. 'I must admit, I have never seen their like before. May I inquire as to their provenance?'

'The seanore,' said the proprietor. 'The nomads of the underwater world.'

Lord Donaldson licked his lips appreciatively. 'Incredible. I understood those devils would skin an air breather as soon as look at them?'

'They do try, every now and then,' said the proprietor, removing a tray of intricately shaped gems from under glass. 'But a few of them hold me with a little more fondness than is usual between surface dwellers and the underwater clans. From what Mister Fisher has told me of your fiancée, something from this collection might suit?'

Lord Donaldson had to stop himself from wincing when Fisher discreetly slipped him the price list, with her ladyship's preferences circled in appropriately red ink. Yes, he could see why Lady Amanda liked this place. His eyes settled on the establishment's name engraved in gold leaf on the marble wall. One word, resonant of all the compressed exclusivity and mystique that surrounded this shop: *Shades*.

The female proprietor lightly brushed the velvet cushion holding the gems, then winked at him. 'Don't worry, your lordship, for a piece that will grace the hand of the fair lady who is to unite the third and fourth greatest families in the Kingdom, why, it's a *steal*.'

Lord Donaldson sighed. To let his manservant lure him

into this palace of licensed larceny . . . someone must have hypnotized him into coming along in person.

Jethro Daunt pushed his way through the dense bush as quietly as he could, disturbing the man-sized leaves far less than he was provoking the plagues of biting insects rising out of the dripping green foliage. There seemed a man's weight of bugs waiting with every step the ex-parson took across the Concorzian colonies. Not that Boxiron was bothered. The black buzzing things could crawl across his shining steel chest without a twinge of visible discomfort from the steamman.

Climbing far faster – and stealthier – than Jethro could, Boxiron had already gained the rise. He was lying down examining the vista below with only the gentle clicking of his vision plate to indicate he was counting the spears and dart-guns ranged against the pair of them.

'It would seem the aborigine you bribed is reliable,' said Boxiron.

'Quite so,' said Jethro, unclipping the telescope from his belt and extending it out for a better look. If the informer had been untrustworthy, then their friends wouldn't be in the clearing at the bottom of the hill, staked out against wooden posts. Daunt adjusted the telescope's magnification. Yes, there was Molly, Coppertracks and Professor Harsh, all tied up along with the survivors among their guides. The aborigines – man-sized grasshopper things – were dancing around their prisoners, lashing their own bodies in acts of self-flagellation. Music was echoing out of the ruined city behind the Jackelians, eerie piercing notes that put Daunt in mind of sawing wood. The beat's tempo was accelerating, no doubt quickening right up to the point when the piled wood under their friend's feet would be torched and the feasting begin.

'There are a lot of warriors down there, old steamer.'

'They will not present a problem,' said Boxiron.

No, they probably wouldn't, even if Boxiron had been alone. Daunt could barely discern the little movements along the line of jungle that indicated Boxiron's drones were slowly moving into position. And Daunt knew what to look for. For the aborigines, Boxiron would most likely be the first steamman they were going to see. The last too, unfortunately for many of them.

'Ready yourself, Jethro softbody. I fight in five.'

'I remain quite certain your upgraded body can shift its gears without my intervention.'

Boxiron said nothing. It was as though he still needed permission to be unleashed, and perhaps that was just as well. Making such judgements should remain the job of a priest, not a knight's, even if the two of them were no longer quite the people they had once been. Daunt still had a yen for mischief and justice, and Boxiron still had a taste for mayhem. Daunt grabbed the gearstick on Boxiron's back, and very quickly, both their tastes were fully obliged.

Dick Tull sat on the kettle-black's worn leather seat as the carriage swayed rhythmically down Cloisterham Avenue, the street crowded with horses and omnibuses and carts laden with milk churns or mounds of black coal, shifting and settling as the crowded traffic moved and halted.

The only other passenger was a clerk who fastidiously kept a pair of calfskin gloves on at all times, even in the carriage's warm cab. He was often in the same carriage when Dick ventured off to lunch. No doubt the dour little scribe returned home for a brief meal served by his wife, then returned to his office to serve out the remainder of his day at work. Usually the clerk had a newssheet to engage him, but a lightning printers' strike had stopped today's editions and so, like

Dick, he leant on the handle of his cane, shaking with the carriage's motions, jolting slightly as the boiler coughed out each belch of smoke.

'An observation, sir, if I may?' said the clerk.

Dick nodded. So he fancied himself an observant man, this grey little jack-an-ink?

'You often board at the same place. A very fine neighbour-hood. Yet you always disembark in the direction of an ordinary to take your luncheon. I was wondering why a fellow who carries as fine a silver cane as you would choose to eat in an establishment where its knives must be chained to its tables? Is this a new fashion for gentlemen I am unaware of?'

Dick used the cane to bang on the roof to let the driver know he was going to exit. 'Food's food. Why pay for five waiters' wages when you're eating just the same? Besides, there's sometimes work to be picked up from the tables there, as well as a good roast.'

'Commissions are to be had inside an ordinary?' The clerk sounded surprised as the carriage drew to a stop. 'Well I never. I had surmised from your hours of luncheon that you might be retired?'

Dick opened the carriage door to the cold and made to step down. 'As much as a man's allowed to be.'

No. The Court of the Air didn't have much of a retirement plan, not unless you included growing old in a porcelain tower in the torpid heat of a far-off island. But then, the Court paid handsomely enough to offset such inconveniences. Airsickness wasn't much of a perk, though. Travelling up to the new aerial city floating up there in the heavens. Creating its own clouds with the exhaust of all those thinking machines. Watching, always watching. *See all, say nothing.* Some things never changed.

Dick pulled his coat in tight and crossed over to see what Sadly was serving today.

'Listen to me and listen well,' said the clan's wise-woman. 'For this is the story of the scar that cuts the world and what may emerge from the deep of the dark.'

The three seanore nomads, the wise-woman's chosen disciples, bobbed warily along the edge of the great trench, for there were strong currents about here said to stir out of the depths. Strong enough to suck many an unsuspecting swimmer down into the maw of the world. A premise far more disturbing to them than the legends which were spun out of such mortal dangers.

The wise-woman sensed their lack of conviction and found their disrespect irksome, banging her rotor-spear in the seabed and sending up eddies of black dust. 'Attention to me. The wisdom of these songs was ancient when the orb of the sun and the rays it casts into the sea were yellow rather than the red that warms your cheeks. I have not dragged you to gaze into the abyss so you might have a tale with which to scare unruly children. Listen you well, to the song of two thieves, one young, one old, who risked all to cast the demons of the mirror-realm back into the darkness from which they crawled.'

The three disciples quietened down to listen to the songs. Perhaps there was hope for them. After all, the passage of time could, or so it was said, make diamonds from even the crudest of coals.